The Cateran
By
W.G.Graham

The young man's haste was due to his determination to reach the *Tigh Tughadh,* his own thatched house, without halting again, having rested only once since bringing down the deer with his long-barrelled horse pistol. .Despite the weight of the burden slung across his shoulders, Andrew MacLaren forced a smile, visualising Fiona, his wife, busy spoiling Calum, their five month old son, in that same house. Aye, it would be good to be home he decided, and the deer, though stringy at this time of year, would be a welcome addition to the pot after such a harsh winter. With an inner satisfaction that all was well within his world, Andrew struggled on.

Close on an hour later, with the rim of the sun sliding behind Ben Vorlich, its blood red rays dipping into the loch, lying like a jewel in the green setting of the braes, Andrew turned the last bend for home, though now apprehensive by the lack of peat smoke from his own fire. This, and the sight of so many hoof prints so close to home.

"Fiona lass, I am home!" he called out, dropping his burden and scattering hens in all directions as he bent his six foot frame through the doorway.

Ignoring the girning bairn in his cot, Andrew's eyes followed the strewn garments across the room to the byre at its far end and saw, through the slats that separated it from the rest of the house, *the thing*, for it could not be human, that lay there amongst the straw. Yet it moved. A hand poked through the slats, strips of flesh hanging from a bleeding arm. Eyes stared up at him, pleading for help, from a face he scarcely recognised. *The thing*, that was the broken bleeding body of his wife.

In an instant the man was by her side, at a loss as to how to hold a body wracked with pain from where the whip had done its work.

"Fiona lass, what has happened here?" he heard himself ask, in a voice he scarcely recognised as his own.

Gently, with all the care he could muster from his shaking hands, Andrew picked at the hay clinging to the back of his young wife where the bare bone showed through, and pressed his cheek to hers, unable to comprehend that this was the same smooth gentle figure he had lain beside that morning.

1

Now he knew the reason for the hoof prints at his door. The raiders must now be well up the glen and confident in their numbers, to have left the sacking of his house until their return.

He shuddered. What to do next? They must not find them here. But what to do about Fiona? Could she be moved? And the bairn? For he knew in his base cowardice he could not bide here to face the raiders' return.

Trembling, Andrew stroked his wife's hair, a movement that brought a further moan to her lips. He would fetch a plaid. He made to rise but the tortured woman clutched at him and gave a gurgle through foam-specked lips, her eyes pleading that he should not leave her.

"I must get you away, for I will not leave you here to face the further wrath of those evil men." The young husband heard his own fear and despair in his words.

"Andrew," Fiona moaned, stretching out a hand as he rose to his feet, "do not leave me."

Desperately he turned away and quickly crossed the room to snatch a plaid from a kist.

"I am here lass!" he cried out, his voice shaking as he hurried back to her, past the still wailing child.

Andrew sank down by his wife's side. "I will have you away in no time, lass." Though he wondered how this could be done without inflicting further pain on this tortured body.

Bending closer in the dim light he saw the sightless eyes, eyes that accused him of leaving her in her final moments. And as he reeled back in shock, he, Andrew MacLaren, knew he would carry the sight of those eyes with him to the grave.

He should not have gone for the plaid but he was not to know how badly Fiona had been hurt. All he had wanted to do was get her and the bairn away; though he knew it was himself he had been thinking of, for he could not face men who could do such evil deeds. Other men would have stayed, stood and fought for what was theirs, but not he. Especially not with a sword, his hated weapon, base coward that he was.

Andrew was never fully aware of leaving the house in panic, passing the screaming child or running through the woods to the brae beyond. The sight of the undisturbed garrons and cattle grazing there confirmed his worst fears, that the raiders thought themselves

2

sufficiently strong in numbers to delay the lifting of his gear until their return from penetrating further up the glen.

The running man slowed to catch his breath. Should this be so, he reasoned, it would not be overlong until the raiders returned.

In an instant he had mounted a garron and was back at the house, halting only to snatch up the child, his fear from within and without driving him from the place.

It was as he turned again for the door that he first became aware of the pistol missing from where it had hung on the wall, the only item, it would appear, to have been taken from the entire household. He cursed. That had been his father's pistol, one of a brace he had learned to use from childhood. Now there was only the one stuck in his belt.

Andrew drew his eyes away from the wall across the room to where his dead wife lay, biting back a sob that he could no longer delay his leaving.

It was first by the loch side, the spray caught by the rising wind stinging his eyes, then up by barren slopes to the crags above, that the young MacLaren rode. Though a longer way to the town of Laidon, hopefully, he reasoned, it would be safer. Yet he was fearful of every shadow in that black stormy night, hushing the child cradled to him to cease his wailing for fear of alerting the entire countryside, not least those he feared most.

After a while, a long while it seemed to the rider, the dim lights of the town cut through the night and he eased his spent beast to a trot, his fears receding with the garron's every stride as he guided his mount up the narrow cobbled street to the home of his in-laws.

Careful of the bundle in his arms, Andrew dismounted and climbed the tenement stairs to the home of his kin, where, rapping upon the door, he waited impatiently for the bolt to be withdrawn, though still at a loss as how he might present the death of his Fiona to her parents. At last the door opened and Rob MacLaurin thrust his young head through the crack.

"Man, Andrew, what brings you here at this hour...and the bairn?" His good-brother's eyes travelled past the man and his sobbing offspring for the sight of his only sister. "And Fiona is not with you?" Wordlessly Andrew pushed passed the youth into the house.

At his unexpected appearance his mother-in-law sprang to her feet from her seat by the fire, the smile on her face freezing from one of pleasure to one of concern as she crossed the short space to take the child from him.

"What is amiss, Andrew? Is it my Fiona? Is she unwell?" The woman's voice shook as she asked the questions.

Fiona's father, swung round from from where he sat to face Andrew. "There is trouble lad?" The weeping of the child almost drowned out the question.

"*It is* Fiona!" the woman wailed, rocking the child back and forth in her arms, her eyes never straying from Andrew's face, willing him to say that she was mistaken.

Andrew slumped down onto a stool, only too willing to share his grief, but still not knowing how it should be done ... in a gentle kindly way. For a moment he sat there staring into the fire, saying nothing. Then at last he began to tell of how he had returned home to find his Fiona dead of a pistol shot ... his own pistol ... which one of the murderers had taken with him, for he was determined to spare the couple the true nature of his wife's death, as well as his own tergiversation.

Angus MacLaurin was up and reaching for his bonnet as the words left his lips. "We best away and advise Himself what has happened here. Aye, and hope no more of our folk have suffered a similar fate this night. Bide with your mother, Rob. We shall not be overlong away," he ordered the young man.

The rain had eased, the town was at their backs and they were on the path to their chieftain, Colin MacLaren's, door before the silence between father and good-son was broken.

"It was not strictly the whole truth you spoke back there, Andrew, laddie."

The words came at the young man out of the darkness. Stunned that his cowardice had been so readily discovered, Andrew opened his mouth to answer, though he did not know what.

"I am after thinking it was to save the pain that you kept your counsel," the elder man went on. "And in this you have my gratitude and respect." Angus drew closer to the younger man.

"Was my daughter...Fiona...violated, before shot with the pistol? This I must know, Andrew, however painful it may be." As if the asking was in itself an indecency to his daughter's memory.

Andrew bit his lip. Would it not have been better, with the exception of his own disgraceful conduct, to have told the truth,

4

since the likelihood of keeping such matters secret for long in the whole of Loch Earn side was, to say the least, remote?

While Andrew struggled to marshal his thoughts, Angus placed a gentle hand on his shoulder. "Perhaps it best be told to the MacLaren Himself, Andrew, when the single telling of it will be enough."

Thus decided, the two grieving men walked on.

It was on the occasion of his father's death, close on ten years since, and he all of eleven years old that Andrew had stood in this same room. He remembered how he had gazed wide eyed at these same rows of books, never in his young life having seen so many and, despite his grief, vowing to himself that one day he would possess a room such as this. Now, here he was once again, drawn as last time by a personal loss.

Colin MacLaren was a tall thin man in his middle years; though of a gentle mien it hid a strength readily called upon in these storm-tossed times. "What trouble brings you to MacLaren's doorstep at this hour Angus, for I see by your look, man, it is nothing less?" The chieftain addressed the elder man not unkindly, as he rose to greet them from behind his oaken desk.

"It is as you say, *Ceann-feadhna,* though I think young Andrew here would be better at the telling of it than myself."

With a nod that this may be so the chieftain motioned both men to be seated, and waited politely for Andrew to begin.

This the young man did, though scarcely aware of what he said, from the effect of the whisky thrust in his hand, the heat of the fire and the events of the day all now having combined to exhaust and confuse him. He had started by telling of how he had found Fiona already dead as he had stated before, except this time he included how the horse whip had done its evil work, the disclosure of which had brought forth a moan of anguish from both men.

Silently, Colin MacLaren rose and crossed to stand by the fire. "It is a hideous thing to have befallen any honest soul, more so a lass so young and bonnie as your own wife. And the pain she must have suffered. In this you have my profound sympathy, although, as father to all my people, I must intrude further in your sorrow.

You were after saying nothing at all was taken from your home except your late father's pistol. Also, you mentioned the fact of seeing an abundance of hoof prints by your door, leading you to

5

conclude the reivers believed themselves sufficient in numbers to be away 'lifting' further up the glen." The chieftain stroked his chin, adding as if speaking to himself, "Thus confident enough to leave the ransacking of your home until their return."

Colin drummed his fingers on the mantelpiece. "This could well be as you say, young man; if so, we may hear of further atrocities before this night is out. Pray God I am wrong!" he said angrily, thumping the mantelshelf.

The chieftain spun roumd to face them then, as if thinking aloud, began, "Therefore I must instantly take steps to thwart their plans, or at least track them down. I will send out horsemen forthwith to see this is done. This is all that can be done in the dark of night. However, our main force will gather at the trysting place by first light. All who own a mount should be there, for it is my intention to find these miscreants ere they leave Loch Earn behind. Theirs will be a slow business with gear and cattle before them, so it is mounted men I will need at my back come dawn."

The MacLaren looked directly at the older man. "Doubtless you will have a mind to be there, Angus?" At the other's nod, "I will see there is a mount waiting." Then, to Andrew, "As you have your own beast, there is no need for me to repeat my offer."

"Is it necessary? Must there be more killing? ... Is my Fiona's death not enough?"

It was the astonished look on the chieftain's face that told Andrew the words uttered had been his own and, above all, to the MacLaren Himself. Staring wearily at his patriarch he saw the man's expression gradually mellow.

"You are not yourself my young friend, or you would not find it necessary to voice such thoughts. For, were you to think again, it would be to realise the import of all knowing that no-one violates MacLaren country or its folks with impunity."

Colin crossed to place a hand on the grieving man's shoulder. "Try and rest, laddie. You will see it in a different light come morning and, if I am not very much mistaken, you will be first at the trysting place...or you are not of the Clan MacLaren."

No word passed between the two men on their way home. Angus, heavy-legged climbed the stairs while Andrew hobbled the garron on the green behind the tenement.

"It is after the reivers you will be going, father?" Andrew heard young Rob say, as he reached the open door, and he saw the young man's eyes gleam at the prospect of helping to revenge his sister's death. "I am old enough now father and there is the sword I have in the practicing. Can I go father?"

"Hold your wheest, laddie, it is not some sort of game we seek to play. Yon old sword would snap as easily as your neck should a grown man stand behind the blow. Now away to your rest and let us away to ours."

Cruelly chastened, young Rob bowed his head and, with a mumbled 'goodnight' to Andrew, timidly closed the door behind him.

"You were over hard on him Angus. Though still young, he has a man's pride," the woman scolded her husband.

"He must learn," Angus grunted, and bidding Andrew a good night took his leave.

Throughout the short discourse, Andrew had made his way to sit by the fireside, his eyes fixed upon the cradle, seeing and unseeing the sleeping child within.

"Here, Andrew laddie, take a sup of broth. You must keep up your strength for the morrow. It will not be long 'til light. When you have done, lay yourself down beside young Rob, and rest awhile," the woman coaxed, thrusting the bowl into his lap.

"I thank you good- mother. I shall bide here awhile," Andrew answered thickly.

"Aye, if it suits you Andrew." The woman fought to steady her voice. "I will in the morning visit Eilidh MacPhater ... her man has a cart, and I will bring my lassie home ... back here ... that is," she amended.

The woman pretended to busy herself. "Have a care when the time comes Andrew, and see that old fool of mine does not let the anger best him. I will want to see you both back home safe and well." As she spoke she drew the covers closer around the sleeping child. "I will away to my own bed. I will see you in the morning. You will both do better for what is before you on a full belly." She turned away from the cradle, saying as she made for the bedroom door, "Do not be worrying, I will hear the bairn well enough should he awaken. I will bid you a good night, or what is left of it."

With dead eyes, Andrew spooned the broth. He had not eaten since breaking his fast that morning. From the depth of the bowl Fiona's face came at him, as he had seen her that morning, when she had handed him his breakfast, and how she had smiled at him, their love making newly done. He looked away, unable to clear his mind of the image of how she had stared at him with those sad accusing eyes.

Setting down the bowl Andrew wrung his hands in despair. It went without saying that all would believe he had done the decent thing by covering his wife's body before he had left. The pain of the whip was nothing to what he had done to her and the lies he had told of how he had found her dead. Again he saw his wife's naked body, a bloody mess of hanging flesh, and thought too of the pain she must have suffered.

Suddenly, he was on his feet, all tiredness fleeing from his mind. In his haste he had left Fiona naked! Uncovered! He must not leave her so ... though even now his brain calculated the risk of returning. But what to do? The child gave a girn and he drew a gentle finger down his sleeping son's tiny hand, before turning for the door.

It was with some trepidation that Andrew sniffed the early morning air for any hint of burning as he climbed the last brae above his home. Then the *Tigh Tughadh* lay beneath him, there, as he had left it, untouched. It was then he saw the men come out of the door carrying the white boards between them.

Letting out a moan, Andrew descended the brae.

"Well, if it is not Andrew MacLaren returned!" the foremost of his clansmen holding an end of the white board mocked. "It is surprised I am to see you here, and I thinking you to be on the far side of Loch Ard by now."

Glaring up at Andrew with all the contempt he had felt for the man since their childhood days, the speaker shifted his burden from one hand to the other. "What manner of man leaves his wife as you have done? Could you not at least have taken the time to cover her decent?" he exploded, nodding down at the board on which the dead woman lay.

The mountd man turned his gaze from his accuser to the body hidden beneath the plaid, angry that his cowardice had been discovered. Angry too at his lack of foresight that the MacLaren

8

Himself would have already sent men this way in an attempt to intercept the reivers upon their return.

"It was the bairn that concerned me most," Andrew stammered, "before yon heathens returned."

"Tush man! No freebooter ... not even Campbells make war on bairns. It was your own self that your thoughts turned to. This I have known since the first day we trained at the sword play: you are a coward Andrew MacLaren; of this now I am certain."

His tirade over, as the spokesman started to lead the grumbling men past the bereaved man, Andrew moved his mount to block the way. "It is my place to be with my wife, Neil MacPhater!"

"Aye you should have thought of that last night," another snapped. "She will rest decent in Laidon Town, MacLaren."

"Aye," another piped up. "Your place is at the trysting. Perhaps it is not yet too late to retrieve some pride. Or is it, as we all know here, you are the craven coward?"

Without waiting for an answer the clansmen continued on their way for, now that Andrew did nothing more to hinder them, they knew what had been said must be so.

It was long after the clansmen had gone before Andrew plucked up enough courage to enter his own house, and when he did so he was careful to avert his eyes from where Fiona had lain. The man shivered, as if the very stones of the place projected their hostility towards him and what he had done here. This, the house of his forefathers, was no longer home to him now that Fiona was no more.

Distraught, Andrew lowered himself on to a stool by the dead fire, dowsed as was the custom in honour of the dead. His jangled nerves drove away any thought of sleep, and the ache in his head prevented him from thinking clearly. Last night Fiona's family had taken her passing well enough under the circumstances......in especial his good-mother, but by this time the shock would have set in. Somewhere in the back of his mind he remembered the woman saying something about bringing a cart here to take her Fiona home. This being the case, there was every possibility of her meeting Neil MacPhater and his company on the way and, even if out of respect for the woman, the man did not relate how he had found Fiona, this knowledge would not remain sacrosanct for long or he did not know the MacPhater very well.

Andrew scanned the room, reflecting on how many important events affecting his life had taken place within these same walls. Firstly, there was the night his mother had passed away. Now in the coldness of this same room he could still feel her touch, a touch that had returned to haunt him as his own wife lay dying. The full consequences of which were still to be concluded.

Then, the night his father had died ... murdered was more the word. He remembered how the rain had beat at the divoted windows ... his grandfather teaching him his cyphers by the fir candle's light ... the cry from outside ... his father leaving to investigate.

Andrew drew a heel over the dirt floor, seeing the room as he had seen it then: his grandfather sitting, an ear cocked for the slightest sound of his father's return, a finger pointed at his lesson, until at last, his patience at an end, the old man had risen and, taking a pistol from the wall and handing him a lighted taper, both had cautiously ventured into the night.

By the taper's light his elder had searched one side of the house, while he had searched the other, ready in an instant to run back to the door at the slightest sound in that wild night.

Instilled in his memory of that fateful night was the thumping of his heart as each step took him away from the safety of the house, too afraid to call out to his father.

Whether it was minutes or hours he searched, he did not recall. But what he did recall was suddenly tripping and the taper flying from him as he threw out both hands to arrest his fall. The feel of something soft, sticky, his face only inches away from the severed arm. The bile in his throat choking him, preventing him from screaming as his eyes followed the severed arm to the dead staring eyes and mutilated body that was his father. Witnessing in that one horrible moment what the claymore had done.

Perhaps that had been the beginning of his fear of the weapon. Or yet again perhaps it was his own inherent cowardice that caused him to loathe it so, a weapon which as a young man he must learn to use.

At first, as laddies, they had learned to fight with wooden swords on the village green, the older clansmen effusive in their encouragement, he backing away as always from his opponent's onslaught while his grandfather shook a mournful head in shame.

The next day, following just such an encounter, his grander had taken down one of his late father's pistols from the wall and had caressed it lovingly, contemplating, it would seem, that had his own son taken one of these beautiful weapons with him yon fateful night he might still be alive. With a grunt he had handed him the deadly weapon of this seventeenth century.

After the most detailed explanation on how to handle the long-barrelled horse pistol, Andrew crooked an arm and fired, and found himself lying on his back from the recoil.

That had been the beginning. With the exception of the Sabbath, tired as he may have been from the day's toil, practice he must. The old man lecturing, 'Soon you will be master in your own house, and in time must learn to defend it, and when The MacLaren Himself calls you to arms some day, as he surely will, you at least must be able to defend yourself, and seeing as you are worse than a gangling lassie with the sword, then it is the pistol you must make your own.'

His grandfather had held out the pistols so that he could read the inscription on the butts. 'Your own father took them from a Buchanan laird. They are the truest *dags* I have ever seen. Use them wisely and you may live long enough to appreciate their worth.' And so the practice had continued.

At last the day had come when he had hit everything...or at least almost everything he had aimed at. This, though, was not enough for his elder who had then schooled him in the art of making his own lead shot, priming, loading and cleaning the weapons. "You have done well Andrew, laddie." He had ruffled his hair. The merest hint of pride in his voice had been the old man's only praise.

At last the young widower slept and when he awoke, remembered that in his dream he had been fifteen years old again and up at the summer sheilings, seeing Fiona through different eyes for the very first time. Then, with the summer over, the cattle driven back to the crofts, he had sworn to see her again though she lived within the town.

Andrew shivered and stared through empty eyes at the house now so stern and cold. His mind drifted back to one night when he stood brushing his hair and smoothing down his *Feileadh Mor*, his great kilt, in preparation for his meeting Fiona on the braeside above the town.

"Aye, love is a grand thing is it not laddie?" he could still hear his grandfather say. "I can well mind even with the help of your uncles and cousins here on the croft you had not the strength left after a day's toil to lay down your head to rest. Now it would seem love has given you Samson's strength to have you traipsing all the long road to Laidon and back. Though have a care it is not your own Delilah that you meet," the old man chuckled.

"You may scorn, grandfather, but Fiona is the lass for me," he had thrown back with all the confidence of youth.

"Aye, you could fare worse laddie. She has a bonnie head on her, yon one, and in more ways than one, I am after thinking."

"You do not disapprove?"

"Would my disapproval make the difference? I think not, see you. For a body when in love only sees and hears what it wishes to see and hear, so that the very wisdom of Solomon himself would be to no avail. Aye, love is an itch you cannot scratch."

Therefore, it came to be that he and Fiona would meet on as many nights as possible throughout the month, his near exhaustion after a heavy day's work instantly revived by the prospect of meeting her. By the time they were both in their seventeenth year they were betrothed.

Neither had his prospective in-laws objected, both considering him a suitable husband for their daughter. After all, did he not have a fine croft and *Tigh Tugnadh* forby?

Old grandfather MacLaren had also added his blessing, well content to see his line continue, especially upon the same land where he himself had been born and raised.

Andrew rose and stood by the open door and gazed vacantly across the land.

He would never feel free of guilt at his grandsire passing away less than a month before he and Fiona were to wed. He had come across the old man sitting by the loch side as if in slumber and, after realizing that the old soul was no more, had sat there staring across loch and brae weeping uncontrollably at having allowed the old body to work so hard so that all would be in order before he brought home his bride.

Now, what good was all of this without someone to share it with?

"Oh Fiona!" he sighed, "that I had not left you alone," knowing yesterday's nightmare was not the end but only the beginning.

Chapter 2

The rocks bit into his chest as he lay there groping in the water, more so when reaching underneath to take hold of the slippery struggling thing in his hands. With a yell of triumph Andrew sprang to his feet clutching the fighting fish, only then did he see the row of horsemen on the nearby loch shore.

"What have we here, Hamish?" asked the foremost of the riders.

"A thief, my lord, I am after thinking!" Hamish nodded.

"And who gives you the right to fish in the burn by the loch of my father, The MacKerlich Himself, think you?"

From where he stood by the burn Andrew scanned the riders arranged along the shore, all clearly enjoying his discomfort. "I was unaware the sea loch belonged to anyone, but I would not be the one to beggar your lord and master by claiming one wee fish, so perhaps I should throw it back and let the line of MacKerlich prosper?" The angry words had left Andrew's lips before he had realised what he had said, the prospect of losing his first real meal in days having prompted him to lash out.

Instantly, Andrew regretted his stupidity, not to mention recklessness. Here he stood, confronted by a score of armed men, whilst his pistol and entire life's possessions lay out of reach on the backs of his two garrons. After all, had he not been at pains these last weeks to avoid any living soul?

Andrew felt, rather than heard, the sharp intake of breath as one of the riders urged forward his mount.

"Hold!" The abrupt command came from the leader.

Andrew studied the speaker carefully, judging him to be about his own age. As the son, it would appear, of the man he had just this minute insulted he would not, could not, let the insult pass.

"I am Andrew MacLaren," he hastened to explain, unable to prevent the tremor in his voice, "and I seek a new place to bide from my native Glen Laidon, by Loch Earn."

"Alone are you now? No wife?" This mockingly said.

"Tis the reason I am here, my wife having passed away with the sickness...not long since and...."

"You became a robber, to boot," the leader suggested coldly.

"I meant no insult ... it was ill said."

The young commander drew closer while at his back there were a few smirks at Andrew's attempt at an apology.

"So it is land you are seeking? Then I am after thinking, Andrew MacLaren, that my father, unlike his fish, has that in plenty. But even should you fail as a crofter," the man laughed, "you will make a bonnie fisherman, for I have never seen a man keep a fish alive as long as you!"

Amid shrieks of laughter, Coll MacKerlich swung round his mount, leaving Andrew, head bowed, clutching the still shaking fish, now long since dead.

Some hours later the traveller found himself looking down upon that self same loch.

"There is your new home, MacLaren. I hope you prosper well." Coll Mackerlich pulled rein, waving a hand at the scene below.

Where marshland met the sea stood a pile of stones: all that remained of a dwelling. A more desolate place he could not have imagined. Andrew stared in horror. "It is a crofter I am, MacKerlich, not a sailor! Can anyone raise anything but seaweed in a place like yon!" he indicated angrily.

"Och well!" the young chieftain laughed, "At least, as you have already proved, you are good at the fishing!" and he threw over his shoulder as he swung round his mount, "Remember your oath to my father. I said I would find you a place. Did I not?"

As the laughing men disappeared, Andrew's anger turned to despair. Now more than ever he wished he had kept his mouth shut back at the lochside. For would a proud man such as Coll MacKerlich not find some way to extirpate his earlier insult?

As for Angus MacKerlich Himself, he who had sat listening so sympathetically while he had told him a tale of how Fiona had died of a sickness and being unable to live on the croft without her, he had decided upon a new place to settle. He bunched his fists ... Only to be given this! This was the MacBeolin place ... or had been at one time, he understood. Now it was nothing more than a pile of rubble.

Forlornly Andrew started down the brae, the water seeping as high as his garron's hochs, until he drew closer to his new home, where mercifully the ground grew firmer.

He would have to act quickly if his intentions were to build some sort of shelter before nightfall, for at best the walls on two sides were no more than two feet high, the whole covered by bush and nettle.

Although, he saw as he dismounted, a third corner stood somewhat higher, where perhaps he could stretch some plaids to form a tent. Then, just as suddenly, what little resolve there had been drained away as he took stock of his dismal surroundings.

What a mess to find himself in. He was as good as a prisoner here; now that he had given his word to the MacKerlich, there was no up and leaving. This he knew was what the younger MacKerlich expected of him, to catch him stealing away like a thief in the night.

Well, Coll MacKerlich if this is your thinking I will play you at your own game! I will make a home of this place, or appear to have done so, and when you have lost interest in me, I will up and away. So saying, Andrew lashed out at the nettles with a foot.

Later, having only just succeeded in clearing away some undergrowth, the rain started. Cursing, Andrew quickly stretched a plaid across the corner of two of the remaining walls, and crawled into the confined space to settle down for the night.

"What a fool I am," he said aloud to the two restless garrons. "You both had a better place than I have at present, back in Glen Laidon."

The thought led him to think once again of his own croft, as he had done every night since his leaving. Had it been only three weeks since he had turned his back on his native glen? If so there was still time to return. It would mean further humiliation, but anything was better than this.

He leaned back against the wall, the rain dripping down his neck. It was no use; there could be no returning, at least not yet awhile.

It was now three years since Fiona's passing. Three years in which he had suffered the contempt of his clansmen. Even on the day of Fiona's funeral no one had come to shake his hand or offer their condolences.

That same day his in-laws had taken his son Calum back to live with them and, when he had protested, his good-sire had challenged him angrily by asking if it was his intention to bring his son up to be as great a coward as his father.

Next had been his kinsmen turning him away from his sharing of the ploughing of the infield, so that by the start of the winter he must surely starve.

The miller too had refused him meal, so that he had to trek the long way to Crieff, where his cowardice was not yet known.

At first the humiliation and loneliness, not to mention near starvation, had driven him close to taking his own life. Then after a while, self pity having turned to anger, he had headed for his in-laws with the full intention of bringing his son home, before his steps had slowed while he weighed up the consequences and difficulties of rearing a small child by himself, before turning to plod a weary way home, bitter with frustration.

At last the day had come when he could stand it no longer. It had been a Sabbath, he recalled. He had sat on the braeside that Sabbath morning watching the good folk of his clan make their way to church, Calum and his in-laws amongst them. Oh, how he had longed to run down the brae, snatch the child up in his arms and hug him tight, even have the courage to take him with him, but all he could do was sit and watch and weep.

At last, self pity having turned to resolve, he had turned for home, saddled the garrons with all he possessed and started for the north, heading he did not know where, only that he could not bide in the glen any longer. As a last act of defiance before leaving he had put his own thatch to the torch. Andrew let out a deep sigh, all for it to have come to this, and sighed again.

It took Andrew the whole of the next day to form some sort of a shelter. He'd started by raising the two remaining walls and constructing a third wall to form a triangle, leaving only enough space to crawl in under two stretched plaids used for a roof, which he covered with bush and whin found up on the hillside. The whole thing he had weighed down with stones, finally crawling in to cook the first hot meal he had had in days, on the fire he'd positioned just outside the entrance.

His modest meal over, Andrew drew his knees up to his chin in the furthest corner of his shelter to reflect on his days work, choking on the smoke blown by a sudden shifting of the wind. He would dearly have loved to stretch another plaid across the entrance, but he had only one left and that too good to be used in such a way. Moreover, it had been woven by Fiona herself. Lovingly, he drew a hand over the kist containing all that remained to him from Glen Laidon. And with these thoughts of home and more pleasant days there, he eventually fell asleep.

Next day was the happiest that Andrew had spent in years, or so he led himself to believe. Here he was on his way home from his new town where everyone and anyone had been only to willing to speak with him, even if for nothing more than out of curiosity, or to offer their sympathy at his sad loss, as well as giving him advice in the working of his land, as all seemed to know his reason for being there.

It was the afternoon of the following day that a second surprise awaited the newcomer. While striving to finish a furrow, the apparition suddenly appeared from nowhere.

"Do you never halt man?" The voice that came at him was firm but soft.

Andrew spun round to face the speaker. "I did not hear or see you approach ... I must have been dreaming," he stammered, his eyes alighting on the young woman who stood there.

"I have been watching you these last days, never halting for a bite or sup. Is it ill health you are after seeking?" she asked with a hint of a smile.

"I have no time even for that!" Andrew laughed, now at ease with this bonnie creature. "Yet in this you are mistaken, for only yesterday I was in Monar Town."

The bonnie head nodded. "I saw you from up there." The lass turned to point back up the hillside. "I bide on the croft on yonder side of the brae, 'tis no more than a mile or so."

The young woman walked towards him. "I brought this for you." She held out the basket that she carried. "It is not much, but I sought to save you time."

Andrew took the proffered basket, while his thoughts lingered on how she did not look a bit like his Fiona, yet she was bonnie in a different sort of way, and of the same age. Suddenly he remembered he no longer had a wife and that his Fiona was no more.

"Should I be holding you from your work, I will away."

The woman's words cut into his thoughts. Andrew dropped his eyes to the basket. "No, no!" he stammered and felt himself blush, only now aware of his eyes never having left the young woman's face. "Forgive my ill manners. You will share a bite with me? There is over much here for one."

"That I will, Andrew MacLaren."

"You know my name?" Andrew exclaimed in surprise.

The woman waved a hand at the empty landscape. "In the circumstances, you are surprised?" Andrew gave a sheepish grin.

17

"Come, we shall sit yonder." She took a step forward. "And seeing as you are too shy to ask the name of the brash lassie who would share a bite with such as yourself, my name is, Kirsty ... Kirsty MacKenzie."

Andrew followed his bonnie new acquaintance to a sheltered spot where she set about setting out the fare, at the same time answering his now ready questions with quiet Highland grace.

For his part Andrew sat watching her every move, learning how she lived with her grandmother, her father having passed away the previous year. He found himself strangely excited to learn that she was unwed, if not a little ashamed that his thoughts should run in such a way, with his own Fiona not long since gone.

She handed him a chicken wing. "So now that you know all about me and mine, what of yourself?" Andrew thought he detected a hint of amusement in her voice, until it was quickly dispelled by her asking, "I have heard you have suffered a great loss, that of your young wife, if I am not mistaken?"

In the past his fabrication of how Fiona had passed away had not bothered him at all. Nor the fact he was now coming to believe it himself. This time the lie would not sit so easily. When he had done, the woman sat silent for a time, the man despising himself for his deceit. Then, as if having come to a sudden decision, Kirsty rose quickly to her feet. "I must away lest my grandmother thinks the *eireallach* has taken me.*"

Andrew's heart sank at the thought of losing such bonnie company. "Och, we are not so close to the water's edge that the kelpie would be having you. What of myself, he who must bide here ... and alone?" he asked lightly, attempting to make amends at having made her so vexed by the story of his wife.

Kirsty chuckled, her eyes gleaming. "I think you are well and able to look after yourself , Mr MacLaren!"

The man rose. "Andrew, if you please, Mistress MacKenzie."

"Then, Kirsty if *you* please, kind sir." They both laughed heartily

"Diabhul!" Kirsty's eyes lost their glint at the sight of Andrew's shelter. "What in the devil's name is yon, man? You will not be telling me that is where you spend your nights? The sound of disbelief was clear in her voice as she strode purposefully towards the shelter.

"It is no chieftain's castle, that I grant you", Andrew stammered, following her, "but until I can build my own *Tigh Tughadh* ..." Andrew patted a wall, "then this must suffice."

Horrified, Kirsty examined the shelter more closely. "You will catch your death man!"

"Do not worry yourself ... Kirsty." He had trouble using her Christian name for the first time. "Once I have my planting done, I will have my own house built in no time at all."

"Then I best not stand in your way. I sought to save you time, and here I am blethering like some old hen wife," Kirsty apologised. She turned. "'Til we meet again, Mister...Andrew."

"What of this?" he asked, holding up her basket.

The woman waved a dismissive hand. "Och, when you have done you can bring it back. My grandmother will also be happy to meet the man who saved her granddaughter from the kelpie!" The woman's laughter still lingered with the man long after she had gone.

With a happy sigh Andrew turned to his ploughing, feeling no longer alone and now not in such a great hurry to be leaving this place after all.

Andrew's intention of dividing the work between the ploughing and the building of his house was thwarted by the incessant rain over the ensuing days, which left him with no option but to make a start on the building of his dwelling.

By the third day the man's spirits were at their lowest ebb. Continually drenched through by day and forced to lie shivering in his wet clothing by night, in a shelter no longer able to afford him protection whilst all around him turned to quagmire, it seemed to him that the very croft had become part of the sea loch itself.

Forlornly, Andrew drew up his knees and fought an overpowering urge to invent some excuse to visit Kirsty MacKenzie, pride alone preventing him from doing so ... that he should present himself in such a sorry state before that young lass. Yet what would he not give for a sight of her again? More so under a dry warm roof.

Dismissing these thoughts from his mind, Andrew turned to channelling some of the water away from his feet, silently praying that by tomorrow the rain would have ceased, which in fact it did, and for the next two days. So that by the end of a week's labour, with the exception of the Sabbath, he had most of the inner and outer walls completed, filling in the intervening space with an earth turned to mud.

Now the difficulty lay in his finding enough timber in this almost treeless land for the door and couples, in especial the rooftree, for it was this that would be the mainstay of the whole building. Perhaps it was time to pay Kirsty a visit, for here indeed was reason enough for seeing the lassie again.

Therefore, it was the very next day, Kirsty's basket in hand, that Andrew made his way to the MacKenzie croft and, while still some distance away, the door opened and Kirsty herself walked to meet him, his heart quickening at the sight of her.

"Oh, you have survived, Andrew MacLaren! I had feared, with so much rain as we are after having, that the kelpie had come right up to your door and spirited you away!" She laughed heartily, coming to take him by the arm.

"It is to be wondered at that it did not, for I believe it would be better to be building an ark than a house!" Andrew responded cheerily.

"Then you best come away in, Noah, and meet my grandmother," Kirsty shrilled, leading him through the door, announcing as she did so, "Grandmother, here is the man I mentioned meeting at the old MacBeolin place the other day!"

"Aye mentioned and mentioned continually," the old woman replied from her seat by the fire.

Blushing, the young woman threw her elder an angry look.

To cover her embarrassment, Andrew handed her the basket. "I am sorry I took so long to return your basket, but I was busy, see you."

"Sit you there by the fire." Embarrassed still, that her grandmother should have said such a thing before a man she scarcely knew, Kirsty's tone was sharper than intended when asking, "You will take a sup of broth?"

"I have scarcely finished eating," Andrew lied.

"What, you will refuse the best broth in the whole of Kintail, made by my granddaughter herself young man?" the old woman challenged, the eyes that sparkled with amusement at Andrew cautioning him to measure his words carefully.

"I did not seek to offend you ... Kirsty," he stammered, at her sharp look.

"Then sit," she commanded, handing him the broth, whilst the old woman cackled at his discomfiture.

The house was quite small in comparison with his own, back in Glen Laidon, he thought, until remembering he had no home; rather, what he did have was a pile of stones on the outreaches of a loch. Therefore, what would he not give to have a place like this, this very night.

The elder MacKenzie interrupted his thoughts. "So it is the old MacBeolin place that you bide, young man. It must be ... let me see ... close on thirty years since his passing. There used to be quite a town here when I was a lass, then folk either died or moved away, until there was no in or outfield left to till. My own son, Kirsty's father, would not move. No, not at all," the old woman stated proudly.

"But how do you manage on your own?" Andrew asked as the old woman reflected.

"Och, we are not entirely on our own Mister MacLaren. There is no shortage of help from the young suitors, you'll understand."

"Grandmother!" Kirsty admonished, blushing. "I have kin who come by when it is needed," she hastened to explain.

"Then you must call on me also; a day's work is worth a sup of your broth anytime, I'll wager." Andrew winked at the elder.

Mellowing slightly, Kirsty shook her head. "You have enough and plenty to do by yourself with not so much as a roof over your head."

Andrew seized the opportunity. "Oh, I have almost all the walls complete. It is the roofing, or the lack of it, that worries me."

"Then this we must remedy," Kirsty nodded decisively. "There are folk in Monar with just such skills."

Encouraged by this, Andrew would have pressed the conversation further had the old woman not interrupted. "It is a sorry plight you are in young man. Whatever possessed you to let MacKerlich, or yon rogue of a son of his, talk you into settling on the old MacBeolin place?"

Believing his hosts were entitled to some sort of an explanation, Andrew related the circumstances in which he had allowed himself to be so easily duped, and the terms that he remain on the croft until one crop had been raised and the rent paid in forfeiture of his goods and gear.

At this the old woman shook her head in condemnation of his gullibility. "You should have seen the place before you gave your word. Can you survive at all man?"

"Aye, that he can, Grandmother," Kirsty interceded, all hostility gone, though perhaps a little too hastily that the man should look at her so. "With a little help from his friends, that is," she added with an encouraging smile.

The remainder of the evening passed pleasantly and to the man more quickly than he would have liked, with him doing most of the talking. He told of his marriage and life in Glen Laidon with Fiona, though he intentionally omitted to mention he had a son because of the obvious questions that would arise. Suddenly, he was aware of the lateness of the hour and, although loathe to leave the warmth of the house for that of his own abysmal dwelling, yet knowing that politeness demanded that he do so, he made his excuses to leave.

Kirsty walked some distance from the house with him before she broke the silence between them. "You must have loved her over much Andrew MacLaren, I am after thinking." The question took the silent man by surprise. "How say you Kirsty ... I ..."

"Och man. The way you talked of her ... and to give up your fine house ... for this ..." Kirsty gestured at the surrounding wilderness, "because you could not abide the thought of living there without her after she had died of the sickness."

"It was so evident?" he asked, ashamed of the lies he had told, for he had taken a liking to this young woman, and her grandmother.

"As evident as Loch Lapaich ... or ... or Sgurr na Lapaich," she threw out a hand, at a loss for words.

"I apologise for my ill manners, Kirsty, it was inexcusable in such bonnie company," he replied, angry at the thought of having upset his new found friend. "I did not mean to offend you or yours. You must be patient with me, if we are to remain good neighbours to one another."

"Only neighbours, Mister MacLaren?"

Stung by the reversion to his surname, Andrew added quickly, "As well as friends ... that is."

Kirsty drew to a halt. "I must be getting back." She pivoted round to look up into his face, her eyes twinkling. "You are a strange man, Andrew MacLaren, as well as naive, I am after thinking."

Then she was gone, leaving the man to ponder on this by himself.

Andrew straightened from his work with the *cas chrom*. Leaning on the crooked spade he stared past the unfinished house to the loch beyond lying still and deep in the warm April sun, shifting his gaze to the whin covered braes. It was indeed a bonnie place, if not wild, and now that fairer weather was upon them, and should fortune favour, he would soon have his ploughing complete.

Bending again to his work Andrew was unaware of the rumble of wheels until the carts had reached the foot of the brae. Startled by the sound he swung round. For a moment he stood there opened mouthed as the procession picked its way over the drier ground towards him, Kirsty mounted on the leading cart.

"I give you good morning Andrew." The woman greeted him warmly with a wave. "See, I have brought those who have the skill to build your *tigh tughadh* for you!"

The cart drew closer and she held out her arms for him to help her down, he, through his surprise, only vaguely aware of her body slipping past him.

"This is Kenneth MacConnach, who will see to the couples and the rooftree," Kirsty exclaimed, releasing herself easily from Andrew's hold.

"And the thatching," the big man added, jumping down and grasping Andrew's hand in greeting.

As the carts drew to a halt others came to make themselves known and offer their services, the stunned man not knowing where to turn until Kirsty came to his rescue.

"Meet Rob MacKenzie, Andrew," she cried happily, introducing him to a man of middle years. "He is a great one to know."

"You have worked well, young man," the older man declared, by way of greeting, and nodding at the house. "You have left a goodly space between the walls, I see."

"I filled the spaces with earth as I have seen done in my own native glen," Andrew replied eagerly at the others interest.

The older man nodded, and walked to what would come to be the centre of the finished dwelling. "You will want the byre here no doubt, where there is the slope … the fire in the middle of the floor ... here." He drew a foot along the ground and Andrew nodded enthusiastically. And a window, here and here ..."

And so it went on, Andrew so engrossed by it all, that he was unaware of Kirsty's absence until the voice of the giant Kenneth MacConnach boomed out to him. "If you help with the wood, Andrew, we can start with the couples whilst the others go searching for the stones."

The old man let him go and Andrew eagerly did what was asked of him by helping to carry the rooftree, the mainstay of the whole structure of the house. At least a dozen men, scattered between the house and loch, hefted boulders for the wall that would divide the barn from the byre, while a half score of women worked at cutting heather pegs and laying out barley straw for the thatch, and in this way the building began.

A little toward noon, Kirsty called to all within earshot to come for refreshments, whereupon the women set out the food.

"This is over much, Kirsty!" an embarrassed Andrew chided, adding louder to the assembled company, "I cannot thank you all enough ... it is all too much."

"It is nothing at all, man! Wait until you work on my castle!" A man of Andrew's own age, though shorter by a head, laughed a reply and had the company joining in.

"Will it have a drawbridge, Gregor?" one asked jovially.

"Aye, and a moat forby!"

Amid further laughter, Kirsty whispered to Andrew, "Yon is Gregor MacVinish. A great fiddler is that one. Sometime you must hear him play."

The bite over and as the company drifted back to their various tasks, Andrew gripped Kirsty by the arm. "It is you I must thank for all of this." He waved a hand at the scene.

"Would they not have done the same in Glen Laidon? Or, need I say, in all of the Highlands, as is our custom?" Kirsty asked.

"Aye, but not so readily for a stranger," Andrew conceded.

Kirsty gave him a startled look. "You are a stranger in name only, Andrew MacLaren." She made a gesture that he should go. "You best hurry, for I see Big Kenneth beckons you there." With this she left him to his work.

It was almost dark before the company finally halted and the men stood around the MacLaren to survey their days work.

"It will be two days before I can return again, Andrew," Big Kenneth apologised. "I have business of my own I must need attend."

"And I also," declared the mason. "But we shall complete your *tigh tughadh* for you on that day. The others are for coming back as well, so it should only be three nights you must spend in yon bird's nest," the man grunted, pointing to Andrew's shelter.

Thanking the company warmly for their assistance, Andrew crossed to where Kirsty stood waiting. "You are not leaving as you came? Should I then walk you home?" he asked hopefully.

The woman shook her head, waving at the departing carts. "There is no need Andrew, Big Kenneth and the fiddler have offered me their company."

"Is it not out of their way?" This said a trifle hastily, that the woman smiled.

"Aye, it is. But who am I to deny them the pleasure of my company, if a simple walk is all they ask in the way of payment for this day's work?"

Kirsty pointed beyond him. "Since you have refused the shelter that others offered you then best you tend your fire there, Andrew, it grows low, and already the night's chill is in the air. Sleep well. I will see you with the others in two days time."

Then she was on her way, the fiddler and the thatcher on either arm, leaving him to stare after her in the darkness, a pang of jealousy eradicating the good day's work.

The company was as good as its word, all arriving on the proposed day and setting to work with a will, so that by late afternoon the work was almost complete.

Once again they were gathered around the knoll to eat a well earned bite when craftsmen, chattering over various problems encountered and overcome, were silenced by raised voices from within the gathering.

"You were told to throw the rope with the stone tied to it *over* the roof for me to catch, but not with my *head*, fool!" This, angrily, to the fiddler from a man of about Gregor's own age and height, who stood pointing to the lump on his head. "I swear it was no accident

Gregor MacVinish. I have a mind to play a tune on *your* head with that fiddle of yours!"

Before the argument could develop further, the big thatcher came between them.

"Will you two never cease your feuding, even on such a day as this?" he laughed heartily at the two life long adversaries. "Now let us all drink to Andrew and his new home!"

The thatcher turned to all around. "To your rooftree, Andrew MacLaren," the company joining him in the old Highland sentiment.

Andrew had barely responded to the toast before he found himself drawn aside by an old man he had seen cutting the divots for the roof so expertly that first day. "I have brought some peat for your fire young man, if you will but help me unload my cart," he said softly, almost conspiratorially."

Obediently, Andrew followed the old man, with a few others following to help stack the peat inside his door. Then, just as suddenly, there were folk all around thrusting gifts into his hands: a three legged stool no longer required, fir candles, dry heather for his bed and so it went on, his thanks drowned by the music from the little fiddler. And so the dance began.

"I told you he was a great fiddler, did I not!" Kirsty shouted into Andrew's ear, above the din, linking his arm in hers.

"That you did, Kirsty," the man acknowledged, aware of the admiring glances of the young women directed at the musician, not least of all from Kirsty herself.

Now the house was full of happy, dancing people whilst others, like Andrew himself, were quite content to watch.

It is to be wondered at how long that happy scene would have continued had not someone called out a few hours later that it was now quite dark outside and should they not all be thinking of leaving for their own homes and leaving Andrew to his?

Then, as quickly as the house had filled, it was suddenly quite empty.

Kirsty would have gone with the rest had Andrew not drawn her aside. "Again, I cannot be thanking you enough for all of this." He waved a hand to encompass the room.

"Thank you, kind sir," Kirsty gave a short curtsey to spare her blushes. "Though I think you favour me over much, there were more than myself with a hand in this." She took stock of the room.

"Now you have a roof over your head, a fire and a warm bed, nothing more than the rest of us enjoy."

Andrew looked past the woman, "and I cannot even repay you by seeing you safely home?"

Kirsty looked out of the open door to the waiting men. "No. I have over and enough escort as it is, as you can see. Some other time, perhaps, Andrew, if you can spare the time that is?"

"Oh that I can Kirsty MacKenzie," Andrew countered. "That I can."

Chapter 3

Gingerly, Andrew lowered himself into the burn, steeling his naked body against the chill, whilst at his back the cascade churned the peat-stained water to a yellow foam, deadening the sound of the approaching horsemen.

"Man! If it is not the fisherman again, Hamish. A great liking this one has for the water, I'm after thinking!" The voice of Coll MacKerlich shrilled above the noise of the falls. "See how he stains the water of our bonnie clear burn!"

Arranged along the banking, the seven horsemen laughed nervously at their leader's humour. He, finding no response to his deliberate insult, lifted Andrew's *feileadh mor* by the point of his sword and, twitching his nose in mock disgust as he held it at arms length, called out, "You will not be telling me, MacLaren, that you wear such a dirt-stained garment? It fairly reeks man!"

"If so, it is MacKerlich dirt as found in the old MacBeolin place that offends your nostrils," Andrew retorted angrily.

Why was it, Andrew asked himself, that this man angered him so? Why could he not learn to keep his wheest? After all, he had ever been a cautious, if not a cowardly, man and here he was again at a disadvantage and provoking a man whose design was clearly to test his mettle.

A few of the horsemen looked away to hide their amusement as their leader charged on angrily. "You are ever brave with the words, MacLaren, though it is there your courage ends I am after thinking. Was it ever the same in your native Glen Laidon?"

At this unexpected mention of his former home, Andrew's head jerked up, his steely stare penetrating that of his adversary, so that the man had to look away.

With a sudden movement the young chieftain sheathed his sword. "Come! We have men's work to do this day," he barked and without another word spurred his mount away.

For a time Andrew was oblivious to the water's chill, for his eyes still held the spot where the MacKerlich had stood. Could it be that this man was aware of his past in Glen Laidon? No, this could not be, for Coll MacKerlich was not the kind of man to keep this secret. Finally, taking his eyes from the spot, Andrew shook his head and turned his thought to more pleasant things.

Riding away, Coll MacKerlich's thoughts still lingered by the burn, convinced that somehow his last remark had struck a nerve. Perhaps there was more to the man's being here than met the eye? Therefore, it would not go amiss to spier further in Glen Laidon sometime. Meanwhile it could rest, for there were more important matters awaiting his attention.

For the next month Andrew was busier than ever. He had seldom seen Kirsty, though loathe not to have done so, it being more important that he finish the ploughing and planting, for all now hinged on his first crop.

Already his newly acquired cattle had left him little enough in his sporran and should the crop fail there would be nothing left to pay the rent, let alone buy meal for the winter. However in this warm day in May, with the sun shining over loch and brae, it was not a day for brooding. So, with the light heartedness of youth, Andrew drove the beasts before him to the croft of Kirsty MacKenzie, for today the woman folk, lads and lassies of the clan were leaving for the summer sheilings.

By the time he arrived Kirsty was, as usual, surrounded by several admirers, all anxious to be of some assistance to her and her grandmother. The latter settled upon the cart surrounded by every conceivable household article.

Andrew halted to pass the time of day with the old woman and wave a greeting to those around. "I have brought the beasts as you instructed, Kirsty," he greeted the younger woman.

Kirsty looked down at him from where she sat on the cart. "You are not coming a ways with us?" she asked in surprise. "Tis a while since I last saw you, Andrew MacLaren. Where have you been hiding yourself?"

Andrew hesitated. Was this an invitation? Did this comely young lass favour his company? He could think of nothing better than to spend the day with one so bonnie, even with the old woman in attendance, but pride would not allow him to be seen trotting behind her like some running gillie. Besides, what chance stood he against such folk as the thatcher for one? "No. I see you have, as usual, more than enough to keep you company. Still, if you will allow, I will see you in a week or so."

Masking her disappointment, Kirsty asked pleasantly, "You will be anxious to see how we fare?"

"Aye, I shall be anxious about my cattle. I should not care to lose any."

At Andrew's stony-faced reply, Kirsty's eyes opened wide in astonishment, and the man broke into a grin, while beside her the old woman slapped her thigh guffawing loudly at the jest.

Angry at being the brunt of the man's humour, Kirsty threw her head in the air. "I think your humour escapes me Andrew MacLaren," she retorted, snapping at the reins.

The woman deigned only to turn her head when some distance away, to smile a measure of forgiveness at the lonely figure standing there.

"Aye, it is not only my humour that escapes you Kirsty MacKennzie, it appears my affection does so as well," Andrew said aloud and, with a heavy heart, watched the line of carts disappear.

Andrew did in fact visit Kirsty several times throughout that same summer, though only once alone and even then for less than half a day.

Looking back on it now, Andrew still felt a slight pang of resentment that Kirsty should have treated him with the same degree of affection as she had shown to others. And why not, he rationalised? After all, he was still little more than a stranger here, with less to offer than those who had known her since childhood. Was he then mistaken in setting his sights too high in the hope Kirsty might feel more for him than he thought she may do?

Perhaps, when the corn was in and by this time next year when there was more to his croft than just a pickle of hens and a few cows, Kirsty would see him differently. This was if she was not already spoken for by that time.

Therefore, it came to be in the autumn that Kirsty shared his satisfaction and relief that his first crop was a success.

Scarcely able to suppress his excitement, Andrew encompassed the field of newly stacked corn stooks with a wave of his hand. "I had my doubts over this, Kirsty. I was sure, with Coll MacKerlich spying on me all the while, that he meant to see me fail. Now I must admit I was wrong about the man, though at times he sorely tried my patience with his snide remarks, and I was scarcely able to hold my tongue." Andrew shook his head angrily, remembering his first meeting with the man by the lochside.

Kirsty nodded at the shorn field. "You need not worry now, Andrew, the corn is in and there is sufficient to see you through this first winter."

"Aye, even after the rent is met. And, who knows, next year may be even better."

"You mean to bide then?" Why, she thought, did this have her heart leaping? True, she had affection for the man ... or was it pity? Love? Now that was a different colour.

"You would have me leave? I have been so ill a neighbour?" Andrew teased.

Kirsty bit her lip. The man had no notion of love, or he would not tease her so.

. "No ... not at all, Andrew, yet there must be better places than this bog land of yours."

The man drew a finger along the gatepost. He dearly wanted to say, "Perhaps so, but where would I find another Kirsty MacKenzie?" Instead he said, "Aye, it will suffice for now. I am quite content."

Kirsty's heart sank; her thinking had been right, there was no love here. This man could not forget the wife he had left back in Glen Laidon. Sadly Kirsty hid a tear.

The winter *ceilidhs* were when the menfolk would gather together in someone's *tigh tughadh* to relate tales of their clan in days gone by. As a newcomer, Andrew was eagerly sought after to tell of his own clan's exploits, and this he would do with relish, it being to him a sign of acceptance by his adopted clan. Only afterwards in the loneliness of his own home would he sadly reflect on similar gatherings in his own glen. It was then he missed his own folk and was for ever wondering how his young son fared.

That first winter he did not see much of Kirsty.

In the course of the winter, Andrew found himself at Monar House, at a great birthday feast held in honour of Angus MacKerlich, Himself. Gregor was there, filling the great hall with his music; this when he was not arguing with his mortal enemy, Kenneth MacCrae.

Winding through the swirling dancers, Kirsty found Andrew in the company of the old divot cutter and spirited the younger man away.

"If I did not know you better, Andrew MacLaren, I would believe you had more interest in cutting divots than you had in seeing me, since I have scarcely rested eyes on you this entire long winter!" she teased him with a mischievous glint in her eye.

"Och, you were not at all starved of attention, Kirsty MacKenzie. Yon young callants were buzzing around you like bees around a honey pot."

Kirsty threw her head back in laughter. "I do believe you are jealous, Mister MacLaren!"

Andrew did not know how to answer. Was she mocking him? A game she was playing? Or was she merely using him to make others jealous? Yet he did not believe this was the nature of the lass.

Kirsty saw the man's sad look and knew instantly her jibe had hurt. She grabbed him by the hand. "Come! You shall dance a reel with me! Show me you are not angry at your Kirsty!"

Reluctantly drawn into the circle of dancers, Andrew decided a man never knew where he was with a woman, especially such a woman as Kirsty MacKenzie.

It was a glorious spring evening, with the long winter past and with a feeling that all was well within his world, that Andrew made his way to the MacKenzie croft. For a moment he took time on the crest of the brae to look down at his own croft, at the neat furrows of planted corn, the cows grazing peacefully by the burn and the diminutive specks of hens scattered around his door. Sighing contentedly, the man again started on his way.

After a while he changed direction and headed for the rock that marked the great hollow. There, he spied Kirsty on the braeside beyond, drawing water from the burn as was her custom at this hour. She saw his coming and and waved a cheery greeting.

"It is a great while since I last saw you Andrew. I was for thinking my tongue had offended you the last time we met." Kirsty paused to search his face.

"No, Kirsty, the fault lies with me. I should have paid my respects to you and your grandmother long since. Nor is it excusable that I did not seek to help you during these long winter months." Andrew shuffled a foot. "It is of this I have come to speak."

Setting down the bucket Kirsty waited for him to go on.

With the whole panorama of the distant mountains as backdrop, a great ball of fire that was the sun sinking behind her, Andrew thought he had never seen anyone look so bonnie. "You have not known me long Kirsty ... and I have little to offer you as yet ... though in that time we have enjoyed each others company ..." It was all going wrong, his well prepared speech clean gone from his head. He started again. "I would know if you harbour any small feelings towards me ... as I have for you ... not *small*," he corrected himself. "Och, Kirsty, it is not what I would say. Not what I would have you know," he cried in despair.

"Oh! You bonnie poor man!" The anguish in the woman's voice startled him. "Why now? Why *this* day? Devil take you, Andrew MacLaren, but you never spoke of this before, never a word of your feelings towards me."

Here was an anger, a despair never before witnessed by the man. "I did not intend to offend you Kirsty, as I fear I have done. It was ungallant, and you scarcely knowing me."

He turned to move away and she caught him by the arm. "You are too late, Andrew, I fear." Tears in her eys Kirsty bowed her head. "I did not know you cared so, when I promised myself to another."

Kirsty felt, rather than saw, the man sag before her. He moved away to the burn side to stand a silent broken man, then eventually, after what would seem to her to be a long time, to ask, huskily, "It is the thatcher? I would not blame you." Then, at the shake of her head, "Rob MacDonnel, the miller. It is he? Am I not right?" Again the bonnie head shook. "Then, for pity's sake, *who*?" he cried.

"Gregor MacVinish," she whispered, unable to look at his anguished face.

"The fiddler?" Andrew exclaimed in disbelief.

"He loves me and has said so Andrew," Kirsty said softly in defence of her choice.

"And what of me, Kirsty? Do I not love you also?" This hoarsely said.

"Aye. This may be true of a fashion. But how was I to know ... really know? You never did tell me as Gregor has done."

"I tried to when we were alone, see you."

"We were never alone," Kirsty moaned. "There lies the pity of it all. There was always your Fiona between us. And I will not share a bed with a woman dead and gone."

Thus it ended.

Whenever Andrew met Gregor on communal work in the glens he was scarcely able to keep a civil tongue, that man's sole crime being his stealing of Kirsty from him. Annoyed and ashamed, yet unable to help himself, Andrew knew the cause of his bitterness towards the man was purely jealously, an ever-increasing ailment as the day of the impending marriage drew closer.

The dawn of that day found Andrew bent to his work with a ferocity which even he was unaware he possessed. This, he decided, would be the longest day ... and night ... of his life. Finally, with all work exhausted, the clansman took himself by the loch side and then eventually to the hills beyond, walking where he did not know, or care, as long as it led him away from Monar's kirkyard, until the gloaming saw his unwitting steps once again by the sea loch's shore.

Seated on a rock not far from where he had first encountered Coll MacKerlich, Andrew reflected on this latest chapter of his life. Oh, that he had never halted here in Kintail in the first place and had instead struck east by the Great Glen, then Kirsty MacKenzie would still be unknown to him.

In this moment of despair, his acceptance into a clan other than his own where everyone treated him as friend and equal meant little to him. For, however he may reflect upon these things, it always came back to Kirsty and it mattered little to him that there should be a few raised eyebrows at his absence from the wedding festivities. But the sight of the woman he loved in the arms of another would surely break his heart.

Oblivious to the silent waters and the surrounding beauty, Andrew shivered, more from a feeling of despair than from the cold. It would soon be dark, or what passed for darkness in this long July day. He stood up, skimming a stone across the grey mirror of the water. "It should have been me lying there with Kirsty this night, in my own thatched house that she herself helped build. The fiddler!" he shouted aloud, scattering the whaups in all directions. "It should have been me!"

It is said time is a great healer, yet time passed slowly from that hot July day to the autumn for the MacLaren. He had not ventured near the MacKenzie household since Gregor had come to bide there. Neither had the happy couple's step brought them to his own door. Yet it was inevitable that, due to communal work, he and Gregor should meet.

It was while working at the kiln that, it seemed to Andrew, their friendship accidentally restarted, though to the fiddler their acquaintanceship had never altered. Strangely it was Coll MacKerlich they both had to thank.

"Man!" the younger MacKerlich cried, looking down from horseback at the smaller figure of the fiddler. "I do believe you have shrunk, man! I fear your bonnie wife is over much for you Gregor. Perhaps you should send her to me at Monar House ... eh?"

Although incensed by the remark, Gregor hesitated. This, after all, was the son of their chieftain the MacKerlich Himself, and did not that man reward him well for his fiddle playing?

Perhaps, he tried to convince himself, the man only jested. However, Coll's further ribald remarks, thrown over his shoulder to all and sundry as he rode off, followed by his laughing 'running tail' dispelled all further doubts to the little man.

Aware of Andrew working close by, Gregor's voice shook with humiliation as he watched the departure of the man who had so cruelly chastised him in front of all.

"I could not answer him, Andrew. It is shamed I am that I could not defend my own wife's honour. All for the sake of the siller," he added angrily.

It was not any sympathy for the man that led Andrew to reply but the fact that Kirsty's name had been so besmirched before all. This he could hardly take.

"Heed not man, there will be other times," he heard himself say. "Come, it is time we were away to our own homes."

Thus their friendship began.

Chapter 4

It was inevitable in these stormy times that war between the clans should come eventually. Leaning back against the wall, the fire darting shadows across the darkened room, Andrew sipped the whisky, and reflecting wearily on what little he had achieved over the last four years of sweat and toil. Though, now under the present circumstances even the most mundane of tasks on the croft was decidedly more inviting that what he had to face tomorrow.

All for the sake of what, pride mostly? Reluctantly, Andrew conceded there was more to it than this, though it did little to dispel the fear gnawing his belly, now that he had resolved to stand beside the only friends he knew. The question was, for how long, before he turned tail as he had done the day Fiona died, and once again found himself ostracised for his base cowardice?

The man refilled his cup. It was not that he was over fond of the spirit, only tonight he'd hoped it would give him some chance of sleep. A sleep that as yet had failed to come, and in its stead half forgotten memories leaped out at him to jerk him fully awake.

Why did it now seem so important to recall the last conversation with his grandfather ? The first meeting with Fiona? Or the names of those who played with him when they were laddies up by the waterfall in the glen, all those long years ago?

Andrew gazed into the fire as if therein lay the answer to it all. Wee Calum would soon be eight years old he recalled, reliving for a moment the last time he had seen his son.

His head swam and he slid down to the floor grinning sheepishly, knowing he had indulged himself of the spirit much too freely. It would not do to see twice as many MacMorrans and their cursed allies the MacKinnons tomorrow. Yet, again with luck he might miss the whole damned sorry business.

Panic stricken at the thought of having overslept, Andrew threw himself from his heather bed and stood shivering in the morning's chill.

Still hazy from the effects of last night's drink he poked at the fire in attempt to coax it to burn. By all accounts, he should set about breaking his fast, but the thought of what lay ahead, coupled by his recent over indulgence of the *usque beatha* left him in no doubt as to his feelings towards food at this very moment.

Instead, yawning, he reached up into the thatch and searched for the weapon he most detested, until his fingers curled around its hilt. *Dia*! How he hated the sword and what it could do to a man. Now, the pistol, Andrew balanced his favourite weapon lovingly in his other hand, that was a different story. Clean, impersonal, no need to come in contact with your foe, to hack, stab or maim.

Thrusting the weapon into his belt Andrew took a last look around the room that was home to him, hoping the fire would last until his return. Then thinking as he closed the door behind him what a daft thought it should be a time such as this. For, was it not much more important that he should see the place again? And if so would he be whole? Or would he be maimed, and have to rely upon others for his very existence as he had seen in others back in his own glen? With a despairing shake of his head, that it would be God's will, he started for the braeside.

It was some time before Andrew caught sight of the first of his fellow clansmen, and altering direction, lifted his step to meet them.

"I give you good morning Andrew MacLaren," Rob MacDonnel greeted him cheerfully as if journeying to nothing more than a Sabbath service. "You are alone I see. Where is the fiddler?"

Andrew hated the man for his coolness. Did he not know what they were about? Had he not seen what sword play could do? "I have not seen him as yet, Rob. Perhaps Kirsty commands he bides at home, and has tucked him under her arm!" he answered in an attempt at flippancy, for there would be time enough for them to find out his own lack of mettle, and walked on amid a chorus of laughter.

As they proceeded across the braes, others hurried to join them, either singly or in groups, swelling their ever increasing numbers.

Suddenly the MacDonnel pointed a finger back down the braeside at the diminutive figure of Gregor hurrying up the slope to join them. "Look yonder, Andrew!" he cried. "Is not that the wee man himself? He must have tickled Kirsty under the oxter, that she has had to let him drop!" he laughed.

In no time at all it seemed, the fiddler was with them, deftly countering their ribald remarks as he sought out his friend.

"I thought for a time you must be acting as rearguard!" the MacLaren poked drily.

"It was a sore thing to leave her, man," the other replied with a shake of his head.

There was silence between them for a time as they walked on, until Gregor without looking at the man walking beside him, asked, "You will look after her Andrew, should I fall this day?" Gregor continued to stare ahead, clearly embarrassed by the question. "I have ever been surprised she chose the likes of me over someone such as yourself. Me of all people !" he thumbed his chest. "I am asking you...no...begging you, will you care for her, for I love her dearly? As I believe you do also in your own way."

As the wind blew at Andrew's plaid, he was aware of how right the man's thoughts were, however nieve. Aloud he said. "That I will, Gregor, though I fear she will not let me."

Gregor drew to an abrupt halt. "And why not?" he exclaimed angrily, staring up at his friend, and stepping out of the way of the passing clansmen.

"Because I cannot play the fiddle, you daft wee man!"

For a moment both men stood there on the open hillside glaring at one another, until gradually an expression of comprehension covered the fiddler's face. "Aye, maybe it is too late for you to learn," he grinned.

The company travelled on for the best part of an hour, Andrew and Gregor scarcely speaking a word, while others, mainly the younger ones kept up a steady banter as they crossed the more gentle braes. Whereupon, reaching the slopes of Carn Eige the final contingent from the town itself converged to meet them.

At last their numbers complete, they gathered round the mounted figure of Coll MacKerlich. "I greet you all in the name of my father the MacKerlich Himself, who unhappily is unable to be with us, for as you all know he has suffered sorely these last years with the rheumatism. Nonetheless, he is with us all in spirit, and has been assured by me his son of a victory this day.

We have been long over patient with these accursed MacKinnons and their underlings the MacMorrans, now our patience is at an end. I will say no more." Dramatically the young chieftain drew his sword, and in a voice that rose angrily, pointed down the glen. "Now let us forward and do what must be done!"

"Is he not full of himself, Andrew ?" The fiddler breathed through his teeth, having no liking for the man, or his insults since that day at the kiln. "At least he has the decency to spare telling us of how we are fighting for the honour of our clan, and how our cause is right and just."

Surprised by this unexpected explosion of feeling, Andrew looked sideways at the friend walking beside him. "Och!" the fiddler went on. "I will not be saying we have not been sorely tried by yon heathen tribes." Gregor slowed to glance around him. "Still there is many a man here under sufferance of having the thatch burned over his head as befits the right of any chieftain to do, should that clansman not wish to follow."

Andrew held his peace, for was this not true of himself?

Gregor appeared not to have noticed, but continued scathingly. "Aye, Angus MacKerlich, the old scoundrel, he is well out of it. Rheumatism indeed! It has never prevented him from visiting the widows in Monar, ere now!"

"Then it is to be hoped when this day is done, he has not an even greater choosing." Andrew sighed.

They had walked on close on a mile when the young chieftain drew them to a halt. There on the near braeside stood the foe, the sound of their pipes reaching them across the glen, their high ringing challenge followed almost at once by a roar as each man took up the ancient slogan of his clan. Over and over it came, like cannon fire, reverberating from the very mountainsides themselves.

A hush had descended on their own ranks, Andrew swallowed hard, and gripped his weapon tighter. There seemed so many of them. He shot a furtive glance at the faces around him feeling as though he was the only one who stood there afraid. One man caught his eye, and winked, lifting his sword in encouragement. Feeling a little better for this, Andrew looked towards the foe.

"You Kenneth! And you Fraser!" Coll MacKerlich flung at his pipers, the hurled words cutting through the silent company like a knife. "I vowed to my father we would not be outfought this day! Neither do I expect to be outplayed! Now play damn you, play!"

In that instant all was transformed as the first notes of the pipes filled the air, and a mighty roar erupted from their own serried ranks.

Now eager to be at the foe, all pressed forward, Andrew amongst them. First, at a walk, then as the distance shortened, to a trot, so that in no time at all they were charging full tilt at the advancing line.

Andrew ran with the rest, his knees weak beneath him, his numbed brain vaguely registering mountains on his left, trees to his right with the glint of a river beyond. Was he really here? To kill or be killed? Was this unknown glen to be his last resting place?

Panting from exertion he ran on towards that ever closing line of howling men who now ran out a longer line in order to give themselves room to wield their terrible Lochaber axes, and flashing swords. He felt sick. All he wanted was to be away from here. Away from a glen he did not even know, or care to know the name of.

There was a sudden volley of shots and a man to his right went down, and instinctively he ran behind the man in front, self preservation paramount to honour. They were almost there now. Already the first line was in contact with the enemy clansmen, each seeking to choose a foe, to thrust, jab or parry. Then he was down, toppling over the man he had used as a shield, and skidding on to his side, with bodies leaping over him, pain as his head struck a rock, and then darkness.

Face down in the heather, Andrew slowly regained consciousness. Slowly he put a hand to his brow, anxious to know how badly he had been hit, until his brain clearing, he remembered he had simply fallen. He struggled to his knees. A few paces away, his back against a rock, oblivious to the conflict raging behind, Ewen Mackenzie sat watching him.

Andrew put a hand up to his eyes to help clear away the blood, and through a crimson mist saw big Kenneth go down, felled by a blow from a two handed claymore, and before the thatcher could recover was again struck by that murderous weapon, the blow splitting him from shoulder to hip. Even from here he was sure he had heard the crunch of bone above the clamour of battle.

A line of the foe were charging at his friends. He saw the swing of the Lochaber axes, the clang of metal on targe, the blood spewing like a fountain from head and breast, the cry of the wounded, the howl of the enraged.

Sickened, all Andrew wanted to do was bury his face in his hands. If the thatcher had died so easily, what chance stood he? He forced himself to look again to where clansmen still hacked and stabbed at each other, either singly or in groups.

Away to his left he picked out Coll MacKerlich, Gregor by his side, lead on his clansmen. "What you lack in height wee man," Andrew muttered as his friend disappeared into the fray, " you make up in courage, for if it was not for the MacKenzie here watching me, I'd be up and away."

Rising, Andrew found his sword, and walked unsteadily to where the MacKenzie sat.

"It is only a wee wound," he explained, pointing to his head. "But what of yourself, man, are you sorely hurt?" he asked putting a gentle hand on the man's shoulder, to recoil in horror as he slid sideways at his touch.

"God's curse, I have been watched by a dead man!" Andrew exclaimed aloud, angry that he could already have been quit of this place.

The frightened man took a hasty look around him to ensure that there was no other witness to what he had in mind. There was none. Only here and there tartan mingling with the heather betrayed where a dead clansman lay. He took to his heels, now in no great hurry to be joining his friends.

Reaching the woods Andrew drew breath, and leaned against a tree to reflect on how last night it would have appeared inconceivable that he should return to live as an outcast as he had done back in Glen Laidon. Now, in the light of day it did not seem so ill, at least he would be alive, not cut down like the thatcher, and how many more?

Andrew knew he was no swordsman, and now that both sides were intermingled his pistol would be of little use, or so he tried to tell himself. He slid down on to the damp grass and held his head in his hands. He was a coward, and God help him, would ever be until the day he died.

He had deserted the only friends he had, who like himself also wished to live, but they unlike him had not turned tail. He shook his head as if clearing it from a nightmare. He must think...form a plan if he was not to be found out.

Rising, the agonised man walked the short distance to the river bank, where, kneeling down he hoped to catch his reflection in the water to find out how large was the cut on his brow, although by its feel and what he had witnessed this day, it would not warrant a second glance. Nor would it convince anyone as reason for him not having been in the thick of things long before now. Now his only hope was to watch the battle from the safety of the woods, then wait until the time was right to join his friends, either in victory or defeat.

Andrew splashed water on his face. The coolness helped to convince him this was the only hope of avoiding recrimination. It was then he heard the murmur of voices, and from across the water made out the glint of sunlight on steel, followed by a glimpse of tartan through the bracken.

Choking back his fear Andrew scrambled to his feet and ran as fast as his legs would carry him, and had barely reached the safety of the woods to throw himself down, before a band of MacKinnons burst into view, fanning out on the opposite bank in search of a way across the shallow river.

"Ten...eleven...twelve!" Andrew counted. "Dear Lord in heaven." he hissed. "should they succeed in crossing, it will be all up with the clan." Now, if he had any thought of saving himself, he better be quickly away.

Yet what of his friends? Especially of Gregor? Andrew allowed himself one callous moment of thought. Should anything befall the fiddler, Kirsty was certain to turn to him for solace, and this time he would not be slow to miss his opportunity. After all, was this not what the wee man had asked of him?

Disgusted that he should think such things at a time like this, Andrew dismissed it from his mind, and instead concentrated on the river as the first man dropped down the banking almost directly across from where he hid.

Perhaps, a warning shot would deter them, two at most, then it was away with him. He would have done his best, he lied. And if the MacKinnons did win across, there would be more than he running for home.

With his mind made up, Andrew set down his powder horn on the ground beside him for ready reloading, and using a boulder top to steady his hand took careful aim as the foremost figure entered the water, firing and hitting the startled clansman and throwing him back against the banking.

In that instant all was confusion as the enemy clansmen halted to scan the woods in search of their unseen attacker.

He had killed his first man! Andrew's fingers trembled as he reloaded. Already two more were some ways across the river, their *feileadh mor* billowing in the current. He fired again, his target swaying and clutching his shoulder, before again coming on, his fellow clansmen close behind.

Now the river seemed full of enemy clansmen, targes head high to offer greater protection. Again Andrew took aim, though he knew his attempt to arrest the advancing foe was hopeless, for already, one had almost reached the banking, with others not so far behind.

But why was he doing this, Andrew thought while again reloading. It would be to no avail, for if his intentions were to save himself he must away. Then why was he up and running at this man, instead of in the opposite direction? He reached the banking, firing at the man scrambling up the banking and hitting him at almost point blank range, who with a strangled moan slid back into the water.

Andrew's head jerked up at the shriek that followed his shot to where a clansman stood midstream shaking his sword in fury, who, with a further howl of rage, followed by his kinsmen came charging at him through the water.

Shaking with fear, Andrew backed away, only too well aware of his fate should he be caught. This, and the fact his pistol was empty, and he would have little time to pick up his sword from the wood before they would be upon him.

He turned and ran, reaching the woods at the same time as a line of charging howling men came out of the trees, sweeping passed him to the river. His own clansmen had arrived.

Sword pumping the air in triumph, Rob MacDonnel trotted back from the waters edge. "You have saved the day MacLaren, but for you, it would be ourselves who would be running with our tails between our legs!" Relief and gratitude covered the miller's face, as others behind him came to slap Andrew on the back or shake his hand.

Rob put an arm around the dazed hero's shoulder and led him back through the woods, all the while explaining how the battle had gone, and how Kenneth MacKenzie, bathing a wound downstream had seen Andrew hold off the MacKinnons and had quickly returned to raise the alarm.

"We had the better of them by that time!" the elated man went on. "Yet, had yon ones won behind us, it would have been a different ending to the tale, I am after thinking."

Andrew emerged from the woods to a battlefield now quiet and still, where a clansman knelt by a wounded kinsman while others, a little less quiet, were in the act of stripping the beaten foe.

Meekly, Andrew followed Rob to where their young chieftain stood.

"You have seen the scum off by the river, then Rob?" Coll asked, pointedly ignoring the MacLaren, his voice loud and somehow intrusive on such hallowed ground.

"Aye, that we have, Coll," the man answered enthusiastically. "Thanks to Andrew, here who prevented their crossing. There must have been a score or more that came at you, Andrew. What say you?" he asked eagerly.

Too embarrassed to answer and knowing the true manner of his actions, Andrew hesitated to answer.

"Och! It is yourself fisherman we have to thank." Coll turned a steely eye on his former adversary, as if only just aware of his presence. "I wondered what had befallen you. Run off at the first shot, thought I." His uncalled for remark against the one who had undoubtedly saved the day, brought a gasp from those around. Coll read their angry faces. Now, it seemed to them this newcomer in their midst was a saviour, a man who had quietly borne his taunts and insults, though to them he need not have done so, for this man was no coward, only a man like themselves who wanted nothing more than to raise his crops and live in peace. Coll gave a short laugh as if what he had said had been in jest. "But where else would a fisherman be if not by the water, think you!"

Nimbly the young chieftain swung onto his garron, and with sword raised high cried out for all to hear. "So let us give thanks this day, for this victory is surely ours!" The cry, once taken up echoing from one end of the battlefield to the other.

From his garron's back, Coll MacKerlich seethed at Andrew's receding back. "Look at you now, MacLaren," he choked, "soaking up the praises of all, whilst pretending to help the wounded. Already in your mind you are hearing the *fear an tigh* at the *ceilidh* tell of your bravery this day. Yet, what of me, Coll MacKelich, he who led in the thickest of battle? Will there be a thought for him? 'Tis strange how events can change all. Though I can still see the look on your face, MacLaren, yon day by the waterfall, and I saw it again this day. It could well be, you are after all running away, and the answer lies deep in Glen Laidon. Bathe in your glory fisherman, for I fear it will be short lived, of this I am certain. As certain as this day is surely *mine !"*

Coll MacKerlich's thinking was in part true, to Andrew to have survived was in itself a miracle: to be regarded a hero, beyond all comprehension. Also, there was no need for him to lie about his absence from the fray, as now all accepted that the reason for his being at the river was the same as that of Kenneth Mackenzie his inadvertent rescuer.

Andrew scanned the recent battleground, still scarcely able to believe his good fortune though careful to avert his eyes or look too closely at those lying maimed or mortally wounded.

Had it been only last night that he had feared this day? Well look at him now! Though he well knew that nothing within him had changed, for was he not still that same base coward of Glen Laidon?

"Andrew! Andrew!" Rob MacDonnel, was at his elbow. "'Tis the fiddler...Gregor, see you!"

Catching the cry of despair in the man's voice, Andrew felt the knot in his stomach as he followed the man across the heather to a mound where Gregor lay, those around the wounded man moving aside to let him through.

At first it was the sight of Kenneth MacCrae kneeling by Gregor's side that surprised him most, with Gregor himself lying on his back, his head cushioned in the lap of his cousin Calum.

A sudden spasm racked the tortured man as Andrew dropped to his side. He saw the partially severed arm, belched and looked away. It was not the action of a hero, but he was beyond caring. It was his friend who lay here.

On the opposite side from where Andrew knelt, Kenneth MacCrae, let out a wail. "Oh you poor man, you will never play the fiddle again!"

Gregor's answer was little more than a whisper. "This will no doubt please you, MacCrae, for you said I never could play the damned thing in the first place."

"And never you could," his rival replied in mock anger.

Gregor struggled to rise. "I'll mind that, MacCrae, when next I thrash you, though it will be no different than before, except this time there will be no need to tie my hand behind my back.

Then it was over. The pistol coming down to take the fiddler behind the ear.

"Be quick before he comes round, he has already lost over much life's blood," the MacCrae commanded, rising.

Now understanding the ploy, Andrew stood back to give Calum room to sever what remained of the arm, and bind the wound as best he could. Within seconds a litter had appeared and Gregor laid upon it.

His glory short-lived, Andrew moved off a little to vomit. There were no victors in war, only victims such as his friend Gregor, or the men he himself had slain by the river, and women like Kirsty whose life and so many more would never be the same again.

As if to mock him and those laying there, the clan's stirring march cut through the air, Coll MacKerlich at the head of the young men passing by, shouting and laughing, laden down with the spoils of war. After all, had they not won?

The stretcher bearers had stuck to the glens and gentler slopes in order to make the fiddler's journey and those like him easier. Now there was only Gregor left, the rest having departed on their various ways, and it was almost dark by the time they sighted the MacKenzie croft, Calum hurrying on to prepare the women for what was to come.

Walking beside the stretcher, Andrew looked down from the last ridge top towards his own house and croft, where the sea loch reached out threatening to engulf the oasis that was his home and failing for the first time to see the harshness of the land, only longing to be back amongst safe and familiar things once more.

Kirsty left Calum by the open door and hurried to meet them, every man there tensing as she grew closer, each reluctant to be the first to meet her look. They need not have feared, for Kirsty saw none but Gregor.

They halted to let her place a gentle hand on her man's brow, averting their eyes while she bent to kiss the unconscious figure, saying nothing as she fell in step beside them as they resumed their journey.

They laid Gregor by the fire, the old woman's malevolent stare sharper than any steel met that day, leaving them awkward and ashamed. This then is the folly of war it glowered. Was it worth it? Not to poor Gregor, nor any like him. Only those who had survived unscathed would hunger for more, then the folly would begin all over again.

The men retreated to the farthest recesses of the tiny room, each looking on in silent fascination as the old woman spread butter on a cloth singed with a hot iron, then bind the wound with the skin of the eel.

It was while watching Kirsty's grandmother at work, that Andrew first became aware of Calum thrusting a cup of ale in to his hand as he spoke to his kinsman standing beside him. "I myself will bide here the night, Rob. Tell my wife I am fine, if you will, and...."

"You best away home to Morag, Calum.and not have her worrying," Kirsty's low but steady voice broke in. "I can look after my man well enough, and I thank you all for bringing him home." She got up from where she had been kneeling beside her stricken husband, as if to usher them out. "I rejoice to see you all safe, and that the clan fared well this day. At least, God willing we will know peace for a time."

Almost guiltily the men looked at one another or grunted a reluctance to leave, though each inwardly eager to be gone from this place of sorrow, and away to their own home. Then, as if exonerated by Kirsty's steady stare they shuffled to the door where they halted briefly to offer a last word of comfort to the two women.

Behind them Andrew hesitated, reluctant to leave. "I will come by tomorrow and see how he fares, Kirsty," he whispered, and wondered where he had seen that same look of sorrow and despair as the woman looked up from where she had again knelt to cradle her man's head in her lap.

"Aye that will be fine, Andrew and I thank you kindly."

For a moment their eyes met, and Andrew knew all the love within her was for the man she held in her arms. He closed the door behind him, breathing in the clear night air, thankful to be alive and going home, but never before having felt so alone.

Andrew kept his promise, calling in the next day and every day after, for the next two months, to help when necessary.

One day towards the end of October when he was walking with Kirsty down the brae from the croft, the woman suddenly broke the silence between them, her voice little more than a whisper. "The man is not healing, Andrew, you can see this for yourself."

"Give it time, lass, it is a sore time for him. I fear the wound gives him great pain at times, though he had said little of this to me."

They walked on in silence, skirting the whin before Kirsty spoke again. "The arm will heal well enough, of this I am sure, it is his mind I fear for. He cannot come to terms with himself. Before this..."she hesitated, choking ."...before this happened, Gregor was a man proud of his art, and his love for the music. Aye, and for that bit extra his skill could bring home to me."

Momentarily, Kirsty's eyes flashed with pride as she went on, as if in her mind's eye she saw those happy days again. "When Gregor MacVinish played his music, no man...not even the MacKerlich Himself looked down upon the wee man. Now the music is no more, and there is no call from Himself for him to come to Monar House. It grieves him Andrew, this and the little he can do around the croft."

Clutching Andrew by the arm Kirsty drew to a halt to stare up into his face. "His comfort is in the drink, Andrew, not with me." There was despair in her voice as she went on. "He believes I find him repulsive, Andrew, and that I seek him in the night out of pity alone."

The woman drew away to hide her tears; never since their marriage had she spoken so freely to him.

Andrew put his arm around her and gave her a gentle squeeze. "Time is a great healer, Kirsty, both for mind and body; though in the end it will be well worth the wait." He drew her around to face him, and wiped away her tears with the tip of his finger. "Come, Mistress Kirsty," he said jovially, for he must lift this sad woman from her sorrow, "we have work to do. It will not be long before Peter MacMaster, returns from the south. I pray he has won us both a fair price for our beasts. I myself asked for..."

And in this way Andrew managed to restore a little comfort to the woman, as they continued on their way.

A gray curtain of rain swept in from the sea, piercing the loch with a thousand needles, driving squawking sea birds for the shelter of the land.

Huddled around the fire, Andrew was glad to be home. It had smirred after leaving Kirsty, and he had only just succeeded in reaching the croft as the rain lashed down. Already it was turning into a wild night and the *snighe;* the rain coming in through the roof sizzled in the open fire, turning his thoughts to those first nights in his shelter, and he allowed himself a moment of pride at his achievements since then, for now he no longer compared his present *tigh tughd* with that back in Glen Laidon.

It was as he was heaping more peat upon the fire that he heard the banging on the door and the voice he recognised as that of Peter MacMaster, he, whom he had spoken of earlier that day to Kirsty, calling from outside, that had him swiftly rising to unbar the door.

"'Tis yourself Peter," Andrew shouted above the wind. "This is no night to be abroad. Come away in man!"

"We must put the beasts in the byre, Andrew, before we are all blown away!" the MacBeolin shouted back.

Once done, Andrew led the drenched man to the fire, and quickly set about placing meet and drink before him.

"Man I am soaked through," Peter shivered. "It is more like hail than rain. To make matters worse my own garron has gone lame, and me wanting badly to see my own fireside this night, and I still have the fiddler's croft to reach as well."

"Do not be worrying yourself, Peter, you can take old Robbie there. He is not as lively as your own beast, but strong enough to see you home."

"I thank you kindly, man. I can walk fine if Robbie can carry the meal, and will be over glad to be sitting by my own fireside once more.

I met Coll MacKerlich in Glen Lyon on my way back," the hungry man began between mouthfuls. "He was telling me he was on some important business and should return within the week." Peter chewed on the meat. "He had sent me down by your own Glen Laidon, on some other matter....'Tis a bonnie part of the country yon. I can well see how you would be loathe to leave it."

Was there some purpose to the man letting him know he had been to his former home, Andrew thought as he busied himself by the fire? And what was this other matter he spoke of? Or was he merely trying to be polite. "Fate does not always allow a man to do what is best." He moved the iron pot aside. "Glen Laidon was in another lifetime, Peter. My home is here now." He rose stiffly. "But enough of that. What price did you manage for the beasts?"

49

After some time, their business concluded, Peter rose, slapping his thigh. "Well it is time I was away if Mistress MacBeolin is to see her man this night." The big man yawned stretching himself by the fire. "Though I am loathe to leave your fire, MacLaren. At least I have dried out a wee bit. And I thank you kindly for the bite and sup."

Peter reached the door and Andrew drew a plaid from his kist and held it out to him.

"Here take this, man, you will be glad of it by the time you see your own peat fire."

Reluctantly Peter took the proffered plaid. "Man, Andrew, this plaid is over good to be wearing on such a night," he protested, surveying its quality.

"It was Fiona...my wife who wove it herself. It was made to keep a man warm."

Peter opened his mouth to speak, then as if thinking better of it said instead. "I will have it back to you when I return your Robbie and fetch my own beast back. I will bid you a good night Andrew MacLaren, and I thank you again."

Andrew opened the door waiting there until his friend had disappeared into the night before returning to his fire, happy at having had some company for a change, as well as being paid both in meal and coin for his beasts. Yet, had there not been something in the man's manner when speaking about Coll MacKerlich and Glen Laidon, that had him feeling uneasy? Was his past about to catch up with him? Please that it was not so. Not after what he had achieved here on the croft, and having won every man's respect after the battle in the glen.

He would have pondered the matter further had the sound of the gunshot not interrupted all further thoughts. Racing to the door he threw it open as the riderless garron galloped passed, and having no doubts as to the cause of the sound, rushed out into the rain.

Andrew came upon Peter MacMaster lying in the mud. Gently he lifted the stricken man's head onto his lap, Peter's life's blood mingling with the rain, seeping through the plaid.

Peter stared up at him in disbelief. "Why, MacLaren? Why

"I do not know, Peter," Andrew answered, steeling a quick look around him. Now realising should the assassin still be near, he himself was unarmed. The scene reminiscent of the night his own father had died. "I will try and get you in by. Put an arm around me."

"It is no use man...I fear I have not the strength. You will tell...Helen...that..."
Andrew bent closer to hear those last few words meant for his wife. Words that never came.

Andrew could not believe what had happened in so short a time. Nor could he put reason to it. With an overwhelming sadness he cradled the dead man in his arms, oblivious to the cold and driving rain, and at a loss on how to tell Peter's wife that her man was no more.

It was a cold autumn day when they laid Peter MacMaster to rest in the kirk's tiny graveyard. Clansmen gathered to offer their condolences to Malise, Peter's brother, while others stood back muttering and shaking their heads in disbelief, each wondering who would wish to harm such a man as this, he a good husband and father, and him only just the other side of thirty.

In the midst of that sober gathering, Andrew, found himself relating for the hundredth time it would seem, the events of that fateful night, and therefore was not immediately aware of the commotion behind him until struck a glancing blow by the garron racing past, to be drawn up on its haunches and wheeled around by an angry Coll MacKerlich.

"You...you murderer!" the outraged rider shrieked, pointing an accusing finger at Andrew, and startling the gathering. "You would dare offer your condolences to the brother of the man you have so foully murdered!"

An angry growl of disbelief at this unexpected outburst rose from the company, as all turned to stare at the man so openly accused, who himself stood open mouthed, a look of sheer incredulity on his face.

"Why should the MacLaren want to be doing such a thing?" Rob MacDonnel cried angrily, pushing through to where his young chieftain sat his mount.

"You ask *me*, MacDonnel?" Coll shrieked. "I will tell you why." His angry stare travelled the assembled mourners. "When the men went south with the cattle, Peter amongst them, God rest his soul, I asked him to pay a visit to a certain district...Glen Laidon, to be precise." Coll stopped for effect, glowering all awhile at Andrew. "This he did. Later I met him in Glen Lyon, as arranged, where he told me of a certain Andrew MacLaren, who had indeed lived in Glen Laidon, and that this same Andrew MacLaren also had a wife and bairn! A wife who one night after being cruelly whipped and molested by caterans, watched in her final moments, her cowardly husband flee for the safety of Laidon town! This then is your hero of the Battle of the Glen!"

"It cannot be the same man...You are mistaken!" Voices of horror and disbelief rose from those gathered there.

"Then ask him to deny it!" Coll howled at them.

Gregor was the first to speak directly to Andrew. "Tell me it is not so, Andrew." The hope in the man's voice willing his friend to deny such an act.

Coll's disclosure had left Andrew weak. It was all out at last. Would he never escape his past? The young chieftain had put it in such a way that no decent man could feel anything other than disgust for him. Nor could he blame them. Here was the pity of it all.

Andrew looked directly into his friend's face, then up at the mounted man, answering with more conviction than he felt, "Aye, it is true, I did leave my bonnie young wife yon night. Though God help me, I thought He had taken her to HIM before I left. It was the bairn I sought to save, and I have suffered every long day since."

The moan that followed his confession chilled Andrew to the bone, but now that he had started he must go on. "Because of my cowardice the brave folk of my native glen took my son away to be brought up brave and true, unlike the father he would never know. "Now you know! Now you *all* know!" he spat out at them daring each man to look him in the face. "But I did not murder Peter Macmaster, of this I swear. Why should I?"

"I will tell you why!" Coll choked. "Because the night Peter brought you home the meal, he let you know what he thought of you as a man, for what you did to your wife. Then, you sneaked out into the night and shot him down like the coward you admit you are. For I believe you did not know of our meeting in Glen Lyon, and of Peter telling *me* of your black deed in your native glen, so by murdering poor Peter, you sought to keep those same deeds secret, for you did not know I also knew."

"What is this, then?" The voice rolled over the assembled men like thunder. "Has this clan of ours forgotten how to honour its dead? 'Tis more a cockfight than a burial!"

All swung round at the angry voice of their chieftain, none having heard him ride up.

"It was my doing, father," the son answered, fighting to control the venom still sticking to his tongue. "Were you after hearing what has past here?"

"No. I was after speaking with the good man the minister himself, when I saw you charge up here as a groom hastening to his nuptials," came the caustic reply.

"I apologise, father." The younger MacKerlich blushed. "I was on my way home this very day when I heard of poor Peter's death, and how he died, and so came directly here to pay my respects, never expecting to see his murderer walking free. "Father!" Coll exploded, "Andrew MacLaren killed Peter MacMaster!"

"If this is as you say, he must surely hang," the chieftain replied nonplussed, as if discussing some minor business. "Though this is neither the time nor place to discuss such matters."

The old chieftain eyes travelled to Andrew. "Young man, you will be pleased to present yourself at Monar House by one o'clock of the morrow, when we shall discuss this matter further."

"What, father! You will give this murderer time to flee the countryside?" Coll shouted, incredulously as if not having heard his senior a right.

Wordlessly Angus MacKerlich put spur to his mount, not answering his son, for he had spoken.

His eyes still on the departing mount, Gregor spoke curtly to Andrew. "I have not paid my respects to Malise, so, if you will be kind enough to start for home, I hope to catch you up."

Andrew could have replied he could well wait, but knowing the real reason behind the fiddler's words, nodded his understanding, and started through the mourners, the nape of his neck tingling from their silent hostility, with most stepping out of his way as if he carried the plague, none stopping to offer support or otherwise. It was Glen Laidon returned.

Next morning Andrew left early to be at Monar House by the appointed time. In a mind still dulled by the double shock of yesterday, he was only now beginning to realise that he could well hang for the killing of Peter MacMaster.

Sweeping a final look over his croft, he was reminded of similar feelings that fateful day of the battle. Then, those he had travelled with had been his friends. These same folk who now looked upon him once more as a stranger, for it was inconceivable to them, that one of their own could have done such a deed and to what purpose?

So much in thought was Andrew that he was almost on the figure before he saw her. Of all folk he wished to avoid this morning it was Kirsty; plainly he could not do so.

"You should not have come Kirsty, Gregor would not wish it. He will not be pleased at your coming." Andrew bridled his anger and shame.

"It is not Gregor who concerns me, it is you Andrew MacLaren." The anguish was clear in the woman's voice.

"Kirsty, I did not harm Peter MacMaster! This I swear to you." It now seeming all important that Kirsty above all should believe him.

"I know this well enough, Andrew. It was never in my mind that it was ever so."

"As to the other business, I am not so innocent." Andrew looked away to avoid her eyes. "It is true what Coll MacKerlich, is saying, and though it grieves me that the whole countryside knows of my shame, it grieves me more of having lied to you. Many a time...." Andrew laughed bitterly. " I was close on telling you, but feared to lose your friendship."

Kirsty reached up to placed her hand on his as she stood by the stirrup, forcing the man to look down in to those sad eyes. "She was always between us Andrew. I can never say I can condone what you have done...forgive...yes...for I think you have suffered enough, and unless I am mistaken there are other women who will give the nod to what I am saying." At Andrew's look of surprise, she hurried on. "Oh aye, Andrew MacLaren, there is many a woman who offers up a prayer that her bed is not empty this night, thanks to what you did yon day by the river. And even if I am mistaken, there is one woman this side of Monar who will ever be your friend."

Kirsty drew her shawl more closely about her and started to walk away, leaving Andrew to stare after her, scarcely able to believe, if not relieved to know that the woman did not despise him, even though he had deceived her more than anyone....and yet what must she have sacrificed to walk all this way knowing of her husband's feelings towards him?

Kneeing the garron forward, Andrew caught Kirsty gently by the shoulder, turning her around. "It matters naught to me now what others may think of Andrew MacLaren, as long as I still know I have you as my friend." Andrew bent to kiss her tear stained cheek.

"Aye ever your friend, Andrew, but nothing more, there lays the pity of it all." With this Kirsty broke free to hurry down the braeside.

Kirsty's support sustained the accused man all the way into town, where he noticed there appeared to be more than the usual activity, a few only returning his greeting whilst others stricken with a sudden deaf or blindness busied themselves about their tasks.

Thankfully the old chieftain did not leave him long waiting before summoning him in.

Although Andrew had been at the house on a few previous occasions it was the first time he had seen so many gathered at the long table, where at its head sat, Angus MacKerlich Himself, his son on his right.

Upon seeing him enter, the chieftain motioned him to sit at the foot of the table.

"You will be in need of some refreshment, MacLaren, I am after thinking," he said civilly.

"I thank you kindly," Andrew replied, clearing his throat from the tremor in his voice lest they believe he had something to hide. "If it pleases you, the ale will suffice."

"Oh! The guilty man has no stomach for a bite, has he not?" the younger MacKerlich cried mockingly, clearly enjoying what was about to happen to the man who had stolen the glory from him the day of the clan battle.

"Wheest your tongue, son of mine, and mind your manners. The MacLaren sits at my table under my roof!"

Coll's eyes bore into Andrew, the rebuke having inflamed his hatred for the man the more, while the assembled company, pretending not to have heard continued politely with their conversations. Andrew's only comfort was that it was the father and not the son who had summoned him here.

Eventually the old chieftain rose, and with a slight movement of his hand, beckoned Andrew, Coll and Malise, the murdered man's brother to follow him, Andrew grateful at not having to state his case here before all.

Angus MacKerlich led them to a small low roofed room almost denuded of furnishings, except for the Highland targes and weapons of a bygone age adorning the walls. The only light in that tiny room filtered through one narrow embrasure, a hint that it was the oldest part of the house.

It was here to Andrew's left in the window seat that the younger MacKerlich threw himself down. Malise retreating to the far corner of the room, whilst the chieftain himself elected to stand with his back to the fire.

"Sit yourself down, man," Angus gestured to Andrew to sit facing him. "I have taken the liberty of asking Peter's brother here, to be present, so he may witness all that passes between us. Also, my son Coll, who you are undoubtedly aware, sees you as the villain in this piece."

Then, commanding of Andrew not unkindly, "It will please me if you tell in your own words what transpired yon fateful night, MacLaren, see you." Then severely. "Omit nothing."

Andrew cleared his throat and, after a hesitant start that brought a smirk to the younger MacKerlich's lips, told everything he could remember that had transpired that wild calamitous night, the old chieftain interrupting only when necessary to clarify a point.

When he had done, the chieftain crossed to a chair by the fireside where he sat, head bowed, transported back in time to that night on Andrew's croft, attempting it would seem to visualise all that had happened there.

Andrew's heart bounded while he waited in that dark silent room, all too aware that his life lay in this man's hands. Yet better him, than that of his son, who would have had him kicking at the end of a rope by this time.

How long he sat there awaiting his fate Andrew did not know, only that it was time enough to have him reflect on all he should have done with his life, and it surprised him not a little that Kirsty should figure so prominently in his thoughts. What a fool he had been to let a lass like Kirsty slip through his fingers!

Eventually Angus rose. Andrew held his breath.

But it was to Malise, the chieftain first addressed himself. "You would judge your brother to have been a proud man, Malise? And if my recollections are not mistaken, a magnanimous one as well?"

"Aye, MacKerlich, this I would say of Peter."

Angus swung to his son. "When you and Peter met in Glen Lyon, did you instruct the man to hold his silence over what had been discovered back in Glen Laidon concerning the MacLaren here until you yourself had returned home?"

"That I did father. It is so."

"And do you think, Peter would have disobeyed you?"

Measuring his words, Coll glowered at Andrew, "No, father, Peter was a true and loyal friend."

Angus gave a satisfied nod. "This being so, and Peter did not speak to the MacLaren about what he already knew of him, there would have been no cause for angry words between them, and as the MacLaren here has already admitted knowing of your meeting in Glen Lyon, and even were he to have guessed as to its nature, there would have been no point to his killing the man, as you also were privy to this knowledge."

Coll MacKerlich sprang to his feet, his eyes blazing. "Perhaps I too was to be silenced!" he shouted, angry at the prospect of his adversary escaping his just desserts.

"Though son of mine, and I love you dearly, you sorely try me at times!" Angus laughed scornfully.

The chieftain turned to face the room's other two occupants. "I say this in front of these good folk here in view of the severity of the occasion. Coll, you have let your emotions cloud your thinking, and for this would have an innocent man hanged, for Andrew MacLaren is truly innocent."

Through the spinning room, Andrew heard the chieftain continue above the protestations of his son. "Malise, already has testified to his brother's magnanimity, as was shown in his civility to the MacLaren, for whatever feelings he may have harboured towards the man he remained silent, as were his instructions."

Here Angus halted to reflect, consider the possibility. "Perhaps Peter was unsure this was the same MacLaren,that he had learned of back yonder, for Peter MacMaster, being a proud man would neither have accepted the loan of the garron or the plaid, nor would he have supped under the MacLaren's roof had he though it to be truly so."

There was silence in that small dark room for a time. Eventually Malise Macmaster, rose, and choosing his words carefully and deliberately, said softly. "I think I speak for me and mine when I say, MacKerlich, I am satisfied in my own mind the MacLaren here did not slay my brother. Though, God alone knows who did, and I thank you for pointing out to me what a blind man should have seen had we ourselves not been so blind."

Nodding his acceptance, the chieftain turned to Andrew. "In the matter of Peter MacMaster's death, I see you clearly innocent, therefore let no man's hand be raised against you. This is my command. However, in the business of Glen Laidon, to which you have confessed your guilt, I leave to each man's conscience, for in this I cannot command."

Once again the elder MacKerlich was to be interrupted by an outburst from his son. "God's curse father! You will not send him away though he deceived us all with his lies? Aye, from the first day he came under this very same roof." The words soat out with all the hatred Coll could muster for the MacLaren.

Angus faced his son squarely. "The deceit was not all on one side yon day if I mind aright, Coll, since this is why you call the MacLaren, the fisherman!"

And with this the audience was at an end.

Chapter 5

In the ensuing weeks, Andrew was determined not to follow the pattern which he had set himself back in Glen Laidon. Therefore, it was with some trepidation he set off than fine winter night to attend the wedding celebrations of Hamish MacDonnel, brother to Rob, skirting the sea loch's shore with the moon reflecting on its steel grey surface, while all around the landscape lay ghost like in a thick covering of frost.

Eventually, veering away from the loch, Andrew topped the brae above the MacDonnel croft, hearing the shrills and hoots of delight from dancers, high above the fiddlers music. The bonfire from the open door announcing the house itself too small to accommodate such a large gathering.

For a moment the man stood there hesitating, then shrugging as if having decided to take his courage in both hands descended the brae.

Warily, he rounded the bonfire and headed for the open door with the intention of offering his congratulations to the newly weds, well aware of a few halting in their dance to stare at him, while others held up their cups in mock salute. Determined not to hasten his step and see this thing through, Andrew reached the door.

As was the custom with all Highland folks, Andrew found himself greeted civilly by the happy couple, if not altogether warmly by some others. And although his innocence of Peter MacMaster's death had been generally accepted, his treatment of his late wife when lay dying, obviously had not. Nor of a man who had left his son to be brought up by others.

Peter's death was still a mystery. Some declared it to be the work of their near neighbours the MacMorrans, and had called for an instant retaliation before that clan struck again, for no man felt safe abroad at night. However, the MacKerlich Himself, had commanded against it, convinced the MacMorrans or their allies the MacKinnons would not have dared risk a further confrontation in the aftermath of all the blood shed in the last encounter. But if not their late antagonists, who?

Kirsty was the first to speak to Andrew with genuine warmth, coming to sit beside him whilst the *tear an tigh*, or man of the house set about telling another tale of their clan's bravery in days of yore.

Gregor, Andrew observed sat in a corner talking to Rob MacDonnel, and that the fiddler should blatantly ignore him hurt him deeply.

His eyes still on Gregor across the smoke filled room, Andrew spoke only loud enough for the woman to hear. "I have not come to the croft these last few weeks, Kirsty. Though I would have liked to have paid my respects to your grandmother, who I hope is well, as I feared I should not be welcome by your husband, who no longer sees me as his friend. Is it my past that disturbs him, for surely he cannot believe me guilty of poor Peter's death?"

"Och! Do not bother yourself overmuch, Andrew, it is his arm...or lack of it that makes him so."

"Gregor's other arm makes up for it, I'm after thinking." Andrew nodded across the room. "He is already well in his cups. Gregor grows worse, I fear. I am sorry lass...It is no business of mine." He hurried to apologise at the woman's quick intake of breath. "Though I have never seen a man change so, and not for the better. There were others who fared worse than he from yon sad battle."

"You are right, Andrew. At first I could see how the drink helped take away the pain...in his mind that is. But sufficient time has passed for Gregor to accept what he is. He has changed, Andrew, as you say. There is a side to Gregor I never knew there to be.
I understand his music means.. meant everything to him. When he played, Gregor felt the tallest man in all of Kintail, now..." She broke off. Andrew nodded his understanding.

Kirsty sat silent for a time, as if listening to the *tear an tigh.* "It took great courage for Gregor to come here this night, as it did you, Andrew." Kirsty squeezed his hand. She squeezed again, tighter this time, apologising for what she was about to do. "I best away and sit by my man. I see him watching us, and I fear with the state he is in, there might be trouble between you. But do not be overlong in visiting us, and my grandmother will be happy to see you....as will I".

Andrew took his eyes off Kirsty crossing the room to sit beside her husband, looking around him at the happy smiling faces. Suddenly with Kirsty gone, and despite all those gathered there he felt a loneliness steel over him. Swallowing hard, Andrew in his solitude turned to listen to the *seanachaidh.*

In the months following, Andrew saw little of Kirsty or Gregor. Nor would the latter be drawn into speaking of his wound or their friendship when they did. Kirsty's grandmother declaring it to be Gregor's brain left behind on yon battlefield and not his arm. Therefore, Andrew decided to reduce his visits to that unhappy household.

The weather too, had played its part. It still being winter, there was little that needed to be done around the croft. Still, he confessed to missing his neighbours company. This, and being kept indoors for the last two weeks had not helped lift his spirits.

At first it had rained, poured was nearer the truth, until the earthen floor of the house was awash. Next came the frost, freezing the land. With the drop in temperature, ice formed along the edges of the sea loch like broken glass, followed a week later by snow higher in places as a man's shoulder.

Andrew stirred the boiling pot, and shook his head in dismay. This would be the third time of bleeding the cattle this winter. His meal too, was almost gone.

"Andrew! Andrew!" The voice shrieked at him above the wind.

Cocking his ear, the man listened. Surely he had been mistaken. It could not have been Kirsty he had heard; not on such a night.

The cry came again, and Andrew ran and threw open the door, a blast of cold air took his breath away, and needles of ice stabbed his face.

"Kirsty lass! What brings you here in this weather?" Andrew drew the freezing woman into the house, his mind racing at what ill tidings could have brought the distraught woman to his door.

"Oh, Andrew it is Gregor! He left the house earlier on, and when he had not returned, I went seeking him. We had words over his drinking...I found him, Andrew. He lies in the great hollow by the big stone. Lord knows what he was doing there. We...my grandmother and I...we cannot get him out. ....The snow covered sides are too steep! All we could do was to throw down some plaids and shawls to try to cover him!" Kirsty's voice stilled to a whisper. "He does not move."

Andrew sat her down by the fireside. "Gently Kirsty," he soothed the woman. "I will away and have him out. You bide here, you are worn out. There are plaids in the kist, and gruel in the pot...of a sort. Help yourself and await my return."

Hurriedly wrapping an extra plaid around him, and pulling his bonnet low over his head, Andrew headed for the door, where he hesitated to look back at the woman sitting head bowed by the fire, a sight of utter dejection. "Do not be worrying Kirsty, Gregor will be fine. This I promise you."

The bitter wind hurled slivers of ice at Andrew as he literally followed in Kirsty's footprints, forcing him after a time to slow his step. So by the time he had reached the crest of the hill he was almost exhausted, and marvelled at the woman's resilience at having come so far.

In order to catch his breath, he turned his back to the wind. Beneath him the whole dead countryside lay wrapped in a white shroud. The only sign of life, that of the loch glistening in the winter moonlight.

Starting again; for he must hurry if he was to save poor Gregor, he plodded down the other side of the hill, his thoughts on how on any other occasion the mile to Kirsty's croft would have been an easy one. But tonight it could take for ever.

Knowing where the hollow lay, Andrew was not unduly worried at the wind hurrying to cover Kirsty's footprints, only that he might not reach Gregor in time. His own brief halt had left *him* frozen, this after sweating all the way up the hillside. Therefore, what hope was there for Gregor having lain there these hours past?

With something akin to panic Andrew redoubled his efforts, the hard packed snow cutting at his bare legs. "I will not let you die, Gregor MacVinish, despite what you are at present, Kirsty has suffered enough! What say you? The man mumbled, trudging on.

All trace of footprints long since gone, Andrew headed for the dark silhouette of the stone that stood sentinel where the hollow lay. Gasping for breath he reached the stone, and plodded on until he came to the rim of the hollow. At first he could see nothing and put up a hand to shield his eyes against the driving wind. Fearing the worst he moved a little to his right. "Aye, there could be something down there," he whispered, and edged closer to the rim's edge, catching sight of the tartan mound below. "They must have thrown down every shawl and plaid they possess in trying to cover you wee man," he murmured. "Though I fear I have come too late."

Andrew swept the natural amphitheatre for a way down. Then he saw it, a cleft in the rock face. Gingerly he lowered himself over the edge, and as he shifted his weight lost his footing on the slippery surface, and felt himself slip and slide until landing in an unceremonious heap at the bottom.

Picking himself up, he trudged to the inert figure. It was a miracle he had seen the plaids at all, for all were almost covered by a white mantle. Dropping to his knees he drew back one of the plaids covering the fiddlers upper body, the snow crunching under the added weight when he struggled to lift the inert body to a sitting position, the skin jerking and relaxing under his blows as he fought to bring some life back into an ashen countenance.

He did not know whether Gregor was alive or not. The only way to find out was to get him back to Kirsty's croft. Wrapping as many plaids as he could around the unconscious man, he hoisted him on to his shoulder, and staggered to the foot of the banking.

Andrew did not know whether he had enough strength to reach the croft, or if indeed he was carrying a dead man.

At last he was there. Summoning up what little energy he had left, he kicked open the unbarred door and staggered into the room, dropping the fiddler to the floor as gently as his frozen fingers would allow, the old grandmother already by his side stripping the clothes off the unconscious man.

"Hang the plaids by the fire, man. These are all we have, see you. Now come, rub his feet and lower body whilst I put these hot cloths to his head," she commanded urgently.

Without question, Andrew followed her instructions, and stood aside while she placed hot stones from the peat fire by Gregor's side.

"Sit him up a wee bit, Andrew, and I will try the *usque beatha* in him. Yet I see no life in the man at all."

Raising the crumpled figure to a sitting position, Andrew did as he was asked, wincing at the sight of the naked stump and thinking how of late those few missing inches of human flesh and bone had affected so many lives.

At first the old woman poured a little of the spirit between the seemingly dead man's lips, ordering Andrew to lay him back when this had no affect, and to once again rub Gregor's body with a warm rag. "We shall try again, though I fear it is too late." Andrew heard the weariness in the old woman's voice.

At her command Andrew cradled his friend in his arms, and again the woman gently poured some more of the whisky down her good-son's throat. Then, slowly, very slowly, there was a slight stiffening of the back, a choking as the raw spirit did its work...Gregor was alive!

Slowly the fiddler's uncomprehending eyes, fought to focus on the man who held him, then to the woman who persisted in pouring the amber liquid down his throat, her voice from afar ranting on about how never of late had he refused such an offer. Then he closed his eyes and returned to peaceful oblivion.

Gregor's breathing was slow and regular as Andrew laid down the man whom he had given up as lost, and was scarcely aware of the woman busily wrapping her patient in all the plaids gathered there.

"He will be fine now. Though God is my witness, I do not know how he has survived this long. Aye, and more thanks to you Andrew, I am after thinking." The old grey head shook in wonder.

"You played no small part in it yourself grandmother MacKenzie," Andrew replied, dropping down on to a stool, all strength having suddenly left him, and peering through glazed eyes that wanted so much to close, at the figure lying there. "He will be in agony when the circulation returns, if I am not mistaken."

"It might well be an act of retribution from the good Lord himself, if you follow my meaning," the other opinioned sourly. "It should be enough that he is alive at all."

The old woman moved to the far side of the fire, enforcing silence for a time by busying herself there, returning after a while to shake the dozing man by the shoulder, and hold out the cup and bannock to him.

Wearily Andrew shook his head. "No. I could not take the bite. Besides, you have little enough yourself as it is, knowing the winter it has been."

"Then his lordship there, must do without." The old woman nodded at Gregor's sleeping figure. "Now, eat! You have earned it," the woman commanded sternly.

Too tired to argue, and scarcely aware of his action, Andrew took the food, the warmth of the room so much an invitation to sleep.

"I think you should rest your head here, this night," the old lady counselled, as he sat nibbling the bannock through have closed eyes.

Andrew jerked himself awake. "I must away grandmother MacKenzie, I have left Kirsty alone at home. She will be anxious over Gregor. I had a mind to tell you...in the midst of things I have forgotten." Andrew staggered to his feet. " I must away. I thank you for the bite and sup."

He had reached the door before the old woman spoke again. "They say you are a great coward, Andrew MacLaren for what you did back in your own glen. This, despite what you did in yon senseless battle between daft men. Though, I am after thinking that your greatest cowardice lies in your fear of love." The old woman turned, and he stepped out in to the night.

The return to the numbing cold drove all drowsiness from Andrew's body. One minute his tired legs would slip on an icy surface, then next he would find himself waist deep in drifting snow. All the while the arctic wind drove him on. The old woman's words still lingering in his ears.

Never had there been a more welcome sight as his own thatched house. Never an unbarred door so resistant. Finally he was in the room, crashing to the floor when his overtaxed muscles at last gave out.

"Andrew! Andrew!" Kirsty cried dropping down by his side.

"It is nothing lass, nothing that the sight of you and a sup of gruel will not remedy." Andrew smiled weaklyup into her distraught face. His jest misfired. "I am weary lass, that is all. Gregor is safely home."

Kirsty helped him to the fire, and quickly filled a cup.

Andrew drank deeply. "I thank you lass...Now of Gregor. It is nothing short of a miracle that he is alive, in this weather."

Kirsty was taking off his plaid and shirt while he told of how her grandmother had brought Gregor back to the land of the living, and continued to rub at his bare skin whilst he endeavoured to keep his mind on the near tragic events of the night.

"Wheest you of Gregor," Kirsty said softly. "It is enough that he lives. God forgive me it was you, who concerned me more, as I sat here thinking to lose you both."

Andrew drew back in disbelief. That Kirsty should fear for him as well as her own man, was natural enough, but not in this way. "You are still distraught Kirsty, you know not what you say. I mind how you came here earlier this night, fearful of losing your man. You could not have changed in so little a time."

Kirsty's eyes dropped to the floor. "God knows I do not wish him dead, Andrew. Nor would I have thought to say such things before...but now?" she stammered, unable to continue.

Andrew drew her close to him. "Give the wee man time, Kirsty. The love will return *mo ghadl* ...for you both. No one can stay out of love with you e'er long."

Kirsty pulled herself away, her eyes filled with tears. "Oh you great fool, Andrew MacLaren," she sobbed. "If only you had spoken of your love for me the sooner."

Pulling her to him, Andrew buried Kirsty's head in his bare chest.

The storm, though having abated in the course of the night, had left its chill upon the land, creeping through Andrew's *tigh tughadh* to the very fireside where the newly awakened man lay shivering.

Pulling the plaids around him, Andrew's thoughts of last night's events were interrupted by the unfamiliar sound of rattling dishes. Rolling on to his side he spied Kirsty at work, and instantly felt an anger at the man who treated this woman the way he did. Also, that this man should have Kirsty in his bed instead of him.

Suddenly the woman looked up, and saw him watching her. "I bid you good morning your lordship." She greeted him with a slight curtsey. "I trust you slept well?"

"I fear I must...I scarce remember returning...except..." he lied, for he clearly remembered those last few words of Kirsty's. He saw her embarrassment and shifted tack. "That smells good, Kirsty, is it for your lordship, think you?"

The woman smiled at him, her apprehension stilled. For, what she had said last night could have been seized upon had it been other than this kind gentle man smiling up at her.

"It is only porridge. You have little else. How do you manage man?" She frowned.

"Seeing you, makes me wonder, lass."

She knew she must say something concerning last night, something to put them both at ease.

"Andrew.... Last night, I said." She started again. "...What I said..."

"As I said, Kirsty, I scarce mind seeing my own fireside."

Kirsty bent to kiss his cheek. "For that I thank you, Andrew, but if I am to play the decent wife, I must away to my man!"

Pulling the plaids around him Andrew got to his feet. "Curb your haste, lass, for I will swear you have not tasted a bite since coming here last night," and gently forced the woman to be seated.

The return journey bore no resemblance to that of the previous night the wind having abated and there now being no need to hurry.

They spoke little, the woman being the first to break the silence when nearing the croft.

"I do love him still, Andrew, though it grieves me to see him as he is at present. Sometimes I fear him also." Kirsty hurried on at the anger clouding Andrew's face. "I have never seen an anger fester in a man so much." Kirsty choked back a sob. "He broke his fiddle, Andrew! His pride and joy...it has gone this far."

"Then he must learn to play the man," Andrew retorted angrily.

Kirsty bit her lip at the double meaning, and was about to reply when the door suddenly flew open, to reveal the dishevelled figure of her husband.

"So the lovers return!" Gregor threw the words at them. "Where else would my loving wife be, if not with my good friend the fisherman?"

Only Kirsty's restraining hand prevented Andrew from leaping at the man, who after his initial outburst sagged against the door jam.

"It is well she is safe, Gregor, after what she went through for you in last night's storm!" Andrew hurled back venomously, adding mockingly, for he could not resist the jibe to hurt this angry inconsiderate man. "But you would be knowing nothing of this I am after thinking!"

As Gregor struggled to answer, the old woman's head appeared around the door. "You best come away in before you catch your death," she urged her grand daughter. "Though there is one other I would not seek to advise so readily," she glowered at the man standing beside her.

Kirsty threw Andrew a sideways glance and started for the door.

"Should you have need of me, Kirsty, you know where I bide!" Andrew called after her.

"Oh! Of that I am sure!" Gregor mocked, his breath rasping. Then using all his strength to lever himself off the door lintel, pointed a finger shaking with rage. "You are no longer welcome here MacLaren, wife deserter!" he shrieked. "Now go!"

Stung by the outburst, Andrew fought to control his feelings. "I do not understand you man, you, who were once my friend." He shook his head. "Do you think I would do such as to harm you or Kirsty? Nothing passed between us last night, of this I swear. Do you not mind the day before the battle in the glen, when you begged me to care for Kirsty should anything befall you?"

Beside himself with rage, Gregor hurled back with all the anger he could muster. "I mind fine, as well as I mind your answer. You laughed that Kirsty would not have you, for you could not play the fiddle. Well, laugh now Andrew MacLaren!" Gregor brandished the naked stump of his arm. "Laugh now, for neither can I!"

Chapter 6

From the garron's back Andrew gazed over the Kyles shimmering in the summer sun to distant Skye, well pleased by the day's transactions, if still not a little mystified as to why the MacDonald should wish to buy the heifers at this time of year. However, now with meal at his back and coin in his sporran he was more than satisfied.

Casting a final appreciative look over that unsurpassed grandeur, Andrew turned his attention once more to his journey home, determined to reach the same bothan as he had used on his outward journey.

Several hours later, alerted by his garron's whinnying Andrew stood in that same bothan doorway waiting patiently for the three horsemen to pick their way through the bracken to where he stood shading his eyes on the leading rider. A tall man it would appear, by the way his legs dangled over his mount, handsome too, he thought, in his late thirties, and heavily armed as were his two companions. Now a little uneasy at having left his own pistol in his saddlebags by the fire, Andrew waited.

Aware of the waiting man's scrutiny the handsome rider raised a hand in cheery greeting.

"Seamus MacIntosh, gives you good day, as does my friend Johnny MacKellar, here," the speaker announced, nodding at a man of about Andrew's own age, though slightly taller and better built.

The MacKellar nodded a silent greeting, pointing a finger at the third member of the party. "And that old bag of bones there, is Duncan Cameron, him you do not wish to meet,"
he said in a grating voice, only the sparkle in his eyes, suggested what he had said of his friend had been in jest.

Andrew introduced himself, and found himself unexpectedly drawn towards the eldest man, seeing in him a softening of the features so patently absent in both his travelling companions. Perhaps it was this, or the way he had of asking, that first put Andrew at ease in this strange new company.

"Have you yourself travelled far today friend?" Duncan asked, dismounting.

"Aye, that I have. As far as Loch Maree," Andrew answered warmly.

"We ourselves saw Loch Broom, this morning." Johnny MacKellar broke in.

Andrew whistled, impressed. "Then it is tired and hungry you must be, for it is a far ways from yon loch. I have the fire lit and you are welcome to share what little fare I have," he offered, now feeling more relaxed.

"We have over enough for ourselves, MacLaren, I thank you." This civilly from their leader. "Though to your company, this I will gladly share, since such as I have kept of late leaves a lot to be desired to an educated man." The MacIntosh winked at his host, and followed him into the bothan.

By sunset all four men were well into their cups, swapping tales and addressing one another as old friends. The Cameron with his gentle mien was especially a teller of tales, and kept the company laughing. Laying sprawled out by the fireside Andrew decided that it had been many a long day since he had laughed so much, and was hardly aware of the MacIntosh struggling to his feet.

"It is time I was away to my own business, whilst I leave you all to yours." He threw the half empty bottle he had been drinking from to the MacKellar.

"Can she not wait another dram, Seamus?" Duncan taunted.

"No, I have kept her waiting long as it is my friend, and I'll wager she is thirstier than you by now, though in a different way if you take my meaning, Duncan. Besides, she is wild this one. Like a brood mare. Wild!" He gestured with his hands.

"Have a care she is not as wild as yon lass you told us of, who did so much to improve your looks!" Duncan laughed rapturously.

"There was none as wild as yon," Seamus snapped, putting a hand to his cheek, his smile disappearing. "At the time I thought she had spoiled my looks with those nails of hers. A bonnie lass wasted, for she angered me so, fighting the way she did." The man fingered his scar. "Aye, I have never used the whip before or since in such a way." He snarled at the memory.
" I will never be forgetting Glen Laidon!"

Glen Laidon! Glen Laidon! The mention of his native glen and what this man had newly said had Andrew's mind reeling. He tried to rise but found he could not. He held his head in his hands, while his friends laughed at his drunkedness.

After the Macintosh had gone, Andrew lay there now more sick from what he had heard than from the effects of the drink, with the pounding of his heart matching that of his head.

This had been a meeting against all odds! Beyond comprehension! After all these years, to meet the man responsible for his Fiona's death, and for the road it had taken him since then. His mind reeled on.

What was to be done? To go after the man, challenge, perhaps kill him? What then?

Return to Glen Laidon, claim a son he did not know and bring him back to Kintail? Would his in-laws allow this, having brought up Calum in the knowledge that his father was a coward? Above all would Calum himself be willing to leave all he knew and loved?

Many a night he had dreamed of meeting the man who had killed Fiona, of killing him and returning to Glen Laidon in triumph, to confront those who had so sedulously ostracised him for his cowardice. Now this seemed so long ago, and with the way of so many dreams it had dimmed with time. No, killing the MacIntosh would change nothing, it was already too late.

Andrew wiped his brow, afraid to open his eyes and find the room still revolving around him. Was it the drink clouding his thinking? Or did he really believe he could challenge such a man as Seamus MacIntosh? That he was a freebooter, or in the case of his own wife, worse, was obvious. What surprised him more, was that his newly found acquaintance, Duncan Cameron, should be likewise. Or did he judge the man too harshly? After all, Glen Laidon had been a long time ago. Perhaps, knowing of how the MacIntosh had come by the scar was only the result of that man's boasting, not that he also had been party to Fiona's demise.

It made no odds, his mind was made up. Perhaps the drink was blunting his fear and reasoning, for come what may, he would confront Seamus MacIntosh, and if necessary, both his confederates. What else had he to lose, other than his life? He had no real friends left since Peter MacMaster's death...discounting Kirsty, that was....and she well out of reach. No, he had naught to lose. And in one way or another it would bring him peace, if not to Fiona herself, God rest her soul.

For awhile Andrew lay with bated breath, awaiting the sounds that would tell him that his companions were asleep, and hoped it would

71

not be too long, lest his courage desert him. Then at last came the deep breathing of sleeping men.

Cautiously, Andrew turned on to his side, and drew his pistol from his saddle- bag. Rising, he tip toed to the door, where he stood for a moment to let his senses clear. Then gently opening the door, strode he hoped not too unsteadily down the hillside.

It must have been close on three hours later, with the first of the dawn's light breaking over Sgurr na Lapaich, that the MacLaren was alerted to the steps coming up the path towards him.

Rising from where he had lain behind the rock Andrew shivered, having realised he must have dozed while awaiting the arrival of his adversary. Now with all trace of drink gone from his head, as were all doubts as to what he must do, he took a long look at the loch below, reflecting that for him this could very well be his last day on earth. "God help me," he whispered. "I have come this far. I will see it through. It is little enough I owe Fiona, to try,"and slipped out from behind the rock to meet the MacIntosh.

"Who is there?" The freebooter called out, drawing to a halt.

"Seamus MacIntosh, it is, I, Andrew MacLaren!" he answered stoutly.

"Oh! It is my friend from the bothan. You startled me there for a time. I thought at first you were another angry husband, see you!" Seamus laughed, relieved that it was not so.

"That I am!" Andrew cried, and as Seamus started forward. "Halt! Come no closer!"

"This I do not understand, Andrew, man. You cuckold?" The man's laughter floated in the still morning air.

Spurred to reply, Andrew shouted, "Not cuckold, MacIntosh, but angry! You spoke earlier of the lass who gave you yon scar, the one you raped and took the horse whip to." Andrew's voice rose to a crescendo, anger having replaced fear. "Well MacIntosh, yon was my wife!"

"Well! Well!" The man sucked in breath. "The Cameron was always telling me I boasted overmuch as to my ways with the fairer sex, now I must heed the man more closely."

"You have scarcely time for that."

The venom in Andrew's voice did not fail to reach his tormentor. "You mean to challenge *me*, man? Me who is known to my folk as The Cateran ! You would......" In mid sentence MacIntosh threw himself to one side, drawing and firing his pistol in one quick movement.

Taken by surprise all Andrew was aware of was the explosion in his chest, and the thought that this evil man had dealt him a mortal blow. He staggered, sobbing, not out of fear but of failure, and was dimly aware through a kaleidoscope of colour dancing before his eyes of the MacIntosh rising to his feet, staring at him in the semi darkness, dumfounded that he Andrew was not yet dead, but at least on his feet and with a loaded pistol in his hand.

Cursing, Seamus backed away. He had never known a weapon to rival his own, always firing when he thought he had out ranged the other. He had hit this man, it was only a matter of time. All he need do was keep out of range.

The MacIntosh was still in the act of unobtrusively backing away, with the thought that should Andrew's shot fail, and he was to come close enough, he would have him with his sword, when the shot rang out. It was the last thought Seamus MacIntosh, The Cateran, was to know.

Staggering, unsure that he could make it, Andrew crossed the intervening space and with an effort of will stooped to pick up the MacIntosh's pistol, seeing through a crimson haze the familiar pattern on the butt . If ever proof was needed that he had in fact avenged Fiona, it now lay in his hands. It was his father's pistol, the one taken from his wall that fateful night when he had left Fiona all alone.

Then as if a dam bursting, his strength gave out and he slid to the ground.

It was too warm for grass and the wrong colour. Besides, it swayed so. Through half closed eyes, Andrew made out the twin peaks of the distant mountains, and squeezed his eyes shut when one waved before him, then once more slipped into peaceful oblivion unable to comprehend what he had seen, or thought he had seen.

It was later, much later, three days to be precise before any semblance of sanity returned to Andrew's tortured mind and body, and this only in brief snatches of consciousness.

The warm grass he had previously experienced had in fact been the warm hair of his garron as he lay stretched over its mane: the twin peaks, its ears. A never ending journey in only one direction it seemed, upwards, ever upwards, whether from the beast's own volition or by some other guiding hand he knew not, and cared less. His sole comfort lay behind a shield of darkness which even the pain in his chest failed to penetrate, until all again was quiet, unmoving, peaceful.

The wounded man awoke believing the place to be his own. At length unable to distinguish any familiar feature, cast his mind back to the bothan.

Certainly this could well be the same place. His saddlebags were there as were two pistols. Two pistols! So he had not dreamed it after all!

Running his tongue over his parched lips he moved his head to the side, startled by the young lass not more than sixteen years old standing there , who upon seeing him awake ran shouting, to the door.

Within seconds, Johnny MacKellar with Duncan Cameron at his heels appeared, the latter smiling broadly.

"So you have survived, my friend. At first we both feared the Cateran had done for you, as you had for him." Duncan's smile disappeared. "How is the wound? Does it give you much pain? You were struck just above the breast, but there is nothing harmed that you cannot do without."

Scarcely able to follow what was said, Andrew flexed his arm and a sharp pain crossed his chest. "The wound seems fine...Duncan," he lied, the elder man's name, only just coming to his lips. "Who is this cateran you mention? Was this the man Seamus MacIntosh?"

"He was, the one and the same. He was our leader, see you." Johnny MacKellar answered in turn.

"Leader? Then where am I now?" The question asked uneasily.

"The Monadliath, where you are safe." Johnny raised an eye at the wounded man's bewilderment. "We could only bide in yon bothan for two days. Then we had to move for your sake as well as our own. It has taken us another four days to get you here. It was a close thing, you having lost so much blood."

This was too much for Andrew's tired mind. Staring up at the roof he ran his tongue over his dry lips. "I killed the MacIntosh for the harm he caused my wife. It was she he took the whip to," he explained weakly. "The rest I do not understand, or what you want of me, by saving my life, and bringing me here?"

Drawing up a stool, Duncan sat down beside the heather bed, having taken it upon himself to act as spokesman. "It is like this, Andrew." He scratched his head and started again. "We had fallen asleep yon night we first met in the bothan, and when we awoke it was to find you gone. At first we accepted this as a call of nature, but as time past, and you still had not returned, Johnny here thought you might have passed out after your wee bit tipple with the drink," he added slyly with a twinkle in his eye. "So we set out to look for you. It was then we heard the shots and came upon you both lying there. Poor Seamus was quite dead, and at first we thought the same of you. Then you started your ranting and raving of what Seamus had done to your wife and such, so we carted you back to the bothan and bound your wound as best we could.

However, folks the likes of us cannot dally overlong in the same place. Besides, the lass the Cateran was visiting yon same night might come snooping about, or find the place we had buried poor Seamus, God rest his sould, so we came away.

Then there was yourself, Andrew." Duncan hesitated at his listener's look of perplexity. "We knew naught of you. To us, here was a man who dared challenge the Cateran himself, and bested him. Therefore, it was to our way of thinking, perhaps you were not all you appeared to be."

"Though I am indebted to you and Johnny here for saving my life, I can assure you Duncan, I am nothing more than a crofter," Andrew cut in soberly.

"This may be as you say, though we did not know this at the time, or whether your meeting Seamus was nothing more than mere coincidence. Should you be..mh..like ourselves, then you were the one to take the Cateran's place...seeing as we ourselves are now leaderless. If not ...'' The man shrugged.

"Since I am not, Duncan, what now?" Andrew whispered wearily, for he was so tired he cared little what happened to him. "Will you or some of the MacIntosh's friends not wish revenge on the man who created this situation?"

It was Johnny MacKellar who first laughed. "I think not MacLaren, Seamus MacIntosh, was not a man much loved, even though he may have had the skill to lead and provide, in especial, provide."

Johnny gestured with a flick of his head. " See you young Una there? She was but nine years old when Seamus found her, and took her in, and has cared for her ever since. Aye, and has cared for many like her over the years, that has been Seamus's MacIntosh's legacy, nothing more nothing less."

"Then I can expect no sympathy from that quarter, MacKellar. It is best that I leave with the least possible delay."

Duncan rose from his stool. "As yet you are in no fit state to travel my young friend. Rest easy, for you have nothing to fear from these folk who had a liking for Seamus. It was always the way considering the business we are in that any of us, the Cateran included may fall by the sword. The Cateran is no more, but one of us will take his place...however inadequately. Aye, it is also to be wondered at, that yon lass who gave Seamus the scar was none other than your own wife! It scarcely beggars belief. It is fate laddie, nothing less."

"Sakes, MacLaren, here is your broth!" The man stood aside to let young Una hand Andrew the bowl. "We should not have tired you with so much talk."

Bolstering himself up on an elbow Andrew took the bowl, and stared wide eyed into its depth.

"What is this floating here?" he asked in disgust.

Duncan poked at the object with a finger. "It will not harm you Andrew, laddie, it is already quite dead."

Laughing, Andrew's visitors now took their leave.

In his dream he was once more on the garron's back, its hair filling his nostrils, except this hair was softer, longer and seemingly everywhere at once. Andrew turned on his side on the heather bed, an expanse of white skin filled his open eyes. He shot bolt upright, a movement that sent a spasm of pain through his chest. "What is this!" Andrew put a hand on the young girl's bare shoulder jerking her awake.

Still half asleep, the young lass tumbled from the bed, alarmed by the tone in Andrew's voice.

"What do you do here, lass? This is no fit place for one as young as yourself!" Andrew berated her.

"It is more my bed than yours stranger. It is the one I shared with Seamus," she pouted defiantly. "And I am no child, as he would tell you if he himself were here."

"No doubt," the man retorted, eyeing the young lass standing there with her clothes snatched up and gathered around her. "So what do your kin say of this? Surely they cannot condone as much!"

"I have no kin, that is why Seamus tended me, and I him," came the stubborn reply. "Since you do not want me in your bed, will you leave me to those who do?" Una took a step closer to add testily. "Or do you not care that I altogether starve?"

Andrew rose shakily to a sitting position, more than ever perplexed by the situation.

"If you will but help me break my fast, I am sure we can come to some arrangement you and I....until I am fit enough to travel, that is," he stammered, wishing more than ever to be on his way home.

Una stood for a moment, her brown eyes staring up at the roof, mulling over what this strange man had said. There were not many men here who would have found her presence so disagreeable. Perhaps his wound had affected his mind?

"I will make your breakfast, then when your belly is full and your strength returned, you may not find it so easy a task to keep me from your bed."

The compromise reached, Una turned her attention to her cooking, her tongue working as fast as her hands while she told Andrew of how, the Cateran Seamus MacIntosh, had found her wandering alone after some clan *creache*, and upon finding both her parents dead after the raid, had brought her back here to bide with him.

"He was good to me whatever folk might say," Una declared adamantly. "He taught me to read and count. Seamus said counting was the most important thing in our line of business," laughing, she stirred the pot.

Andrew's eyes swept his shelter while Una went on, wondering how he could have confused this place with his own. This appeared to be cut into the very rock itself, the natural crevices acting as larder and cupboard. The entire place, as was the young lass, none too clean. Therefore, it was with some apprehension he hoped the porridge would taste somewhat better than the broth she had fed him these last few days.

Later, his hopes dashed for a better sup than before, Andrew took himself outside, totally unprepared for what awaited him there. Cliff faces, sheer, and almost entirely blocking out the sky rose on all four sides. The stronghold stretching some two hundred yards long, by almost half that in breadth. Ranged at intervals along the walls stood bothans or rude shelters, similar at least from the outside to that which he just left. Rocks, some as high as a man's waist stood in the centre of an open arena, around which a group of men lounged, or sat chatting: obviously the meeting place of the band.

Upon seeing Andrew standing there hesitantly, Duncan Cameron hurried from the group to meet him. "So you are up and about, I see," he said cheerfully. "Does your wound give you much pain?" He drew closer at Andrew's shake of his head. "Are you up to taking a wee stroll around our domain?"

The man led Andrew in the direction of the farthest wall, where he indicated with a flick of his hand. "This is where we pen the cattle. There is little grass here even in high summer, as you can see."

Duncan turned slightly, pointing to the cliffs almost directly opposite to Andrew's own dwelling. "That is the only way in."

"Where?" Andrew furrowed his brows.

"There. If you stand here you can see it well enough."

At that moment the entrance was betrayed by a man emerging from behind the rock.

"It is a bend in the rock" Duncan explained. He pointed upwards. "We have it guarded forebye." Still bewildered, Andrew followed the pointing finger. "You will see nothing my friend. Rest assured the sentinels can see both within and without, no one can approach without being seen."

Andrew's next question was interrupted by the excited shrieks of children at play from the opposite side of the arena, bringing the first smile to his lips.

"How many are there here?"

"Children you mean? A score or more, by my guessing"

"No, in total," the crofter corrected himself, turning his eye to the women at work.

"Seventy or so,:thirty one able body men to care for the rest. That number I do know, for our lives depend upon it," Duncan explained with a twist of his lip.

Astonished by this answer, Andrew inquired, "How many know of this place? Surely such a vast number cannot stay completely anonymous?"

"Only those we can trust," Duncan answered, knowing what lay behind the question. "There is nothing , or no one of importance here that would warrant betrayal. Besides, there is another way out known only to the MacKellar and myself. Content yourself,we are all quite safe here."

"So there will no objection to my leaving when the time comes?" Andrew stole a glance at the men by the rocks watching him, sizing him up it would appear, no doubt wondering how this slip of a figure could have bested their leader, their Cateran.

"You are afraid some may prevent your leaving? I think not, Andrew. You were not yourself most of the way here, and there is always the blindfold when you chose to take your leave."

Following Andrew's look to where his compatriots stood by the rocks, Duncan suddenly realised the man's fears. "Perhaps you are thinking your slaying of the Cateran may have rendered your life forfeit." Duncan gave a shrug. "It would be dishonest of me to say you are loved here, since it is you who have created the situation. Some such as young Una... liked, or should I say depended on Seamus, while others may have had cause to fear him. However, what all these folk did have in common was the security that his leadership provided. Now that has gone."

Duncan kicked out at a stone. "Oh, there were hard times, there is no saying different. At times we scarce could find a bite, but always Seamus won through somehow, and we survived. Aye, there will be some who will not be forgetting this over quickly." Andrew's guide started to move back the way they had come. "So if you see no liking in their eyes for you, this will be the reason, yet I think they will fall short of murder."

"And what of Una?" Andrew asked. "This I cannot understand of the lass, that she should tend my every need, I who have slain her guardian."

"'Tis no strange thing my friend, Seamus used the lass....in more ways than one I am after thinking. Nor would it have sat well with him had Una chosen to sit at another man's table. No, there was no love between them, be assured on that score. Una would gladly see you in the MacIntosh's place if only to take care of her as did he."

Unconvinced by the Cameron's reassurances , and wanting nothing more than to be away from this place, but knowing he could not for the weakness still upon him, Andrew with an inward frustration followed his benefactor back to the rocks and the awaiting men.

Fearfully, Andrew eyed the men watching his every approaching step. Some with no more a hostile appearance than those back in Glen Laidon or Kintail, while there were others he would not wish to turn his back on. Hard evil looking men armed to the teeth, even here in the midst of their stronghold.

"You have enjoyed your stroll Andrew?" Johnny MacKellar asked cheerfully coming to meet them. "Come, let me introduce you to those here."

Stepping forward, Johnny rhymed off names Andrew knew he was never likely to remember, and he thought again how it would take a braver man then he to challenge any one of them, at the same time grudging a fleeting moment of admiration for the man who had controlled these, and others like them for so many years.

Introductions over, Andrew leaned against a rock more to recover from his nervousness rather than from his wound.

"The pain is still bad, Andrew?" Johnny asked, with a slight smirk at his fellow caterans.

Andrew saw it, and replied with a forced stab at bravado. "It will pass. He was a goodly shot, that one."

There was a general murmur of agreement from those around, whereupon a giant of a man came to lean against a rock opposite Andrew. "Maybe so, but you must be better yourself, MacLaren? Seamus was handy with the *dag* , see you. Especially yon long barrelled one he prized so dearly, and better still with the sword, I am after thinking."

Sensing this quiet confrontation, Andrew took his time in answering.

"I would not be knowing about that, seeing as it did not reach that length."

"And had it done so?" the giant asked quietly.

"The world is full of ifs and buts, my friend, suffice to say, he lies there and I stand here." Andrew prized himself off the rock and with the sweat running down his back, steeled himself to walk unhurriedly back to his bothan.

Two weeks later Johnny MacKellar asked while walking with the crofter, "Now that your wound is healed, you will have a mind to be leaving for home no doubt?"

"That I have Johnny, and I thank you again for sending word to Kintail, and advising them I am well. At least I am easy in my mind that others are minding my croft in my absence. Since it is over a month from my leaving for the Kyles and there is a harvest to be won, I must return to do my share."

"You sound a happy man, Andrew MacLaren. I envy you your life."

Surprised by the sadness in his companion's voice, yet not knowing how to respond, Andrew turned his thoughts to home; the tang of the sea loch in the air everywhere the gorse thick upon the braes; the brown road leading to Monar Baile. All this now brought on an impatient urge to see these treasured sights once more. "I am, and it is to you and Duncan that I owe that it may continue."

Inevitably the day of his departure dawned. Andrew took a last look around the place that had been home to him these last few weeks, now not so hostile as he had first believed it to be. He had made a few acquaintances, and those who had chosen to snub him, had in no way attempted to prevent his leaving.

"I will away then Una. I thank you again for your kindness toward me and tending my wound." Andrew slung his saddlebag over his shoulder.

Una busied herself by the fire, loath to turn to see him leave now that the time had come. "You will not be back?"

"No Una, I will not."

"You will not take me with you?"

Andrew had not expected the question, but now that it had come, he could see how it would have made sense to one placed as was Una. He fumbled with the straps on his saddlebag, searching for the right words, words that would not hurt. "This lass, I cannot do. You are over young, see you, and you must mind what decent folk might think, were I to take you under my roof."

Una swung round flinging herself into his arms. "Do not go, Andrew! You have shown me a great kindness, also....that....that." She turned her tear-filled eyes up to his face. "....and demanded nothing in return."

81

Taken aback by this unforeseen emotion for a man who had slain her protector, Andrew gave her an affectionate hug. "Wheest lassie." He drew back to wipe her tears. "Johnny and Duncan will see no harm befalls you. Here, take this," he pressed a coin into her hand. "It is not much, but should times grow hard, it may help a wee."

Gently disengaging himself from the young girl's embrace, Andrew walked outside to meet the assembled company, where women were taking a last farewell of their menfolk.

Duncan saw him and walked across the arena to meet him. "We are ready, Andrew. Your garron stands there." Duncan pointed towards the entrance where Robbie stood burdened by that same meal Andrew had purchased back in the Kyles.

"You could least take the meal, Duncan, it is little enough for having saved my life."

Duncan shook his head, a glint in his eye. "No, nor the coin in your sporran. Neither are we thieves," he chuckled at the man's surprise, "at least not to our friends." He nodded in Una's direction. "I see you have taken your leave of the lass."

Andrew could not trust himself to speak, but instead started towards his garron, the Cameron calling out at his back. "She has taken a liking to you man, and will be full grown in no time at all! See the raven hair, and the eyes to match. She will be turning many a head in no great time at all, I am after thinking. You are a great fool Andrew MacLaren!

The last remark spun Andrew round to stare past the man to the young lass standing forlornly in the bothan doorway, his thoughts on when he had last heard those self same words.

The Cameron was right, it had taken all of his willpower when lying beside that slender figure to think only of her as a child. Swinging round he hurried on.

At last all being ready, Andrew followed the caterans round the bend in the rock, where to his surprise he immediately found himself in a defile no wider than a cart's width. The steep sides void of all vegetation, until nearing the top where overhanging shrubbery almost succeeded in blocking out any rays of light or warmth from the sun. Now he could well understand how easily the stronghold could be defended.

Johnny MacKellar fell in step beside him at the end of that dark and dismal place. "We will accompany you as far as Loch Mhor. You must then turn south, as we go about our business, the other way. Follow Loch Ness to its end, then it is the road to Glen Garry you must take. Will you be knowing your way from there?"

From the garron's back, Andrew nodded his understanding. "This reiving, is it necessary think you?"

"It is a way of life, my friend" Johnny kept his eyes on the road. "As a Highland man yourself, this you must know. Except, for us it is necessary, and not for the sake of pride alone, as is the way of many a clan chief. No, Andrew, since we have neither grain, cattle or land of our own, we must take to 'lifting' another man's.

"You have not always done this Johnny, I am after thinking."

The MacKellar side stepped a stone on his path. "Once, I lived with my family. That was a long time ago. Or so it seems. Suffice to say the land was hard, though not so, as to prevent others seeking it. Then I met the MacIntosh." Johnny gave a shrug, breaking off to shout instructions to a fellow cateran.

Feeling he did not know the man well enough to spier further, Andrew fell silent.

An hour or so had passed when Duncan Cameron came hurrying to join the company, shaking his head in silent signal to the MacKellar before turning his attention to Andrew.

"See yon big stone down yonder?" he asked of Andrew, pointing a finger at a solitary standing stone. "Yon is the trysting place. It is there all come to join the caterans. Broken men like ourselves who have lost land and home to others who were strong and greedy enough to take them."

Johnny cut in. "It is also where messages are left, or where a body would wait to deliver it in person."

"You mean this is where you glean your information of the district?" Andrew asked admiringly.

"Aye, if you put it that way. It is wise to know what business transpires in some of those great halls of the gentry, Andrew my friend. Aye, more than you could ever imagine."

"But why tell me this Johnny?" Andrew asked uneasily, for they had not bothered to blindfold him when leaving the stronghold.

The man shrugged. "Who knows my friend when some day you may have need of it." Johnny hesitated, struggling to find the right words. "We have taken a liking to you Andrew, Duncan and myself that is. Therefore, if matters should not go aright for you in Kintail...now or at...some other time..." He stammered to a halt at a loss for words.

"What the man is trying to say Andrew," Duncan gave a laugh of mockery at his companion's inability to express himself. "Should you for whatever reason wish to find us, though...." He laughed again. "I cannot for the life of me envisage why. Wait you by yon standing stone. Someone will make themselves known to you."

"Is this why you did not have me blindfolded? You think we may meet again?" Andrew asked puzzled.

"Aye, this and the fact Johnny and myself are for telling you that we were never party to yon sad affair concerning your late wife." With this, the two men turned sharply away, leaving, a happy crofter to stare in wonder at these strange mens rapidly retreating backs.

By this time their journey had taken a gradual descent from the fastness of the Monadliath, though still sufficiently high to overlook a wooded stretch to far Loch Ness, when Johnny acting as captain called a halt, telling Andrew, "We shall rest here awhile before journeying further, for we must in our business arrive in what darkness there is this summer's night."

"Then I must take my leave of you now, for darkness is no friend of mine if I am to see Glen Garry before nightfall, and old Robbie here is not the swiftest of beasts, especially burdened as he is with the meal you would not presume to take." Andrew threw a sly look at Duncan, and mounted his garron. "I will thank you both again, and I am ever in your debt." He bent down and held out his hand for both men to grasp. "Look after yourself, for who is to know, we may yet meet again, as you say." Scarcely had he raised his hand in a farewell salute when the first shots rang out, and the crest of the hillside erupted with armed men, sunlight on steel as the host bore down upon the resting caterans.

"Scatter....for your lives!" the MacKellar shouted above the noise of confusion, simultaneously slapping Robbie on the rump, and sending the startled animal forward. "Save yourself MacLaren!" he cried out at Andrew fighting to control the beast.

Heeding the man's warning, Andrew, bent low, charging the laden beast forward as a second volley rang out bringing the garron to its knees while he himself catapulted over its head to land sliding and skidding on the grass, amongst spilled grain.

Mindful that poor Robbie was done for, and he likewise if he did not take to his heels, Andrew scrambled to his feet and sprinted for the safety of the woods, all the while anticipating the pain in his back which would follow the pistol shot he was certain must come. For surely no marksman could fail to miss so large a target as his back, it being the width of Loch Ness, to him at this stage.

Fear and momentum lifted Andrew clear of bog and burn as he ran for the shelter of the woods which stubbornly refused to draw closer, and was almost there when the cry of warning reached him. Shaken at someone being so near, he swung in mid flight, to recognise the running figure of one of the caterans.

"Not in there!" the man shrieked. "'Tis the home of the monster, I'd rather face ten foes than yon!" he gasped swinging away. "Come! Follow me!"

Instinctively, Andrew changed direction to follow when a shot rang out, bringing the man down.

Self preservation stronger than superstition, Andrew turned once again in the direction of the woods, and plunged deep into its shelter, pausing only briefly to regain his breath and listen for any sound of pursuit. There being none he slowed to a walk, the only sound now in this cathedral stillness, the snap of twigs beneath his feet.

Had Duncan and Johnny escaped he wondered? What of the other caterans? And who had been their attackers? Andrew trod on.

Now deep in the woods Andrew sat down on a fallen tree. He knew he should turn and find out what had happened to his two friends but lacked the courage to do so. No, he would bide here until morning, when he reasoned, it should be safe enough for him to venture out, perhaps then he could begin his search.

It was the call of nature that awakened Andrew next morning. Despite the encroaching chill of the night and the occasional nocturnal visitor, he had slept soundly; with no sign of the 'monster' he had been warned existed here within.

His toilet complete, now that he thought it comparatively safe to find his friends, Andrew decided to retrace his steps. Kintail could wait a little longer.

It was then he heard it, a sound that sent shivers up his spine, awakening old superstitions long since forgotten. Again it came, this time high and unnatural, freezing him in his tracks.

Perhaps it was a wounded hare he assured himself, at the eerie sound hurling though the trees. Andrew halted remembering old childhood memories of tales told around the fireside at night to hurry misbehaving bairns to their beds.

Terrified yet curious, Andrew steeled himself forward, both pistols drawn. A little way through the undergrowth he came upon a fallen tree, and stepping over it heard the sound again. He peered to right and left as far as he could see through the foliage. He saw nothing. Again he dismissed the sound as a wounded hare, when the ungodly shriek filled the air once more, driving birds scurrying for the safety of the heavens.

Visibly shaken Andrew turned to run. No, he would find out what was amiss here, he told himself. The sound came again, closer this time somewhere to his right, he believed. A spasm of pain cut through his chest from his old wound, not only from the effort but from what he saw through the parted branches.

A tiny figure lay there, a leg trapped beneath a newly fallen tree, the outsized head on the diminutive body staring up at him.

"You are a dwarf, see you!" Andrew exclaimed both in surprise and relief that this was no monster...at least not to his way of thinking.

The giant head stared back, eyes bulging from beneath long black matted hair, watching Andrew's every move.

"How long have you lain here man?" Andrew asked drawing closer to the trapped man.

For answer the prisoner clawed frantically at the axe lying out with his reach.

Gagging at the smell of excrement, Andrew thrust his pistols back into his belt and stepped over the axe, his eyes searching for a branch strong enough to act as a lever. Picking up one that lay at his feet he wedged it under the fallen tree close to the dwarf's trapped leg.

"When you feel it give, get your foot out and quickly."

Dog like, the dwarf cocked his giant head to one side.

"Do you understand what I intend?" Andrew gasped, the pain in his chest worse through his exertions. Suddenly he halted in his work as the realisation hit him. "Surely it cannot be? *DIA!* You are deaf as well as mute I am after thinking!"

Andrew stood back, the trapped man glaring up at him. What was he to do? He could not just leave him here?

Scratching his head, frustrated and not a little annoyed at finding himself in such a situation, Andrew, his initial shock over, mimed his intentions to the dwarf, and again set to work. For a time there was no visible reaction, until redoubling his efforts and wincing at the pain in his chest, the tree moved fractionally, the dwarf instantly wriggling free to snatch up his axe and balance precariously on one leg to defend himself.

Andrew backed away, his hands held up in front of him in a gesture bidding the tiny man not to be afraid.

One hand holding the branch of a tree the other gripping his axe, the frightened man stood there, his eyes fixed on his rescuer, then, all strength suddenly deserting him, crumpled to the ground.

It took Andrew most of the morning to clean the unconscious man and dress his wound, and it was whilst searching for water to proceed with this task that he had come upon the bothan that was clearly home to the dwarf.

Fascinated, Andrew spent some time exploring the tiny abode. There was the usual household articles found in most Highland homes, except those made of wood which were expertly carved, the explorer suspecting these to be the dwarf's own work.

Then there were other such things the tiny owner had acquired: plaids, querns, targes, bonnets, sporrans and a beautiful exquisitely two handed claymore. Whistling with astonishment, Andrew left this Aladdin's cave to return to his patient, puzzled to know how so small a man could accumulate such a vast horde. Doubtless, he thought, some could be found on the mountains, either by accident or design, but there was more to it than this. Unfortunately, the owner could not be questioned as to why he lived here, and to Andrew, all alone.

At last, his nursing complete and in a dilemma as to what to do next, Andrew sat back to await his patient's return to consciousness.

Clearly Christian charity forbade him to leave the wee man in such circumstances, but with Robbie gone, and his own home well out of reach by far, the only alternative was to carry the poor unfortunate soul down to Loch Ness, and hope to come across some honest body either in town or croft willing to look after him. Though it was to be wondered at, who in their right mind would be sufficiently brave to tend such a repugnant figure, when it had taken all of his own courage to bring himself to touch the man, having to turn away from that evil smelling mouth when working on a countenance entirely covered in facial hair.

Angrily Andrew rose. By all accounts he should have been well on his way back to his own home by now. The man roundly cursed yesterday's attackers whoever they may have been, and wondering how many of the caterans, Johnny and Duncan included, had escaped.

He looked across the tiny space to find the dwarf watching him. To stand here, he sighed would not remedy the situation, therefore, he best make a start.

By mid afternoon, Loch Ness still lay a grey smudge on the distant horizon. Andrew sat the injured man down and stared down the mountainside with lack lustre eyes, failing to catch even the mere wisp of peat smoke in all that vast emptiness. His wound too, was becoming more painful by the stride. In the last hour he had rested more than he had carried.

Andrew shifted his despondent gaze back to the source of all his present troubles, his thoughts on the time lost that morning when trying to convince this tiny pathetic creature, of his good intentions. How the man had become increasingly aggressive, signalling for him to leave him, and for a time he had thought of doing just that, though in all conscience he could not.

Slowly...very slowly, fear and suspicion had lifted from the tiny man's face. He had nodded his consent that he would come with Andrew, but not before he had attempted to take with him as many of his possessions as he, or more so, Andrew, could carry.

Eventually the dwarf had seen reason, and had settled on a bonnet and plaid, though loathe to leave his seemingly beloved two handed claymore behind.

Andrew looked up at the sky. It was coming on to rain. Already the grey stone of the mountain glistened in a sun too weak to chase away leaden clouds from the sky. It was then he heard the voices, they came from three men rounding the shoulder of a crag.

Even from that distance Andrew could not fail to recognise the bulk of Fergus MacAlister, the same who had challenged him that first day by the rocks in the stronghold, who looking across the hillside spying him, pointed a finger in his direction, alerting the others to his presence.

The Cameron, for it was indeed he, lengthened his stride, crossing the hillside to meet him.

"So we meet again, Andrew MacLaren, I think fate has made it so!" he called. "Though I thought by this time you either dead, or warming your feet by your own fireside in Kintail!"

"That, I should be doing, Duncan if it was not for him." Andrew jerked a thumb over his shoulder at the dwarf.

Duncan approached and drew to an abrupt halt, his two companions now by his side, each staring in awe at the crumpled figure lying there.

"*DIA*! I have never seen such an ugly soul!" The big MacAlister whistled.

"Then you have never seen your own reflection, MacAlister!" Duncan laughed. Prompting him to ask, "Where in God's name did you ever find such a creature?"

"This morning in the woods, the same woods I ran to when we were attacked. He is a deaf mute...at least," Andrew hesitated, unsure. " he has not the gift of speech that is ..."

" You found him in the wood of the monster!" This from the third member of the party, a young fair haired youth who Andrew had only seen once before. "This is *ann- spiorad* an evil spirit!" he exclaimed drawing his dirk and making the sign of the Cross.

Andrew ran a hand through his hair. "He is nothing other than a frightened wee man with a broken leg, who can do no harm."

"You would not be saying this should you have lived in the same land as I," the youth exploded, turning his wrath on the dwarf, who watched wide eyed from his silent world, now clearly alarmed. "Even as a child I was reared to fear *coille ann-spiorad,* and have heard of grown men disappearing on the mountains nearby, never to be seen again." The youth turned to Duncan, soliciting his help, his understanding. "From time to time we left there, sheep, goats and hens, forbye food we could ill afford, in the hope this would favour us with a good harvest, and keep the sickness from the herds. Many a time it did not." He spat at the dwarf. "Then came the night of the great *creache*, our whole town burning, and my father with a hole in his side as big as your fist, rushing us up to the caves, away from that mad, black night." The blade in the young man's hand shook while he relived that night.

"My mother never did come to terms with living like an animal. She passed away that first winter. It was then my father took my young sister to kin on the far side of Ness, and he and I became caterans, as you well know, Duncan."

Duncan nodded sadly. "You were not much more than a bairn yourself Dugald. Aye" he sighed, "your father was a goodly man, God be with him."

"Then let us put an end to this!"the giant MacKellar spat angrily, drawing his dirk and advancing on the diminutive figure huddled against the rock.

With a sickening realisation of what was about to happen, Andrew thought it had been better to have left the *troich* in the safety of his own woods rather than have him murdered here. He looked down at the frightened bundle of humanity, feeling an unexpected affinity towards the man.

What must it be like to live alone, incarcerated within yon woods, and for how long, only the good Lord himself knew? Four years in Glen Laidon had been more than enough for him, and he neither deaf or mute; as had been many of his fellow clansmen?

Brought up in Highland superstition he could well understand the fear of the men here. And if the truth be known, was himself a little in awe of the *troich,* recalling the man's bothan and what it contained, and still more than a little uneasy as to how the tiny figure came by it all. Now that same tiny figure was snarling and kicking out with his one good foot at the enormous MacAlister standing over him, dirk drawn, supported by the young man Dugald by his side.

To Andrew there was but one choice to save the dwarf. However, should this fail he would not put his own life at risk, in especial against the MacAlister. Why should he, over such an issue?

"You are both braver men than I, that you would take the *troich's* life, and chance having the evil eye placed upon you." Andrew clicked his teeth, affecting an air of nonchalance, as if marvelling at their boldness.

"What mean you, MacLaren? Explain yourself," the big man insisted angrily, his dirk still held at the ready.

Though appearing to be indifferent to the man's intention, Andrew's heart beat faster and thrust from his mind the consequences were his ruse to fail. "If he is *ann-spiorad* as you deem him to be, and clearly knows what you are about, would he not curse those about to take his life?"

"Then you do concede he is the evil one." This from Dugald.

"No. Though I have naught to fear, should this be true, as my intentions were to save, not murder him."

"If he is not?" MacAlister queried, dropping his dirk a little, now not so sure of his design.

"Then it is as I have said before, he is nothing more than an ugly wee man with a broken leg, who has no more the gift of casting a spell on you, than you or I. Therefore, if you will help me carry him to folk kinder than yourselves, we can see an end to this affair."

Interceding for the first time, Duncan inquired, "And where would you take him Andrew MacLaren, seeing as there is no croft or *baile* this side of Ness? And should there be, none will see him different than we do ourselves."

"Then I will tend him, if you will assist me in taking him back to your *daingneach*" Andrew replied stubbornly.

"To our stronghold!" Duncan exclaimed, thinking he had not heard aright. "MacLaren I am after thinking you still have the fever of your wound upon you. Even should we agree, how will you feed and attend his needs, with you all the while champing at the bit for Kintail? Besides, we have little enough ourselves after yesterday's fiasco, with half our numbers missing."

"You have lost so many?" Andrew asked aghast.

"Aye. You are the first met this day. We have seven lying back home, and seven more besides ourselves, searching for those unable to win home unaided."

The dwarf momentarily forgotten, Andrew speired. "How did this happen? Who were they who attacked you?"

"MacKeiths. The very folk whose cattle we came to lift, met by accident, see you." Duncan slapped the wet rock with an open hand. "Damnation that they should be on the mountain in pursuit of their own business at the same time as we ourselves were abroad."

Duncan glared down at the dwarf. "Ill fortune would you not say, MacLaren? This taking place so near yon woods. Do you still think it wise to have us carry the *troich* back home to the greeting he must surely receive when it is known who he is, and whence he came?

Andrew never knew why he insisted in helping the tiny man, when all could have been resolved by him simply walking away. "I will not take him back to the woods, neither will I leave him here to die. Though, I know the meal poor Robbie carried is lost, I can assure you, I will endeavour to return with enough meal for both of us, and hopefully others forbye...at least 'till he is sufficiently well recovered to journey home," Andrew replied stubbornly.

"....and once in Kintail we shall never see your face again, MacLaren," the giant scoffed.

"You have my word on this. Besides, how long think you would the man survive if my returning from Kintail was overdue?"

"True." This from Duncan. "It would sit even better should we ourselves have full bellies," he mused.

"How can this be, Duncan? I have not the means to offer more." Andrew replied, a little put out by the notion.

"No, I grant you, though it could be so when next we strike the MacKeiths."

"Still you mean to strike that clan, and with so few?" Dugald exclaimed, absently putting away his dirk, the dwarf thrust from his mind.

Duncan made a face. "Aye, when we are ready, whenever that may be."

"It should have to be when the MacKeiths little expect you, ...straight away, if you had the numbers that is," Andrew suggested.

Duncan looked down at the dwarf who was looking from one to the other, obviously at a loss as to what it was all about, though guessing however wrongly, that it was he who was the subject of the discussion.

"An excellent idea Andrew. As you say, yon folk will not be expecting a lifting so quickly from those whom they have so recently put to flight. Who knows, Andrew". he chuckled, "you may even win back your own meal!"

The MacAlister sheathed his dirk. "It is settled then, we shall lay our plans before Johnny."

Silently Andrew cursed himself at how easily he had fallen into the Cameron's trap. The man's reference to the meal had left him with no option, other than that he should accompany them on this foray by way of payment for the help given him during his healing. Not that he relished the prospect of another battle, for with so few around him he would have little opportunity of beating an unobserved retreat...or in other words to run away without being seen.

"Aye it is settled. Now, who will be the first to carry this sorry wee man?" Duncan laughingly inquired.

"Is there no learning in you, Duncan Cameron for one of your age?" Johnny MacKellar, now acting as leader, stood arms akimbo in front of his friend. "We have over and enough dissension here as it is, without you adding to it by consenting to bring this....this," Johnny almost choked on the words, his finger pointed stiffly at the dwarf.

In the half light of late evening back in the *daingneachd,* or stronghold, Andrew could have sworn there was a twinkle in the eye of the Cameron as he turned to face him. "Did I not say as much, Andrew. You should deem yourself fortunate that your services are so sorely needed, or...." He drew a finger across his throat. ".that would put an end to your tiny friend here."

Already a crowd, mostly women and old men had gathered around the small group of men, where once more the dwarf was the centre of attraction.

With a feeling of misgiving, Andrew brought it upon himself to answer the MacKellar. "Is it agreed then Johnny, if I help in the lifting, the *troich* can bide here 'till he heals?"

Despairingly that man glared back. "Why in the name of all that is holy, did you not leave him be man? Do you not see by bringing him here, all future misfortunes will be laid at his door? For to many, if not all, he is nothing other than *ann-spiord* from the depths of yon accursed woods!"

Johnny kicked out angrily at a stone. "And should all go well in the lifting, and you yourself survive, who is to nurse him while you are away in Kintail? For there are more folk here who would rather tend him with a knife than a spoon!"

This was a problem Andrew conceded, darting a quick look at the dwarf busily fending off pokes and prods from those sufficiently brave to venture close.

Andrew's unexpected answer came in the form of Una rushing through the gathering to throw herself upon him, clasping and hugging him, all the while crying, "I knew it! I knew it Andrew MacLaren that you could not do without your Una!"

"It is not you lass, that brings him back." Despite the seriousness of the situation the MacKellar managed a smile, a finger pointed at the dwarf.

Una swung round, aware for the first time of the dwarf huddled on the ground, a strapped leg thrust out before him, free, at least for the moment of all molestation.

"Oh you poor wee soul!" she cried out in horror, kneeling down beside him. "You have hurt your leg!" Gently touching the binding asked. "Does it pain you much?"

"He cannot hear to answer you, lass," Andrew explained softly, crouching down by her side. "His tongue cannot form the words, though when at first I heard him, I likened his shrieking to that of a Spey wife." Andrew jerked his head up to those around him, "Although there are those who would have him as *ann-spioad"* he spat at them in disgust.

Una saw the look on Andrew's face. Now she realised beyond all doubt that his concern for this pathetic foul smelling creature, had indeed been his sole reason for returning. Her natural guile also told her, should she agree to nurse this pariah who clearly meant so much to the man, it could well prove a means of keeping her Andrew MacLaren, that bit closer forbye.

"Och, he is no such thing, of this I am sure,"she pouted.

Una stood up. "We must carry him inside, lest he catches his death of cold. Come Fergus! You can lift him and more by yourself," she demanded of the giant.

Obediently the big man acquiesced. "Una!" He held his nose. "You must do something about his smelling see you, before he drives us all off the mountain!"

Laughing with the rest of the company, Una cried excitedly, "That I will Fergus. That I will!"

From the sidelines Andrew watched the trio disappear towards the bothan, and felt a singular affection for the lass, who, however unwittingly had defused the situation...at least for the time being.

Chapter 7

It was with a spring in his step that Andrew MacLaren at last turned his face to Kintail, more than satisfied and relieved by the events of the last three days than he had ever dared hoped, with Una's tending of the dwarf more like a bairn, than a man old enough to be her father.

The caterans for their part had kept their distance, hastily crossing themselves should the forbidden subject of the *troich* arise. The lass having treated it all with quiet amusement, and not with the fear and revulsion he would have expected from one so young.

For his part the dwarf seemed to trust her, though still apprehensive of others, in this strange new world, and mercifully unaware of being regarded as an evil spirit who's presence was sure to bring disaster to an already shrinking company.

Therefore, it was with a promise to Una to return as soon as events allowed that he left the *daingneachd*.

Still a matter of discussion around the stones by the men in the arena was the absurd simplicity of the 'lifting' from the MacKeiths. In and out like a poke at the fire, was how Duncan had described it.

Even now Andrew shivered at the thought of another such raid. This, and the fear of his own base cowardice coming to the fore. Fortunately, Johnny MacKellar who, acting as captain had stationed him: no doubt with his pistols in mind, in a position to halt any sign of pursuit. There having been none, his reputation remained intact.

Now at last there was only one brae between him and Kirsty's croft. Strange how he still thought of it as hers and not that of the old lady or Gregor's. Puffing, Andrew crested the brae, and took time to draw breath and stare away at the great mountain in the distance that told him he was home. For this was where out of nothing he had made his own.

A few hurried steps later, Andrew saw Kirsty by the same burn where he had asked her to be his own. For a time he stood there watching her at work at laying out the sheets on the grass to dry. Until, as if sensing his presence she looked up at the same time as he started to stride down the brae, she rushing to meet him at the cognizance of his step.

"Andrew! Andrew MacLaren it is you!" Kirsty threw her arms around him pressing her cheek against his.

This was a welcome indeed, Andrew thought, stroking her hair, to be holding Kirsty in his arms. "Come lass," he said at length, reluctantly releasing himself from her hold. "You must mind your station, see you. What would your neighbours be after thinking if they were to see you in the arms of other than your own good man? And you wearing your hair in the *curtch* of a married woman."

"I would not care!" she challenged with a laugh that sent a thrill through him, as she held him at arms length for inspection. "So you have returned at last. Sakes, Andrew MacLaren," she said with a twinkle in her eye, "I had given you up as lost." Then soberly, "Are you all now healed?"

"I have the pain now and again, as I have at present. It is ever the same when I spy a bonnie lass."

"You had ever the way with words Andrew MacLaren," she said jovially, taking him by the hand. "Come, you must tell grandmother and me all that has befallen you since you left for the Kyles!"

Andrew drew her back. "What of Gregor? You know he has no liking for my company."

Kirsty tugged his hand. "Gregor is in the glens helping with the harvest and shall not return 'till dark."

"This is why I myself am here, to help with the harvest and tend my own crop."

For a moment Kirsty's hand slackened its grip before tugging Andrew on again. "Have no fear on that score Andrew, your crop is in. It was the first cut in the glens."

"The first?" Andrew exclaimed in surprise.

Reaching the door, Kirsty cried out to her elder, to guess what grand body had called to pay his respects, having that old lady call back in mock seriousness 'that it could not be the King, for he mucks out the byre on a Tuesday, and it could not be the MacKenzie Himself!'....Andrew stepping inside the door to reply..."for he helps the King muck out the byre on a Tuesday!"

Laughing, the old woman trotted to the door, to warmly hug her unexpected visitor.

"It is good to see you again, grandma." Andrew kissed her cheek.

"And you also Andrew, laddie." She ran a critical eye over him. "You are well?"

"Never better."

"You can sup some broth made by my grand daughter herself?"

"How can I refuse the best broth made in the whole of Kintail." The old woman chuckled, remembering that first night they met.

Kirsty drew up a stool and asked eagerly, while Andrew supped, "Tell us how came you by your wound, Andrew. It was on your way home from the Kyles, so yon messenger said."

Spooning the broth, Andrew began to relate how he had met the three caterans at the bothan. His killing of Seamus MacIntosh, the one and the same who had brutally murdered his Fiona, taking an ill disguised pleasure in seeing the look of pride on the younger woman's face, while her elder nodded her old head in approval. Andrew ending with his wounding, and the reason for his subsequent delay for returning, by finding the *troich*.

When he had finished, Kirsty inquired guardedly, "And this Una? What of her.?"

Andrew took a sudden interest in his broth. Only a woman would be capable of asking such a question considering all else he had been through. That his taking revenge on a man who had been responsible for the death of his wife, was of little importance compared to Kirsty's curiousity of another woman, though she herself already wed.

"She is but a child Kirsty," he answered still engrossed in the bowl.

"Child enough to have nursed you back, as I see you now."

Detecting a hint of jealousy in her tone, Andrew swung a little towards the fire, lest she see his pleasure at the thought of her still caring for him, and asking of the older woman, "Is it too much to be asking for another sup of your grand' daughter's very excellent broth, grandam MacKenzie?"

Exasperated, Kirsty jumped up from her stool. "I have chores of my own to attend to Andrew MacLaren, if you will but excuse me," she flung at him hotily. Would the man never change?

"And I myself Kirsty, for however pleasant the company, I must away to my own home. As it was the thought of this and seeing you both that sustained me these last few weeks."

Kirsty's annoyance at the man drained away. Sinking back down on her stool she darted a furtive glance at her elder.

"It is best it come from you Kirsty, Andrew will learn of it soon enough for himself," the old woman advised sorrowfully.

Andrew's eyes flew from one to the other.

"It is the croft, Andrew, Coll MacKerlich has given it to Fergus MacRae, seeing as you were not here to meet the rent."

Andrew clutched the bowl he had been about to put down. "How can this be?" His voice dry, challenging. "The rent is not yet due. Even if I were yet absent, the crop itself would meet the rent and more, this, Coll MacKerlich knows full well!"

"Folk said as much," Kirsty agreed. "It was Coll himself who declared you would not return, as the death of Peter MacMaster was still on your conscience."

"That is but a sham!" Andrew cried. "A ploy! His father cleared me of all blame. How is it that Angus MacKerlich bows to this outrage, when he himself rules here and not his son?" Andrew cried angrily, jerking round at the old woman's grasp.

"Lord! You will not be knowing of this either!" she exclaimed. "Angus MacKerlich, passed away some weeks ago."

"Dia! Then all is done." With shaking hands Andrew laid down the bowl.

A few brief minutes ago he had known the joy of being home. Now in its stead there was this. "So I have nothing...nothing more than I carry in my sporran," he whispered hoarsely.

"In this you are wrong," Kirsty consoled, a glint of a tear in her eye. "There is still the garron you left behind when heading for the Kyles, and your kist is in the barn."

"But how?" Andrew gasped.

Kirsty picked up Andrew's empty bowl, and ran a finger absently around its rim. "Coll MacKerlich declared, should you by chance return, you would leave Kintail as you came."

So the younger MacKerlich had won after all, letting him prosper, all the while intending to take it all away. Revenge no doubt for all the glib replies the proud young chief had not appreciated.

"I thank you lass....I thank you both," he corrected himself, rising. "It is time I was away, for the day is not yet spent."

The old woman grabbed his arm. "You will not fight for what is rightly yours? Did the croft come so easily, that you will let it slip away?"

Andrew looked away from those angry old eyes. Here was more spirit than he could ever hope to have.

"It would avail me nothing, for Coll MacKerlich has long awaited this day to see me fail. Any pursuance of this matter on my part will only lead to trouble. No. It is best I leave."

"Back to Glen Laidon, now that you have slain your cateran?" Kirsty asked, her intention to hurt: make him think again.

"It was never in my mind," Andrew grimaced.

"Then where?"

Andrew shrugged.

"Then surely you will bide the night?" the old woman asked anxiously, letting go of his arm.

Aware of the embarrassment this would cause upon Gregor's return, Andrew shook his head. "No. It is best I leave now." He made for the door.

"Then you will wanting your garron and kist," Kirsty sighed, for a day that had started with so much promise.

Andrew sat astride the garron on the braeside where he'd first set eyes on what was to become his croft. In his minds eye he saw again the first shelter built: the field so deep in mire that the garrons could not work, and had cost him a day's toil with the *cas chrom*: that first day he had met Kirsty: the clansfolk rallying around to help build his house, though him little more than a stranger: Gregor and his music that had brought his home alive under the thatch: faces like the mason, the thatcher, slain at the Battle of the Glen, these and many more. Thoughts that cut through his mind as scythe to corn.

From bogland to what lay before him now was what his own honest labour had created, only to have it stolen and given to another.

Angrily, Andrew swore an oath. "It is a deed some day you will live to regret Coll MacKerlich. Of this I promise you."

Had the man glanced some way to his right he would have seen the figure of a woman watching him, as she had done that first day of his coming. Now, as she swung away she whispered softly, "Fare you well Andrew MacLaren. God go with you, wherever you may choose to be. But do not forget she who loved you so."

With tears running unashamedly down her cheeks Kirsty ran back down the braeside to her own croft.

Andrew sat with his back against the standing stone. Half the day gone and not a sign of anyone coming he thought dejectedly. If in

99

another half hour he was still alone, he must try and find his own way to the *daingneachd*. Though, it was the high corries which perplexed him most, for he had no wish to lose his way and wander half the night in yon wild desolation.

Closing his eyes Andrew returned to his reverie, picturing for the hundredth time the croft left behind. The corn harvested and stooked. He could remember every back breaking inch of ground to his *tigh tughadh*. It had not been much but it had been home.

"Coll MacKerlich! You have no right!" he called out, squeezing his eyes even tighter shut.

"Have no right to what?" The youthful voice surprised him.

Andrew snapped his eyes open. Dugald Ferguson looked down at him from his garron.

"Sakes, Dugald, I did not hear you approach, so deep were my thoughts," he apologised, and a little embarrassed.

Dugald made a gesture of understanding. Dismounting, he disappeared behind the resting man. "Nothing! It has been a wasted journey this day!" he exclaimed, coming back round the stone. "Except to find you here, that is, MacLaren. Though, none expect you back so soon, if at all."

Andrew's return to the stronghold was met with quiet surprise by both the MacKellar and Cameron, the latter announcing cheerfully his assurance of Andrew's return, though he conceded, not so soon.

After Dugald had taken his leave, Andrew briefly informed both men of the circumstances which had prompted his early return, Duncan declaring, that now he too, was as they, a cateran.

"For the present, I grant you, Duncan," Andrew replied, crossing the arena with his friends, "at least until the dwarf is healed. How has the wee man progressed since last we met?"

"See for yourself, I am sure his nurse will be overglad to see you, and so soon."

Andrew handed over the reins of his garron to Duncan. "Here is the meal I promised. Share out what you think the *troich*, Una and myself will be needing." Before the man could spier further, added. "Do not bother to ask, Duncan," he cautioned, and apprehensively made his way to the bothan.

Una was at her spinning when she heard his step. Andrew thought he had never seen anyone look so pleased to see him, not even his precious Kirsty, for here was a look of a different kind.

"Andrew! Andrew!" she exclaimed in delight, running to envelope herself in his arms.

"And so soon!" he quipped. Then adding at her puzzled expression,. "It is the singular greeting on everyone's lips since I sat by the standing stone," he laughed.

Una laughed back, not so much at the jest, but that Andrew had come back. Now her fears could be dispelled. She would hold him here, even though it be through the *troich*.

"Come!" Andrew held her at arms length, and surveying a figure that every day was rapidly growing to womanhood. "Tell me how you have fared since my leaving, though in truth it is not so very long ago." He put an arm round her and led her back to the fire. "Is there much trouble at the dwarf's biding here? Fearing her answer.

The brown eyes that had welcomed him so warmly, dimmed a little. "Only a few," she pouted. "Mainly from those who have lost their men near *coille taibhseach*. They blame the poor wee man , or *ann-spiord* as they call him, though he is no evil spirit. Of this I am sure," Una replied defiantly.

Suddenly the young girl's face lit up. "If only they could see the poor wee soul, then they would not be thinking of him as such. Come! See for yourself!" Una tugged at his arm leading him to the bothan next door.

They found him by the fire, shrouded in plaids. A grin appearing from ear to ear displaying a row of rotting yellow teeth, at the sight of Andrew,

Una skipped across the room to kneel behind her patient.

"What have you accomplished here, lass? It is nothing short of a miracle! I would scarce know the man as the one I found in yonder woods!" Andrew exclaimed scarcely able to believe the transformation of the man.

Una was delighted at the praise. "I have cut and combed his hair, and washed his clothes. See he has the crutch when nature calls," she ran on excitedly. "I rebound his leg. It mends well Andrew!" Breathless she awaited further reaction from Andrew.

"This I do believe Una, if the rest is anything to judge by. You will not be telling me you shaved him as well?" Andrew proclaimed at that enormous face now free of all hair.

Una reeled back in laughter. "No, Duncan did that. Though at first the *troich* thought he had come to cut his throat! He is a fiery wee man Andrew." She rolled her eyes to the roof, not wishing to further elaborate. "I had to sit by his side."

"Och!" Andrew threw his hands in the air in a wild gesture. "You have won him over in no time at all lass. It is easy to see who reaps the benefit here. There he sits shinning like a new pin and you not even having the time to wash." Although he felt a pang of guilt at what he had said, considering all that the lass had achieved he was determined it must be said if he was to share her bothan , if not her bed, for Una herself was none too clean.

"In this you are right," Una blushed, brushing back a strand of unruly hair, though. inwardly fuming at the insult. Who was this man to tell her when to wash? Something The McIntosh had never done. Had he no understanding how inconvenient, not to say, unnecessary it all was, here in the *daingneachd?* She would let the insult pass… for now....but when she had him safe..."

Una heard Andrew go on, "Though I have no room to boast, for I myself have neither bathed or eaten since this morning."

She crossed to Andrew's side, and looked back at the dwarf now dozing by the fire, and thought of how the man was a mystery, but not wild as she had first expected. Nor had she any fear of him. True, he still treated others with suspicion. And why not? He who had only known silence and loneliness, and for how long she did not know. To her, he was simply a poor wee man with a broken leg, who by his ill-favoured features, she reasoned, had had to live alone. Though, when he was well again, what would become of him? What was more important, what would become of her beloved Andrew? And why had she taken to him so? Had she forgotten her Seamus so easily? Una smiled to herself. There was still time aplenty, the *troich* would not heal so quickly, or appear to do so with her in attendance, Una chuckled, and who was to know, perhaps in time her crofter would fall in'love with her.

"If it is the sup you lack, this I can quickly remedy, I have some broth upon the fire." Una took his hand. Andrew stifled a moan. This would be the next delicate step in Una's edification, Andrew thought as they left the dwarf to his slumber.

"There is not yet sufficient to meet the winter's need!"
"Aye, but mind there are not now so many mouths to feed."

"You are wrong, man, there are not so many fighting mens mouths to feed."

Although aware of his presence, some chose to ignore Andrew, while others for his benefit, loudly forecast disaster now that they sheltered the devil's disciple in their midst.

Perhaps, Andrew thought, he had made a mistake by bringing the *troich* here. Would it not have been better to have tended the wee man where he had found him? Or better still not to have found him at all?

Johnny MacKellar interrupted Andrew's unchristian thoughts by asking of him, "What say you Andrew? Fergus here has just this morning returned from Moray, where he says there is meal and cattle aplenty for the taking, if we had but the numbers."

Andrew ventured a little closer to the circle, his docility plain to all there. "I fear I do not have the skill to make a judgement in this. I myself have had little experience in such matters."

"You did well enough at the last lifting, Johnny replied spiritedly.

The MacLaren's reluctance was plain, Johnny knew. The man was ...still was a crofter and knew little of lifting another man's gear, but then it had been the same for most of them at one time or another. Besides, he had something else in mind for the man.

"Come Fergus, tell Andrew what you were after saying about Moray," Johnny requested of the giant. "Do not let his modesty be fooling you, for was it not his idea to attack the MacKeiths straight away? Or so Duncan would have me believe."

Again Andrew had the feeling of being manipulated one more time.

Andrew lay with his back to the ridge, huddled like those around him against the evening's chill. "It is time. Have the men await my signal, see you," he said to Johnny lying by his side.

His heart pounding, Andrew crawled to the ridge top, where he peered cautiously down at the tower scarcely visable in the semi darkness beyond a line of trees.

However, it was not the tower itself which arrested his attention, but the ridge opposite, lying some distance beyond the intervening cornfields.

Fighting to contain his fear and impatience Andrew bunched his fists. So much...no all depended on this, his plan. Should anything go awry, he left the thought unfinished, and again scanned the ridge.

Johnny, now the late MacIntosh's successor, had made him 'captain' of the raid a shrewd move on his part, for should this raid fail, the MacKellar could not be blamed. On the contrary, it would most likely be he and the *troich* that the blame would fall. He, for his dismal planning, and the *troich* as the evil one who had brought down misfortune on them all.

His plan had been simple enough, set fire to the opposite ridge, have the men in the tower rush out to save the stooked corn lying between ridge and tower, whilst he and the caterans stole down and lifted the cattle during the confusion. What he had not expected was that the cattle should be so well guarded, now all hinged on those watching the herd also being coerced into helping with the fire, thus removing them from guard duty.

"Where are you man!" Andrew snarled through his clenched teeth. "Nothing!"

Once more he swung his gaze to the trees below. Somewhere between those trees and the tower lay the reason for their visit. He heard the lowing of the cattle, and counted again the number of herdsmen their earlier reconnaissance had detected.

His gut tightening Andrew once more averted his eyes to the opposite ridge, this time grunting with satisfaction. There it was, nothing more than a glow at first, until bursting into life the fire was in no time at all sweeping the ridge from end to end.

"Are you blind? Can you not see?" Andrew fumed, as the tower below remained silent, deserted, except for the gleam of light from the windows.

Then, with as much spontaneity as the fire itself, the tower suddenly gushed forth with running men, shouting and clambering away across the cornfields to meet the blaze.

Andrew rose quickly and signalled back down to the waiting caterans who sprang up the ridge, where at their head he led them over the other side and down into the trees below.

Leaving them there Andrew hurried through the woods, where, once on the other side he slowed his step to peer through his screen of trees at the bellowing cattle milling around in contagious fear,unfortunately, for the caterans, still surrounded by their ever watchful herdsmen.

Would these watchmen never move? Would they ever keep their vigil? Even now they remained at their posts while the fire, hungry to be at the corn stooks roared and crackled, sending sparks and ashes heavenwards, enveloping the newly risen moon in black filled smoke.

"The MacAlister and the lads have done their work well, I am after thinking."

Startled, Andrew swung to find Johnny by his side. "That they have. As for us, should the herdsmen not move and soon, all is lost," Andrew choked.

As if in answer to his fears a figure came pounding towards the herd from the direction of the tower, shouting to the herdsmen that they should follow him.

"Seven," Johnny said evenly, after the departing herdsmen.

"Aye, five we counted earlier," Andrew answered relieved.

"Then two we did not see. You were right to keep us hidden, Andrew. Had we missed yon two, all was up with us."

More so for me and the *troich*, Andrew mumbled to himself.

Now that the last of the herdsmen had gone, the caterans burst from the woods, flanking the milling cattle and driving them between tower and woods.

Andrew hurried to position himself to where he could see all before him. Now, should either those in the fields or the tower, raise the alarm, he would be the first to know. He moved a little closer to the tower, where Duncan Cameron and another rider whirled past him, leading a half dozen garrons towards a barn a short distance away, and although it had taken the men no time at all to load the garrons, to Andrew it seemed an eternity before they were back and heading over the ridge once more.

The cattle however, were a different matter, stampeding here and there, with caterans struggling to drive them in the same direction as the departing garrons.

Instinctively, Andrew made his way back to the woods lest his own line of retreat be cut off by any coming from the tower, his pounding heart ever awaiting the cry that would announce their discovery.

With painful slowness, the caterans at last had the herd behind the cover of the woods. Now anyone from the fire who may happen to look in this direction, even if they could see this far through smoke and night, might well deduce that beasts frightened by the encroaching fire and minus herdsmen had in fact scattered to the hillside beyond.

Andrew leaned against a tree. Now his fear was that the fire itself could now prove to be more hindrance than advantage, with the likelihood of folk from the district hurrying to the aid of their kinsmen, for, should any of these come unexpectedly upon the caterans and raise the alarm they would find themselves greatly outnumbered. Therefore, with a wary eye on the fiery scene below, Andrew decided to give the caterans a little more time before starting after them. Though, should the alarm be raised before this, he would run after them, fire a warning shot and take himself off into the night

It was in fact close on an hour before Andrew started after the reivers, following a trail which even a blind man could not fail to miss, and marvelling at the distance covered by his compatriots in that time, when a shape suddenly materialised from behind a rock. Startled, Andrew stepped back and drew his pistols, hearing Dugald's youthful voice ring out an assurance.

"It is you Dugald?" Andrew cried, rushing on before that youngster could see or hear his fear. "I did not think to find you so far travelled in the dark."

"We are only just ahead," the youngster replied spiritedly, "Already Johnny has sent on the garrons with the meal; better half a bannock than none, says he."

In no time at all they were reunited, Johnny sending Dugald back to resume his watch.

"It is done!" That man cried exuberantly. "And it is you we must thank, MacLaren!"

Andrew, not so inclined to share this optimism, grimaced. "It will not take much wit to follow this trail, Johnny, surely despite your progress they will be at our heels ere long?"

"I think not. Yon fire will burn 'till morning, by which time we should ourselves be safely in Strathdern. Duncan is already away with the garrons, and I have split the herd, and have given Hamish

MacBain, instructions to go by Finhorn waters, whilst we ourselves pass the night in yonder corrie."

Sensing Andrew's dubiety, Johnny hastened to explain. "It is broken country here about man. We stand to lose all, should we venture further this night. Come! Rest easy, your work is done...at least until morning."

Despite the MacKellar's assurance, Andrew spent a sleepless night, treating every sound with fearful suspicion, pistols at the ready.

It was in this way he greeted Fergus MacAlister's return, his pistols only inches away from the big man's upturned face. "*Dia!*" the big man exploded. "First, it is young Dugald, rising like *ann-spiorad* from the ground, then it is you MacLaren from this boulder top! Is this the way to greet three men who have covered half of Moray since last we met?"

Lowering his pistols, Andrew jumped down from the high rock where he had lain. "The fault is mine, Fergus, I was half asleep when I heard you approach. At first I thought we had been discovered. It is an ill greeting for men who have worked so hard this night."

Johnny crossed from where he had been lying to join the four men. "Where have you been hiding, MacAlaister? I thought to see you long since!" he cried in mock surprise.

As the big man struggled to find words, one of his company provided an answer.

"It was the fire itself, see you. Man, we ran about yon ridge like scalded cats, unable to see through the smoke or how you fared, while all below was like pandemonium!"

" Aye, and with all the district rushing to help, we thought it time to leave," added a third.

At last having found the right reply and not wishing to be outdone, the giant rushed to interpose. "This is why we are so long in coming. I believe we circled the very shores of Lochindorb itself!" The giant's exaggeration bringing uproarious laughter from those who had risen from their beds to greet the newcomers.

"Come. We must have our rest and be on our way by first light," Johnny interrupted, gesturing for silence. "For, I warrant by this time our unfriends will be knowing their cattle have not strayed this far without some assistance."

Chilled, Andrew awoke, surprised at having dozed at all throughout the night. Sitting up he gathered his plaid about him, and reached inside his jacket for a bannock he had left for today.

Shivering again he yawned at the mist shrouded mountains, and of cattle uneasy in the eerie morning's half light, their coats glistening wet. Already men were up and about, some stamping their feet to keep warm. He jumped down from his rock bed and leaned on the big stone, chewing his bannock, as Johnny crossed to speak to him.

"This mist will favour us Andrew, should we start this instant, as our unfriends will not be so very far behind, I'll warrant. Though, even they must move slowly." His greeting without preamble.

"No doubt you are right, Johnny." Andrew took a last bite of his bannock. "I for one will not take it amiss to be out of these high corries."

"You will bide and act as rearguard, though? Since you brought neither sword nor targe, I cannot see you drive the beasts with the flat of your pistols, if you take my meaning." This more a command than question.

Hating that dreaded weapon the broadsword, and having decided should it result in his being chased the length and breadth of Moray, he would run the faster without it, Andrew replied, "Aye, Johnny, but I shall not be so very far behind as to miss you, see you."

Andrew waited only the briefest of intervals before starting after the protesting cattle, having no wish to face a foe which might suddenly appear out of the mist.

A little later, the mist thinning now that he was out of the higher corries, with its treacherous cliff and scree, with the herd now somewhere on the lower slopes, driven at a trot round bog and mire, Andrew made for a ridge where he could rest, and at the same time keep an eye on the cattle and the crest above. Although, he knew, it would be impossible for him to halt any great numbers that might follow them, even should he wish to try, which he had no mind to do. His only hope being, to fire a shot or two in warning, then, he chuckled he would be down amongst those cattle before his pistol shot.

Andrew reached the ridge and sat down on the grass. Inhaling the morning air, he took in that kaleidoscope of colour all around. What was he doing here? He was no robber of other mens cattle, especially no leader of such men, most of whom he feared.

The MacKellar was the one he feared most. Aye, he was the cunning one, appointing him as cateran leader, so that should anything go sour, it was he who would shoulder the blame, and when it did, perhaps challenge him in front of others.... Show that he could best the one who had slain the MacIntosh himself.

Andrew kicked the grass at his feet. What would he give not to have made yon journey to the Kyles, then he would not have lost his home, to be living here like an animal, risking life and limb for the very bite to eat. He would even stand Coll MacKerlich's mocking to be back home. There was the trouble, once again he no longer had a home.

Andrew drew a hand over his knee. Perhaps he could start somewhere anew? Even as the thought entered his head, he dismissed the idea. He knew what he had endured to make a life on the old MacBeolin place, and had no wish to repeat that experience, even should there be another Kirsty MacKenzie, at the end of it all.

What of his return to Glen Laidon and the chance to see his own son again? If he were to show the clan....,especially his in-laws the stolen pistol, and relate how he had avenged his Fiona, surely they would forgive him; perhaps not wholly, but enough to let him settle there? Naturally, it would not be on his own croft, for no doubt this would be in the hands of someone else after all this time, for they would not let good land go to waste. Nor would he wish to settle back on his own croft, his own *tigh tughadh*, not after what had happened the night Fiona died.

He stood up. He had no place to go. It was all wishful thinking, he would have to remain here, at least for the time being, be on his guard at all times, and await the MacKellar's inevitable challenge.

"It is done! We are safe at last!" Johnny MacKellar, punched the air in triumph, as an out of breath, Andrew MacLaren trotted towards him.

"You are sure of this, Johnny, it is still some ways home?" Andrew wiped his brow, not at all convinced.

"You will presently see for yourself my friend. Look yonder," Johnny pointed.

At first to Andrew there was nothing to be seen but empty braeside, then in an instant a score or more of heavily armed clansmen appeared upon the slope.

"That is why. These are MacPhersons, see you. The Moray men will not now venture closer. Come. I will introduce you to Neil there."

"*Dia!* MacKellar, whose loss is this I'm after wondering? And how many slain to win such a herd?" was the newcomer's first words.

"Where they came from, it is best you do not know, Neil. As to how many slain, not a one, thanks to the MacLaren here, whose whole plan it was," the cateran announced proudly, slapping Andrew on the back.

"You will be making the MacIntosh green with envy at your planning MacLaren!" Neil MacPherson, exploded pumping Andrew's hand vigorously. "He prides himself in this, does that one!"

"Where have you been hiding that face of yours MacPherson?" Johnny asked mockingly. "Seamus is no more, and you not knowing it. Has the entire Clan MacPherson been asleep?"

Embarrassed by the shape the conversation was taking, Andrew made a discreet withdrawal leaving the explaining of the late MacIntosh's demise to the MacKellar, and heard a low whistle of astonishment at his back as he did so.

As the two men talked, the MacPherson clansmen busied themselves driving a number of the herd back up the braeside. Perplexed Andrew asked of Dugald, "What is this Dugald, have we robbed, to find ourselves in turn robbed? And for why?"

"It is the way," Dugald deigned to answer with a twist of his lip. "For portion of the herd we can pass freely through MacPherson land, an arrangement that has worked fairly well in the past, for we are safe from pursuit from this point on."

Dugald drew closer to his bewildered listener, his voice low, conspiratorial. "Do not concern yourself over much MacLaren, they do not know Hamish has passed through earlier unobserved."

At last the 'raiders callop' paid, and pride preserved, both parties took their leave.

Chapter 8

They heard the pipes long before they had emerged from the defile. Then there were folk all around them, laughing, slapping their backs, dogs scampering back and forth, barking excitedly, all adding to the noise.

Laughing, Duncan fought a way through the happy throng to Andrew. "It was a master plan you had there, Andrew MacLaren, and not a soul lost!" The man ran a critical eye over the women and bairns herding the cattle to the pens at the farthest end of the compound. "There is enough here to last 'till spring at least."

"So you and Hamish met no trouble?" Andrew speared, happy to be safe once again, and not a little pleased at being treated the hero in this piece.

"We saw not a soul. Still, you will hear of this and more before this night is out. Away and see Una, man, then hurry back to the festivities." Duncan jerked his head at the folk already dancing around the peat fires in the arena, to emphasise his point.

Una was tying a ribbon in her hair when Andrew found her. She saw him, and ran to engulf herself in his arms. "You are the brave hero returned are you not Andrew MacLaren?" she cried, snuggling his chest. "Oh, the proud lassie I will be this night, dancing with my man!"

Kissing her, Andrew broke free and walked across the room to his kist, where for a moment he stood hesitating , then having made up his mind, bent to open and rummage through the kist until finding what he wanted, turned to face the lass.

"It was my wife's ...my own Fiona." He held out the dress to her. "I do not know why I had a mind to keep it. ... If you will not take it amiss, Una, I should like you to have it...for all the kindness you have shown me and the *troich*."

The dress had been his final link with Glen Laidon. At the time he could not bear to leave the garment behind, for it was as if by having the dress with him he was not leaving Fiona behind but bringing her with him.

He had been on the verge of offering it to Kirsty, and was glad he had not, for now he knew it would not have been appreciated, seeing as that lass had held the notion that it was his late wife who had always stood between them, then the dress would have been the final insult, whereas the opposite was the case with Una.

Una clapped her hands in sheer happiness and ran to take the dress from him, her dark eyes wide with delight. Holding it up in front of her, she swung around to see it swirl.

"Andrew! Andrew! What can I say?" she shrilled, the tears running down her cheeks. For to Una that this man had given her his dear wife's dress, could only mean he had more than a distant liking for her.

The picture of Una holding up the dress against her body, transposed Andrew back to Glen Laidon and the last time he had seen his wife wear the garment, and suddenly weary he leaned against the kist.

"Away and see to the *troich* whilst I make myself presentable," Una command but not too sharply. When her man had closed the door behind him, Una winked to herself. "When this night is done, there will be more than the *troich* to keep you here my bonnie man, I am after thinking."

There being neither body nor message, the caterans left the standing stone behind.

Andrew's eyes travelled over the empty landscape, and beckoned the *troich* to follow.

It was good to be out of the confines of the stronghold after the winter's captivity. Not that the time had passed slowly, for there had been plenty to occupy both mind and body these past chilly months. The man chuckled at the diplomacy he had been forced to employ by having the widow MacCrae show Una new dishes to serve. This, he conceded she now did reasonably well, considering the meagre sources to hand, as well as keeping herself a great deal cleaner.

The bothan itself was now quite watertight where it met the cliff, thanks to the dwarf's skills, which had not surprised Andrew after seeing the tiny man's own home.

Thankfully, the tiny man himself was no longer the target of mischievous bairns. Now these same miscreants were ever eager to be at his door to receive wooden toys carved by him, his huge face creased in smiles at their obvious pleasure, with a few even allowing themselves to be patted on the head on occasion as they departed clutching some new prized toy.

At night by the peat fire flame, Andrew had sat with the dwarf conversing in sign language in an attempt to unravel the mystery of the man who had spent so long in isolation. Clearly he had no name. Neither could he read or write, or tell his age, but by drawing marks on the dirt floor Andrew had reasoned the man had spent twenty years: probably half his life within those wooded confines.

This was as far as he had got, beyond which, was total mystery. Who his kin were, or had been, or how he had come to be there, even Una with her uncanny instinct for understanding the man could not unravel.

Riding beside the dwarf, now mounted precariously on a garron, Andrew felt an unexpected fondness for the man. Una too, would miss him, as so aptly demonstrated when the tiny man had shown his intentions of returning to his own home.

Una had hugged and wept over him. He, clearly embarrassed had studied the floor shifting from one foot to another.

Neither would the dwarf accept any great quantity of meal or other goods, untying them from his garron as quickly as Una had put them on. At last, the lass defeated, he and the *troich* had started on their way: a few souls in the *daingneachd* not unhappy at his departure.

Suddenly, the dwarf tugged at Andrew's sleeve, and pointed down the mountainside to a herd of deer bounding towards them, gesturing that Andrew should draw his pistols. However, the lead stag having caught their scent veered away, with the entire herd following, climbing and leaping majestically up the mountainside out of sight.

As they vanished over the crest, Andrew felt the dwarf's eyes on him. He, unable to explain that although any meat was welcome, these deer were not worth the killing. Still the man continued to stare, his eyes bulging, fists clenched tight, then just as suddenly, relaxed. Puzzled, Andrew coaxed his mount on, happy to be on the move again, though feeling more than a little uneasy.

By winding round snow speckled braes they avoided the higher slopes and passes still deep in winter snow, until at last they arrived at *coille taibhseach,* where, at its sight the *troich* was off his mount, disappearing into its folds, his friend instantly forgotten.

For a time Andrew sat there listening to the dwarf run hither and thither in the encroaching darkness, until deciding to see what the wee man was about, dismounted.

By following the tiny footprints in the snow Andrew came upon the dwarf. The hairs on the nape of his neck tingling while watching the man caress and lay his cheek against a giant tree, bend to stroke a sapling no more than a foot high, then hurry to another to repeat the same process

The muscles in Andrew's throat constricted, and a strange eeriness came over him awakening old superstitions. Perhaps after all this man was *ann-spiorad*, since what he did here was nothing short of unnatural. The dwarf turned, a smile on his lips, waving affectionately at the trees nearest him as if greeting long lost friends.

Suddenly the realisation that this was the tiny man's family struck home to Andrew. And why not he demurred? What else, or who else had the tiny man for company these last long years? Would it not be as natural to watch nature grow as one would a child? Even though Andrew was sure the dwarf had not seen him watching him from behind his screen , the tiny man walked directly to where he stood. How had he known he was there? Once again Andrew was to witness that strange eeriness creep over him.

However, it was not long before both men sat round the fire in the confines of the dwarf's tiny bothan, eating well of what remained of Una's food after their long journey.

Now relaxed, the episode of the trees almost forgotten, Andrew sat with half closed eyes while the dwarf rummaged amongst his treasures in a small alcove built into the rock, and was not at first aware of the silver goblet or the bottle of wine thrust into his hand until his host shook him by the shoulder . Grunting, the dwarf filled up his own cup, and so it started. Before long another bottle was produced and yet another, having Andrew wondering how came the man by so much store. The importance of which faded with every quaich, until he was fast asleep.

The first to awaken, Andrew rose and went outside to relieve himself. Done, he made his way back through the trees. The morning was cold. Perhaps it would rain later. He shivered, his mouth thick with the after effects of the drink. Suddenly a shattering noise assailed his thumping head. He drew closer to the bothan where the dwarf was in the act of throwing out of his abode all of his household treasures, until one by one a untidy pile lay at his feet.

Feeling sick from the drink, Andrew leaned on one of the garrons for support,while the dwarf spread a plaid on the ground, Why,

Andrew thought had he indulged so much in the drink? He had never done so before, nor with so little a conversation amongst revellers, he grinned.

Now he realised why the *troich* had refused the meal from Una, for all along his intentions had been to return to the *daingneachd*. His head still pounding, Andrew stepped forward halting the tiny man in his work. Pointing in the direction of the stronghold then at the bundle on the ground, he drew a hand across his throat.

Shrugging, the dwarf cocked his enormous head on one side and awaited an explanation.

Andrew scratched his throbbing head in frustration. "How can I make you understand, man, that the caterans...or most, see you for what you truly are.....a dwarf, but it would not be the case should you return with these." He threw a hand at the bundle. "For were they to see such gear they would quickly return to their former thinking that you are indeed *ann- spoirad*."

Still, the dwarf continued to stare at him, as a dog would his master. Andrew threw his hands in the air. With such a throbbing in his head he had little patience left.

"How think you they will make of this?" Andrew kneeled to pick up a silver goblet. "Or does every Highland cheil possess a quaich of such distinction think you?" he asked angrily.

With a shake of his head, Andrew rose. "If only you had the speech, *troich*, no doubt all could be explained, but should you return to the *daingneachd* so burdened, then I would fear for your very life, no matter how rich you may make your new found friends."

Suddenly the embryo of a plan formulated in Andrew's fuddled brain. He threw his friend a sly smile. "Still there is no need to leave it all behind. First, we eat or in my case drink water that is." And with a hand on his shoulder guided his perplexed companion back inside the bothan.

An hour or so later saw Andrew and his companion on their way back to the stronghold. His garron brushed the branch of a tree and he felt the snow wet on his leg. At last, he thought a thaw was on the way. He reached down and took a drink from his flask. Never again he thought, but did everyone who had over indulged in the drink not say the same?

He glanced at the dwarf riding beside him, a great claymore at his back. He had refused to leave the weapon with the other goods he had left behind in the tiny bothan.

Andrew shook his head in bewilderment, thinking on how the dwarf had led him to a cave deeper into the woods where he had shown him a further horde stashed there. The entrance to which had not been sealed. And why should it have been, for no man in his right mind should wish to venture into woods with such a reputation? Andrew scratched his still thumping head at the thought that he himself fitted such a description. When through their usual sign language he had brought this to the dwarf's attention the tiny man had merely rolled a rock well over his own size and weight in front of it, leaving Andrew to marvel at such a feet of strength.

The setting sun threw ever lengthening shadows against the rocks when Andrew and the *troich* emerged from the defile to the noisy revelry of, Fergus MacAlister, and his kind.

Taking in the scene at a glance, the tiny figure stiffened in the saddle, oblivious for once of the children gathering around him as he dismounted, his huge claymore at his back.

Throwing down his half empty bottle MacAlister staggered towards the tiny man. "Well! Well! 'Tis the *troich* returned to defend us all! Upon my word I have never seen a *claymore*, carry *a man!*" he bellowed.

Encouraged by the resulting laughter, the MacAlister suddenly hoisted the diminutive figure face high before him, in the same instance that the dwarf head butted the big man, who, with a howl of rage slackened his hold to clutch his blood splattered face.

Instantly a hush descended around the arena. The dwarf quickly moving back to reach for his weapon, while the MacAlister , backhanded wiped the blood off his face and strode to where his own sword lay, turning as quickly as his inebriated state would allow to advance weapon in hand upon the tiny figure.

"Hold!" Andrew quickly dismounted, fearing murder would be done to the man he had sacrificed so much to save. "You cannot fight the *troich*, MacAlister! Look you the size of the man! Have you no pride at all?"

Angrily, Fergus wiped his face and thrust Andrew aside, and with all sign of drunkenness appearing to have gone, snarled at Andrew,

"He had no call to do as he did, MacLaren, his height, or lack of it will not save him now!"

Despairingly, Andrew swung to face the fast growing crowd for help, astonished to find both Duncan and Johnny in their midst, the latter shaking his head in signal not to interfere. Frustrated that his own recent status had been so easily brushed aside, Andrew could only watch.

"When I finish slicing you from head to toe, wee man, there will not be enough left to fill a bannock!" the giant growled, shaking his sword angrily at his diminutive opponent.

Anticipating the outcome of this uneven contest between this David and Goliath, the crowd fell silent, even the dogs sensing the despair in the foreboding silence, scurried off.

The circle widened at the giant's advance upon his adversary, who, instead of awaiting the expected onrush sprang forward, taking the big man by surprise, catching his oppenents sword by its hilt with his own claymore, and wrenching it from his grasp in a movement quicker than the eye could follow.

For a moment no one moved, so rapid had been the *troich*'s action. Suddenly as a dam bursting, all rushed forward to congratulate the tiny man, leaving the MacAlister to explain to anyone who would care to listen, that it had been the drink that had hindered him, or all would have ended differently.

Amidst the compliments from the astonished onlookers, the *troich* pushed through to present Andrew with MacAlister's sword.

Andrew knew what he had to do. But did he have the courage? For the truth be known he was still afraid of these wild men,

Since his successful planning of the Moray raid, he was no longer seen as a simple crofter turned cateran, but a man capable of planning and providing as had the MacIntosh, though in fact it was still Johnny and Duncan who ran the everyday affairs. Therefore, to ensure his own safety and that of the dwarf, it was essential that he now display no weakness.

With racing heart Andrew held out the sword to the vanquished giant, and in a voice all could hear, commanded; for this is what he must do, "Fergus MacAlister, you are indeed fortunate the only blood spilt here this night was your own, for had the *troich* suffered harm when I commanded you to halt...." Andrew clapped a hand to his pistol, "I would have killed you myself."

Andrew's countenance had not changed as he spoke, though his heart had felt to burst through his chest. What would the big man do? What would he do, should the giant challenge *him*? Or could this be the opportunity Johnny MacKellar, had patiently awaited?

While he awaited the MacAlister's reaction a murmur of astonishment at Andrew's assertion rolled around the gathering, all now eager to hear the big man's reply to this newcomer. The gathering further astonished by the man submissively taking the sword from this same newcomer, and without a word spoken, pushed his way roughly through his fellow caterans.

Andrew lay on the grass, his eyes closed against the glare of the summer sun, knowing that each day was taking him that bit further away from leaving this new life he had set himself. What disturbed him most was, that it was becoming that bit easier to bide here. Here, he was respected, now no longer a subject of ridicule or derision. Of course it was still a struggle to survive, no different from life on the croft, except that was, to let an honest man do the back breaking, while he and his like reaped the reward of his toils.

Now and again Andrew felt a pang of guilt over this, for he knew how soul destroying labour it could be to raise cattle or crops only to have them stolen in one swift blow. Was this *him*? Was he becoming another Seamus MacIntosh? Had he ruined lives by his reiving as had that cateran? No. He could never do what the MacIntosh had done, even though the 'lifting' of another man's cattle was a way of life throughout the Highlands.

"Well! Well! It must be hard put you are to lie there having to do all that breathing by yourself, and not a body to help you!"

Andrew screwed up his eyes as the shadow of Duncan Cameron, fell over him.

"Aye that it is Duncan, all day and every day without a hint of help," he answered lazily.

Duncan gave a guffaw at Andrew's quick reply and sat down beside him, his gaze lingering over Una and the others splashing water about in the lochan below.

Andrew drew himself up to a sitting position nodding to where the MacAlister stood waist deep in the water, the dwarf mounted on his shoulders. "I would not have believed it possible, not after yon night when the *troich* disarmed him. I feared the big man would have

118

sought some means of satisfying his pride, either with the *troich* there, or myself,... or us both. I believe his over indulgence of the drink that night was his...our saving grace. Though I am led to believe it is to you Duncan that the credit must go for the man's lack of reprisal."

The elder man shrugged. "Fergus came to see no sense in it. The *troich* and yourself would now be sorely missed. Besides, as you say, Fergus put his besting by the *troich* down to the drink. It has helped him to save face, you understand" he chortled. "Though I think he still cannot get over it."

"Speaking of the wee man, I have always meant to have a word with you, Duncan."

"Oh, aye, Andrew, and what would that word be about, see you?" Duncan asked, amused by the antics of those in the water.

In great detail, Andrew related his perception and uneasiness concerning the tiny man. From the time of seeing the deer, the incident of the trees, and how, although unable to see Andrew hidden as he stood watching him, had known he was there. Above all, the *troich's* uncanny instinct of anticipating impending trouble, such as the sword fight with the MacAlister.

"It seems not altogether natural, Duncan," Andrew confided to his friend. "I know fine, he is none other than a dwarf...no evil spirit...but..."Andrew broke off with a shudder. "You take my meaning, Duncan?"

Duncan chewed on a piece of grass. "That I do. Though, tell me this my friend, if you were confined to a prison such as yon woods, with every hand met, set against you, none to offer friendship, and even if it were so, could not so much as pass the time of day with you , would it be so strange to turn your attention to the trees around you?   To watch them spring from seed, grow, mature as we ourselves do, in the knowledge that they at least will not seek to harm you?

As to the other matter, I do not myself know, but I am after thinking, even here one acquires a sixth sense for danger. Is it any wonder then, that the wee man may rely on this the greater, since he lacks another two?"

Andrew scratched his jaw, mulling over his friend's words.

"Do not be worrying yourself, Andrew, laddie. When all found it easier to destroy what they feared, or had been brought up to fear, you stood up and proved them wrong. The result is there for all to see." Duncan gestured towards the lochan. "You have given the *troich* a chance at happiness. For how long, only the good Lord himself knows, but every day must be better than what he has known."

Rising, Duncan touched Andrew on the shoulder, his tone changing. "However, it is not on this subject I sought you out. Johnny awaits us. You may mind me telling you when we walked yon first day, of another way out of the *daingneachd*, known only to Johnny and myself? Well we both think it best, since you are now *ceann cinnidh* that you should also know of this."

Andrew stared at his elder, whose declaration had come as a shock to one who had never looked upon himself at having taken the place of Seamus MacIntosh, only as another poor soul having sought refuge amongst others as unfortunate as himself.

True, it was to him all looked to for the planning of the 'lifting',though, to him this was far enough. He was no warrior. Any one of them could best him in a fight. Now here were his two friends offering to tell him their most cherished secret regarding the safety of the stronghold.

As to him being made *ceann cinnidh*..chieftain, how could fighting men like, Fergus MacAlister and his kind follow him, obey *his* orders, when he knew nothing about such matters?

"You are wondering why any should wish to follow you?" Duncan asked having read his thoughts. "Sometimes it is best to follow one who is always that wee bit of a mystery in his thinking."

"Then you have the right man there, Duncan, see you, for my own thoughts are often a mystery, even to myself," Andrew sighed, trying to make light of the situation, though his heart felt as though it reverberated off the side of Carn Leac.

"Besides, Andrew laddie, you have the head for the planning."

Duncan started to lead the younger man around the rocks that littered the braeside. Perhaps, Andrew thought he should think of leaving now while there was still time, for should he accept this accolade of leadership, he could no longer walk away and return to being a crofter.

His instincts were telling him to quit now before the responsibility for these folks lives overwhelmed him. Or was this what the MacKellar also had in mind for him? He could not see that man give way to him, he little more than a stranger. Then again why would he and Duncan have trailed him over every gully and corrie, or show him passes where none should be, not to mention paths through the great forest of the Monadliath, if for no other reason than to make him chieftain..their *ceann cinnidh.*? Or show him short cuts and hiding places, besides teaching him the diplomacy of living within others lands. How it was permitted to take the occasional deer from the hill, fish from the loch, but never another man's cattle within the boundaries of his own domain, which in turn guaranteed their immunity when returning with a *'spreidh'* of cattle so long as the tribute or 'raiders callop' was paid to the owners of the land through which they passed, thus creating a buffer between them and their pursuers.

Then there had been the intricate network of spies and recruits via the standing stone to learn and digest, enabling the caterans to be in the right place at the right time. All this his two companions had taught him in a relatively short space of time.

Andrew rounded a boulder at the Cameron's back. "Does everyone see me as leader?"

"Aye, Andrew, even the MacAlister added his consent ...and none too slowly, see you."

Andrew stumbled after the man. He took a slight look back down at the lochan at folk laughing and splashing in the water, they whose lives he was now responsible. How could he come to terms with this, knowing how the fate of Iain MacLean, caught and hanged this past month, and he with a wife and four bairns left to feed had affected him?

"You have no thought to my refusing?" Andrew asked of Duncan's back.

Duncan strode on. "You have little choice man...as we have," he threw over his shoulder. "For it was yourself who slew the MacIntosh....left us leaderless... tamed the MacAlister...with a little help from your friend that is." The mountain breeze blew Duncan's laughter back at Andrew. "Left us all dependent on your planning for our lifting, as it was with Seamus."

Though he could not see the Cameron's face, he was sure it held that same smile he had seen, when he Andrew, had first spoken of attacking the MacKeiths. Once again Andrew had the feeling of having been duped. So, with little choice, he followed on.

121

Johnny MacKellar led Andrew to the last bothan but one from the cattle pen, leaving Duncan outside to keep guard on the door. Weaving in and out of the paraphernalia long since discarded, Johnny reached the far wall of the room, where he threw aside the peat stacked there, to reveal a passage large enough to admit a crouching man.

Tapers lit, Andrew followed his guide through the narrow tunnel, to a chamber beyond, which was sufficiently high to let them stand fully upright.

"There is room for fifty or more here, whilst it needs only one to guard what you have just this minute crawled through," Johnny exclaimed holding his taper high.

"Aye, a man would not be at his best fighting on his hands and knees if he were to chase a body in here through that wee crack," Andrew agreed, surveying the aperture with interest.

Johnny swung on his heel. "Come, follow me, mind you keep to the middle of the tunnel now, for there are passages to the right and left which I fear drop down to the very bowels of the mountain itself," he warned, leading the way. His voice echoing as he said over his shoulder, "there are tapers at intervals on the walls. The MacIntosh and I put them there some time ago in case of an emergency, which I pray to the above, we may never have. Can you not just see the panic of bairns and old folk, when guided through here in the dark, even with no one at their heels? And the time it would take?"

Following his companion through the narrow passage's twists and turns, Andrew tried to picture in his mind what it would be like to shepherd three score women, bairns, and old folk, through such an eerie frightening place, where draughts from caverns on either side threatened to extinguish the tapers light at any moment, and walls echoed with the intermittent drip of water, whilst deep within the bowels of the mountain came the constant sound of distant rumbling.

At long last, and much to Andrew's relief he caught sight of a chink of light a little way ahead. Thankfully they had reached the end of the tunnel.

Reaching the source of the light Johnny pushed a boulder aside, and kneeling down, cautiously poked out his head, then, satisfied all was clear scrambled out into the sunlight, quickly followed by Andrew at his heels.

"This surely cannot be the corrie we passed through yesterday?" Andrew asked incredulously, staring down the mountainside, his eyes not yet accustomed to the sudden sunlight after the blackness of the tunnel.

"The very same. It was done intentionally," Johnny replied, nonchalantly, as if what they had just negotiated had been nothing more than a skip over a burn.

"But it took over two hours to reach the stronghold from down yonder!" Andrew exclaimed, mystified.

"So you see the value of it all. Do not be tempted to use it as a shortcut, for its true worth remains only as long as it is held secret. No one must know of its existence. That my friend, includes your Una."

Andrew blew out his breath at what he thought was an absurdity. "Aye, I understand, Johnny, but who in his right mind would wish to use it as a walk in the sun. I would not be tempted to use it I am after thinking, even if the devil himself was at my heels."

They were almost three quarters of the way back along the passage when Andrew stumbled, and one of his pistol that had fallen out of his belt clattered down one of the caverns. Alarmed at the thought of having lost it, he bent down, shinning his taper over the void.

"Johnny!" he called out to his friend, swinging a leg over the edge. "One of my pistols has dropped over the side. The drop is not so far, that I cannot fetch it. It will take but a moment!.

"Be careful man,!" his friend cautioned from above, " some of these shafts lead straight to hell, I am after thinking. Can you see well enough?"

"Fairly well!" Andrew called back, now out of sight of his companion, and by the tapers flickering light saw where his pistol had fallen and, accidentally loosened a rock from the wall when he bent to retrieve it.

Something made Andrew look at the hole where the rock had been. He stepped closer, and in the tapers shadowy light saw what appeared to be two leather pouches. Puzzled as to why they should be here Andrew was about to shout up to Johnny to tell him what he had discovered when a sudden notion made him think better of it.

Lifting out one of the pouches Andrew emptied the contents into the palm of his hand. "Dia!" he exclaimed staring at the pile of coins, for there were enough to feed and clothe a man for many a good day. Andrew's heart raced. Quickly replacing the coins in the pouch, he shouted up to Johnny that he had not yet found the weapon.

With some trepidation the finder reached for the second pouch, his heart pounding at what he may find. Then there in his hands, glittering up at him in the eerie light lay four rings, two of gold and two set in stone. Scarcely able to contain his excitement, Andrew quickly replaced his find in the niche and scrambled back up to his waiting companion.

"I thought you were away conversing with the devil himself !" Johnny tittered at Andrew emerging out of the darkness.

"It was deeper than I thought, Johnny," Andrew stammered, his mind racing. The look on Johnny's face convincing him the man knew nothing of the pouches, which left only Duncan, whose reaction he would shortly test. Though, he wagered as three only were aware of the tunnel, his find no doubt belonged to the late Seamus MacIntosh.

But how had that man come by such wealth? He himself had only seen rings like these once before, and that was on the hands of *Macailein Mhor*, chief of Clan Campbell, when he had come to visit his own MacLaren chief, in Glen Laidon.

"I wish I was a crofter again...though now I could leave this life and own a hundred crofts! Maybe my own clan!" he said half aloud with a smile.

"What was that you were after saying?" Johnny asked, a step or two in front.

"Nothing, Johnny. I was just saying, I wish we were out of this place."

Four, Andrew counted to himself. He had found the pouches in the fourth cavern from the entrance. This he must mind for the future, for his brain still reeled at his good fortune and the enormity of finding the cache in all of that great place.

It was not until the entrance was again sealed, and they were outside in the sunlight that Duncan, still standing guard, asked Andrew what he thought of their secret escape route.

Making a moue and studying the man's reactions, Andrew declared his liking for the idea, if not the tunnel itself, and went on to emphasis his point by relating how he had dropped his pistol and had to drop down into one of those heathen pits to retrieve it.

"Dear as the weapon might be to you, seeing as it was your own father's, I myself would have left it there, for you will not be finding me leaving yon passage ways for all the gold in *Lunnain.*"

Now a little more assured that the hoard had been the MacIntosh's, Andrew merely smiled.

Chapter 9

Both Duncan and Johnny had been right in warning him to be careful of this dandified object across the table, whose speech, as was his attire, entirely Lowland, from his powdered wig to manicured fingernails. This then was Kenneth MacSorley of Quoich.

To say he, Andrew was uneasy was an understatement, for was not this tryst of Crief close to his own native clan country. He drew the bottle to him, glad both his friends and more mingled outside the tavern. Some, already having relieved unsuspecting Lowlanders of their pouched siller, and later, it was hoped their cattle as well.

The dandy pushed his empty plate away, and lifting a glass of claret to his lips sipped lightly, his eyes darting furtively around the crowded room. "I have asked you to do me the honour of joining me...Mister..eh," he spoke quietly in the Gaelic.

"MacLaren," Andrew answered evenly, and at the other's knowing smile, "at least that is how you may address me at present, sir."

The dandy gave an ill disguised smirk. "I have a business proposition which I am sure will interest you, considering you are in this same line of business as myself."

"And what line of business would that be, Mister MacSorley?"

"Cattle, sir! Cattle! What all the vast Highlands depend upon for their very existence."

Quoich took a sip of his drink and sat back to await Andrew's reaction. When none was forthcoming he pushed on, despite having the temptation to tell this cateran cur to mind his manners, for was not he, Quoich, himself a gentleman born? "I may be a few years your elder Mister MacLaren, but...and I say this with pride, I am still in my prime." Andrew stifled the urge to laugh, that MacSorley was about as close as he himself was to his mother's milk. "And though I have the choosing of most eligible ladies of society in *Dun Eideann*, it is the Lady Isobella Grant, I wish to make my own."

Quoich designed his next question to establish their different stations, as well as humiliating this landless churl. "You do not know the lady, MacLaren? No...? Had you the pleasure of having done so, you would understand my ready desire for her. However, she finds it in herself to reject me. Me! Kenneth MacSorley of Quoich!...that red headed...And with a temper to match, I can assure you," he stammered, unable to bring himself to believe that this; indeed any lady, should be so ill disposed towards him.

Lowering his voice, Quoich leaned across the table. "Here is my proposition, MacLaren. For three years past, yon lady has found herself without the assistance of her brother, who had the misfortune of having himself killed," the man scorned, "which now leaves the fair Isabella to run her own affairs...with the dubious aide of a factor: and not over successfully, I may add. Now, I believe she and her brood of a tribe can hardly survive another winter...more so without cattle..if you take my meaning?"

Andrew could very well take his meaning, and was already feeling a great sympathy for the unfortunate lady. He eyed the man coldly. "I could never be party to the starving of women and bairns, MacSorley, not even to help you fulfil your amorous ambitions. You must find yourself another man."

Andrew rose and Quoich held out a restraining hand "Hear me out sir...at least...if you please." He glanced around to ensure no one was listening. "Do you not see my plan? Should you play your part aright, and help relieve Mistress Grant of her cattle,yon lady will be left with no other choice than to turn to me for assistance, which as a Christian man, I will give only too willingly," Quoich spouted, sitting back in his chair, a smug look on his face.

"Leaving the lady with no other recourse than except to wed you in return for the lives of her kinsfolk," Andrew added scornfully. "Surely if she appeals to The Grant Himself."

"Be assured, her patriarch will not interfere. It is to his advantage that this match should take place." Quoich's eyes travelled over Andrew's face. "Come man, there is a great deal of siller in this for you and yours should it be done aright."

Andrew sipped at his glass to give himself time to think. It appeared which ever way this unfortunate creature turned, she was already doomed, and, although he neither liked this man or his proposal, who was he to moralise? To refuse would not halt others hastening to do this dandy's bidding. Also, there was the matter of their own survival to consider; a matter of which he was now responsible. Hesitating no longer, Andrew nodded his agreement.

With a hint of triumph in his eyes, Quoich leaned forward, sliding a leather purse discreetly across the table. "There is more siller there, than you will find in a lifetime of reiving MacLaren, and that only half. The rest is when the task is done."

Weighing the purse in his hand, Andrew quickly dropped into his sporran away from prying eyes, aware that it was no mean sum.

"When will it be done, MacLaren....if indeed that is your name? I need to know exactly, so that I may absent myself from home, for it essential than not even the merest hint of suspicion should fall my way."

"That I can well understand," Andrew scorned. "Let us settle on two weeks from this day."

The numeral seven was roughly the shape of the glen they followed, with Gleidh House at its junction their objective before nightfall. The rain never having ceased, the lower slopes had become a quagmire, the scree above slippery underfoot.

Head bent against the stinging rain which threatened to drive them all off the hill itself, Andrew snatched a quick look ahead at the snakelike procession of the caterans slipping and sliding on the wet scree, and wishing wholeheartedly that he had never heard of Kenneth MacSorley, or his accursed scheme, although, Johnny and Duncan harboured no such qualms, advising that there was more to this than met the eye, or they knew nothing of gentry or their ways.

Putting a hand up to wipe his face, Andrew peered into the low cloud base obscuring the front of the column, and at the same time heard the clatter of falling scree and Johnny's warning cry.

Almost immediately a figure shot through Andrew's line of vision, followed by an avalanche of rocks, hitting and passing the falling man as if vying with one other to reach the bottom, each onlooker there feeling every thud and thump that hit the stricken man, until, he finally slithered to a halt.

Young Dugald was the first to reach the injured man, shouting up to Andrew that it was Angus MacVie, and that he was sore hurt.

Again silently reiterating his dislike for this whole situation Andrew descended the slope to where the injured man, his head cradled in someone's lap, lay wracked in pain.

MacVie grimaced up at him. "It is my leg clean broken Andrew, and my back feels as though the wife has been at it again with the besom." He tried to smile through the pain.

"Never mind, Angus, we shall have you back home in no time at all. We would not be wanting your wife to be missing even one day at the thrashing of your back."

Having no wood to set a splint, Angus's own sword was placed along the leg and bound, while others tied plaids to targes to form some sort of litter.

"It will take five men to see him home," Andrew said, standing back and looking at their handiwork. "One, to act as relief and guide, the other four to do the carrying." He took a sharp look at the men clustered around the injured man. "You four there who have given up your plaids and weapons, see Angus home." Then in afterthought, "Take young Dugald with you, his eyes are keen and will keep you out of trouble."

"With five of our numbers gone, it will be a hard task lifting a *spreidh* of cattle, should we also run into trouble, Andrew," Duncan announced heavily, now at his leader's side.

Andrew clicked his teeth demurring. Although their numbers had risen since attacked by the MacKeiths at 'the wood of the monster,' they were now reduced to seventeen, excluding the sentinels left at home, and the returning party.

"Then we must keep well hidden." Andrew turned sharply to Dugald. "You will do well to go by yonder corrie we skirted earlier before descending to the glen itself, Dugald. At least your numbers will not raise too much alarm should you be seen." Adding to erase the youth's despondency at being sent back, "I am relying on you Dugald to see them all safely home. You must also decide where to pass the night, and see to Angus's comfort."

Immediately the cloud lifted from the young man's face, to be replaced by pride at being given such a responsibility, and the trust this new cateran leader had placed upon him, for the MacIntosh would never have done so.

"That I will, *ceann cinnidh*! That I will!"

A little later, watching the litter disappear into the mist, Duncan proclaimed softly for Andrew's ear. "We were right in our thinking to make you our captain, see you, for you have the way with you, Andrew."

"Perhaps, Duncan. Though I wonder if we should not all be going yon way ourselves?" "No." he decided with a grunt, "we must go on. Keep to our arrangement. See an end to this."

With almost three quarters of the journey covered, darkness began to fall and with it a drop in temperature, turning the rain to sleet, and making their unknown way even more hazardous. Men slipped on wet grass, and with bare legs cut and gashed from heather long since dead, the weary band hoped fervently to be quit of the hills before all light was gone and they froze to death.

Squinting against the sleet, Andrew could just make out the pin point that was Gleidh House, and thankful that they had almost reached their destination led the caterans on the long descent to the end of the glen. It was as they reached its floor that the figure appeared, running and bounding towards them, arms flailing in warning.

Johnny was the first to recognise the rapidly approaching figure. "It is Dugald! How can this be? We left him heading in the opposite direction, some hours past."

It was in fact Dugald Ferguson, who came to a halt, panting and gasping before them.

"What is this, Dugald you have left your charge so early?" Andrew chided.

Dugald gulped for breath. "It was Angus who directed me to find you, and as fast as possible! ..He said… you would wish to know all was not right. He thought...no...I am wrong...he said...."

Andrew held up his hand. "Do not waste the time you held so dearly in your haste to find us, by stammering, Dugald. Calmly now, tell me what is so important Angus thinks I should know?"

Now partially recovered, Dugald related how when resting in the trees from a slow descent from the ridge top, they had witnessed a party of two score horsemen head up this same glen, with a similar number of running clansmen at their backs.

"It was Angus who recognised him!" Dugald exclaimed in near desperation. "They were led by MacSorley himself!"

A slow whistle of astonishment escaped from Duncan.

Andrew swivelled to face him. "Quoich, in person? And it was I who told him the very day of our being here. *Dia!* If I am not very much mistaken, there will be the same number at the watch tower 'tween hill and loch at the farther end of the glen."

"Then it is a trap!" Johnny and Duncan echoed.

"Nothing less," Andrew agreed. "Now it is too late to retrace our steps. Besides, we are already too far spent to face such numbers, and with the darkness upon us, we cannot again take to the hillside."

"We cannot bide here, Andrew, we shall all freeze to death by the morrow," Johnny replied, too cold to cogitate.

"This I grant you, Johnny, though I am after thinking we can play this MacSorley at his own game. Come! We must lose no time in reaching Gleidh House."

Three men stood at the door of Gleidh House, two supporting a supposedly injured third. Apprehensively, the caterans waited some distance away in the shadow of the trees, while the merest chink of light showed the door to be open, and cautious denizens peered into the night, their remonstrations halted when the injured man collapsed in a heap in the partially opened doorway. In a flash the waiting caterans were up and through the door before the startled occupants could react.

Unsure of the *troich's* reaction in such a situation, Andrew grabbed him by the arm. The gesture also gaining him time until it was safe for him to follow, for though every day he gained in confidence, he was still unsure of these wild men at his back, especially if things were to go awry.

Once inside the house, Andrew hastily took in the scene of caterans already devouring meat and wine from the rudely interrupted meal, with the entire household lined up against a wall, save the lady herself who continued to sit calmly at the table's head, indignant at this gross intrusion to her privacy.

Instantly, Andrew forgave the MacSorley and his devious scheme to win the lady. And who could blame him, for was she not beautiful in the extreme?

Andrew judged her to be a few years his elder, though still too young for the ancient Quoich, who must be in his forties at least...he reasoned. The hair more auburn than red, the blue eyes that glared at him sparkling with a quiet anger, her swan like neck, flushed blood red by this effrontery.

"And *you* must be master of this rabble!" the lady asked highly.

The question and tone of her voice jerked Andrew back to reality.

"You must forgive my friends, it is long since last they ate," Andrew answered, not a little ashamed by his companions' behaviour.

131

"Longer still when my clansmen learn of your presence here, I am after thinking, sir!"

Andrew recovered himself. "I hope not, for all our sakes. Now time is of the essence. Come lady, I should have a word with you in private."

The lady turned a cold eye on him, and for a moment Andrew thought she was about to disobey, and who could blame her? Who was he to command her, in this her own house?

He saw her eyes shift from him to the dwarf, then to two caterans arguing over a serving lass. He swallowed. Could he in fact control these men? If not all was lost within and without.

He motioned politely, that the lady should follow him into the adjoining room. Still seated and making no effort to move and continuing to stare her hostility at him, Isobella Grant, howled indignantly, "*You*, expect *me* , to treat with the likes of you?

Andrew was aware of the room suddenly quieten, all heads turned in his direction. He must not lose control of the situation. He cleared his throat. "I beg you to do so, for I believe you may learn something which may serve us both."

Angrily the lady threw down her napkin, and with an almost imperceptible glance at a clansman pinned against the wall by two caterans, who was almost the equal in stature to their own, MacAlister, rose to follow Andrew, who himself turned in the doorway to command Johnny, as that man was also about to follow. "See no one escapes from this house, Johnny. Keep a careful eye out for our mutual friend, he can now not be so far behind, though I believe he will wait somewhere down the glen so that he will catch us in the act so to speak, for he must make it seem wholly a coincidence that he finds us here."

Seeing Johnny colour at his exclusion from this colloquy Andrew attempted to soften the insult. "I will not be overlong my friend, when I assure you all will be revealed." So saying he gently closed the door.

The room was small. The lady crossed to sit on a high backed chair, and with a clipped wave of her hand motioned Andrew to do likewise. This he did, feeling a stirring in the blood at the sight of this lovely creature opposite, who despite her situation, sat, it would appear nonplussed, awaiting his explanation.

Feeling the disadvantage he was certain the lady purposely placed upon him, Andrew quickly related his encounter with the MacSorley; a slight grasping of the chair arm her only reaction.

"As you can see, Quoich has played me false, and hopes to ingratiate himself with you by catching a thief at work, whereby placing you forever in his debt," Andrew concluded drawing a deep breath of relief now that he had said his piece.

"Then he is mistaken sir! Even had his ruse succeeded, I would no more choose him for a husband than I would ...that, that.. *troich* of yours!" came the haughty reply.

Andrew twitched his ear. "Come Mistress Grant, you do the tiny man an injustice, he at least tells me no untruths."

For the first time the lady smiled, and despite the urgency, Andrew was quite content to sit and drink in such beauty, thoughts of Una and Kirsty clean gone from his mind.

"So, cateran, why tell me this? Is it absolution which you seek, if so, you cannot gain it from me."

Andrew forced himself back to the present situation. "I have a plan...Mistress....or should I say, Lady Grant...one which may work to our mutual advantage."

Now less than an hour later, the caterans found themselves being rowed up the far side of the loch that lay from Gleidh House to the head of the glen, thus completing the numeral seven.

Duncan tapped Andrew lightly on the shoulder. "You were right in your thinking, man. There they go!"

By the light of a pale moon in a sky turning to snow, Andrew faintly made out the horsemen on the far shore of the loch heading in the direction of Gleidh House.

"What I would not give to see MacSorley's face when he arrives from the other end of the glen and finds the nest empty!" Duncan chuckled.

"It is not his face I would be seeking, Duncan, should I have met the man this night, for by morning he would be missing his vitals," Johnny grimly assured his friend. "Aye, and had not Andrew here conspired with yon lady, we should be the kernel in the nut by now."

A half hour later the caterans, plus a score or more of Grants landed a mile or so upstream of the tower that guarded the head of the glen. The latter headed by their own giant leading a wearisome band of caterans into the hills, urged on by what the MacLaren and the lady had planned. Thus by morning all was complete.

Standing in a hollow, a brisk breeze ridding what little trees there were of snow, Andrew watched the last of the Grants except one, drive MacSorley beasts over the rim of the brae. This Grant, tall as their own MacAlister stood beside him, waiting.

"Give my regards to your mistress, Lachlan, and tell her I send her these beasts with the courtesy of, Kenneth MacSorley of Quoich who unfortunately was not at home when we called," he chuckled. "Tell her also, I especially crave her forgiveness for any unpleasantness that might have arisen from our recent visit."

The grinning giant tugged at his ear. "Since I know the lady fairly well, she will be seeing the humour in it herself, if I am not mistaken, that we should have lifted that man's cattle from his own doorstep, whilst he waits at ours."

The big man held out his hand. "Should your step bring you to Gleidh, you will find a welcome, of this I am sure, in especial from the lady herself I am after thinking."

Surprised and not displeased at this confession, Andrew waved a farewell before starting back with their own portion of the MacSorley herd, to the Monadhliath.

He had calculated and recalculated the distance from where he sat the garron, to the cleft rock in the open field, and from that rock to the ridge opposite. Now satisfied that the distance was almost equal, Andrew settled down to wait.

The mounted man's nervousness transmitted itself to his mount and he put a hand down to calm the beast, telling himself, it would not be long now.

Andrew was still amazed by his own transition, from simple crofter, afraid of his own shadow to this. Not that he was any braver than the night he had left Fiona to die, only now more cautious, wiser.

After the battle in the glen back in Kintail, he had been sure he'd never have to risk life and limb again. He had never been more wrong.

He had decided not to tell either Johnny or Duncan of his intentions, for should the truth be known he did not know whether of not he could bring himself to carry out what he thought must be done. Perhaps what he was about to attempt was not altogether wise, but how many caterans would now be lying in the heather if Angus MacVie had not broken his leg yon day? With he himself swinging from a MacSorley gibbet to impress all, and mainly a certain Isobella Grant. Andrew spat.

The day was still and clear, much warmer than the day of the intended 'lifting' at Gleidh, with its early threat of snow. Hearing a noise Andrew looked up to where Quoich sat mounted on the opposite ridge, a score or more of mounted men and clansmen by his side, now all hinged on Quoich's next move. Would the dandy, seeing him alone, venture across the intervening space by himself? Or would he bring his entire train with him? Already he had gambled on the first, believing Quoich would not wish anyone to know what had passed between them, lest they learn of their master's treachery and broken word.

His heart racing, Andrew waited, for timing was now all important if he was to survive, as well as succeed this day.

At last, Quoich started down from the ridge. Andrew spurred his own mount forward and drew up by a cleft rock to await the other's approach.

"And how many of your rabble have you hidden yonder, MacLaren?" Quoich challenged angrily, pointing to the ridge at Andrew's back, drawing up his own mount.

"None MacSorley, since it is you who are master of deceit, not I," Andrew retorted. "But since you doubt my word, I will await your inspection."

Thus rebuked, MacSorley seethed, "You played me false, MacLaren...if that is indeed your name. You were paid good siller to lift Grant cattle, not mine!"

"Nor was I paid to be used as a popinjay, MacSorley of Quoich!" Andrew hurled at the man. "Your only truth was in telling me you would not be at your own home yon day, though somewhat careful to omit telling me you could instead be found at Gleidh House!"

His eyes blazing, the older man blushed crimson. "The bargain between us MacLaren is nul and void," he choked, spittle forming at the corner of his mouth. "Return my siller and no more will be said of this."

"I believe the bargain was for double the sum received?" Andrew smirked.

"Do not quibble man, I have seen fit not to have asked for the return of my cattle. However, my message was plain, that you must bring the siller with you."

Andrew chanced a quick glance at the ridge, and satisfied that none of Quoich's men had moved, withdrew the leather pouch from his coat.

With a smile of triumph over this gee gaw, Quoich stretched out his hand to receive it, in the same instant that the dwarf leaped out of the cleft rock, and with one swift blow from his claymore severed the greedy outstretched hand.

With a howl of pain, shock and disbelief, Quoich grasped the shattered stump, wrenching the cravat from his throat to quench the blood flow, all the while whimpering at the object on the ground that was his hand.

The dwarf at his back Andrew quickly swung his mount around throwing a final warning to the distraught dandy. "Let all know, Kenneth MacSorley of Quoich, how I Andrew MacLaren, the cateran deal with those who would seek to betray me and mine!"

With his words ringing out to meet the Quich's rapidly approaching riders Andrew put spur to mount.

Chapter 10

Stretched out on the heather, Andrew turned his attention from the herd grazing amongst greener folds of the Monadhliath, to that of the women and bairns guddling in the burn further down the brae. Screwing up his eyes against the sun's glare and through narrow slits watched with unashamed pride, Una in the burn, her skirts gathered up around her knees. It was now a year and more since his coming here. He saw Una splash water on one of the bairns and smiled at how she was still a child at heart, though in some other ways a woman full grown.

Perhaps it was both these qualities that drew him to her. This laughing bubbling Una, who had brightened many a dull day by brushing aside the ever demanding worries of leadership.

Leadership! The word brought a scowl to Andrew's face. That, he had never heard of the word, or its meaning, in especial after his meeting with the MacSorley those months past.

Without closing his eyes he could still envisage the look of anger and frustration on Johnny MacKellar's face when he had informed him of that very same encounter.

"Was it not enough that you took his pride, without taking his hand as well?" Johnny had exploded. "You should have at least consulted Duncan and myself before venturing on this ploy, seeing as it concerns us all! It was wrong! Wrong!" The man had punched his open hand. "The likes of yon will not let this day rest. He will seek you out, MacLaren, and us with you. More's the pity."

Not a little angry himself he had shouted back. "It was what I believed best, not for myself alone, but for us all. You said yourself yon night on the loch how you wished to face the man after realising what he had intended. Had we been caught in his trap, how many would be alive today, think you? What of the old folk, women and bairns who rely upon us for their very existence, had we fallen yon day? How many lives would Quoich have accounted for in the end had his evil scheme succeeded?"

It was then that Duncan had interceded in an attempt to defuse the situation. "Andrew has a point there, Johnny. Though I agree with you, the lifting of the man's cattle, leaving his larder the emptier was deed enough in itself...without the other, but what is done, cannot be undone. Let us hope since we leave Kenneth MacSorley alone, he will do the same for us."

"Andrew! Andrew! I have brought some folks to meet you!" The dreamer became suddenly aware of the voice cutting into his reflections, and the figure of Dugald Ferguson striding up the slope, accompanied by two strangers attired in the garb of the Lowlander.

"What have we here, Dugald? And who are these two fine gentlemen?" Andrew asked, rising warily.

It was the smaller of the two, who seized the opportunity to answer. "My name is Sean McMahon, from Erin's Isle, your lordship," he responded in the Gaelic. "And this fine fellow is my friend, Davie Hamilton from your own Border country, or so he has led me to believe."

Andrew's eyes travelled from the smaller middle aged Irishman bobbing so submissively before him, to that of his tall fair haired companion, inquiring. "What brings you both to this side of the Highland Line, my friends?"

"Pure necessity your lordship, pure necessity," the Irishman moaned forlornly. "Indeed, if it was not for my young friend Dugald here, we should both be swinging from the gallows tree by now. And that's for sure."

"And what was your crime?" Andrew asked, his curiosity aroused.

"Sure, and it was only for throwing some dandified laird's bonnet in the loch, 'twas all."

"And for this he would have you hanged?"

"Well, seeing as he was still wearing it at the time may have made the difference."

Unprepared for such an unlikely answer, Andrew threw his head back laughing. "As you say, McMahon, that could have made the difference! And your friend here?"

"Och!" The Irishman responded with a flourish, "He sent in the son to help the father. Only I swear he could not swim a stroke either!"

Convulsed in laughter, Dugald slapped the Irishman's back, evidently much taken by his new found friend. "Can I be taking them to the *daingneachd*, Andrew? They have a notion to join our band," the young man asked eagerly, his eyes sparkling with admiration for the new comers.

"This I have no doubt, considering they have little choice in the matter," Andrew consented. "Mind you look after them well, Dugald. We shall talk presently of your errand, and how you came by these folk. Perhaps, your friends will also tell us the names of the gentlemen they endeavoured to teach to swim?" Andrew suggested, as a smiling Dugald led his acquaintances away.

Having strode up the braeside while the conversation was taking place, Una reached Andrew's side slipping her hand in his. "What manner of men are those who do not wear the *feileadh mor?* she asked as the three men disappeared out of sight.

"Saxons" Andrew replied evenly, his eyes on the spot where the three had crested the brae. "Irish and Border, to be precise, Una."

"I heard your laughter. What 'twas said?" Una chuckled inquisitively.

"Later, Una. Later." For he was still unsure of their new aquaintances.

"Then come sit by me Andrew. It is long since last we talked. You are ever busy when I seek your company. Have you grown tired of your Una?"

Andrew sat down and put his arm around the lass. "That is daft woman's talk, Una. You well know the burden placed upon me."

He saw that he had hurt her, and gently squeezed her shoulder. "Forgive me lass. But our numbers grow daily as do our needs, and we lack the men necessary to lift a *spreidh* often enough to fill our bellies. None know this better than you."

He squeezed her shoulder again. "Enough of this talk." The timbre of his voice changed to one of happiness. "Did you catch a fish or two in yonder burn?"

"No. I nearly did. Wee Sheena caught it before me!"

"Wee Sheena! She must be all of six years old," Andrew cried in mock alarm. "Is it to the bairn's fire I must go with bonnet in hand to beg for my supper this night, and me supposedly *ceann cinnidh*!"

Una pushed him away, and Andrew pretended to fall on his back. She fell on top of him gazing down into his eyes. "Will it ever be like this, Andrew? Say that it will never change," she entreated, her eyes sparkling.

"Never is a long time, lass," he whispered up into that bonnie face.

"Then some day you will leave the *daingneachd,* and your Una? she pouted, burying her face in his shoulder.

Holding her tight, Andrew nibbled her ear. "Not 'till I build you yon castle you are ever on about."

Una rolled on to her side. "Tell me again, Andrew," she begged, happy once more, for Una was a lass, who, when not bubbling with exuberance was sometimes given to bouts of depression, and this fantasy of the castle Andrew had made up on just such an occasion to lift her flagging spirits.

"Well, I was after thinking, if I were to command all the folk from the eldest to the youngest to bring a stone to your door each day, we could have your castle built by the time I was a hundred and four years old. This, of course does not include the turrets, see you. For by that time you will be a hundred and four years old."

Tears of laughter ran down Una's cheeks. She drew the man to her. "I love you Andrew MacLaren," she said between kisses.

"And I you," was the whispered reply.

At the same time as Andrew was conversing with the Irishman and his friend, Fergus MacAlister, accompanied by the dwarf was similarly engaged with Iain MacKinnon at the standing stone.

"The *ceann cinnidh* wishes that you bide with MacSorley. He sees you to be more service there than with us at the *daingneachd*," the big man stated flatly, for he had no liking for this man before him.

"You are after saying the MacLaren prefers the likes of yon, to me? MacKinnon's face twisted contemptuously, pointing at the dwarf, standing by the garrons.

Angrily the giant hurled back. "Do not let the *troich's* lack of size mislead you MacKinnon, one sign from me and it would liken a wolfhound with a hare, see you!"

Startled by the venomousness of the attack, MacKinnon struggled to make amends.

"Crofting is no easy thing amongst folk not my own," he whined, shuffling a foot.

"Then it is more fool you for leaving your own kin for the likes of yon MacSorley, though no doubt you had your reasons."

"Condemnation slips easily from your tongue MacAlister when you are in no such position yourself. Neither you or the MacLaren know of the risks I am after taking; not to mention the long road here to tell you what you must know. Should Quoich learn I have an ear within his household and betray his every move, my life would not be worth a bole of meal."

"You price yourself over highly, MacKinnon, I should have said much less," Fergus scoffed. Besides, man, and are you not well paid for your trouble?"

Iain MacKinnon frowned. "That I am,but the risks are that much greater since yon man lost his hand, now there is no pleasing him, and there will be none 'till the MacLaren is found."

Uneasy at this and its implications, Fergus replied evenly. "It is indeed fortunate for us that you should be in the MacSorley employ. I will tell the MacLaren of your news, of which he will thank you....I am sure. I will also advise him of your wish to join us." Then to pacify a man he did not trust, "Be careful, see you, for as you so rightly say, it is a long ways back."

Iain MacKinnon waited uneasily while the giant mounted his garron, who with the briefest of waves, followed by his companion, were gone.

Bitter at the rejection meted out to him by the big man, and not quite knowing why, the informer decided to follow the riders. At least if he was not permitted to live like a cateran, it could do no harm to find out where they themselves lived.

The flash of an idea when it came to Iain MacKinnon had him draw rein. What would Quoich not give to be in possession of such knowledge?

A life of grandeur instantly stretched before him. No more toiling for a crabbit one- handed man, or grovelling to that big obnoxious dotard who had just left. Not to mention coming face to face with the man he had never met, the elusive cateran, the *ceann cinnidh,* Himself. Convinced the MacSorley would meet his terms, elated, Iain coaxed forward his mount.

The two would be beyond the trees by now, and climbing towards the high corries. Therefore, he must keep out of sight, difficult enough in that barren land, but should he be seen, all was lost.

A good half hour later Iain halted, scratching his head in perplexity, certain both men would have passed that way, and was not immediately aware of the figure until it was almost on him, the dwarf having appeared from nowhere.

Thinking as quickly as his startled brain would allow, MacKinnon pointed to his right, simultaneously turning his mount in that direction, and indicating to the dwarf this was another way home. Iain did not look back until the *troich* had disappeared out of sight.

It was good to see the *daingneachd* again after all of this time, although at the time he had been equally glad to have left it behind.

Andrew's decision to visit Kirsty and take her three fine beasts, his right as *ceann cinnidh* had been met by a tearful tantrum by Una, and an expression of relief by Johnny and Duncan; who ever since the quarrel over his attack on the MacSorley had never been the same towards him, now and again the pair having a knack of finding a string of domestic chores to keep them well out of his way.

Regarding his place as *ceann cinnidh*, he was now not so sure. Perhaps, this was the opportunity Johnny had sought; to be rid of him and with it the MacSorley threat of vengeance.

He had not seen Kirsty and had never intended doing so, reasoning that there was sufficient animosity towards him without the fiddler adding to it. Instead, he had left the beasts grazing by her door, each with a sprig of Spurge Laurel tied to a horn, so, even if she did not know what had become of him, she would at least know it had been a MacLaren who had left them there.

He regretted not having seen Kirsty again, though in truth he found himself thinking of her less with each passing day. No, it had been a ruse to see the bonnie Isobella Grant once more, and suspecting the scene this would have created should Una have found out, he had made Kirsty and Gregor the reason for his visit. Also, knowing the close proximity of Gleidth House to that of the MacSorley, he had also refrained from mentioning it to both his friends.

Andrew jumped the burn, skirting the whin bushes, breathing in the cool refreshing mountain air, at the same time recalling his return visit to Gleidth House, where his reception had been polite, if not altogether warm.

"You must tread warily," Isobella warned, surprised by his return. "Quoich has spies everywhere, and swears to see you hang."

"Surely not here in Gleidh, Lady Isobella?" Andrew asked more humorously than he felt, now not so sure that his coming here had been wise.

The lady led him into the anti-chamber where they had first conversed in private.

"No. Though, even so there is danger." She sat down, facing him across the room. "Why did...why did you find it necessary to do what you did?" The woman's voice was disapproving, cold, unable to understand such an un- Christian act.

For the hundredth time it seemed to Andrew he must answer this same question, not least of all to himself. Did he not see that same hand in every dream? Relive the fear when chased by Quoich's men, knowing should a chance shot have brought down either man or beast, it would have meant the end, for him and the *troich*. Then later that day when safe, and out of sight of the dwarf had vomited his stomach clean with the sheer terror of what he had done.

Realising his host awaited an answer Andrew shrugged. "It was necessary." Happily she did not press him further.

For the next few days, Andrew enjoyed the lady's company, and found her an able and charming hostess, if not somewhat cool to his advances. He having to struggle to restrain himself from touching her except in the most formal of ways. Then, as if prearranged, and in order to thwart his plans, Neil Stewart, presented by Isobella as her cousin germane, arrived.

Well dressed and educated in the ways of the south, Neil Stewart, instead, became the focus of the lady's attention, leaving the cateran to feel uncomfortable as well as ignorant regarding the subjects of their after dinner conversations.

"Tush, Neil, we are embarrassing Mister MacLaren, are we not?" Isobella declared during such one conversation. "Perhaps, mister....Andrew would be telling you how he saved all here, including my unworthy self from the clutches of the MacSorley?" The lady rolled her eyes heavenward in mock terror.

"Aye, MacLaren, Isobella has hinted as much. Tell me how you came by this. How it was you who saved my bonnie cousin here?" Stewart asked, a mischievous twinkle in his eye.

Humiliated by the game they were playing at his expense, Andrew felt he had been mistaken in coming here in the first place, both having succeeded in making him feel the cateran he was...a broken landless man. The *troich* himself would have been more capable of contributing to the conversation than he had done.

However, pride alone prevented him from surrendering so easily to such blatant breach of Highland civility, answering with as much sagacity as he could muster. "It was nothing at all Mister Stewart, my single thought was that there should be meat on the table when once again I visited Gleidh." With a deft flick of his knife he held up a skewered piece of meat from the table. "Even should it only be MacSorley meat," he confirmed, looking from one to the other.

For a brief moment there was silence, both cousins staring at one another wide eyed, until the lady threw back her head, her laughter filling the little room, followed by that of the Stewart.

"Well said MacLaren!" Neil Stewart howled. "You have put us both in our place. Here let me fill your glass." Content, Andrew sat back in his chair.

Only too glad to have been rid of the Stewart and to have had the lady to himself even for a short while after her cousin's leaving, Andrew now rode with Isobella Grant up that same glen the caterans had been at so much pains to avoid those months past.

"So, you too are leaving Gleidh?" she asked, letting the garrons drink their fill by the burn.

"That I am, however reluctantly. I also have responsibilities to fulfil." He looked away from the woman to the crags on either side and to the glen stretched out before them, the trees gently swaying in the summer breeze. Somewhere in the distance the sound of women singing at their work, all of which reminded him of Kintail and his own Glen Laidon.

Still looking away from the woman, Andrew spoke softly. "I fear I have overstayed my welcome. Perhaps it was ill done to have come at all.....It was a mistake, see you."

The woman gently touched his hand. "The mistake is in your thinking this. My gratitude for what you did for me and mine will not win you my bed, Andrew MacLaren. If this is in your thinking, then you are no better than Kenneth MacSorley. Do you not know, a woman must see something more of this in a man? I think you are such a man, Andrew, and if so, come again to Gleidh, when you may find me more charitable."

Hidden by the trees on the hillside, the watcher saw the running gasping man, stagger, rise again in desperation to reach the tower.

Andrew glanced to his left hearing rather than seeing the caterans driving the bellowing protesting beasts before them. Now satisfied that all was in order and that the running man would reach the tall grey building and raise the alarm, waited.

In no time at all the tower came to life. The door flying open and men bursting out, all running in the direction the gasping man had indicated, to disappear in the evening's gloom in pursuit of the thieves.

A little later a cateran came panting to Andrew's side on the hillock where he stood overlooking the tower, to inform him those chasing after the caterans from the tower had been neatly caught in their trap. While a second band of caterans had slipped in by the open tower door at their backs, and a third was already on their way home with the stolen cattle.

Andrew snapped his fingers in triumph. All had succeeded, and again he had kept himself well out of harms way.

Below him a heavily laden figure stepped out of the tower's open doorway, searching for the garrons Duncan should already have had waiting.

Andrew cursed. "Where was the man?"

Then as if in answer, the Cameron appeared, leading a half dozen mounts around the hillside at a gallop, in the same instant that a shot rang out, and the burdened man by the tower door crumpled, chattels clattering at his feet.

Sweeping the battlements, Andrew caught the tell tale wisp of smoke from the musket shot, and ran as fast as his legs would take him down the hillside, his own safety momentarily forgotten for the figure standing just inside the doorway, staring uncomprehendingly at the dead man was that of the dwarf, the tiny man unaware that should he step out into the courtyard he too would become an easy target from above.

Almost at the foot of the brae and only a short distance from the tower a shot tugged at Andrew's sleeve as he knelt and fired at the dwarf, his shot thudding into the door lintel, inches from the tiny man's head, sending him scurrying for the inner safety of the tower.

Another shot rang out and Andrew threw himself into the cover of the whin, unable to think what to do next, though glad that Duncan had had the foresight to wheel away the garrons. All had gone as planned until now, he fumed. However, they could not very well bide here for long, as the shots would be heard in the nearest *beale-tean*, and every clansman in the district would now be scurrying here at the sound. Nor could the caterans in the tower get out until the musketeers on the battlement were dislodged. Even his own pistols, fine as they were for their time, were quite ineffective at this range.

While Andrew mulled over the situation, unknown to him, an enterprising Irishman inside the tower had taken the decision to urge on his fellow clansmen into piling every combustible they could find under the trap door leading to the battlements. The first Andrew was to know of this was when flames suddenly shot into the night sky, and the foremost caterans came running from the building carrying everything they could throw onto the hastily reappeared garrons.

Seeing this, Andrew leaped out of the whin. "'Tis enough!" he shouted. "We must be gone...there is little time to spare!"

Needing no further instruction, Duncan lashed at the beasts, and with only the briefest of acknowledgment to Andrew, was gone.

A little later out of breath, Andrew drew up on the hillside beside Johnny who had watched the scene below unfold. "We must see to our prisoners and be gone before half the countryside is at our heels," he panted.

"Aye, you are right. They will have to be as deaf as the *troich* not to have heard this commotion," Johnny fired back, clearly alarmed.

Andrew looked past him to where the giant MacAlister was still hard at work tying up prisoners from their trap. "You do not have enough rope there, Fergus, not all are bound."

"No, there are a wheen more than I expected."

"You will not let them follow us to Loch an Daimh?"

"No."

"How will you prevent this?"

"Like so!" the big man answered, cracking two heads together, but not before entering into oblivion, one remembered the name Loch an Daimh.

By midnight, plunder laden garrons, driven cattle, followed by a cateran rearguard found themselves in the prearranged gleannan.

"Is there no pursuit?" Duncan asked of Andrew.

"None as yet. We will not know 'till Dugald comes up." Andrew shivered in the raw cold of night. Shapes and shadows all around, aroused his fears of being followed.

"It was Jamie Donald, slain by yon tower, I am told, he with a wife and bairn, too." Duncan kicked angrily at the young heather.

"I should not like to consider our losses had the tower not been set alight." Andrew answered wearily. Somewhere a burn tinkled in the distance. Andrew scanned the resting men. Some talking quietly while they ate, others, already exhausted, lay asleep.

"And who have we to be thanking for setting fire to yon tower?" Andrew asked, the sound of his own voice unnaturally loud to him.

"It was the Irishman, McMahon," came the answer out of the darkness.

"And modest forby, I am after thinking. Have I the right of it, Sean, it was yourself that saved the day?" Andrew inquired, drawing closer to the resting men.

"'Twas nothing your lordship, a wee something in return for my board and lodgings, so to speak."

Amid the muffled laughter, Andrew responded. "You did well, Sean. It was quick thinking,
see you, for an Irishman that is!"

He sat down as the moon drifted out from behind a cloud, giving him a glimpse of the glen ahead, and the brief glimmer of a pool shimmering in the moonlight before all was returned to darkness. He took a bannock from the inner folds of his plaid.

"Does the ruse work, think you?"

Andrew glanced up at Johnny standing over him, his face in shadow. "If it does not, we will know soon enough, for this is as far as we dare travel, even in this August night, Johnny."

Johnny, grunting made to move away, Andrew put up his hand to stay the man.

"Will you sit by me for a time Johnny, there is a matter warrants discussion see you, and has ever been on my mind?

Andrew munched on his supper, aware of the man's uneasiness, for the MacSorley matter still lay between them. "I have been mulling over the fact, Johnny, that our numbers are over great in the *daingneachd* as you yourself well know. Already there is over much squabbling when more than one family share the same fireside, and matters worsens daily. Do you take my meaning? Noncommittally the MacKellar waited. A little annoyed, Andrew continued. "We cannot turn folks away who are as unfortunate as ourselves, nor can we afford the risk of alarming the clans whose land we bide in, by our ever increasing numbers. This much and more you taught me, Johnny. Therefore....I was after thinking," he hesitated. Was the man never going to speak, at least show some interest, support or otherwise? "I was after thinking,".he continued, "that it is time to

147

seek another stronghold, perhaps in the Cairngorms, with either you our myself as *ceann cinnidh*?"

Encouraged by the slight gasp from his friend, Andrew went on. "What say you, Johnny? It will also provide a second sanctuary in case of discovery."

"Only the very trusted should know of both," Johnny volunteered at last.

"My very thought," Andrew patronized, encouraging the other to go on.

"I can see your reasoning, Andrew, the *daingneachd* is to overflowing, and there is ever trouble where women and bairns are concerned. But how am I to choose who will accompany me?"

"So it is you who will leave? Even though it is I who am the usurper, for the stronghold has been your home longer than mine?" Andrew asked in surprise, though relieved, for he did not wish to start again. Nor did he wish to be further away from Gleaidh House.

Now warming to the subject Johnny did not appear to have noticed the question.

"I will have to seek a place, as safe as the one we have at present. It will be hard to find, man. I fear it will take time."

"Och we are not so hard pushed for that as yet man." Andrew breathed easily, now that a glimmer of friendliness had returned between them. "As for those who will follow you, I believe you only need to ask."

With a satisfied grunt, Johnny rose.

As the darkened gleannan lightened in the August dawn, Dugald shook his chief by the shoulder, awakening the man from a dream in which Kirsty and not Isobella Grant, had been the principal player.

"We are safe, Andrew. You have them chasing in the wrong direction, see you. They will all be miles away by the shore of Loch an Daimh by now!"

Andrew heard Dugald's excited voice from afar, and wondered what the youth was doing in his dream. At last comprehension sifting into his brain he struggled to his feet, mumbling. "You have done well Dugald. It is sleep you will be needing yourself, I am after thinking." He stifled a yawn. "You can follow the herd later, for driving cattle is a slow business."

Dugald stared after his departing chief who had wandered off to see all was well. "'Tis you who needs the sleep more than I. What must it be like to be old?" With this Dugald settled down to rest.

Andrew and the dwarf looked on as the caterans left the shores of Loch Laggan, to head for the Monadliath, whilst they themselves; on foot this time as all garrons were laden, turned west for Loch Oich, and the southern tip of Loch Ness.

This coming from the south was not the MacLaren's usual approach to Kintail, but he thought to be wary of the MacSorley, at the same time avoiding Glen Moriston, for the present.

It had been the dream back in the gleannan that had first given him the notion of visiting Kirsty, hoping to find her returned from the summer sheilings, and in her own croft. Should Gregor also be there, then so be it.

The weather had held for the entire journey, both men having enjoyed the hunting and unrestricted joy of travelling amongst braes coming alive with heather, cooling under a waterfall, or guddling in a strange burn. Andrew never failing to be amazed and mystified by the dwarf's uncanny instincts, though he be as deaf as the stones of Carn Dearg.

At length Andrew crested the last brae, and with a ponding heart gazed down at what had once been his own croft with the sea beyond. Inevitably, his eyes turned to the fields ripe with corn, and admitting however reluctantly that the present owner knew his business well enough...... though he himself, would have done this or that differently.

Dismissing this unexpected yearning for his old home, Andrew led the dwarf in the direction of Kirsty's croft experiencing a strange stirring at the prospect of seeing her again.

Why should this be, this arousing of old passions, and of memories best forgotten? The worst of it being, now that he was here, he could not remember what any of that damned dream was all about.

At last they were there, passing the burn where he had first learned of having lost Kirsty,then to the hollow where Gregor had lain in the snow, it all flooding back from the recesses of his mind to lie before him now. Then, lending emphasis to his thoughts, there was Kirsty herself...and was not the bundle in her arms a bairn?

He saw her stare at their coming, not at him in particular but at the dwarf, then step back quickly into the doorway, calling to someone within.

Andrew waved and quickened his pace, calling out a greeting to her as Gregor emerged from the doorway, and now that he was nearer knew that the bundle in her arms was indeed a child.

"Kirsty!" he called again excitedly, forgetting both Gregor and the dwarf. "Is it true? Am I right in thinking you are a mother?"

"Andrew MacLaren ! It is none other than yourself after all this time!" Kirsty called back in surprise. She swung to Gregor. "See who we have here! Andrew MacLaren, come to visit, and his...friend!"

Andrew drew to a halt, not knowing what reception he might receive from the fiddler.

"It is long since last you visited your friends," Gregor greeted Andrew, though failing to disguise the embarrassment in his voice.

Andrew bit back a retort that it was he Gregor himself, who had driven him away from this same door, instead, mellowing and glad that all animosity was in the past, said with a rueful smile. "I bide a far cry from here Gregor. Besides the *troich* and I are not always welcome at the doors we chap."

"Maybe so, but this is not one of them. Come away in man!" He turned to the dwarf. "You will be hungry no doubt, and if Andrew has not already said, I am Gregor MacVinish, and this is Kirsty and Col, my wife and son."

In response the dwarf vigorously pumped the outstretched hand all the while smiling and grunting his approval.

"He is a deaf mute, Gregor." Andrew explained at Gregor's puzzlement

"Oh the poor wee man. Come you both inside,"Kirsty implored.

Andrew stepped quickly into the house. "Grandmother MacKenzie, it is I Andrew MacLaren, returned to help the king and you muck out the byre!" he called out remembering his last visit, then at the empty house swung to face Kirsty.

The woman nodded, dropping her eyes to the floor. "She is gone, Andrew, these five weeks past. She was taken peacefully enough in her sleep."

Andrew opened his mouth to offer his condolences, and strangely sad at the old woman's passing, for he had loved her in his own way, when Gregor broke the silence.

"Where have you been hiding since last we met?" he asked, as Kirsty handed him their son, and hurried to set the meat.

"Aye, you have the right of it there, Gregor, for hiding is the word. In the wild Monadhliath to be precise."

"I knew it was you who left the beasts with the sign of your clan badge upon them," Kirsty cried triumphantly, above the clatter of plates. "Gregor would not hear of it, would you husband? Though I knew it to be the badge you wore since that first day we met.

"So you did not return to Glen Laidon?" Gregor interrupted, scowling at his wife.

"No. There was no more there, than there is for me here in Kintail." and was not surprised when neither begged to disagree.

Little was said during the supper, until striving to break the silence that had arisen between Andrew and her husband, Kirsty asked, "Tell me Andrew, how have you passed your days since you left? And how came you by your silent friend? Is he the one you found in the woods you mentioned yon.....?" Kirsty saw her mistake. She should not have mentioned Andrew's last visit, when Gregor had been away.

To cover her mistake, Andrew began to relate his adventures since losing his croft by the loch, carefully omitting any mention of Isobella Grant, or the MacSorley, also glad that Kirsty could not inquire about Una without further alerting her husband to his last visit.

"But what of yourselves, and of Col your son? How old is he?"

"Five months!" Kirsty proudly announced. "Whose looks do you think he is after taking? Honestly now," the woman challenged, with a sly smile.

Andrew stroked his chin in pretense of being in deep thought. "'Tis a most dangerous question to be asking a man, I am after thinking. I think I will let the *troich* answer instead."

They all laughed, staring at the tiny man, who in turn cocked his enormous head to one side and grinned, stretching out his hands to hold the infant.

Andrew bit his lip. He had forgotten how grotesque the sight of the dwarf could be, how he, as had others recoiled when seeing him for the first time.

True, he was cleaner and tidier now, but even so his presence still left folks ill at ease. So here he was holding out his hands to Kirsty, beckoning her to let him hold her first born, her only child.

Kirsty did not hesitate, though the look she threw her husband was for one of support as she set down the infant in the tiny man's lap, and drew back to await her son's expected scream of disapproval, if not outright terror. Instead of which that young man simply beamed, bubbling his pleasure up at his new friend.

"He has a way with him," Andrew chuckled, clearly relieved as all were, tickling the bouncing infant under the chin. "You should see the bit toys the wee man fashions for the bairns back in the *daingneachd*."

Amused by the dwarf's antics and their son's obvious joy, both hosts smiled politely.

"Grandam MacKenzie would have dotted on him. Of this I am sure, Kirsty."

"You are right, Andrew. Spoiled him she did." Kirsty's eyes glistened, and Andrew wished he had held his tongue.

Gregor rose stiffly. "I will away to the croft, I have a few odds and ends to attend to. You bide here and talk to Kirsty, Andrew."

Col held up a hand to his father, his tiny fingers clasping and unclasping.

Gregor shook one of the bairns fingers. "I will not be long wee man."

"He would not have you leave Gregor. You are indeed a fortunate man," Andrew conceded, his thoughts returning to his own lost child.

The dwarf held up one of Col's hands and waved it at Gregor, who had reached the door.

"Before you leave Andrew, you must take a look at the calves we have from the beasts you left awhile back," Gregor said.

"That I will, Gregor," Andrew answered, pleased that all seemed right between them again, and if Gregor was aware of his previous visit, he had endeavoured to let it pass as nothing more than that.

"Aye, you do that." Gregor gently closed the door behind him.

"That was tactfully done, Kirsty, I am after thinking," the cateran commented on the fiddler having left them alone.

"He is a changed man, Andrew, more so since Col's coming.

"And the drink?"

Kirsty beamed at Col curled up sleepily in the dwarf's lap. "Never a drop, not so much that you would notice."

"Did my leaving help?"

Kirsty leaned forward to wipe the child's chin. "In some ways, though I believe he has at last come to terms with losing his arm. With you gone, so also has gone the threat of his losing me. Or so it seemed to Gregor's way of thinking."

"I am glad lass. I said it would work in time, did I not?"

Andrew drew a gentle finger down the dozing infant's cheek, his voice low, contrite. "You were ever right in your choosing, Kirsty...had you chosen me.!" He tried to make light of it. "You would now find yourself living in some bothan in the high Monadhliath."

"Halt Andrew! Have a mercy!" Kirsty pleaded, gently taking the sleeping infant from the dwarf, and briefly smiling her appreciation at the man.

Her countenance changing she grew stern, her mouth quivering at the corners. "What have you done, telling of your living amongst wild barbarians? And to crown it all, saying you are now their *ceann cinnidh*? This I find hard to believe, unless they are using you so."

Now close to tears, Kirsty rocked her child back and forth in her arms. "Andrew, you are not a savage. A more gentle man I have yet to meet. You of all people cannot live by the sword!" Kirsty hugged her child to her for comfort, her emotions spent.

"Gently lass." Andrew reached out to touch her. "It is not all as it appears. There are good men yonder, see you. Homeless, broken men like myself, who are there through no fault of their own. Should you speak of barbarians and savages, then vent your spleen on the proud chiefs and lairds who cause this plight.

Andrew rose, surprised at his own conviction and the feeling of the necessity to vindicate these caterans...his own folk. Then it came to him, they were his own folk.

Proudly Andrew looked at the *troich*. For as Kirsty was just after saying, was he not in fact their chief? Their *ceann cinnidh*.

Chapter 11

Crossing the narrow glen the cold October wind blew straight off the shoulder of Creag Meegaidh, chilling them to the bone.

Trudging along on the flank of the reluctant herd, Andrew sighed in weary content at the success of the raid, at their sacking of the mill for much needed grain, and their' lifting' of the black cattle they now drove before them.

It had been some time ago now, yet he was worried still, unsettled in his mind since his last meeting with Kirsty. She had been right of course about his way of life, though wrong, for he was more coward than the gentle man she believed him to be. Even on this raid he had succeeded in keeping himself safe by reason of command, and was not a little surprised that others had not yet come to suspect. Or was it that they were too blind in their trust not to see? It was of no consequence. It was what he knew within himself to be the truth that mattered.

Kirsty had asked...no implored him to think again about his life at his leaving. He in turn had made light of it all by presenting her with two cruisies taken at the sacking of the burning hall. She had accepted them with good grace, yet her look had told him this was not the Andrew MacLaren, she had known. His own thoughts, were if not, then who was it that had made him so? Yet he was too ashamed to admit that the blame lay solely with himself.

Before his visit to Kirsty and Gregor his mind had constantly whirled with thoughts that with the siller and stones he had found, he could again become a crofter, either in Kintail, or back in Glen Laidon. He knew of course deep down, he could never settle again in either place, for if the truth be told, he sighed, he had become besotted with the bonnie Isobella Grant.

As to his being *ceann cinnidh* ? Even after this time he could not bring himself to believe he was one of them...a cateran, though he now looked upon them as his own folk. Had Kirsty also been right here? Were they in fact using him? Were they indeed waiting until he became unsuccessful before avenging themselves on his slaying of the MacIntosh. His eyes on the ground, the man scolded himself at his over active imagination.

When they had finally left Kirsty, Gregor and the bairn, it had been for Glen Moriston and the delectable Isobella. Once in sight of the house the dwarf had quickly left Andrew for the company of Lachlan Grant, a peculiarity which he was not slow to notice. Was it that the dwarf had an aversion to meeting the lady, for it was not that the tiny man was a misogynist? Or was it something else? Something the *troich* could see, that he, Andrew could not..or did not wish to see.

Andrew hit out at a beast who had the intention of returning home.

Again he returned to that last meeting with the lady which this time had been so different. The look on her face when sitting by the fireside in the small antechamber when he placed the ring on her finger; one of the four found in the cavern, and remembered her every word.

"Andrew, is this not worth a king's ransom?" Isobella cried with delight, her eyes gleaming in that beautiful face. Suddenly her expression changed. "No, Andrew, it is too much!" she cried, tearing the ring from her finger.

Surprised by her sincerity, yet pleased that she should value his gift so highly, Andrew asked, "Why not Isobella, you have little enough in the way of luxury yourself, seeing as you have the clan to think after."

"You think it badly done, as I am a woman?" This testily.

"No! No!" he scolded. "'Tis ever hard here in the Highlands, lass, we must take...or give while we can."

He slipped the ring once more over her small delicate finger, his hand lingering at the touch. Then she lifted her face to kiss him, and he knew nothing except at last, the sheer ecstasy of holding Isobella Grant.

At length she pushed him gently away. "I would have you in my bed, Andrew MacLaren,"she said coyly. "If I knew for certain that unlike the MacSorley, you did not mean to buy your way there."

"Then I shall take the ring back, and you may judge for yourself," he teased.

"Only if you vouchsafe the *troich* does not stand guard beneath the bed!" Isobella chuckled with a wily smile.

"Stand *beneath* the bed!" Andrew bellowed.

"Aye, stand. For have no fear, MacLaren, small as he may be...if naught else, he is to you a watchdog," she laughed, leading him by the hand. "Aye! A watchdog!"

155

Jerked back to the present by a stumble, Andrew was startled to discover how far they had travelled since his mind had wandered to more pleasant things, and he could still find himself stir when thinking of that first night with the lady.

Lying back spent, she had asked how he came by the ring, and he had fobbed her off with a hint of future baubles, and other similar treasures.

"Then why risk life and limb on the 'liftings', when you have this and more to your name?" she queried, holding the ring up in the semi darkness, and admiring its sparkle. "You will not ever be so young to clamber up and down yon wild braes. If you have other such treasures as you hint, it is a place of your own you should be after seeking."

Ever be so young! Andrew breathed; that was not what worried him. True, there were those in the *daingneachd* who may never see another summer, and it strayed into his mind that this could be he in no great a time at all, should he not wish to veer his course in life.

No, it was the others that worried, frightened him, men such as Peter MacPhail, broken by some sort of seizure, and unable to lift a hand to fend for himself. Calum MacDonald, a man who had run with the deer, now wanting a leg. Andrew remembered how he had halted at his door and how he had heard him howl in pain, and the shame in the man's eyes at having to be helped to the stones to pass the time of day with his fellows. Was this his destiny? Though he often cast his mind from it, it could just as easily be his own fate. Andrew shuddered at the vision of these hapless men, and the only too recent sight of Gregor and that empty sleeve.

Propped on an elbow, Isobella stared down into his face. She traced a finger across his bare chest. "*Dun Eideann* is a bonnie place Andrew. You could live like a lord there, sup with the gentry, and never have to worry where the next bite was coming from. Aye, and safe too, Andrew, safe."

Thrusting the last dark thought from his mind, Andrew opened his eyes at the change in Isobella's voice.

"What would I be wanting in a place like yon, lassie? It is a great towering place, I am led to believe, smelling and dirty, with folks living on top of one another."

He felt her recoil. "It need not be *Dun Eideann* then my love, it could be a fairer place, see you, as long as we are together."

Andrew was scarcely able to believe his good fortune, that in so short a time the lady was willing to sacrifice all, in order to be with him. He drew her close. "You must tell me then, how many more of these baubles it will take."

They were crossing the glen now at its narrowest point, heading for the gentler slopes beyond, with the herd stretched out before them, Duncan cantering passed, leading a string of burdened garrons, when they came at them, as if out of the very ground itself. A long line of mounted men: no Highland, garrons these, but heavy cavalry mounts, carrying breastplated helmeted Lowland soldiers. Two score or more, charging in one long terrible line, sabres glinting in the afternoon sun, bearing down on the unsuspecting caterans.

No shout of warning necessary, the caterans fled for the side of the glen, Andrew amongst them, terrified cattle scattering cateran and trooper alike.

His lungs bursting, Andrew maneuvered to keep the panic stricken cattle between him and his attackers. Already a horseman had overtaken a running man and with one powerful stroke had severed the head from his body, then wheel away to attack another.

As a man on a treadmill Andrew ran on, running, gasping, yet never nearing the shelter of the hillside, afraid to look back, ever expecting the sabre thrust that would end it all. Suddenly from his right, a trooper cut off his retreat, bearing down on him with frightening speed. No where to go, Andrew halted and drew his pistols, unsure where to aim at this armour clad foe, who, with a yell of triumph standing upright in his stirrups to deal the fatal blow charged on. Steadying his hand, Andrew fired, and was already on his way to the glen side before the stallion had hit the ground.

At last reaching the side of the glen Andrew scrambled up the slope, while to his right, the giant MacAlister fought off two horsemen. Somewhere further back shrieks of dying caterans filled the air.

Throwing himself down, Andrew watched the scene of decimation below. Caterans running to reach the safety of the glen side, as drowning mariners to the shore.

Suddenly Johnny MacKellar, appeared out of the mingling cattle, unaware of the trooper at his back, those on the hillside shouting and waving their warning to no effect.

Andrew cursed. It was too far across the open ground for Johnny to reach the glen side, for already a trooper was almost upon him. Gasping, wide eyed, Johnny stared up at the rocks and the shouting waving caterans, and in a moment of understanding whirled around to throw himself to the ground as the trooper hurled passed. Then he was up again and running for the safety of the rocks, only to find himself cut off by that same trooper having wheeled his mount around, and come charging back at him.

Sword drawn, Johnny stood his ground awaiting that fearful onslaught when the shot rang out, and the trooper reeled from his saddle, the voice of Andrew MacLaren, smoking pistol in hand shouting to him to hurry away.

Once again amongst the rocks, the MacKellar by his side Andrew looked down upon that carnage on the glen floor, where wounded and captured alike were being done to death. Except for one unfortunate man, who lay spread-eagled on the ground a rope tied to each limb while four horsemen coaxed on their mounts, jerking the ropes ever tighter.

Andrew clapped his hands to his ears to drown out the high tortuous scream of the dying man. Certain even at that distance of hearing the tearing of flesh and bone, until mercifully the screaming stilled.

Now all was quiet in that place of death, the troopers advancing in military line, to halt and stare up at the survivors amongst the rocks high upon the heather slopes. Waiting, until out of their ranks a mounted tartan clad figure emerged, who with a flourish doffed his feathered bonnet in mock salute to the silent clansmen above.

"MacSorley!" Andrew seethed. "Kenneth MacSorley!"

Heads bowed, the caterans silently turned to climb to the crags above.

They converged on the summit, each man alone within himself. Stunned men, heads bent in silent horror of what was left behind.

The big MacAlister though wounded himself, helped another along.

"Who was the man?" Andrew asked the giant, and was shocked at the sound of his own voice, for of all the carnage all knew to whom he referred.

"MacVie," came the simple answer as he passed by.

Johnny MacKellar panted up to the ridge top, Andrew asking of him. "Did Duncan win through, Johnny, think you?"

Johnny collapsed on the ground. "I was over busy myself to notice, except to see him ride hell bent up the glen," he answered testily.

Andrew studied the ground at his feet. "The blame is mine Johnny. You were right in your thinking, I should not have vented my spleen upon the MacSorley...I see that now, God help me, now it is too late."

"It is a burden you must bear, MacLaren, more so as *ceann cinnidh,.*" Johnny seethed, with no thought of thanking Andrew for his life, not when this same man had been the reason for it all, the cause of the death of so many. "Though none could have foreseen this day's brutality...Lowland mercenaries they must be, for no Highland man is unworthy of such inhuman deeds. Quoich must want us badly, or more so you, to have engaged such barbarians."

Andrew drew a sad look over the straggling column. Ten out of thirty two he counted who had followed at his back, with not one lost in the lifting. "God's mercy on me," he whispered, "that my folly has cost us this."

And what if the MacSorley had caught him? Andrew shuddered at the vision of the tortured MacVie, and the bile rose in his throat. His own death would be as nothing to that of that poor man.

Andrew walked along the line of silent resting men, where those unscathed helped the less fortunate.

"He is too far gone to be moved," he heard one whisper.

"Merciful Lord he does not know it," another replied.

Andrew kneeled down beside the dying man and his two companions. "Who might this be? He has newly come to bide in the stronghold."

"'Tis young MacPherson, *ceann cinnidh* , and he just three months wed." One man answered, looking up at his chief despairingly.

"And he cannot be moved?" Andrew's eyes travelled over the unconscious figure, scorning himself at the futility of the question. "I will bide with him awhile. You both best be on your way after you have rested." He rose to avoid their looks of appreciation, for he alone knew that his intentions were anything but kind.

Later from a ridge two miles away from the ill fated glen, Andrew watched the remnants of his band cross this wider glen floor, first

159

having arranged to fire his pistols in warning should any of the enemy horsemen come in sight.

Midway across, at the point of no return, the caterans, amid furtive glances to left and right, quickened their step, half carrying half pulling their wounded companions with them. The watching man sharing their apprehension as they broke into a desperate run, dragging their wounded with them, scrambling for the cover of the further slopes, until they had disappeared amongst whin and fern.

Now that his companions were safe, now totally spent, Andrew returned to sit by the dying man, his thoughts on a day that had lasted for ever. Was it only yesterday that they had set out on the 'lifting'? Or was he mistaken, had that been in another lifetime?

Andrew heard the dying man moan, and settled him more comfortably against a rock.

Blood ran down his hand and he pulled away the wounded man's shirt, wincing at the sight of the belly wound and the young man's life blood spilling out.

He stood up. There was nothing he could do. Oblivious to the cold as was the dying man, Andrew returned to his vantage point to cast an eye up and down the empty glen. At least those who had survived would now be safely home, or nearly so, and by tomorrow it should also be safe for him to follow, which had been his sole pretence for biding by the dying man.

Through an eerie darkness on that desolate ridge, Andrew heard the whisper, and bent down to cradle the dying man in his arms. "You will ask her to forgive me. It is not that I would not bide the longer..." The words no longer coherent drifted away, borne on the bitter mountain wind. The body relaxed and Andrew knew the end had come.

Gently laying down the lifeless figure on the barren rocks, Andrew edged around the rock which had helped shelter them both, that by doing so he could distance himself from his guilt.

Now more than ever he wished to be away with Isobella Grant. Away from the harshness of the land and men like Kenneth MacSorley and his like. Or who was to say that his returning to the stronghold would not result in his own death. Surely there could be no better opportunity afforded to Johnny MacKellar than this to have him deposed as *ceann cinnidh*.

160

Curling up against the cold, Andrew wished he himself had died this day.

Andrew heard the wail of the lament long before he had reached the defile. The sad eerie notes of the pipes echoed through the black empty mountains, crying their anguish, telling of his failure.

As a man to the scaffold, Andrew trudged on, mustering his strength to face the final tribulation. Then he was home.

Except for the lone piper and sentinel above, the place stood deserted, peat smoke from silent bothans the only sign of life. Andrew quickly made for his own bothan, believing his return to be undetected until the dwarf stood in his way, the entire gigantic face creased in welcome.

Andrew nodded a tired greeting, bewildered yet again by the tiny man's knowing of his return, but also regretting at not having taken him with him, for he above all people may have been capable of warning them of the troopers coming.

Though mid day, Andrew found Una dozing by the fire, and touched her on the shoulder, jerking her awake.

Una slowly opened her eyes and seeing him threw herself into his arms. "Oh what terrible thing is this Andrew!" she wailed, sqeezing him tight. "And you ever the brave man waiting by the side of Ian MacPherson, and all alone on the mountain, see you! Is he....?" she shuddered at Andrew's nod.

"Aye. I must tell his young wife this is so, and give her what little things her man possessed." He threw himself down on a stool, the despair welling up inside him, staring unseeing into the fire, unable to bring himself to tell Una the truth, that he above all men was the least brave.

At last he asked in a whisper, "What of here , Una, the place is deserted? Where are all those who have returned?"

Una drew herself closer to the man. "Johnny, Fergus, Duncan and Dugald have gone back to where...to where it happened. They mean to take the long way round to seek out the wounded, should any have survived. They left before it was scarcely light."

The distraught man pushed her gently away, gazing into a face that was no longer a child but of a woman grown, recalling the Cameron's words the day he had left for Kintail. She **was** bonnie.

The shining black hair, the sparkling eyes wet with tears, awaiting him to speak.

He stood up, angry that she should seek his assurance that all would be well. "You call me brave, and they returning to yon place!" He took a step further away, lest he contaminate this innocent lass with his guilt. Almost afraid to ask, "And the others,....the women folk? How do they see all of this? Or more so me?"

Una's face clouded. "I do not take your meaning Andrew? Why should they choose to think ill of you? Is it your thinking that as *ceann cinnidh* they would hold you responsible for what has happened?"

"No, not as chief, but as a man who wrongly sought vengeance on the MacSorley." Andrew expounded emotionally, striding back to grip her tightly by boths arms and pin them by her side. "It was Kenneth MacSorley, behind the deed, Una!" he raged. Angry at himself and not this young lass who stood so helpless before him. Begging, wishing she would show some revulsion for what he had done.

Instead, Una said gently, "You did what you thought right at the time Andrew, so that no one should seek to use the likes of us again. You stood up to the MacSorley and his kind, and in so doing defied the gentry, the lairds and tacksmen. Aye, and the very chiefs themselves! Those who would force us to live as we do. If anyone is to blame for yon black day, it is not you, Andrew MacLaren! None here points the finger at you, least of all the women. Of this I am sure."

It had been a long speech for Una, and one filled with a sincerity which Andrew could only respond to by hugging her tight, her words as balm to his jangled nerves.

Later, when she released herself from his embrace where they had lain, Andrew was asleep. He was dreaming once again of being on the ridge, piling stones on the dead MacPherson. Returning to hand the dead man's possessions to a young bride, who, shaking with anger, threw herself upon him, scratching and biting, covering him with her blood. Then when the shaking had finally ceased, it was to look up into the anxious face of Duncan Cameron.

"It is a dream you are after having laddie and one best forgotten I am after thinking," Duncan said in a voice full of concern.

Andrew shook his head as much to clear it from his dream as to bring himself awake, peering around the now darkened room and wondering how long he had slept.

"You are back Duncan, I see. And the others, they are safely back?" He shivered though the place was not cold.

"That we are." This from Johnny coming into the light. "We must talk, asses the situation, since you are the last returned."

"*Dia*! You found no more?" Andrew croaked, his mouth dry.

"No. Mores the pity."

"How many do we number?"

"As many as you see here."

Andrew peered around him at the ghost like faces in the peat fire flame staring quietly at him, and he mentally counted, Duncan, Johnny, Dugald and the big MacAlister, hunched in the corner, and Col Fraser, the elder. Horrified he exclaimed, "This is not all... surely...to have survived?"

The MacKellar spread his hands, taking it upon himself to answer. "No . There is the *troich*, Mc Mahon, and the Lowlander, who are at present relieving two of the four sentinels left behind during the lifting, two more having succumbed since we left yesterday. We can count on thirteen only unscathed, whilst four lie sorely wounded."

Andrew stood up, and leaning against the small window stared out disconsolately at the empty amphitheater. "The blame is mine. The deaths lie at my door," he declared, his voice choked with emotion.

"Self recrimination will not help at this juncture, not with so many bellies to fill, and the winter almost upon us!" Johnny retorted harshly.

"You did not save the meal, Duncan?" Andrew spun round to confront the man, ignoring the MacKellar.

"It was all a man could do to save himself!"

" Both the meal and the garrons?"

Duncan nodded curtly.

"Then we must seek out the chieftains who benefit so generously from our raids. Advise them of our plight. It will be to their advantage when we come into our own again."

Johnny MacKellar's unexpected laughter filled the darkened room. "Poor innocent MacLaren, great chieftain of the caterans." His lip twitched in mockery. "*Dia!* Do you not see, we are of little use to them now! More a nuisance I am after thinking. To be sure they

163

gained from our liftings, and benefited from the raiders callop when we passed through their lands, and for this they protected us from our pursuers. Of course..." Johnny's lip curled in sarcastic contempt, "they also turned a blind eye to our occasional taking of a deer from the hill, or salmon from the river. Now they owe us nothing. As for coming into our own again," Johnny stared directly at the man whom he had helped become leader. " we are indeed caterans, broken men, with over three score, old and young mouths to feed, and us with not enough to see the month out."

An angry murmur of agreement followed this outburst, and although inwardly seething at this humiliation, Andrew was determined not to give the MacKellar a second chance. Fighting to remain calm answered, "The chieftains have their price. "We have a barn full of chattels, barter these for grain and meal." Then a little more sternly to the man who had deliberately debased him in front of the others. "You Johnny can select who will accompany you. I suggest you first pay a visit to your friend Neil MacPherson."

Open mouthed, Johnny watched Andrew stride to the open hearth, then turn to face the gathering; ordering, in a voice seething with anger. "The women folk!.....all who are able,... to the gathering of the peat,...old men and bairns to the river and the burns. The rest of us to the hill for the deer! Let this be known to all that we start at first light."

No sooner had the door closed on the last of the departing caterans, Andrew lowered himself on to a stool. Had he gone too far in his demands? It would not do to alienate these men, who were all that stood between them and starvation. Still, Johnny should not have humiliated him so. Now that it seemed the man had no wish to challenge his leadership, he must show who was in command here. And Andrew swore, never again to admit to self pity in front of such men as Johnny MacKellar, for was he not their *ceann cinnidh?* At least until they had it otherwise.

"This is all the selfish chieftains would give!" Andrew exclaimed, his eyes on the young lads herding the beasts to the byre.

"Do you think me a soft headed Campbell?" Johnny retorted angrily. "Did I not say it would be so. Those high lords see no reason to help a spent force. We are more liability than asset to them now. No..." he continued. "I offered little, knowing I should get as much in return.

164

This trade was not what Andrew had expected from those whom he had help better themselves.

"Did you get meal forbye?" was his next question.

"A bole or two, nothing more." Johnny swung away from the cattle to walk beside the crofter turned cateran chieftain, grudgingly admiring the man's organisation. A man no longer willing to accept blame for what had past, who had found it in himself to offer condolence to widow and mother alike, but never to apologise: a man who always looked to the future for their survival, and so had left the past in the past.

His eyes lingering on a passing, lass, Johnny asked, "What now? We cannot mount another lifting at this time of year, for cattle will be in the byre by now. To have them out would be nothing short of a *creach*. Lifting is one thing, but to raid, perhaps murder honest folk, another."

"Did I voice any such thought?" Andrew spat. "When you have supped, bring the men to the stones, for I would speak with them awhile." Andrew grasped Johnny by the arm. "You think me naive, Johnny? In some matters you are right, but this I do know, yon Lowland churls did not happen on us by chance, we were betrayed, see you, and by one of our own." At the look of astonishment on his friend's face, Andrew drove home his point. "Think you well on it, Johnny, as I myself have done. How many knew of our plans and of our crossing yon glen that day?"

Johnny's shoulders rose and fell in a gesture of disbelieve. "No one here would do such a vile and wicked thing...and for what reason, Quoich's siller? I think not. Even so, who would wish to risk their own life as well as that of their kin?"

"So the traitor lies without the *daingneachd* ? One we trust, one in our employ,one knowing Quoich's business to boot. Do you know of such a man?"

Johnny demurred. "No, I cannot single out any one in particular for there are many in just such a position, but I will make it my business to find out."

"Then do so my friend, though quietly, see you. Discreetly if you please."

Chapter 12

Andrew looked up at the mounted men, then at the row of silent watching women. Here and there an old man or woman stood by their door, these too, silently awaited the horsemen's departure. The only sound to break that awkward silence, the cry of a bairn or champing of the garrons at the bit, these anxious as their masters to be away...away from this silent mournful place.

"You will be gone three weeks, a month at most then?" Andrew confirmed, addressing the Irishman.

"Aye sur, that we will. A month at worst, three weeks at best. It all depends whether it is Edinburgh or Stirling that we must travel. Never fear your lordship, we will be back with all you ask for, and more."

Andrew thrust a finger at the horsemen. "McMahon, every life here depends on you." He encompassed the troop with a withering stare. "And you Hamilton, Fraser and Dugald there, make no mistake, for should you fail in what you seek, or worse still, return too late to win through the passes before the snow, then we shall all must surely starve."

"Rest assured, sur, you will see us all back with time and meal to spare," the Irishman reiterated, turning his mount and throwing a cheerful farewell to the crowd, followed at his back by the rest of the horsemen chosen for the venture.

"Was it the right decision think you Andrew?" Una asked, after the horsemen had gone. "It is a great gamble you are after taking."

"McMahon seems to know what he is about, and has knowledge of *Dun Eideann*, and where to sell our gear without the wrong questions being asked."

He would dearly have wished to have given McMahon the siller he had found in the cavern, but knew he could not do so without raising the question of how he came by it.

"But should none of them return...in time that is?" Una was saying.

"It does not bear thinking about lass. Och! Cheer up, see you, Col Fraser is no dotard, and McMahon has a fondness for young Dugald, and will see no harm befalls the lad."

"You should have sent, Fergus," Una said firmly with a nod of her head.

"I could not spare him, Una. Besides, the big man does not have the English, and would himself have stood out as do yon castles in either town." Andrew drew the shivering lass close. "Come lass, the winter's chill is already in the air."

"Were it but the cold, I should be well content, Andrew my love. Were it but the cold." And again Una shivered turning for home.

Two days later MacKellar and the dwarf returned to the stronghold, the smaller man's agitation clear upon entering the compound.

"What is amiss with the *troich*, Johnny?" Andrew asked inquisitively at the dwarf running passed him as fast as his tiny legs could carry him, his great claymore clanking at his back. "See! He is at McMahon's door! Now he goes in!"

"Now he comes out!" Johnny guffawed. "Sometimes he is not quite right in that great head of his, I am after thinking."

Disturbed by his friend's obvious agitation, Andrew started towards him, he in turn throwing his head back renting the air with an ear piercing inhuman scream that brought forth young and old to their doorsteps.

Impatiently, Andrew gestured to the dwarf to cease, who wild eyed swung to point vigorously at the Irishman's bothan.

"He senses something," Una gasped, hurrying to calm the man.

"Then ask MacMahon!" Johnny snapped, annoyed by folk coming to stand and stare.

"He is not here!" Andrew retorted, and went on to explain the Irishman's absence.

"There is many a mile to tramp, and not much of it to my liking before they again have Ness at their backs," the MacKellar said in answer to Andrew's explanation, while watching Una's attempts to calm the dwarf. "One sniff of what our men carry, and half the countryside will be at their heels...besides...."

"This is why I reasoned, four was best to go," Andrew broke in impatiently. "such numbers need not arouse too much attention. It is their return journey that worries me more, when, should fortune favour, there will be a string of laden garrons at their backs. But since I know not when, I could not name a trysting place."

At last calm, the dwarf freed himself from Una, and came to stand before his chief. Pointing once more at the Irishman's bothan, he jerked round to stare at Andrew, then drawing a finger across his

167

throat swung swiftly on his heel, leaving bemused onlookers muttering amongst themselves, to slowly disperse.

Andrew called out to one of the elders, shuffling to his home. "Ewen Finlay, a word in your ear if you please. Will you bide awhile? But first I must speak with my friend the MacKellar here." And at the old man's nod turned again to Johnny. "Your journey, was it rewarding?"

"The *troich* and myself waited at the standing stone as you advised. There were upwards of a dozen who knew of our intentions yon day, men who had gleaned information on our behalf for that very raid. Four who rent land from Quoich himself."

"Do you think it likely 'tis one of the latter?"

Johnny looked across the floor of the stronghold. "It does not necessary follow. We have used and trusted these same men in the past without complaint."

Johnny halted, his eyes twinkling, but not from the lass who smiled at him in passing. "We then followed your suggestion of paying our respects to the Lady Isobella; who by the way sends you her kind regards, and fondest memories," Johnny chuckled. "Who also charges me to inform you she is disappointed you did not deem to come yourself."

"Aye! Aye!" Andrew replied impatiently. "On with it man. What news did you learn from the lady?"

Savouring Andrew's embarrassment, Johnny answered slowly. "Firstly, tell me man, what is amiss with the *troich*, that prevents him from entering the front door of yon house? At the very sight of the place he was away to find his big friend Lachlan."

"I do not understand it myself," Andrew reflected, kicking out at a stone. Then urgently. "First things first, man, what did you learn at Gleidh House?"

"That Isobella Grant is a bonnie woman, as I thought when first I saw her the night of the raid, though over fond of her cousin to my way of thinking!" Johnny laughed heartily.

"Her cousin, Neil Stewart, was there?" Andrew asked, and wishing he had not heard aright.

"Aye, it was he rather than the lady who offered the information that Quoich has disbanded his Lowland mercenaries as he sees his task at an end...at present, but not complete. He means to seek you out at a later date my friend. Stewart says MacSorley thinks you finished and only a matter of time before he finds you. He has set a price on your head believing one of your own will betray you in the end."

Silent as he was, inwardly Andrew's heart had skipped a beat. Would the betrayer be this man standing next to him? It would make sense. In one deft blow he could gain an amnesty from Quoich and also gain leadership of the caterans. Now that they were so few at least in fighting terms there was no need for a second *daingneachd.* .Then again, perhaps he judged the man too harshly. Or was now the time for him to be away with the rings and siller from the cavern? Away out of the Highlands before Quoich knew he was gone, to be beside a certain lady for the rest of his life.

Aware that Johnny waited, Andrew said grim faced, "Then the traitor is not here amongst us, and does not know the whereabouts of our *daingneachd,* or Quoich would already be chapping at our door. You have done well Johnny. You had better away and rest."

"The lady sent you these." Johnny pointed to where two tethered garrons stood where he had left them across the arena. "She apologises that she could not send better, or reciprocate by doing what you did for her and hers when they themselves were in need, but hopes the meal and flour will help."

Andrew placed a hand on Johnny's shoulder. "Everything will help, my friend, everything," he sighed wearily. "However, I must speak with old Finlay whose bones I hear rattling with cold, even at this distance." So saying he left Johnny to meet the old man.

Together the old man and young chieftain walked the length of the stronghold to its furthest corner where most of the elderly lived in bothans not set into the cliffside, but instead stood separate and independent to one another. Here in this cul-de-sac they halted.

Andrew lifted his face to the cliffs above, to the narrow waterfall which never gushed, but dripped rather, never quite dying in summer, though halting each winter to hang long pointed icy fingers at the rocks below.

"It is a rugged part of the *daingneachd* , Ewen, and a body cannot always see what is going on by the entrance, hidden as it is by this bend. Why did you elders settle for this place?"

"It is near the waterfall, see you *ceann cinnidh,* and saves our old legs when fetching water. Besides, man, we are long past the hustle and bustle that never seems to cease up yonder." The old man jerked a nod. "We are content here in our *clu-nead*."

"Aye, it is a sheltered nest," Andrew returned politely. "Now you must forgive me for not summoning...eh! inviting you to the meeting at our fireside the other night, but..."

"You need say no more. There is no reason why you should explain your decisions to the likes of me. After all, you are leader here, are you not?" the old man admonished. "So you will have a word with old Ewen you are after thinking to yourself. Now that winter is upon us and not enough meal in the barns, you fear the old folks will fare the worse. In this you are wrong, young MacLaren. Folks ancient as we, do not need any great sustenance to fill our bellies. Look you instead to the sick and the young, it is they who will be needing your help. Of this I am sure."

At a loss to understand how the old man had fathomed why he had wanted this word, Andrew stammered, "You are a wise old man Ewen Finlay, it is your counsel I should be seeking by the peat fire flame."

Ewen spat, burying the spittle with his foot. "It is not that I am wise, see you,it is, just by the time you have reached my age you have spent all the draftness the good Lord has given you, so that there is nothing left except what the young mistakenly see as wisdom."

Appreciating the humour, Andrew put a kind arm around the old man's shoulder. "There is something more I would ask of you, Ewen..."

Looking the younger man in the eye, the old man smiled. "Aye. I thought that was not all you would be seeking from a wise old man!"

The first of the snows fell two weeks after McMahon and his party had left for the Lowlands. Andrew bade Una a fond, if hopefully a short farewell and trudged ankle deep towards the defile, crossing paths with Duncan Cameron. Both men halted, while old Ewen wound a slow and cautious way down from the rocks above, followed by three equally old and slow cronies.

"I give you good day Ewen Finlay!" Duncan called out cheerfully. "Is it birds nests you have been after up there?"

"You should be knowing not to ask such a daft question at your age Duncan Cameron!" the old man replied indignantly.

"Never mind him, Ewen. You have all done well." Andrew struggled to keep a straight face. "Though I fear your services may no longer be required should this snow keep up, as it seems sure to do."

"You may be right," Ewen answered, reaching the floor and ignoring Duncan. "And I for one will not be sad to see the end of this. These old bones are not what they used to be. I have seen the day when this weather would not have bothered me at all." He shrugged, leaving the rest unsaid. "I best away to my fireside then."

Silently both men watched the older ones plod away to their homes, with Andrew wondering if this would be he in the years to come, praying that there must be a better way to live and end his days.

"You have a way with you Andrew and no mistake. I never thought to see old Ewen, no more so his friends stand sentinel up in yon rocks above, and in such foul weather as this," Duncan wagged his head at the disappearing sexagenarians, adding with a bellow. "Although I am after thinking, they spend more time climbing up and down than they do at their posts!"

Andrew grinned. "Still it is necessary, we cannot be guarding here and out hunting to boot. I fear if Quoich learns of this place he will seek us out whilst he can. Therefore, I asked old Ewen to organise the sentinels so the remainder of us can hunt and rest."

"So in some ways we must bless the snow, and in other ways curse it," Duncan reflected.

"Only if McMahon and his party do not return in time."

"Then let us hope they do."

"We caught only three hares and a bird amongst us Una," Andrew winced throwing himself down on the stool, snow cascading from his plaid.

"Never mind, Andrew, there is always tomorrow." Una handed him a bowl of gruel, and took his bonnet from him."

"Not if this snow does not let up. We shall be snowbound by the week's end, and never a sight of the men returning from the Lowlands." Andrew shook his head sadly, stretching out his hands to the fire.

"They are only three weeks gone Andrew, they could be here any day now."

171

"Who is that at the door?" Andrew asked, annoyed that his short rest had been disturbed.

"Sim MacColl!" Una answered, stepping aside on the doorstep to let her guest enter.

"'Tis yourself, Sim" Andrew greeted his unexpected visitor civilly. "Will you take a cup of ale with me? I myself am just newly returned from the hunt, and was after telling Una here, three hares and a bird were all we caught amongst five of us."

Sensing the man's uneasiness, Andrew set down his bowl, not having failed to notice Sim's refusal of Una's proffered drink.

MacColl was not a man he knew well, and what he did know, did not much like, rumour having it that his wife's own unpleasant demeanour added to her husband's continual beligerent mien. Therefore, his greeting was more out of civility than any general feeling of warmth, for he would much prefer to relax in Una's cheerful company than play host to the likes of Sim MacColl.

"Is there something amiss, Sim, that prevents you from sharing a cup with your

ceann cinnidh ?"

Unprepared for the directness of the question, Sim rubbed his chin. "It is Mairi, my wife, see you," he stammered, stealing a quick glance in Una's direction. "She is after telling me, your Una was at her door inquiring about the food we have stored for the winter days." Encouraged by neither hosts having challenged his accusation Sim went on. "What we have saved, we have done without, and ours to do as we will, not to be given to those with eyes bigger than their bellies."

Andrew held up his hand. "There is no fear of you losing what is yours Sim. Una called at my instructions, as she did at every door, in order to know who has plenty, and who has not,so that no one feasts whilst another starves . Only then can we share fairly amongst us all."

Andrew toyed with the spoon in his bowl. "It was my intention to ask Mairi, if she would take the task of planning out our stores should Sean McMahon and his party find themselves unable to win through before the snows block the passes, then we shall need your wife's thrift to ration fairly 'till the Spring at least. What say you Sim? Will Mairi have a mind to help?"

172

Sim swallowed hard. This was unfair. It had been Mairi's idea in the first place to confront the MacLaren over the matter. He himself seizing it only as an opportunity to retaliate for the way the man had ignored him in favour of others. Even that grotesque *troich* was more thought of than he.

Sim focused his anger on the cold gray rock of the bothan wall. Had he not stood guard more often than most? Why then was he never privy to the MacLaren's thoughts as were other men? And now that the opportunity had presented itself to vent his anger on the man, he had confounded him with this suggestion. A suggestion he dare not refuse, or Mairi would give him no peace at all.

Aware of two pair of eyes on him, Sim MacColl shrugged his agreement. "I will tell Mairi your mind. I think it likely she will see her way in doing what you ask. Forbye, is it not right that we should help one another in a time like this?"

"Then it is done? Mairi can give her answer on the morrow." Andrew pretended to be pleased. "Come Sim, talking is thirsty work, now it is time for that cup of ale."

Later when lying together in their heather bed and gazing sleepily eyed at the fire casting great flickering shadows on the wall, Una broke the silence. "You promised me yon task you have given to Mairi MacColl, should she choose to take it, Andrew. Yon is a bitter spiteful woman, who is altogether tighter than a fish's arse."

Andrew turned her face to him. "It is a bonnie turn of phrase you have there lass,"he chuckled. "I gave her the task because of what you know of her. We shall be sorely tried these coming weeks in the Irishman's absence, so it will be someone hard as Mairi MacColl, we shall be needing. Besides, I fear yon bonnie couple could be the trouble makers that every company can do well without. Hopefully in this way, in charge of the victuals, she herself must bide impartial."

"You are a cunning man, Andrew MacLaren," Una admitted admiringly, cuddling up to the man. "I must be wary of your wiles," she added in mock seriousness.

"*Me* cunning? You would say that of me woman? Me who found you firstly in *my* bed!" Andrew tut tutted.

"Do you object MacLaren? Perhaps you would find it more to your likening in someone else's bed?" Una countered coyly.

"Ah woman! That is indeed a cunning question." And with this both embraced laughing.

Cautiously riding his garron haunch deep towards the trees below with only the occasional black rock breaking the vast whiteness between him and the horizon, the rider's thoughts were on how grand it was to be away from the mountain fastness and to contemplate the future without interruption or suggestion. Now for the hundredth time he scanned the endless vista in the hope that by some miracle four black dots would magically appear to herald the party's safe return from the Lowlands. Andrew found nothing and turned his gaze over Ness, seeing in his mind's eye Gleidh House and Isobella Grant.

The MacKellar had been right, he should have seized the opportunity to visit the lady before the winter set in. Now it would be spring at the earliest before he warmed her bed and saw that bonnie face again.

Happy though he may be with Una, it was the companionship of this beautiful woman which he craved, considering her both a means of self gratification and escape; an escape away from this way of life and its never ending struggle for survival.

At first, life had been easier than the daily routine of the croft, but had not the lady herself so rightly said, how long could he go on, another five, ten years? And if so to what purpose? To have him end his days another Ewen Finlay, and his like?

Andrew guided his mount around a rock. Should he somehow manage to better himself, gather enough siller together and lord it with the delectable Isobella Grant, in some Lowland town, would he be content? Would he in fact fit in with the society Isobella was sure to desire? Again he remembered his humiliation at being unable to participate at the level of conversations the lady and her good cousin had enjoyed back at Gleidh House.

Then again, what of Una? It was true the lass filled a need, and he loved her in his own way, albeit she was nothing more, nothing other than a lass of the mountains. Therefore, if the truth be known, he lusted after the lady of Gleidh, and loved wee hapless Una, but he could not hold them both. It was one woman he needed with two women's qualities, and she, he feared was already wed in Kintail.

Andrew had reached the woods when the deer bolted out, almost colliding with his mount. Drawing his pistol he had no more to do than lean out of his saddle and shoot the panicking animal behind the ear. It was to be the caterans' last kill of the winter.

"More snow has fallen since last night." Una shivered, starting to rise from the heather bed. "It will be another cold day I am after thinking."

Andrew's eyes wandered over the white expanse of the lassie's back. "Then bide here where it is warm and safe," he coaxed, pulling her back down beside him and, engulfing her in his arms.

"Warm...maybe. But safe?" Una exclaimed in mock alarm.

Andrew rolled her on to her back straddling her when the door crashed open.

"Have you not the civility to knock at another man's door!" Andrew shouted at the roof, incensed by the rude interruption, before realising it was the agitated figure of the dwarf who stood there.

Oblivious to Andrew's embarrassment, the dwarf ran forward and pulled Andrew by the arm, pointing to the door.

"He is like a dog at times, running back and forth, bidding you to follow him," Andrew snarled, still angry at his lovemaking being so rudely interrupted.

"Quickly Andrew, dress yourself, the man is fair disturbed. There must be something far awry!" Una cried, gaining her composure and drawing the plaids more tightly around her.

"Aye, within that great lump of a head of his!"

Although still angry, Andrew condescended to wrap himself in his *feileadh mor*, and follow the man to the door where a garron already stood saddled and waiting, the dwarf running to hold the reins and gesture impatiently for him to hurry.

With a final curse Andrew swung himself into the saddle, and pulling the dwarf up behind him guided his mount through the defile and into the white expanse beyond, all the while the dwarf urging him on from behind.

After some distance down the mountainside, amid much grunting from behind, and a black hairy hand pointing in a specific direction, Andrew steered his mount haunch deep to the same woods as the day before.

"Do not be telling me, *troich* you smell a deer? It is too much to ask that there should be another today." Well aware that the tiny man's agitation was caused by far more than this, however welcome the catching of another deer might be.

It took Andrew longer than the previous day to ride the garron around snow drift and ice covered rock. Suddenly, and without warning, his guide was off their mount and kneeling by a rock, head cocked to one side, listening, clenching and unclenching his fists, then with a final thrust of a finger at the woods clambered back up beside his chief.

Warily Andrew scanned the eerie deserted treeline, his breath crystallizing in the bitter cold air, where here and there the slight breeze shook loose snow from off a branch.

Andrew gripped his reins tighter, surely it could not be Quoich, or his kind, not up here in this weather? Whatever it was that had attracted the dwarf he meant to go no closer.

However, his companion had no such qualms, for once again he was down, his diminutive figure almost completely lost in the deeper snow as he battled towards the first row of trees.

"It cannot be Quoich, for the *troich* is not fool enough to attack single handed?" were Andrew's thoughts. "See! He has not drawn his claymore! Then it is something other."

Curiosity having replaced fear, Andrew dismounted, and plunged into the snow after his companion. Ahead of him the *troich* plodded on, so that at times it appeared to Andrew that a giant head only, rolled over the snow. Now and again the man would let out that unnatural howl the cateran had come to know and hate, until reaching a rock the tiny man kneeled down.

A few seconds later Andrew reached the rock, gasping in disbelief at the dwarf huddled over the lifeless body that lay there next to the ashes of a dead fire.

Swiftly, Andrew and the dwarf rolled the inert figure on to his back, the blond hair spilling out from beneath the bonnet.

"Dugald! Dugald Ferguson!" Andrew exclaimed, the dwarf nodding and gesturing wildly at his side.

Between them they lifted Dugald to a sitting position, wiping away the snow from off his face wetting the blue tinged lips with *usque beatha* from a horn before tilting his head back and trying again when after a time there was no sign of life.

Desperate now, Andrew looked anxiously at the dwarf who in turn began to rub vigorously at the unconscious man's hands and bare legs, while Andrew applied more of the raw spirit to the lifeless lips.

Suddenly the dwarf was away, plodding deeper into the woods to return in no time at all clutching an armful of twigs.

"Where did you find these man?" Andrew wondered, as the tiny man went about building a fire.

Bit by bit as the small fire held the dwarf added larger branches, both rescuers choking in the smoke while they continued to rub at the frozen flesh.

Despairingly, Andrew drew the still unconscious Dugald to the fire and had almost given up when suddenly there was a cough and the frozen face began to stir.

"He is alive *troich*!" Andrew shouted in relief, laughing hysterically at the antics of the dwarf dancing up and down in delight.

"He sleeps safe now" Una whispered, tip toeing across the floor.

She read the look on Andrew's face. "Your questions must wait 'till morning when he is stronger in mind and body."

Andrew slumped down by the fire. "If we only knew what has befallen the others." His gesture one of despair. "I searched the woods where we found Dugald, but there was no sign of life...or otherwise. Were they robbed on their return? Are all dead except Dugald? How came he by yon wound? 'Tis a sword slash across the neck and shoulder, if I am not mistaken."

"Aye,. I have seen many such as these," Una agreed. "The poor laddie must have been taken from behind, the way it crosses the shoulder. Doubtless he will be telling you himself in the morning."

Una put an affectionate arm around her man. "You yourself should rest Andrew, it has been a trying day for you."

"For the *troich* too, bless him." Andrew sighed wearily. "Whatever gift the man may possess has been proved this day. How did he know something was amiss, and so far away?" Andrew shook his head dumfounded. "If it had not been for him, poor Dugald would still be lying in the snow, never to be found 'till spring at least, if at all."

Una pressed her lips to Andrew's cheek, and then gently drew away. "The man has a gift, in this there is no doubt. Perhaps the

177

same lies within us all, had we but the time and wisdom to look for it, for all we favoured folk seem to do is talk and see, but listen little."

Andrew drew her to him. "At times lassie, you are wise beyond your years. I am indeed fortunate to have a lass....no a woman such as you." The man stroked the raven hair, and thought again of Duncan's words and how right the man had been.

They came to peer in through the tiny windows of the bothan or stand stamping frozen feet in the bitter cold, every living soul it seemed who lived in the stronghold, had made their way here to stand and wait, for, the news had travelled like wildfire, that Dugald Ferguson, was returned and sorely hurt.

As chieftain, Andrew had kept all out, except Johnny, Duncan, Fergus and Sim MacColl, with Una the only woman present, who still fussed unceasingly over her patient.

"When you are ready Dugald," Andrew softly coaxed the wounded man. "We all here would be knowing what has happened since you left these four weeks past."

Dugald cast a weak eye around his eager audience, still unable to believe he was alive. Propping himself up to a sitting position, he began.

."We reached Tummel in good time, and spirit, with the McMahon never ceasing to tell us all the while the high price our gear would fetch. How grand it would be to see the looks on the faces of all back here when we returned laden with flour, meal and such like.

Next day we skirted Tay. I was watching McMahon and Coll Fraser, who were ahead at the time, and I myself was in the act of guiding my garron away from the cliff edge of a crag, when I saw the flash of steel, and Coll go down." Dugald closed his eyes to shut out the memory. "So unexpected did it come, and so horrified to see Sean do such a thing, that next I knew, I myself was over the cliff." Dugald ran a shaking hand across his eyes. "It was the Lowlander, Hamilton who had done for me. I do not mind much more, except seeing and unseeing at times."

Later, I was found by an ancient by the name of MacDonald. It was he as much as the *troich* who saved my life," Dugald blushed.

"What happened then, Dugald?" Fergus MacAlister asked sympathetically.

"The old man could not shift me by himself, Fergus, so I lay there until Rob, his son came to carry me home, where his wife Helen tended my wounds.

At first I feared something broken, but thankfully only cracked and bruised was I. Though the cut in my back nipped like the devil for days." Dugald shuddered, attempting to smile, aplogiseing for his weakness.

And no wonder Una thought, standing behind her patient, it was almost to the bone, an inch deeper and you would not be here Dugald Ferguson.

"Try as I might," Dugald was saying, "I did not have the strength to rise, and did not know what to do for the best, whether to follow those evil pair, or try and win back home to warn you of what had happened, for I knew full well all would be waiting our return." Dugald coughed, and shifted himself a little.

"When I told the MacDonald's wife something of the affair, she advised I should not follow yon pair to *Dun Eideann,* but rather that I return and warn you all here."

Finally exhausted the young man fell back on his makeshift pillow, hiding his eyes behind his arm. "Try as I might, I could not rise from my bed. I was there a week!" he moaned at his lack of resolve.

Dugald took his arm away and scanned those gathered around his bed. "Rob MacDonald, helped me as far as Tummel where he left me with his own kinfolk. It was a hard thing for me to believe how weak I was. Folk there would not hear of my leaving until I was well enough. Then the snow came, and I knew I must be away before the passes closed. I cannot mind overmuch of the journey....of reaching the woods, or lighting the fire, which I must have done." He gave a wan smile. "I only remember the cold....the rest you know.....at least as much as myself." Dugald trailed to a halt.

Una patted the youth's hand, and moved to Andrew's side, who, taking her by the hand tepped away from the bedside to let the others have a word with the wounded man. All there acutely aware of the courage it had taken for one so badly hurt as Dugald to survive a journey in such weather.

Comprehending the upshot of what this would mean to every living soul in the *daingneachd*, Andrew drew Sim MacColl, aside.

"It is all up to Mairi, now Sim. We shall need her thrift all the more now that we understand what Dugald is after telling us."

"Aye, that there is no other help for us *ceann cinnidh*." Sim muttered. "None at all, God help us.

Chapter 13

"We must bring the *troich* to live with us, Andrew." Una put away the pot. She had made up her mind. It was the Christian thing to do.

"What ever for? You know how the wee man lives. It is not so different from when he lived alone in the woods!" Andrew threw his eyes to the roof, dismayed by the thought of their privacy being invaded.

"We must make sacrifices, in especial the *ceann cinnidh*. Cathal MacAlister has taken in Dugald and tends his wounds."

"Dugald is still sorely wounded, the *troich* is not Una," Andrew countered, soberly.   .

Disconsolate, he peered out at the mounting snow. December, and still it came down. Was there no end to it? Was he to be altogether cursed with more deaths on his hands?

Rob Donald, the last of the wounded men from the debacle in the glen had died a week ago. Since then, five more, though these had been bairns and old folk, which was not unusual throughout the winter here in the *daingneachd*.

Without taking his eyes from the window, Andrew conceded with a sigh. "If you think it right to have the *troich* here, I will not object. But mind you..." His voice rose in warning, "we shall not have our privacy, see you. Have you thought of that my bonnie lass?"

"No doubt we will manage," Una giggled. "After all the wee man is deaf."

"Deaf may be, but blind he is not," Andrew muttered as Johnny MacKellar pushed open the bothan door.

"I give you good day," Johnny greeted them, knocking snow off his brogues and crossing to hold out his hands before the fire. "If you will both forgive my intrusion I came to have a word at Mairi MacColl's request, she thinking it would be best that it come from me. It seems the meal will not last the week." Johnny cast his eyes to the fire, awaiting the reaction to his words.

"There is not!" Andrew exploded. "And why not, pray tell, when Mairi herself, assured me there was sufficient to last the month at least?"

Johnny examined his outstretched hands. " Mairi found a bole or more sour. It is no fault of hers. The fault lies with our 'lifting' sour meal." Johnny spun the words over his shoulder.

Would it never end? Was he to be ever cursed? Andrew swung on Una. "What has to be done lass?" He gestured helplessly. "Three more months to spring, and less than a week's supply of meal left."

Una bit her lip. "We shall have a word with old Mistress Finlay, Ewen's wife, and be well advised by her," she declared with a nod, to convince herself as well as both men, that this was the right course to take ...indeed perhaps the only course.

"It is the beasts we must slaughter, some to be bled, others we must kill whilst there is still meat on their bones," Johnny broke in.

"We shall visit Ewen Finlay," Andrew reiterated. "Have Duncan meet us there Johnny. I will accompany Una so she might have a word with Mistress Finlay."

"What think you of the meeting, Una?" Andrew asked, throwing some peat upon the fire.

"It went well, Andrew, Ewen's wife and the old body MacIan, told me of ways to subsist that I never knew before."

"Will Mairi MacColl, be knowing of them?"

"I think not, at least, not all of them."

"Then acquaint her Una, but gently if you please. Gently see you."

"To be sure, Andrew. But what of your own talk? Meal we may lack, but ale we do not. At least if this night is anything to measure by."

"Och! We had not overmuch," Andrew chuckled, sitting down more heavily on the stool than intended. "Ewen's suggestion was well taken. Keep the milch cows, and slaughter all else whilst there is meat on their bones. ...Or was it Johnny who did the saying?" Andrew belched, passing a hand across his eyes, and crumpled onto the bed. "Och had we but the sense of our dumb friends to sleep the winter through," he slurred. "Come to bed, lass," he coaxed, his arms outstretched.

"Away with you man I have other matters to think upon!" Una scolded him brushing aside the offending hands, but not before Andrew had caught and drawn her to him.

"We must make the best of it my brave lass, since this will be our last night alone, thanks to your generosity," Andrew chuckled, nibbling her ear.

"And if you are not after behaving yourself, Andrew MacLaren, it will be your last night! Company or no company!" Una replied, and not all in the best of humour.

"I am sorry, Duncan, all words are empty at this time." Andrew spoke softly, afraid to awaken the shroud covered figure that lay there.

Duncan stared through unseeing eyes. "She was wife to me in everything but name, Andrew. She was wed to Fergus MacLachlan, the same that suffered the gallows in *Eilginn*, only months after I myself came here." Duncan gave a sigh. "I courted her when the time was decent ...och! That was a long time ago, when times were kinder." Duncan trailed off unable to keep the pain from his voice.

Sensing the man's return to those days, those kinder days, when the MacIntosh had been *ceann cinnidh*, and believing this is to be what Duncan referred: and was perhaps even now cursing the day he had ever met Andrew MacLaren, was confounded to hear him continue.

"It is strange how we mortals are adept at remembering the happier days, and inept at recalling the bad. Perhaps it is His way of helping us through life. Och, we saw harsh times too, but we were younger then, and I had my Catrona. Aye, may be that was the difference."

Then as if to exonerate his young chief, Duncan lifted his head to explain. "Catrona was never strong in her latter years, at least not in body. The life here, especially the winters, lessened her days. This winter has been one too many for *mo ghradh*."

Shocked, Andrew realised how old Duncan himself had become, the graying hair, the white face lined and drawn. Or was it that he had ever looked this way, and him never seeing it, having taken it for granted the man's ever willingness to complete each task set, without complaint, to mediate, counsel, obey. Now, to think of it, Duncan was no youngster, nor had been his wife, peace be with her. Neither had he come to know her well, scarcely their conversation ever having reached past the time of day, and she the wife of his most faithful follower...no friend.

Overcome with self loathing, Andrew made his excuses to the man and stepped out into the cold raw air. For a moment he stood there looking skyward, imploring the heavens to let him return to where he would never again be held responsible for another body's life...or death.

The dwarf sat in his new home whittling at the toy dirk, smoothing the wooden blade with a stone. He saw Una watching him hold up the toy to his eyes for closer inspection.

It was liking to a dam having burst and Una was upon the tiny man, beating at him with her fists, wrenching the toy from his bewildered grasp and throwing it into the fire, yelling and shouting, until Andrew was upon her pulling her away.

"What is amiss, Una!" Andrew bawled at her, his eyes wide in disbelief, pulling her roughly off the dwarf, unable to fathom what the lassie had done to someone she cared so much about. "What hurt as the *troich* done that you should treat him so?" He roared at her again, angry and alarmed.

Una beat at his chest, as he held her to him. "'Tis enough! He sits there carving toys for bairns who will never live to see them! Make him stop Andrew! Make him stop!" She buried her face in his chest, her fury spent.

Still angry, though also sad at what had happened, Andrew sat her down by the fire. The dwarf cautiously venturing forward with a cup of *usque beatha,* then retreating to the furthest corner of the bothan to sit forlornly, knees drawn up to his chin, anatomizing the scene from beneath knitted brows.

"You must not talk like this Una, the spring is not so very far away, when you will see the bairns by the wee man's door as you did before," Andrew scolded, voicing a conviction he was far from feeling.

"Will the MacMaster bairns be there...or Donald ..or MacPhersons'?" Una wept, angrily. "....and who is to know how many more He will be taking to Him in the long winter months to come? Spring you say! And this only the third week of the year!" Una mocked, with an accusation in her voice Andrew had never heard before.

"Steady lass. Do you not think every life lost does not hang the more heavily on me, seeing as I am the one responsible for what has come to pass?"

Una saw the pain in her man's eyes. "Forgive me Andrew." She gulped back a sob. "It is just the way of a foolish lassie. I was not thinking how you must be seeing this....And the *troich?* My anger was ill judged. I did not mean to hurt him thus."

"Then tell him Una. See how dejected he sits, not knowing what offence he has given. Go to him. He is a man with a man's feelings. Do not have him thinking you have lost your kindness for him, and he not knowing why."

Wiping back her tears, Una went to the man who sat head bowed apprehensive of her coming. She kneeled down whispering gently, though he could not hear, hoping that he at least would understand, and engulfed him in her arms.

Embarrassed for them both, Andrew turned his back, the tiny man's tears rolling down his gigantic face, while held in the arms of the lass who had first shown him a kindness, when first they met.

The rich smell of roasting meat filled his mind, engulfing his body. He was sitting at the head of a long table in a great hall, Una across the board. Except it was not Una, but Kirsty with auburn hair. When he turned away at the fiddler's music it was Gregor who played the tune, and when he turned again, it was his own wife who served the fare, the blood flowing from her breast, bright red upon his plate, mingling with the roasted meat.

Jumping up he ran out onto the broad green sward, and heard above him the hammers noise of the masons working on four incomplete towers. They waved to him, two, only having one arm. Fleeing back into the hall he picked up the meat from the table and thrust it down his throat, choking and spluttering at its taste, then he was awake, his eyes open, glazed, unseeing. Finally his head and eyes cleared, and he was aware of the dwarf spooning the broth down his throat.

If he had been dreaming, this at least was real. He found a tiny morsel in the corner of his mouth and chewed at it lovingly, and to his delight, found his mouth filled once more, languishing momentarily in its magical taste, before all again returned to darkness.

Andrew reawakened in the early hours of that first day of February, surprised to find himself fresher and stronger than he had been in a long time. Had he been ill? Weakly he levered himself onto his side, and took in the sorry sight of the emaciated form of Una by the fire, bent over a cooking pot, where every movement the young lass made, appeared to be with the greatest effort of will.

Running his tongue over his dry lips he forced himself to speak. "What, up so early *mo ghaol* and it not quite light? Is it pron or skilling yet again?"

Una levered herself round at the sound of the voice, surprised to find her man awake. "Neither my clever man," she coughed, carefully holding out the bowl to him. "Here take this, see if it is to your liking?" she offered, attempting to sound cheerful.

Andrew sipped the broth, his eyes widening in disbelief. "This is neither pron or skilling, and unless I have taken leave of my senses, there is the taste of meat here as well. So last night, my tongue did not deceive me. It was no dream!"

"If it was Andrew, then it is one I also shared, though, I think it is the *troich* we must thank for this." Una supped hungrily, licking at what was sticking to the corner of her mouth. "How, or where he came by it I neither know or care, for it is food Andrew! Food!" She sank down by the fire.

"But where is he that supplied this fare? Why not here to share what he so mysteriously came by?"

Slumped against the wall, Una spooned weakly at her broth. "He has already broken his fast and will be back shortly, so I believe by his gesturing.

She looked up at the window. "It has not snowed for a week or more. Do you think we have seen the last of it, Andrew, though it is still bitter cold?"

"Perhaps lass. Even so, outside the *daingneachd* is as barren as it is inside. "Besides," he moaned, "we do not have the strength to hunt."

At the door's opening the man looked up at the dwarf, who smiling at them both filled his own bowl and came to sit by them.

Gesturing, Una inquired as to where he had been, the dwarf pointing to the cooking pot then outside.

"He has been away feeding others I am after thinking. But with what? Andrew exclaimed understanding the signs.

"Then you best not be knowing," Una decided, with a definite nod of her head. "As long as it fills the belly, the mind can aye bide at rest at what the eye cannot see."

"Is that an old saying of your clan, Una lass, or is it as ancient as my last drawn breath?" Andrew chuckled.

"That I will leave to you, my clever man," Una laughed through a cough. "That I will leave to you."

"There is only one garron left," Sim MacColl informed the company sardonically.

"This we know full well, Sim, but how long will it last amongst us should we slaughter it now? There is not so much meat on the poor beast that its back does not already meet its belly," Duncan replied sourly.

"It is better than nothing at all, and cannot be worse than pron or skilling," Hamish MacKenzie, volunteered.

Andrew studied the man, one of the four left behind the day of the slaying in the glen. A nonentity, Hamish performed his tasks when asked, never complaining or offering an opinion. In fact since coming to the stronghold he had never heard him speak at their counsels, either indoors or by the stones outside. Now to hear him speak at all proved to what extent that ill fated day had drawn them all that bit closer together.

Andrew studied the circle of drawn faces, some leaning against the stones or sitting hunched on boulders, each with the express purpose of conserving what little energy they had left.

"You are for slaughtering the beast, then Hamish?" he asked, his curiosity aroused now that the man had ventured this far.

"Aye, that I am, *ceann cinnidh,* what other choice is open to us? All the cattle are gone and so are the dogs after these last two nights." Hamish eyed the company accusingly.

"The dogs!" the big MacAlister exclaimed. "How know you of this, Hamish?"

"For mine is also missing, Fergus, a mongrel if ever there was one, forever wandering away, but never so long as to miss his bite, see you." Hamish gave a little shake of his head. "I cannot be thinking he has grown tired of my comany, and instead has gone for a dander in this weather to Ness side or such like, now that I can no longer keep him in the manner he has grown accustomed to."

Andrew scanned the smiling faces. Even Duncan managed a grin. The first smile he had seen on the man for awhile, and could have saluted Hamish for his humour.

"What think you has befallen the dog, then, Hamish?"

187

"It takes no thinking, man, the dog was eaten, as was Shona MacFarlane's and the widow Donald. Either this, or they have all conspired to desert together!"

There was an amused silence for a time, each man alone with his own thoughts, none more so than Andrew. So this was what the *troich* had been up to! He put a hand up to hide a smile at the thought of having eaten someone's pet.

"So it is agreed then, we slaughter the garron?" Andrew said in all seriousness, fixing his eye on one of the stones, in an attempt to prevent himself from laughing aloud, not so much at having eaten a dog, but the way in which Hamish had put it, with the man muttering as they dispersed. "Aye, seeing as we have eaten all the dogs."

Una sat with her arm around the old man, listening, sympathising.

"She weaved her own winding sheet, lass," Ewen whispered, lest he disturb his wife's last long rest. "We have never been parted for more than a day or two these last twenty years or more. It will be no different now."

"Hush. Do not be talking thus, Ewen. What would your wife be after saying if she heard you speak so?" Una gently scolded the kind old man she had known for years.

His thoughts on how reminiscent this scene was to that of Duncan Cameron, only this month past, Andrew ventured gently. "We shall need your help and guidance, Ewen, if any of us are to see the spring. There are only eight able bodied men left, and poor Dugald still abed with yon terrible wound."

"A grand help I am to anyone Andrew, when I could not help she who was nearest and dearest to me," the old man replied with a twinge of bitterness.

Out of the corner of his eye, Andrew caught Fergus's nod and knew what he must say. "Ewen, would you have us lay your wife to rest...?"

"Lay her in the barn? Is it the barn you are afraid to say, Andrew?" Ewen completed Andrew's question for him. "Have her rest with the others...so many others," he sighed, unable to disguise the pain in his voice.

"Aye, Ewen, there is no burying 'till the spring. No other place to lay them at present. It has been done before as you yourself well know, having seen more winters here than most."

"This is right laddie. Though now, I should like fine if I could but sit by my wife awhile."

"To be sure Ewen. We shall leave you be, and return when you say the word."

Outside, Johnny MacKellar, came to stand beside Andrew. "Will the dying never cease? Look at the bothans, not a sign of peat smoke from over half, and you telling me not so long past, to find another *daingneachd* as this one was past overflowing."

Whether the statement had been said in criticism or not, none knew, except that it was too much for the Maclaren. "You are saying the blame lies with me?" Andrew retorted, rounding angrily on the man. "That my encounter with MacSorley spawned these deaths! Is this what you imply Johnny? If so speak plainly man, so all may hear," The angry man roared, beside himself with rage.

Opened mouthed Johnny made to move away from the mourner's door, to have himself gripped by the arm by his incensed *ceann cinndh*.

"Answer me man!" Andrew shouted with all the pent up rage stored these last months. "I, who thought you my friend. You, who has scarcely spoken my given name since yon day of the slaying. If you are indeed my friend, you at least owe me the truth! " the leader choked. "As you all do!" he flung at the astonished onlookers, none ever having seen this placid man so consumed with rage.

Andrew swung back to MacKellar. "I never sought the task of leader, it is you who have made me thus. If you see yourself better, then say so! Now! But should you not, then I am *ceann cinnidh* and I give you my word Johnny MacKellar, you *will* need that *daingneachd* in the Cairngorms, for in time...and not so very far distant." Andrew gulped for breath. "All the wild Highlands shall know of Andrew MacLaren, the cateran!"

Without waiting a reply from an astonished MacKellar, Andrew swung on his heel to be followed by an equally astonished Una, running to catch up.

Mercifully it thawed. Frozen footprints disappeared as had so many of their owners. Sudden avalanches left bothan roofs bare. Icicles dripped from frozen rocks. The waterfall came to life.

Exhilarated by the earth's awakening Una stood by the open door laughing and weeping in turn.

"Oh Andrew, the land is free at last, you can take the men and go hunting! Surely you will find a bite amongst you all!" she cried excitedly without turning round to face the man who sat so forlornly by the fireside.

"A man hunts and fights better with something in his belly" Andrew answered sourly, for he could not bring himself to think of trudging outside of the defile. Was not the entrance itself a lifetime away, his mind's eye journeying over that vast expanse of wilderness. "We all have lived too long on pron and skilling, husks of oats that would not fill a bairn newly weaned. How far can we travel on an empty belly? Forby, the creatures at this time of year are as scrawny as we ourselves."

At her man's mournful discourse, Una's joy quickly dissipated. Angrily she swung on him. . "So this is the great Andrew MacLaren that all the Highlands will come to know! Brave words my bonnie man," she snapped. "But what will the Highlands come to know ,that he let all perish who came to love him?" she ended with a rasping cough.

Instantly, Andrew was by her side his pessimism over the hunt forgotten. "Una, this cough lass, it worsens daily...and the sickness?" He asked anxiously guiding her to the heather bed

Una allowed him to lower her on to the bed, gazing weakly up at him. "The cough will pass when my insides are full again, and the sickness will also pass, of this I promise you."

Andrew stared down at the ailing lassie who had reminded him of his boast to the MacKellar. A boast he had made not out of vainglory, but of anger, as he saw again the withered shape of wee Sheena lying there, her mother beside herself with grief, and he unable to do a thing about it. How he had tried to make light of it with the bairn by telling her it would not be long until she was back gurdling fish in the burn, all the while knowing it would never be so.

How many more bairns lives was he to be responsible for? Why was it that no man had taken a dirk to him? Was it not so, that it was his taking revenge on the MacSorley that had led that man to harry him and his? Why had the MacKellar not seized the opportunity to make his peace with that lord by surrendering him to him? Maybe then the bairns would still have a chance of survival.

Andrew took Una's hand, resolving that something must be done to save her and the few who were left. "We shall start at first light," he said hoarsely. "If you are well enough to be left by yourself that is?" he asked anxiously.

Una closed her eyes. "I will find the strength, Andrew, as you yourself have newly done."

"It was kindly done," Johnny MacKellar said, trudging through the snow beside Andrew. Hunched against the wind driven snow, his vision swimming with every step, Andrew did not answer. "That you should have left Duncan behind on the pretext of him being the only one there knowing the other way out of the *daingneachd*, should it be attacked," Johnny continued, hesitantly.

"Duncan is no fool, the ploy did not deceive him," Andrew answered sourly, for he had not forgotten the last time Johnny and he had met.

"Still it was a kindness,.... Andrew," Johnny persisted. "A thing I must mind when you make me *ceann cinnidh* in the Cairngorms when the time comes, see you."

Startled by the man addressing him by his Christian name, Andrew jerked up his head in time to see Johnny quicken his step to catch up with the big MacAlister. So the rift had healed, or appeared to have done so. It was as much as he could expect from the proud MacKellar.

They travelled slowly, stopping often to lean against icy rocks and catch their breaths, until the cold forced them on.

Andrew studied his six companions, men, who in less harsh times would have covered this same distance in no time at all, and without a halt.

"Have a mercy Andrew!" Rob Sutherland pleaded. His rasping cough almost brought him to his knees. "I cannot take another step," he wheezed.

Andrew drew to a halt, shaking the snow from off his *feileadh mor*, and stamping his feet to keep them warm. "We have but started Rob, and must make the other side of the standing stone whilst it is still light."

"But it is miles, Andrew! And in this wind and snow we will not reach half as far," the man moaned, leaning against a rock.

"In this you are right Rob should we halt as often as we are after doing."

Fergus breathed warmth into his cupped hands, and moved away from where some snow had thawed. "I think Rob should turn back, Andrew, even should we reach the cave, what use will he be at the hunting?"

"You are right, Fergus, the man looks poorly." Andrew thrust his hands under his plaid. "Sim...Sim MacColl! Will you be returning with Rob here, see that he wins back safely, if you will."

"That I can, though, I am strong enough in myself to go on should someone else feel so inclined to return with the man." Sim looked around him at the frozen shivering bearded men. If this did not impress his *ceann cinnidh*, then what would?

Before anyone could answer, Andrew spoke again. "This I know, Sim, and I thank you for wanting to bide, but Rob will need your strength to see him through." He stamped his feet again and turned to move away. "Tell Duncan when you see him, where we are headed, and not to expect us for a day or so." Andrew, with a final salute, moved off.

"We shall manage fine, though it is more a crack in the rock than cave, Fergus." Hamish MacKenzie said throwing down the bundle of kindling. "Yet at this time it will serve as well as Kintail's castle itself, if we are not to freeze this night."

While he spoke the dwarf appeared out of the gloaming a dead hare dangling from his outstretched hand.

"*Dia, troich* !" Johnny exclaimed. "And where did you come by that, and so soon?" The dwarf offering a lopsided grin at the man's obvious pleasure.

Later, sitting back contentedly, the shadows flickering across the small cave roof, Andrew drew a look around the men crowded around the glowing fire, still overawed by the fact, these men, wild in their own way, should accept him as their leader...he, Andrew MacLaren, coward, turned cateran, erstwhile husband, etc.

It was the best hare ever," Johnny declared above Andrew's thoughts.

"That it was," the giant agreed.

"For myself, I wish I had not eaten the damned thing," Hamish attested sourly. "Now my belly craves what my mouth cannot deliver. Man, it leaves me hungrier than ever." The comment received by the company with a few chuckles, for what had been said was true, as each there strove in his own way to turn his

192

thoughts away from food. The silence broken only by the crackling of the fire in that eerie darkness, until eventually all were asleep.

"We shall separate here and meet back by the standing stone. Do not venture too far. Mind, you will not be so strong as you think you are. So gang warily.

His warning over, accompanied by the dwarf, Andrew started down the hillside, while the rest made off in different directions.

Close on two hours later, his frozen hands thrust deep in his *feileadh mor*, Andrew watched the dwarf plod a weary way over a barren stretch of snow covered hillside towards him, two hares slung over his shoulder.

"A blessing on you *troich"* Andrew muttered aloud, screwing up his eyes against the glare of the snow. "You have saved us all yet again. His last words interrupted by a flurry of snow, quickly followed by the feet, then the body of Hamish MacKenzie, sliding past.

"God's curse! the man cried, coming to an abrupt halt. "I am after thinking I have slid down from the summit of this accursed mountain, and not a sign of a bite. I tell you Andrew, all living creatures with a brain at all are well on their way to sunnier climes than these!" Hamish let out, brushing himself down. "It is only daft humans who bide here in the winter."

Fergus was the next to return, followed shortly by Johnny, each empty handed.

The dwarf had almost reached them. They saw him, Johnny expressing what was in all of their minds. "It is the wee man we must again thank for our survival, though two hares are not sufficient to see our journey back to the *daingneachd* , far less feed anyone therein."

"Come, let us meet the man, should there be any game at all, it will be by the lochan," Andrew speculated, leading the men to meet the dwarf.

However, having better knowledge of the area, it was the MacAlister who led the way through the melting snow that clung to dripping tartan, with the big man constantly changing direction in as many steps to tread withered grass that thrust defiantly through a captive mantle of snow, and now and again raise a warning hand to skirt unseen bog and mire, until they came at last to the saucer of rock that held the tiny lochan.

"It is still not thawed!" Hamish cried aloud in dismay. "No creature will be coming here, and, even so, it will be by dark!"

Wearily all slumped down, should by some miracle their combined stares melt that frozen surface.

"We must spread out and find what we can," Andrew commanded sternly. "Sitting here will only serve to freeze us more. Come!" he barked, forcing the reluctant company to their feet.

They fanned out in a wide arc, upwind of any living creature headed for the tiny lochan. Cold hungry despondent men, each convinced of the futility of it all.

Suddenly the hare was darting past, this way and that, doubling back on itself in panic. In an instant Andrew had his pistol drawn and cocked, cursing at his shot going wide. Then, with a howl of rage threw the empty weapon after the departing animal, chasing after it through the melting snow, until finally exhausted turned to retrace his steps and retrieve his half buried weapon.

At first, the screech of steel failed to penetrate Andrew's numbed and dismayed mind as he cleaned his pistol with a fold of his plaid, and through the vapour rising from his hot breath from the chase, saw the figures of Hamish and Fergus step determinedly towards each other, their angry voices echoing across the emptiness of the barren mountainside.

"It will not be you who will tell me Fergus MacAlister, that I am dumb! You a MacKenzie!" the giant stormed, shaking his naked weapon at his adversary.

This was all he needed Andrew thought hurrying to intervene. Were they not badly off as it was?

"Aye! You MacAlister are dumb, see you!" Hamish shouted beside himself with rage, and pointing at the mess of pulp and feathers on the boulder top. "When I said to hit the wee bird, I did not mean you should drive its head through its arse!" Both adversaries closing on one another, weapons held at the ready.

Andrew pointed a shaking finger at the boulder, and despite feeling a weakness after his chase and the seriousness of the situation fell to his knees laughing, as one by one the company, adversaries included, joined in. The dwarf not to be excluded jumping up and down and slapping his thigh.

Andrew rose weakly to his feet wiping the tears from his eyes.

Recovering from his laughter Johnny walked to Andrew's side. "That was a close call," he breathed out heavily. "Are you not the wise one? It could easily have ended badly. Sad it is that we have come to this. We must be nearing the end of our sanity."

Andrew nodded at the boulder, his smile gone. " Aye, and over as little as yon. There was not so much in yon poor wee bird as you would find under your fingernail." He drew away from the others, adding conspiratorially to the MacKellar, "We must find a bite soon. Think you also of the folk at home, who depend upon us wholly. Sorry it is that we should quarrel amongst ourselves!"

They left the lochan as they found it, weary and empty handed. Except for the two hares caught by the dwarf, they had caught nothing more. Walking, stumbling, until near dusk they caught their first sight of the woods, when involuntarily the smallest man's step quickened.

"It has turned to frost, by morning all will be ice," Fergus proclaimed, totally weary.

Andrew shivered and drew his plaid closer about him. "Aye, Fergus, I will not be displeased to see the *troich's* home, this night."

Plodding through crystal glistening snow they approached the woods.

"Dia !....yon is the wood of the haunted, *coille taibhseach* , see you!" Fergus drew to a halt, his face clearly betraying his fear of the place.

"It is home of the *troich.* The same hurt dwarf you yourself helped carry back to the *daingneachd,* and who you now call your friend, Fergus," Andrew chided, biting his lip impatiently, and inwardly cursing that it should have been enough to have reached this far at all in their present state without him having to use what little strength he had left in assuring this giant of a man that he had nothing to fear within these same woods.

Hamish MacKenzie came to his chief's rescue. "MacAlister, if you are afraid to enter yonder, perhaps I can arrange for the *troich* to take you by the hand?" he voiced in mock seriousness.

"Aye, MacKenzie, and I can arrange to take you by the neck!" Fergus growled, taking a cautious step forward. While behind him, Hamish winked at Andrew.

At last in the folds of the woods, the dwarf disappeared, leaving the company to follow and gaze around them at this strange new world, all uneasy and not quite knowing what to make of their being in such an infamous place.

This time Andrew need not hunt for his friend, there being his footprints to follow, and cast his eyes heavenward in silent prayer that the dwarf would have completed his ritual with the trees before they had caught up, it being out of sheer necessity that these men had entered these woods at all, given their superstitious fears and the infamy of the place.

"In the name of the Holy Father what is this?" Fergus exclaimed, clearly shocked by the dwarf caressing and examining the trees.

"Do not alarm yourself, Fergus." Andrew silently moaned at the failure of his prayer. "I thought as you do when first I witnessed this. It is as Duncan explained to me. This is all the *troich* has known as a family, prior to our meeting. Can we ourselves ever begin to imagine what it must feel, to live alone in a silent world, never to hear the sound of human laughter, a kind word, or in turn to speak our thoughts and fears, and have a body there to listen?" Andrew stopped, unable to express his feeling adequately to the big man who stood beside him so consumed with fear and superstition.

Fergus glared at the dwarf, and making the sign of the cross walked towards the tiny man who stood smiling at him.

With bated breath Andrew waited, as did the company, as did the entire silent woods it seemed, his mind in a turmoil of rushing thoughts. What was Fergus thinking, brought up in folklore and superstition? Would the dwarf again become the devil incarnate? Would the big man's mind turn to their misfortune and in some way see their starving as the *troich's* fault....the devil's game?

Out of the corner of his eye Andrew saw Johnny watching him, judging him as he had done before. This time however he was at a loss. Short of shooting Fergus there was no stopping the giant when roused. Therefore, with self preservation uppermost in his mind, he waited, while Fergus, with a stern shake of his head pointed to the trees, then putting an arm around the tiny man encompassed the waiting men with a wave. Gradually a look of comprehension spread over that enormous face, turning to a monstrous grin, the *troich* nodding up at his gigantic friend.

Relieved, Andrew drew back, Hamish rushing to pump the dwarf's hand and slap him on the back, who still grinning broadly, bidded them to follow him.

Now less apprehensive, the company made an exaggerated show of approval at the sight of the tiny bothan, all helping to clear away the snow from the door, and quickly lighting a fire in its dank interior.

"*Dia!* I swear it is colder in here than it is outside!" Fergus uttered through his chattering teeth.

"The wee place will warm in no time." This from Hamish, stamping his feet.

Meanwhile, the dwarf returned from his alcove, carrying a satchel of meal and a bottle of claret tucked under each arm, Andrew thinking how fortunate it had been that they had removed the chattels on their previous visit, though mystified as to how he had missed these.

"Is there no end to the man's resourcefulness?" Hamish cried wagging his head in approval at the grinning dwarf, and eagerly grabbing the welcome vituals.

"Man this bothan is near airtight, not a draught except from the hearth, and Hamish's ranting!" Fergus let out in admiration of the dwarf's work. "You were thinking aright when you brought him to the *daingneachd* yon day, Andrew, and I never thought to see the day I would enter *taibhseachd coill*e, far less a bothan therein!"

Andrew grunted his understanding, pleased by the big man's transformation, as well as that of the rest of the company, who only a short time ago could scarcely find the strength to put one foot in front of another.

"We shall cook one hare and a little meal," Johnny suggested looking around for approval. "We must try and save what we can, should we fail in the hunt."

Later, their appetites less than satisfied, though appreciative as to what they had had, they settled down to pass the dwarf's wine around, Hamish mouthing a tune he had learned as a child, or so he would have them believe.

Sprawled in a corner, Johnny sat with a contended look on his face, pretending to hear what Fergus was saying, or make out what Hamish was slurring in the opposite end of the tiny room.

It had not taken the wine long to reach their heads, and already Andrew could feel himself doze, yet his brain would not let up. There was still food to be found, and each day they grew weaker, with scarcely enough food to sustain themselves, least of all those back home. And should they here survive to the spring to be lifting cattle again, how were they to resist Quoich should he in turn find the stronghold?

Draining the last of the bottle, and mindful of his last bout of drinking here in this same bothan, grinning, and not knowing why or caring less Andrew let the wine take him into fitful slumber. The cares of today could wait until the morrow.

It took them two days to retrace their steps, halting at their small cave shelter. Except this time, once again, thanks the dwarf, they carried two scrawny deer slung between two poles, a brace of fowl and a dozen hares. It was in this way they at last sighted the mountains of home.

Looking around him, Andrew saw no sign of the dwarf, who without warning had taken himself off a few miles back, presumably in the hope of securing further supplies for the hungry caterans, and he was not immediately aware of the two men until they had rounded a rock.

"It is good you should both be coming to help us, for we are all but spent!" Andrew shouted, recognising the figures of Sim and Duncan plodding to meet them. "The snow is over deep here, unlike below."

It was something in their look that made Andrew halt.

"It is Una," Duncan's voice trembled. "You best away, and quickly."

Before the pole he had been carrying had hit the ground, Andrew was off, running, slipping, cursing the impeding snow, now all thought of tiredness gone, until he was through the defile and throwing open the bothan door, and taking in at a glance those huddled around the prone silent figure that was his Una.

At his coming, those there moved silently away, leaving him to kneel by the bedside, Mairi MacColl whispering in his ear that it was hopeless, that the end was near.

"But why, it was just a cough she was after having! It is simple nourishment she lacks, as do we all!" Andrew cried despondently, searching the sober faces for reassurance.

"That as may be Andrew, if it was nourishment for herself alone she lacks. Yet, seeing as it is for your bairn as well, that is a different pass."

198

Andrew stared at the woman in astonishment, who nodded confirmation. "Do not be telling me you did not know she was with child? That she had the woman's sickness?"

Andrew held his head in his hands. "The sickness!" he moaned. "It was the sickness, and she never once saying what ails her, and me so dim as not to see it."

He took Una's hand in his, feeling that same coldness he had felt at his own mother's , and Fiona's passing. This time he did not mean to let his cowardice win. He would hold this hand, for never again would he live with guilt.

Drawing Una close Andrew pressed his cheek against her's, whispering her name, tears unashamedly filling his eyes. All the good times came flooding back: the summer days on the braeside, her laughter at something said: their lovemaking, and how it had first came about. Now this bonnie lass no more than a child was, dying. "Oh Una my love, do not leave me. We ourselves are now a family. It is my bairn also you carry there."

He gripped her hand urgently. "Una! It is I Andrew! I have food. I will feed you well...you will be yourself in no time at all! Una! It is me Andrew." He shook her attempting to awaken her from a deep sleep. "You must not leave me lass," he pleaded.

As if in answer, Una returned from her own silent world, to open tired sad eyes at the man she had loved since first they met. "Andrew, it is you returned. I was sore afraid I would not see you again."

"Do not talk so. I have what we sought to fill you this night, for you and the bairn."

"It is over late. I am tired Andrew, see you. Tell me again of the house you will build for me."

Closing his eyes Andrew fought back tears of sorrow. Sorrow that a young lass such as this should depart a life barely started. Sorrow for what she must have borne when parted from her kin, only to be used by the MacIntosh. Had he himself been any better, kinder? Sorrow that she was not to know no other life than here in these wild mountains, and above all, sorrow for what he himself had done to this lass, and what he had meant to do, for was it not so that half his thoughts were ever in Glen Moriston?

Choking back the tears Andrew started his story, a story told in happier days, speaking as he would to a child, of the house he would build for her.

"Tell me of the room where we shall sit together, Andrew," she whispered.

And so he described the book filled room he'd seen in his chief's house those long years ago in Glen Laidon. "But forget you not the hall with its great table, Una, where you will sit at its head, in a dress newly come from *Lunnainn,* with the servants hurrying and scurrying at your command."

"Will there be meat upon the table?" Una struggled to ask.

"Aye lass, there will be meat, for I swear you will never again know hunger," the man sobbed, stroking the raven hair.

" The towers? Will the towers be done?"

"Aye there will be towers, Una."

"Then all is complete," she sighed heavily. "I will go and prepare our home, Andrew. But you must bide awhile, 'till all is ready."

"That I shall, Una, but it will be a sore trial without you *moghaol*." Even as he spoke Andrew knew it was already too late.

Later, while the evening shadows lengthened, Andrew rose from the bedside of a bothan now cold and empty, as indeed was his life, whilst from outside came a high eerie unnatural cry.

Chapter 14

Two months after Una's passing a different Andrew MacLaren, accompanied by the dwarf strode for Glen Moriston. Still numbed by his loss, Andrew now feared Quoich less. Yet, mindful of his responsibilities, he had compelled Johnny and Duncan to include Ewan Finlay in the secret of the second exit from the stronghold, having convinced both men, that with the fighting men away hunting and such like, there was no one who could lead the women and children to safety in the event of an attack. Though reason dictated that with only old men to defend the defile, there would be little time for any to escape. And if so, to where?

It was to this end, despite the lack of able men that he'd sent Johnny and Sim to look for an alternative *daingneachd* in the Cairngorms.

While Andrew and his companion approached Gleidh House, Iain MacKinnon, with well founded apprehension, awaited the arrival of the giant and his young friend at the standing stone. Reflecting, of his having told MacSorley of the caterans intented 'lifting' in Athol, those months back which had subsequently lead to their trapping in Glen Tilt.

That Quoich had spiered no further on how he had come by this information had been a relief, so when he had volunteered to find out more of the MacLaren's whereabouts or intentions, his master had become quite enthusiastic, without outwardly appearing to be so in front of someone as lowly as he.

While Iain MacKinnon stood there brushing away the hordes of insects buzzing around his head, he remembered the last conversation he had had with his master regarding this same meeting.

"If we can but capture one at this standing stone, you are after telling me about, MacKinnon, I will make *him* talk, then we can be done with the MacLaren and his tribe. Aye, in especial the MacLaren." Quoich's eyes shone, adding casually in afterthought, "You have never met the man?"

"No my lord" Iain answered. "I have only met his ..spies..for want of a better word, once or twice," he lied. "They are not likely to tell one little known to them as myself of where they hide. They would much rather I bide here and pass on to them what I know of your affairs, hence this forthcoming meeting."

"And what would this information be, MacKinnon, that you will tell them at this meeting of yours?"

"That you my lord are no longer interested in catching the MacLaren. This you will leave to one of their own."

Quoich raised an eyebrow at this liberty, while Iain went on to explain. "Maclaren will not be taken where he hides in the Monadhliath, nor will you capture one of his own at this standing stone. No, it is best we wait until the fox leaves his lair, then we set our trap. And that trap will be well sprung in Glen Moriston."

He remembered how Quoich's eyes had widened at this, and more so when he had told him of having placed a watch on Gleidh House, all this he had done on Quoich's promise of a reward when the MacLaren was taken.

Aye, Iain sighed, watching the caterans draw near, it was no bad thing to serve two masters, even though there was one he had never met.

Fergus raised a hand in greeting, happy to see another face, even if not one he truly liked. "I give you good day Iain MacKinnon," he said cheerfully.

Iain forced a smile, shocked by both mens emaciated appearance. "And you Fergus MacAlister. And your friend, Dugald is it not?"

"It is that, Iain." Fergus jerked a thumb in the lad's direction. "A wee bit sore from a sword blade, see you."

"From the day you were trapped in the glen, Dugald?" Iain asked sympathetically, surmising that it was there that the youngster had come by his wound. "I heard all those against you were mounted."

"What would you be knowing of the slaying?" Dugald inquired suspiciously, taking a step forward. "With you having Quoich's ear, and not warning us."

"I swear I never heard a word, Dugald! Quoich had those mercenaries bought before they had crossed the Highland Line. None knew of their coming," Iain vouched, if somewhat nervously.

"That is as it may be," Fergus interrupted, a restraing hand on Dugald's arm. "But someone knew of our being in Glen Tilt yon day, the troopers did not happen there by chance."

Feeling weak at the knees, Iain endevoured to lean nonchalantly against the standing stone. "In this you are right, Fergus. Though I fear many knew of your intended lifting." He put as much concern into his voice as his fear would allow. "Quoich too, has his spies, see you. It is just as I have been saying, Quoich knows of the MacLaren's visits to Gleidh, and has set a watch there, this I found out from the man himself. So, how come he by that information, think you? There are more eyes and ears than mine in yon man's employ."

"Quoich is after knowing Andrew visits Gleidh?" Dugald exploded. "and him..,." He stammered to a halt at Fergus's angry glare of warning.

"It is good you are after telling us of this..MacK...Iain." Fergus cleared his throat ridding it of what he had to say to this man he neither liked or trusted. "I will inform the MacLaren himself upon our return, of how it was yourself who gave the warning, of which I am sure he will be truly grateful," he assured the man. There it was out. Fergus spat on the ground at his feet, ashamed at the necessity of having to flatter such a loathsome individual. "...Now to other business....." And he spat again.

The big man started, and Ian, listened while thinking, at least they could not say he had not warned them. So in this way he had protected himself from both masters.

"Oh MacLaren, I am gladdened to see you here in Gleidh!" Neil refrained from adding 'well' at the cateran's skeletal appearance.

"And I you, Neil," was Andrew's honest reply. "for if the noble lady will forgive my rudeness, it is you I am after seeking rather than she, this visit."

Isobella frowned in mock annoyance. "Come sir, that was poorly said. I no longer attract you so?"

Sitting at the tableAndrew found it hard to match her good humour, and scarcely able to refrain himself at the sight of the supper, though not rich, it was to him a feast.

"If you will but allow me to explain my disparaging remarks," Andrew countered through a mouth crammed with food and ignoring the looks of shock at his ill manners. "You may not find me so churlish."

Here he commenced to inform them of the sad and disastrous events since last they met, and as both parties sat lost in their own thoughts, concluded. "So as you see, it is you, Neil whom I must turn to at this time. I need meal for my folk and soon. Secondly, you must help me find the murderers McMahon and Hamilton."

Neil Stewart let out a long low whistle. "Tall orders, Andrew, my friend, both will take time and siller, I fear."

"Siller I have in plenty. Time I have not," Andrew answered impatiently. "There are still folks dying in the *daingneachd*, Neil, even as I sit here filling my belly."

Angrily, Andrew threw two rings upon the table, for he had gambled everything on the Stewart's help, having learned that the man would be here in Gleidh. "One, is for the beasts I require forthwith. The second, for expenses incurred in your inquiries as to the whereabouts of the Irishman and his Lowland friend. It is to *Dun Eideann* I believe them to be, though this is for you to find out."

Lifting the rings Neil examined them closely. "It is not for me to inquire of a gentleman how he came by these." He glanced up at Andrew, awaiting his answer.

"In the same way I came by the one the lady wears...or should be wearing, though I do not see it on her finger," Andrew replied accusingly.

Blushing, Isobella hid the offending hand. "Times remain over hard here in the glen, Andrew despite your welcome services yon winter.....I sold the ring. What good is a shining stone when bairns starve, an experience of which you are well aquatinted I am after thinking," she added with some severity.

"I crave your pardon, Isobella, I spoke out of turn," Andrew dropped his eyes to the table. "I must see if it can be replaced. Now what think you, Neil, are both my orders still as tall?" he asked lifting his eyes to stare at Neil.

Arrangements made, Neil Stewart, left Gleidh early next morning with the date set to meet the cateran with as much meal and gear as one of the rings would purchase, and if possible any news gleaned of the men Andrew so urgently sought.

That same night, despite his longing for the lady, unable to fulfill his needs, Andrew lay back staring dejectedly at the ceiling.

"There is another on your mind this night, Andrew MacLaren." Isobella spoke out of the darkness beside him.

"I lack the strength after these long winter months without victuals," Andrew offered, out of shame and frustration.

"The lack of strength lies not in your loins my bonnie man, but in your mind. Think you, as a woman I do not know when you have another in your thoughts?"

Andrew raised himself on to an elbow. "It is true lass, though I have need of you...wanted you from that first night, and could not get you out of my every thought, all the while I loved Una, and did not know it....and now she is gone."

Isobella rested her cheek on Andrew's bare chest. "I cannot command you to forget her my love, though I can help, even before we are in our bonnie house."

Aye, Andrew thought, will this house also be one to be held in the imagination only?

"It is over much Isobella, and doubly appreciated! " Andrew enthused, studying the laden garron. "I will send back the beast when I see Neil again."

"There is no need, old Hamish here, nears his end, though he deserves better than your cooking pot, Andrew," the woman jested fondling the animal's ear.

"I promise you Isobella, he will end his days in healthy retirement," Andrew laughed.
He cast a look round for the dwarf. "However, it is already late and the *troich* and I must take our leave, if however reluctantly."

"Your friend has already done so." Isobella pointed up the brae where the tiny man stood by Lachlan's side. "Your companion dislikes me, Andrew I fear. Though I swear I have given him no cause."

"It is his way," Andrew assured her. "He feels his ill features more in the presence of the fairer sex, though he is never reluctant to follow me here, even if it is only to see his big friend." Then with an apologetic chuckle. "Besides, Isobella, there are times when no one knows what goes on within yon great head of his." Andrew drew the protesting woman to him. "Enough of the *troich*. Come here," he commanded, kissing her full on the mouth.

"Have a care Andrew MacLaren, there are others who may not find the sight so seemly," the lady warned, catching a glimpse of Helen the maid quickly hiding behind the slightly open scullery door.

"Then perhaps we should return indoors and complete that which last night I could not," Andrew teased.

"Away with you man. Have you forgotten how late you said was the hour? Where now is your impatience to be gone?" Isobella scolded, turning for the door.

Toying with the garron's bridle, Andrew grinned. "'Till we meet again Lady Isobella Grant of Gleidh." He bowed in mock solemnity, and grinning still, set off with the garron to meet the dwarf.

By midday the two men were half way to the dwarf's bothan where they intended biding the night, when walking through a narrow gully, the dwarf suddenly halting, drew his claymore.

Instantly responding to the tiny man's unerring instincts, Andrew dragged the garron around, in the same instant that both sides of the gully erupted with rushing men. Letting go of the frightened animal, Andrew fled back the way he had come, the dwarf at his heels, both men running, gasping for breath until coming upon a space on the gullyside free of their attackers, the friends ran as fast as their feet would take them, with a dozen or so of MacSorley's men at their heels.

Fighting to catch his breath, Andrew was the first to almost reach the top, while further down the hill the first of Quich's men were almost upon the dwarf. Drawing his pistols and with what breath he had left Andrew turned back upon his opponents, taking the chasing men by surprise, and mortally wounding two from his shots, the dwarf cutting down another from his great claymore, before they were off again.

Through the folds of the hills they ran, the dwarf now well behind, Andrew searching for a place to hide. Suddenly the incline was before him and he found himself scrambling and clawing at the whin in indecent haste, the tortured body of MacVie torn and bleeding as the horsemen ripped it apart swimming before his eyes. He urged himself on, determined that MacSorley would not capture him, even should it mean saving the last shot for himself.

At last upon reaching the top, Andrew threw himself down behind a rock to find all beneath him, quiet, empty. Perhaps his pursuers were in full cry in another direction, after the dwarf?

But where was the tiny man? Now he felt ashamed at having been too afraid to look back.

Even as the thought left his brain, the dwarf burst into view, his short tree stumps of legs pumping, his gigantic head rolling from side to side in near exhaustion, where at the sight of so steep an incline before him, still gasping for breath turned to face the foe, claymore at the ready.

Above, Andrew worked on reloading his pistols as Quoich's men fell upon the solitary figure. Not that he need go to the *troich's* aid, for none knew he was there. Instead, he could be away while the tiny man kept them occupied below.

Yet, even in his cowardice the thought of deserting his friend was repugnant to him. Was not this the man who had saved most of their lives at one time or another? The same man who had found them meat when no other could. No, MacSorley you shall not have the *troich*, Andrew vowed.

As a man attempted to get behind the dwarf, Andrew fired. The man fell, and in that briefest of time it took for his adversaries to look in Andrew's direction the tiny man was away, running in the opposite direction from the slope.

For a moment Andrew believed the foe would split up, some to follow him, others to chase the dwarf, instead all followed after the tiny man. Was it, he thought that they saw their task the easier by catching the *troich*, unaware that should they capture him they could not make him tell where the *daingneachd* was? Yet he could not let them take the man...his friend.

Once again his pistols fully loaded, Andrew started after the dwarf's pursuers, and when in range of the rearmost, fired, causing them to turn and chase after him. And to his horror as he swung away, found himself running along a cliff edge, terrified by the sight of the corrie floor far below.

With a gulp of realisation Andrew knew he was trapped. Cautiously his foe converged upon him from either side, forcing him back against the edge.

So this was the end...the bullet he so long knew would have to come, if he meant to deny the MacSorley his pleasure of seeing him slowly die. Still, his cowardice rather than his will to live prevented him from raising a pistol to his head. He looked again at the drop below then at the men almost on him, and without another thought launched himself into space. If he was to die, then at least this way would be quick and clean. And then he was crashing and bouncing, turning and twisting, to end in a final thud in earth and whin below.

For a moment Andrew lay there unable to bring himself to move, in fear of how badly hurt he may be. God that he could move at all, if not, Quoich would have him at his mercy, to do even more evil things to him.

Cursing the stupidity of his decision, Andrew tried very gently to move one limb after another, and blessed his Maker when none appeared to be broken. He ached all over, but the worse pain was in his thigh from where he had landed on the boulder.

From where he lay at the foot of the corrie he could not see the cliff top, and judged this being so, his adversaries in turn could not see him, although, he reckoned it would only be a matter of time before they made their way down by some easier route than he himself had taken, to verify his fate. Therefore, he must make a move, or try to do so. He must not grumble, for it was a miracle he was alive at all.

Staggering to his feet Andrew was surprised to find he had not fallen all the way to the bottom, the reason perhaps for his survival. And the cliff overhang having shielded him from above, he hoped he could make his way along the scree unseen until he found an easier way to the foot.

A little way further along the scree, the cliff overhang ended. He looked up and saw how lucky he had been. Now he must find the correct way home, for he was truly lost. Nor must he encounter the MacSorleys who would no doubt come to investigate his end by him heading in the wrong direction. So thinking, Andrew kept on going.

Andrew was sure he would never rise again for every bone and muscle in his body felt broken or torn. Nor had being hunched up in this niche overnight helped. So now that it was light, he must be on his way again. He tried to rise but fell back unable to clutch the rock with his swollen fingers. His face too, felt the size of the *troich's*; where ever that man may be. He tried to rise again and this time succeeded in getting to a standing position.

A little beneath him a burn gurgled and he staggered to it, stumbling and tripping until gingerly kneeling to slake his thirst and splash the icy water on his burning face, convinced that somehow it helped relieve his pain.

Andrew had no idea where he was, but believing he was well away from the *troich's* bothan, started in what he thought to be the right direction.

How long he walked he did not know, but eventually unable to go on, he gently lowered himself down behind a rock to rest and contemplate.

He looked up at the gathering clouds. It would rain soon. Had his friend escaped, was his next thought.

That there was no familiar land mark worried him, this and the fact that his rests well outweighed his steps. Yet, though he grew steadily weaker he felt no hunger.

He heard a noise and drew his pistol. Had MacSorleys men found him? He peered around the side of his rock. A deer trotted past. Oh had it been on some other occassion!

At least he had not yet been discovered by yon evil man or his breed. He stifled a moan of pain and struggled to his feet. He must keep moving, even if only to prevent himself from stiffening. Yet for how long could he go on in this condition? He wiped the blood from his torn knee with the hem of his kilt. If only he knew his whereabouts. He gave a cough, and winced at the pain his old wound from the MacIntosh still gave him, even after this time. Worse, each winter too, he thought, levering himself up over a heather banking.

It was eventually towards evening that Andrew first sighted the gray mountains of home. Now hungry, and still in pain, Andrew staggered and stumbled around an outcrop of rock, the sudden illusion of, Fergus MacAlister bounding towards him having him pass a hand across his eyes and pray that it should be so.

"It is a mercy Andrew. We all feared you dead, the way the *troich* has been wailing these past hours!" the illusion called out.

Andrew leaned weakly against the rock. "It is yourself Fergus. Man, I am happy to see you," he coughed, clutching his ribs. "The *troich,* he is safe? That is music to my ears. We were almost taken by the MacSorleys, shortly after leaving Gleidh, and found ourselves separated in the chase. I did not know whether he had survived."

"Survived he has. Around midday it was, he arrived home and leading a garron which like yourself has seen better days!" Fergus chortled, glad to see all that Andrew was not as bad as he had feared ,by the dwarf's lamenting.

"The garron as well!" Andrew exclaimed in astonishment. "How he has come to recover that animal I cannot myself imagine."

"Best you ask him yourself, for the rest of us could never understand the man at the best of times." Fergus put an arm under Andrew's. "Come man, you look a bonnie sight, and in need of some attention, I am after thinking. You must let Una...", he stopped. "I will have the wife take at look at that dunt on your head," he corrected himself. "Then again, maybe it is a bite and a sup you are in more need of," the giant suggested, helping Andrew along. "Put your weight on me. We are not far from home and you can thank that wee man for pointing me in this direction, though Lord alone knows how he himself knew."

Once again both men were left to marvel at the tiny man's supernatural qualities.

"Will this suffice, Andrew?" Neil Stewart threw an arm at the column of packed garrons at his mounted back.

"Aye it will Neil...and more, and so soon, see you. It will help save many a life are my thoughts. Have you encountered much trouble on your way?" Andrew's words were rushed.

The rider straightened proudly in his saddle. "None that Stewarts cannot best."

Neil ran a jaundiced eye over Andrew's tiny company, suggesting not a little scornfully. "The Stewarts best see you further on your way, for there's many a greedy man's larder will not long lie empty should they see all that stands between them are those that are at your back."

"These caterans of mine will do me very well sir!" Andrew retorted reproachfully, the inference not having gone astray.

Momentarily stunned by the MacLaren's obvious resentment at what he saw as an insult to his band, Neil was quick to make amends. "I mean no slight on their prowess Andrew, it is their numbers, or lack of them that makes me speak thus. I should not be wishing to see you lose all of this now, so close to home."

"Then I should welcome you and your Stewarts a bit further, Neil, if this is the case," Andrew replied, a little less curtly.

Neil dismounted to walk beside the MacLaren. "I have other news which you will want to hear. I have made inquiries in *Dun Eideann*, and though it is early days, I am certain I will bring you news to your liking, when next we meet."

"You believe the rogues to be in the Maiden City?" Andrew asked eagerly, slapping a passing garron, the unintentional slight all but forgotten.

"In a way. Should I learn more, how may I relay this to you without you traipsing all the long road to Gleidh? Though I surmise," Neil gave Andrew a knowing look, "that it is only the road back you find overlong."

Andrew ignored the innuendo. "I will draw you a map showing you how you may reach the place known as the standing stone," he answered simply.

"Then it is done. This I shall do." Neil looked back at the long line of garrons. "We shall bide another mile or so, then we must turn back before dark."

"That will suffice well enough, I am after thinking. Even we caterans will manage on our own, see you, Neil." Andrew allowed the Stewart time to digest the barb, then with a chuckle, slapped his friend upon the back.

Standing by an outcrop of rock, Johnny MacKellar, pulled down his bonnet against a sudden gust of wind, and nodded in the direction of the receding shapes of the Stewart clansmen far below. "I heard you speak earlier to the Stewart of the standing stone, why is this Andrew, when we are so close to home? Is it you do not trust the lady's cousin?"

Andrew followed his friend's stare to the glen below, the Stewart clansmen now almost invisible in the fading light. "It is in our interest that Stewart believes we bide closer to the standing stone than here. I do not mistrust Neil himself, Johnny, but I know none at his back, should he tell them of our intended meeting."

"I take your meaning Andrew, and if in this you are content, so it is with me."

Johnny surveyed the swiftly scudding clouds darkening the glen below, the last of the retreating Stewarts now invisible. "Laying this aside, how come we by such wealth, Andrew, surely the lady Grant is over generous with her favours?" Johnny turned to run an eye over the milling cattle and burdened garrons.

"That!" Andrew answered flatly. "Is why I would like a word in the ear of Duncan and yourself."

Puzzled, Johnny followed his chief down the line of straggling beasts until they came upon the Cameron who had watched their approach. That man gesturing with a flick of his hand, "How will eight...no six, since two choose to lord it over the likes of myself, strive to drive this mass of reluctant meat and horse, up wild Monadliath, will you be after telling me?" Duncan chided, pretending to be annoyed by heir lack of help and succeeding.

As Johnny rolled his eyes heavenward, Andrew commanded. "First a word in your ears, for I fear I owe you both an explanation for this day's work."

Moving out of the way of the straggling herd, Andrew began. "When first you showed me the second exit from the *daingneachd* yon day, you will mind, Johnny, I lost one of my pistols and sought to retrieve it from out of one of those dismal caverns?" Perplexed both men stood silent, allowing their chief to continue. "I found a leather bag with siller and a pouch with two rings set in stones." When neither spoke or corrected him, Andrew went on. "I thought at first they belonged to either of you, and since there was no complaint when they went astray, I stood convinced they belonged to the MacIntosh."

Again the listeners held their counsel. "One of these rings I gave to Neil Stewart, the result of which you see before you. The second, that he might find the Irishman and the Lowlander." Andrew shifted one of the pistols in his belt to give the men time to reply. Now he was convinced of the complete ignorance of both men, not to mention more than a little ashamed of the lies he had told, for it was not his intention of informing them of his having given the fair Isobella Grant another two jeweled rings.

It was Johnny who spoke first. "For myself, I know nothing of the siller or the rings you mention, nor do I believe does Duncan, though he can speak well enough for himself," the man answered, glancing at his friend the Cameron.

Duncan nodded, answering in turn. "It is as Johnny says, I know nothing of this matter. The MacIntosh was ever deep, and how he came by such things I know not. Still, it is pleasing that some good has resulted from this, and it is commendable that you left nothing for yourself, Andrew." Duncan hitched his targe more firmly on his shoulder." But do not let us stand here gossiping like three old hen wives, we have work to do." Impatiently he swung towards the herd taking Johnny with him. Leaving Andrew to stand and stare at their receding backs, acutely aware of neither having bothered to inquire the amount of siller or the value of the rings, or why he had not confided in them sooner.

At a loss for words, Andrew strode after his two companions.

Chapter 15

It was high summer again. Andrew marvelled at how quickly time had flown since his first coming to his new home. Now he barely remembered ever having been a crofter at all, so much having happened to affect his life, for better or ill.

He was still not fully over the loss of Una, and in fact had only once visited the lady in Glen Moriston since his encounter with the MacSorleys.

Andrew let his eyes roam over the company resting on the edge of the hill. The 'lifting' had been a success despite their lack of numbers, and now they must away before the Moray countryside was raised in alarm against them.

Chewing a blade of grass, Andrew reflected on the amount of work to be done before another winter set in. At least there was one consolation, they had an abundance of meal and cattle to see them through the worst of winters, that was God willing, Quoich did not discover their whereabouts.

As a precaution he had been unwilling to sanction any man joining them who had lived in MacSorley country. The result had been an increase of two only to their numbers, and these, brothers from Athol.

There also had been the business of the second stronghold to consider. This had necessitated Johnny's absence on numerous occasions, and when he had done so had taken with him one or two of their numbers, thus leaving the remainder more hard pressed.

He would have completely abandoned the idea of a second stronghold at this juncture, had he not been fully convinced of its importance against the day the present stronghold might be discovered. Not for himself, but mainly for the women and bairns, who, if there was no second sanctuary to turn to, would surely perish.

Putting these problems behind him for the moment he struggled to his feet, calling out to the half sleeping men that it was time to be on their way as there was still far to travel , when he heard the sound of screaming , the sound coming from the ridge at their backs.

"What noise is this Johnny, think you?" Andrew cried out to his friend.

"It is the sound of women in distress I would be saying Andrew!" The big man already starting to scramble up the slope, with the rest of the company close behind.

On reaching the top, the caterans looked down on the scene below, where a dozen or so clansmen were in hot pursuit of four or five women and bairns, who in turn were thrashing away at driving milch cows before them, while four of their own kinsmen ran to intercept the pursuers.

"There has been another lifting to our own, I am after thinking," the big MacAlister extemporized.

"You are wrong there, Fergus," Duncan shot back. "What decent man would solicit the help of women and bairns in a 'lifting'? No my friend, here is nothing more than the strong taking from the weak."

"Then let us put it to rights!" Fergus exclaimed, drawing his sword and looking at Andrew for approval.

"That we shall, Fergus, but hold awhile," Andrew cautioned. "Johnny! Take Sim, both Rattrays and the *troich* and get behind yon clansmen. Hurry, for our friends are sorely pressed," he commanded, drawing his pistols.

In no time, his command obeyed, Andrew gave the signal to attack, with the giant to the fore yelling and bounding down the hillside, sword waving, targe thrust forward, anxious to be at their throats.

Those of the foe who had worked to get behind the four struggling men, now swung to face this new and unexpected challenge, and realising they had little to fear from so small a number confidently launched themselves at the would be rescuers, three alone converging on this unruly giant of a man. Andrew drawing to a halt to shoot the nearest of Fergus assailants through the head, leaving the MacAlister to deal with the remaining two, at the same time as the rest of the caterans attacked from the rear.

Now that the tide had turned, the enemy clansmen scattered in all directions, the *troich*, unmercifully putting an end to one lying wounded.

"And who have we to thank for our lives?" An out of breath man asked Andrew, a curious eye on the dwarf.

"My name is Andrew MacLaren, and I suspect, like myself you are also a landless man, if I am not mistaken?"

215

"You judge aright my friend. There is over much proud fighting and stupidity in *Cataibh* in these sad times, and we amongst its victims." The man sheathed his word. "I myself am Alasdair Federith, and yonder with the wee wound, is Peter my brother. The two others which your timely arrival helped save, is my wife's cousin, Calum Gunn, and his son, Rory. The rest are our wives and bairns."

Quickly naming his own party, Andrew commented, "We ourselves are headed south, and in some haste if you take my meaning. Therefore, further introductions can wait, except to say the *troich* there, is a deaf mute, should you be thinking to talk to him and believe when he does not answer that he has taken a dislike to you and yours."

While Alasdair smiled his understanding, Andrew hurried on. "We, as you, are landless caterans, and I their *ceann cinnidh*. Speak amongst yourself...but be quick should you wish to join our numbers." Andrew tucked the pistols back into his belt, conscious of the caterans relieving the dead of whatever valuables they possessed. "Our single offer is your own fireside, and in return ask that you share in our daily tasks. Should you decide otherwise, no grudge is borne and may God go with you."

Having spoken his mind Andrew was in the act of moving away when the Federith, spoke. "It needs no consultation my friend, we have no choice, except to lose what little we have to the next bold clansmen who see our sorry state. No, if you find us acceptable, we shall gladly follow on."

"Then tell the others Alasdair Federith, and we shall be on our way," Andrew smiled warmly.

Duncan was on his way out of the defile when he met Andrew returning home. "I am glad to see you safety home again," was his greeting. "I was not in favour of your journeying to Glen Moriston alone in the first place, not since your last narrow escape. She must be worth the risk, see you."

Duncan looked around him and at the cliffs above. Surely there were plenty women here in the *daingneachd* who would be only too willing to satisfy his needs without him traipsing all the long road to Gleidh.

Though he had a fondness for the man, it would do them all no ill should he be taken by the MacSorely, for it was then, and only then would they feel entirely safe. Although Glen Tilt, was some time past, that man was never likely to forget his oath to catch the MacLaren nor the reason for losing his hand.

"In part, Duncan," Andrew assured him, "though I thought it best to leave the *troich* behind, for his presence would surely have alerted anyone but a blind man of my also being there.

No, I went alone and approached Gleidh by the head of the glen, that way it was safe enough, there ever being folk coming and going in yon place. Besides, I had another matter on my mind, for I had hoped that by this time Neil Stewart would have had word concerning yon two rogues, it now being months since last we heard. Isobella too has heard nothing from her cousin in as many weeks. This I also learned.

Later I journeyed to Kintail to see Kirsty and the bairn. Col is a fine wee lad. One to make a father proud," Andrew grinned at the recollection; trailing off at the thought of his own son, and the bairn by Una he was never destined to know. He swatted at a fly, and forced himself to sound cheerful. "What of here, Duncan? Is all well?"

"Och nothing much has happened at all, except the usual women's bickering." Duncan rubbed at his arm. "Dugald returned yesterday from the standing stone where Iain MacKinnon informed him of his master's to and froeing. Also, that Gleidh House is still under watch. But you would be knowing this yourself, or you would not be standing here, I am after thinking."

Andrew nodded his affirmation. Duncan wagged a finger. "You must not forget, MacKinnon is the man who first warned us of this, and has given us a goodly service."

"That he has, Duncan, and I must thank him when we meet, though I have never before met the man."

Duncan took another rub at his arm. "Mackinnon also told Dugald, yon fall you took when you arrived here swollen and bruised had the MacSorley thinking for a time you may be dead, unfortunately he has learned since then this is not so. It is a mystery how that man comes by such information." Duncan clicked his teeth.

"Aye. It is as you say, Duncan. Perhaps had he been fully convinced of my demise, his vigil would now be at an end."

"Aye, for it will never be, until one of you is no more," Duncan said solemnly.

Andrew shuddered. How many years would it take to end the vendetta? Knowing what Duncan had said was true ...until one or both of them were dead.

It was the middle of the night when Andrew awoke from an uneasy sleep. In the far corner of the room the dwarf snored incessantly. He turned on his side and drew the plaid around his ears, his hand falling on the empty space where Una had lain.

Was it this that had awakened him? Despite the *troich's* company the bothan remained cold and empty without her. Then why did thoughts of Isobella Grant, inevitably follow those of Una?

Eventually as before, Una's image blurred to that of Isobella and their last meeting.....

"The quaichs are bonnie, Andrew! I shall not ask how you came by them. Nevertheless at this rate we shall have our bonnie house in no time!" Isobella cried in admiration of the dwarf's treasures.

That evening Isobella sat up, letting the bedcovers slip from her bosom. "Neil, was after telling me a while back of a house this side of Stirling which he assures me would be to our liking," she purred softly in Andrew's ear. "If we can but find the siller."

Without moving his head Andrew fondled a breast. "And how many more silver quaichs will it take lass?" he asked sleepily through half closed eyes. He was tired and the walk to Gleidh grew longer each journey, as had the walk to the woods to pilfer the *troich's* treasure.

"Many more, *gaolach.* But not many more such rings I am after thinking."

"Then it will take time, my bonnie lass. It will take time," he yawned.

"Not over much time, Andrew, I am hoping. Neither of us grow any younger. I myself will be reaching my second score in a year or more, see you." Then teasingly. "Will you still love me when I am old and fat, think you?"

Andrew stifled a yawn. "That I already do, lass."

Pretending to be offended, Isobella pulled his ear, and buried her face in his.

Again Andrew dozed. This time his thoughts turned to Kirsty and his visit there.

It had been harvest time he remembered when passing his own croft, the corn golden ripe in the afternoon sun, and as usual when nearing his former home had halted to run a critical eye over the land, admitting however reluctantly that Calum MacKenzie, who occupied the croft since his evacuation knew his trade well. Though it still rankled at the labour he himself had lent to a land started as bog and mire.

With thoughts of what should have been done had he still lived there, he quickened his pace up the brown braeside to Kirsty's croft, hearing the song of the reapers when still some distance away. At length he gained the top, and sat down to watch the women below, stooping and rising in perfect unison to their song, each endeavouring not to be the one to cut the last sheaf of the ill omened *cailleach* which had they done, foretold of their dying an old maid.

The day's toil over he had walked home with Kirsty, young Col toddling between them. They like Gregor happy to see him again. Andrew recalled how after a time at home their talk had inevitably turned to the harvest, and later when Gregor had left to inspect the croft, the bairn safely tucked up in his cot, Kirsty had asked of him. "Is there no peace for you at all, Andrew MacLaren? This poor lass Una of whom you speak so dearly is gone, as is your Fiona, and nothing will bring either of them back. This Una, I see you still grieve for over much. Yet life must go on."

Kirsty had crossed to where he had sat by the window, and stood there , a glint of a tear in her eye , desperation in her voice, " My poor Andrew, you must make a life of your own, well away from the Monadliath. Suddenly, vehemently, "You are no cateran, Andrew MacLaren, it is a crofter you are my gentle man, and this you must be again."

It was then he had fallen asleep, or awakened, he never was quite sure.

Andrew rolled out of his heather bed, yawned himself into his *feileadh mor*, and mouthed a good morning to the *troich* breaking his fast by the fireside.

Outside he yawned and stretched again, crossing the arena as Dugald emerged from the bothan opposite.

"You are about, I see Dugald," he greeted the young man civilly.

"Only just, Andrew," Dugald answered sleepily. "I myself was about to taste Cathal MacAlister's bannocks. She bakes over many for that big husband of hers...or so she says."
Dugald gave a knowing wink.

"She mothers you well, Dugald. Is it not about time you sought a baker of bannocks for yourself? Is there none here who takes your fancy? Though I fear your choice is somewhat limited since the starving."

Dugald bowed his head to hide his blushes. "Aye there was ever one, but she is lost...to us both, *ceann cinnidh*"

So unexpected was Dugald's answer, Andrew could only stare at the man. Then recovering from his surprise, said piteously. "This I did not know Dugald." Yet it made sense now that it was shown to him, Una's age being more in keeping with Dugald than his own. "Then we both mourn her passing," he whispered.

Andrew broke the uneasy silence that followed this revelation, this time cheerfully. "Duncan tells me you will be after reaching your majority this year. Is this a fact?"

Sensitively, Dugald scratched the side of his neck. "It is, though the precise date is unknown to me."

"So you will be a man fully grown, and with it comes responsibility. This is why I have decided to send you northwards. Fergus has it from the messengers at the standing stone there is much to be gained therein from up yonder. You will take the Rattrays, Rob Sutherland, Federiths and both Gunns, who know the country well."

The command brought Dugald fully awake. "And Fergus ,will I not also have the big man?" he stammered, having scarcely been anywhere without the giant's comforting presence, except when journeying south with the Irishman, and it needed no telling what had resulted from that!

"No. We shall have need of the MacAlister. He will be away with Johnny and some others to the Cairngorms."

"You are telling me, I must lead without him?" Dugald blinked, unable to digest the enormity of his responsibility.

"Aye,that you must. Though I am ever sure you will lead just fine, Dugald, just fine."

Dugald watched his chief stride across the arena, his heart pounding at his good fortune. The very fact that none of the original band were numbered amongst his followers demonstrated the faith placed in him. Fully determined to fulfill this obligation of trust, Dugald swung away to the MacAlister bothan with an even greater appetite than when he had wakened that morning.

Facing the Stewart across the table in the self same inn where he had first met MacSorley of Quoich, Andrew battled to contain his excitement. "You have found them...both...man?" he exclaimed louder than intended.

As curious heads turned in their direction, Neil shrugged the insignificance of his news, though secretly delighted by the MacLaren's reaction. "'Tis true, both, Andrew my friend, and in *Dun Eideann* as you so rightly judged.

Davie Hamilton is the proud owner of a tavern in some back street there. As to the Irishman?" Neil threw up his hands. "It is hard to know what yon man is doing. Whatever it may be, he still keeps himself well acquainted with the Lowlander, both having enhanced their fortunes through the playing of the cartes, so I hear tell."

"So we must seek them out!" Andrew banged the table with his fist.

"Gently my friend," Neil cautioned, more than a little embarrassed by his friend's enthusiasm. "We will form a plan, less we lose one or both." Leaning back in his chair, Neil Stewart, studied his friend awhile, then leaning forward began to reveal his plans to the man.

Dugald emerged from out of the wildly cheering crowd, striding proudly to meet his chief, a wide jubilant grin encasing his youthful countenance.

With a wave of his hand he encompassed the bellowing cattle at his back. "Two score or more, *ceann cinnidh*! This after all 'raiders callop' has been met!"

"Well done young Dugald!" Andrew acknowledged him with a grin. "And how fares it with your band?"

"Rob Sutherland suffered a cut to his arm, though it will not take long in the healing."

Andrew shifted his look from Dugald to the entrance of the defile. "And besides cattle, what else have you gathered on your journey, Dugald?"

Dugald's smiled disappeared. "They came to our aid when we ourselves were chased after the 'lifting'," he hastened to explain.

Andrew furrowed his brows. "You brought them here?" The leader's eyes roamed over the seven wild looking men who had emerged from the defile. The first catching up a lass and snapping a kiss, then dropping her as he strode on, leaving the embarrassed victim to take to her heels amid peels of laughter from his own clansmen.

Dugald shuddered, and turned back to his chief. "Think you they will make trouble, Andrew? They fought well enough when seeing our plight. Besides, we are ever short of numbers are we not?" Dugald expounded enthusiastically, and hoping he had not made a mistake in bringing them here.

Silently, Andrew observed the approaching MacDonnels, wild unkempt men, armed to the hilt. It was men like these who still chilled him to the bone, freebooters who had never turned a spade or tossed a sheaf. Andrew shook his head. "Only time will tell Dugald." He took a step forward, wrapping an arm around the young man, the strangers momentarily forgotten. "I have doubly good news for you my young friend. Firstly, we have found MacMahon and Hamilton!"

"Where!" Dugald cried excitedly breaking free of Andrew's hold and turning to face him.

"*Dun Eideann*!" Andrew witnessed the look of shear hatred in Dugald's eyes, which was quickly followed by a glint at the prospect of meeting them again. "But hold, there is a second news."

Andrew swung Dugald round by the shoulder and pointed down the stronghold to the fires already lit by the stones, the smell of roast and baking wafting in the evening breeze, filling their senses with sweet aroma. "'Tis in your honour, Dugald. Come, let us join the company!"

Later when all had eaten their fill, there was no trouble when a MacDonnel took a lass to dance to the fiddlers tune. In fact despite the amount of drink consumed, the newcomers were remarkably well behaved. Relieved by this, Andrew sought out old Ewen Finlay.

"Ah! There you are, Ewen I could not find you amongst the revellers. A word in your ear if you have a mind." Andrew drew the old man aside, sadly noting his old friend's deterioration since their last meeting. Now more stooped, unkempt, with ever a trickle of saliva at the corner of his mouth.

"You are not after seeking me out, and have me climb yon accursed cliff?" the ancient uttered despondently.

Andrew chuckled, sitting down beside the old man. "No, Ewen, you and yours have done very well in this. However, it is the business of the sentinels that I crave your counsel. Now that we are greater in numbers I would have you draw up a list so that each man can take his turn at the watch. However, there is some difficulty in this. Shortly some of us who saw 'the starving', will leave for *Dun Eideann*, and will leave the safety of our home in the hands of our new found friends." Andrew leaned closer to the old man, lowering his voice. "I do not want more than one MacDonnel to stand guard at any one given time, see you, Ewen."

"I take your meaning, *ceann cinnidh*."

Now that there was once again a purpose to his life the old man struggled to his feet, and throwing back his shoulders looked his chief straight in the eye, proudly declaring, "Rest assured, *ceann cinnidh* it will be done."

After having spoken to old Ewen, Andrew went to sit down beside Johnny MacKellar, pretending not to have noticed some of the revellers discarding to the dogs more than they themselves had eaten in a full week during 'the starving' as it was called by these same folk.

"The plan is set, Johnny, we shall leave for our capital in three days time. I fear your new *daingneachd* will have to wait our return."

"Have no fear on that score, the place can wait until hell itself freezes over so long as we catch yon evil pair." The venom in the man's voice startling Andrew.

Johnny sighed, nodding in the direction of the revellers. "And to think we lived on nothing better than water with some matter floating in it, which we would not now give to the dogs, and..." He pointed disgustedly, and spat. "Look at the likes of yon wasting....wasting." The man could not go on. "It is an affront to those ever absent."

223

"I understand your feelings, Johnny my friend, but do you also think it so wrong to have them live for today? Let us all enjoy ourselves while we may, for, who knows what tomorow may bring."

It was then the harmony was broken. At first there was only laughter which both leaders put down to high spirits, until gradually those around them began to steal furtive glances in their direction.

Catching one of the women glancing at him Andrew spiered, "What is amiss Mistress Donald, is it something Johnny and I are missing?"

"You have not seen?" the woman asked in surprise, throwing a hand in the direction of the stones. "It is the *troich* and yonder MacDonnel devils!"

In an instant both men were on their feet pushing through the crowd to where swords drawn, the MacDonnel leader stood facing Fergus, with Dugald between them failing to calm both men.

"What is happening here?" Andrew asked, the crowd standing aside to let him reach the front.

"This lout!" Fergus exploded. "This excuse of a man, who has the gall to cry himself MacDonnel insulted the *troich* , see you, Andrew! I was about to teach the rogue a lesson in manners this very minute."

"Do you not think we should let he who has been insulted be the teacher?" Andrew answered tongue in cheek.

Calming himself, and understanding his leader's meaning Fergus gave a chuckle, and drew aside as the dwarf himself appeared at a run, naked claymore in hand.

"Will you also be holding his sword for him, big man? Or do you hold him up instead?" the MacDonnel guffawed amongst uproarious laughter from his fellow clansmen, one of whom collapsed in a heap, holding his sides in exaggerated mirth.

"It is to be hoped the MacDonnels hold their weapons better than their drink," Fergus suggested above the laughter of the caterans.

"Enough! I will have an end to this!" Angrily, the challenger threw off his bonnet to reveal a long black mass of matted hair. "It gives me no pride to dispatch such as this!" He pointed his sword disdainfully at the dwarf. "Yet all should know, neither I, or my name will stand insulted!"

"How managed the *troich* in this MacDonnel, seeing as the wee man can neither hear nor speak?" Johnny MacKellar asked advancing on the speaker. "Perhaps you and yours sought to make sport of our friend? Or do MacDonnels choose their opponents by their lack of size, think you?"

All was silence then, even the drunken reveller, now miraculously sober, rose to his feet. Fergus restraining the dwarf who stood looking around him in silent wonder at what was going on, his hands clasped tightly around his weapon.

Andrew thought he had never witnessed so bizarre a scene, as the dwarf once free from Fergus's hold advanced on his opponent, the razor sharp claymore held out before him. The MacDonnel, a smirk on his face circling the tiny man he thought so easily to best.

With a shake of his head Andrew signalled to the dwarf what he must do. All around, the caterans laughing in expectation of what was to unfold.

"See Thomas, the *ceann cinnidh* tells the *troich* not to fight!" A MacDonnel cried jubilantly. "Just you be giving him a prick or two with your sword and the score will be settled. There is no point us offending these good folk, see you!"

"It is what I myself was after thinking, Rob. This I will just be doing,"the challenger shouted back. So saying, lunged at his tiny opponent who quickly taking a backward step to avoid the downward sweep of the weapon hit the MacDonnel midriff flat bladed, swiftly followed by a second blow to his protagonist's head with the hilt of his claymore, the doubled up MacDonnel sprawling unconscious on the ground.

An explosion of cheering from the caterans followed the dwarf's easy victory, while the bewildered kinsmen of the defeated Thomas gazed down at his prostrate body, then around them at the circle of caterans, Andrew to the fore.

"Now you will understand why I shook my head at the *troich*. I was telling him not to kill your kinsman that was all. Now, let us all forget this, and hasten back to the festivities!"

Reluctantly, Dugald walked to where Andrew stood, amid shouts of laughter from the good humoured caterans. "It is my doing, I should not have brought the MacDonnels here. I have failed your trust," Dugald mumbled despondently.

"That you did not, Dugald. Do not judge yourself so harshly. After this night's work, the MacDonnels will either bend the knee, or depart our company. The former I am after thinking, seeing as at present they have no other place to go. Though being bested by the shortest of us all will sorely hurt their pride, so you must advise them they have not been the first. And should they choose to bide, they must abide by our laws. This responsibility, Dugald lies with you."

Andrew looked to where the dwarf stood beaming up at his big friend the MacAlister. The *troich's* enormous head rolling from side to side in pride at what he had done, together with the slaps on the back received from the passing caterans.

Andrew looked back to Dugald. "Some of us leave shortly for *Dun Eideann,* you will remain here and see the *daingneachd* safe."

"Then I have not to have my revenge? After all was done to me I am to bide here, when all are gone?" Dugald pleaded, sorely vexed, and not a little angry.

"You will be avenged my young friend, never fear. Though I am sadly thinking, you attach little importance to you office? If so, then I must choose another."

Dugald's mounting anger at being excluded from those leaving for *Dun Eideann* suddenly lifted, as he came to realise the responsibility his chief had once again placed upon him. "You will leave me in sole charge after this night, never fearing your trust may be misplaced?" he hastened to know.

Andrew looked past the young man to the dispersing revellers, and to others not yet so disposed to give up the night, still dancing to the fiddlers tune. "Should you believe this is what I think, then it is for you to prove me wrong," he said simply. Adding with a grin. "What say you, Dugald Ferguson, on this your day of birth?"

Chapter 16

Against such a throng of people the coach inevitably drew to a halt, much to the delight, rather than the annoyance of its two occupants.

Holding a pose he believed to be in a fair imitation of those gentle born, Sean McMahon pretended disdain for those close enough to gape in by the windows. That the coach bore no escutcheon helped deepen the mystery, as those fortunate or unfortunate to be pressed against its sides argued adamantly that they alone knew the real identity of those within.

"I believe it is you, Davie who despite your rough attire, are taken for Lord Carnwarth!" The Irishman chuckled in delight at the whole affair, the coach jolting forward amid angry protests from Grassmarket inhabitants. "Last time we halted I was Marquis of something or another, now I am merely your travelling companion." He gave an exaggerated sigh. "How a man can fall from grace in so short a time is hard to bear."

At length the capital left behind, the two miscreants sat back to reflect upon the events which had found them thus.

"You are sure you have the right of it Davie, this high born gentleman, seeks to purchase
your ..."

"Humble establishment," Hamilton concluded. "However, should I have been mistaken, would we now be sitting here in a coach neither of us could dream of possessing in a lifetime?"

"Ah! There you have me Davie my friend. It is just that I can not believe our good fortune."

"*Our* good fortune? You are not equal partner in this, Sean. It is I who had the foresight to invest in yon *humble establishment*, whilst you were off squandering your ill gotten gains."

"Did I not help at the cartes? Was it not myself who won yon first wagers, enough to buy yon humble establishment? Och, it was ill fortune to lose what little I had on projects of my own," Sean moaned with a sly look at his friend.

"That as may be. Put it behind you now. Do you know this place?" Hamilton nodded in the direction of the mansion coming into view.

"Me! How should I be knowing of such a place if you know not, and you native born?" Sean postulated as the coach swung up the gravel driveway of the large house now some way distant from Edinburgh.

However, there was no time for a suitable reply before the coach came to a halt and the door flung open by a lively postillion.

"Well! After you, seeing as you believe yourself senior partner in this business," Sean mocked, waving his friend towards the open door.

Throwing his companion a withering look Hamilton stepped down from the coach following a manservant the short distance across the drive and into the great house, Sean at his heels, neither scarcely having time to glimpse the portraits and ancient armour lining the walls of the massive hall before being instantly greeted by their elegantly dressed host, standing in front of an enormous fireplace.

"Ah! It is Mister Hamilton, I do believe. And this is your witness, Mister....eh?" Their host looked from one to the other.

"McMahon, sur...your lordship. Sean MacMahon, to be precise, if you please," the Irishman replied with a flourishing bow.

"Ah ! Yes!" their host acknowledged, motioning them to follow him into an adjoining room which matched that of the great hall itself for spendour. "Come my friends, sit you here,"their host bid them to be seated while he himself made his way behind a small but exquisite oaken desk. "A glass of claret perhaps ? Then to business."

Without waiting an acknowledgment their host poured out two generous measures of wine for his guests, and one for himself. "It is a wine I am certain you will both find to your liking." He raised his glass in salute. "To a successful conclusion to our business, gentlemen."

The toast returned, Hamilton and McMahon sat back to study their host with interest.

Smiling, the man sat down. "Doubtless you are asking yourselves, why all this secrecy? Well it is a simple matter to explain. My patrician, for reasons best known to himself, wishes to purchase your tavern, Mister Hamilton. Of course this you already have surmised." He went on at Hamilton's nod. "I have taken the liberty at my master's request of having a paper drawn up, which will transfer your establishment to his name."

228

The man laid out the document in front of the Lowlander. "You will see, the amount to be generous in the extreme. However, as part of the transaction, you are obliged on no account to reveal the identity of Ubi Supra."

"And who might this fine gentleman Ubi Supra be, may I ask," McMahon asked wrinkling his brows.

Unable to suppress a smile, their host explained. "It means that on no account will you divuldge the above named. Is that quite clear?"

"So we are to be paid for keeping our mouths shut, is this what you are saying?" McMahon shot out. "What kind of an establishment does this Ubi...person mean to have, plainly one that does not want his peers to know about. One of ill repute, perhaps?"

Sensing trouble from this pugnacious little man, their host sat back steepling his fingers.

"The why and wherefore are no concern of yours should your friend here decide to accept the sum offered," he said, with a hint of impatience in his voice.

The Irishman sipped at his glass, and gazed steadily at his Lowland friend, similar thoughts coursing through their minds.

"It is a tidy sum, Davie, but since there is more here than meets the eye, there is nothing to lose by asking for a wee bit more," McMahon advocated in the Gaelic, smiling at the man behind the desk who appeared in ignorance of the suggestion.

"We must not be over greedy, Sean, or we might lose all," Davie cautioned with difficulty in the same tongue.

"Gentlemen, I sense there is some consternation over the sum agreed. Is this so?"
Their host confronted each in turn through raised brows. "If in fact the sum appears to be inadequate, then I fear my patrician will seek alternative premises, as per his instructions to me should such a situation arise. Nevertheless, let me charge your glasses whilst you reconsider the proposition."

"The sum is sufficient," Davie Hamilton concurred, daring the Irishman to contradict, while his host refilled his glass.

"Then it is settled." The man rose clapping his hands together in finality. "Now it lacks nothing more than your signatures to conclude our business," he said sliding the document across the desk top to Hamilton.

With the document signed and witnessed by the still protesting McMahon, their host rounded the desk. "I will have the coin brought to you forthwith. Now if you will allow me a few minutes in its arranging, I will return with the least possible delay." He bowed slightly, offering them a reassuring smile. "While I do so, please help yourself to another glass of wine."

The door had hardly closed before the Irishman was on his feet, crossing the floor to stand with his back to the hearth. "You are daft Davie Hamilton. Do you not sense something amiss when you are offered such a sum in coin? This great lord, whoever he may be, has no liking to be known as owner of your *humble* establishment. Whatever sum we may have mentioned would never have been missed by the likes of yon!" Sean cried angrily, encompassing the room with a hand, at the rich tapestries and book lined shelves.

For a moment the greedy man's eyes alighted on the neatly cut lawn beyond, before returning to stare malignantly at Hamilton. "There is more here in this one room than we could ever hope to own in a lifetime!" he continued to remonstrate. "What would a few more pounds Scots, mean to this lord, think you?"

"Sit yourself down, man," Davie commanded sternly, growing increasingly impatient with his friend, and wishing for nothing more than to be free of this place with a bag full of siller. "You are in fear of wearing yourself out man. Have I not signed the damned thing, and you witness to it? We are rich man! Rich! Would you spoil it all now for the sake of your greed?"

At Hamilton's resolve to ask for nothing more, Sean shrugged his shoulders in resignation.

"Well if this is to be the case, let us at least help ourselves to yon man's wine."

Sean crossed to the desk. Pouring out a measure of wine for himself and Davie he lifted the glass to his lips, hearing the Lowlander say with some conviction as he sipped, "It is better wine than I could ever hope to sell in my place, Sean."

"Aye Davie, a wee bit more will slide down bonnily," Sean acknowlwdged refilling both their glasses with a flourish

"Mind you do not spill it on the man's bonnie desk, Sean," his friend warned at the red wine running down the side of the Irishman's glass.

"I will buy him another to replace it, should it spoil the piece," Sean cackled surveying his friend through the bottom of his upturned glass. "Smooth and relaxing, I am after thinking myself, Davie."

Suddenly the figure of his friend blurred. Alarmed, Sean studied his now empty glass. "A wee bit too much so," he slurred, groping at the desk for support. The indistinct figure of Hamilton slouched in his chair.

Sean slid to the floor, a cheek pressed against the polished wood, while above him through a haze of mist the never ending figure of his host frowned down at him from a great height. Then all turned to darkness.

When next Sean awoke it was to the uneven jolting of their former transport. Fighting against his bonds he struggled to a sitting position and in the dimness of the coach, made out the postrate figure of Davie Hamilton on the seat opposite, spewing vomit on the floor.

Choking back a bout of nausea he looked away, casting his eyes out of the window, rapidly opening and closing them until the twin landscapes merged into one in the encroaching darkness.

"Are you awake, Davie." he asked stealing a glance at his friend, the smell of vomit strong in his nostrils. "I am after thinking we are in a bonnie mess, whatever the cause."

Davie tried to sit upright. Failing, he leaned against the side of the coach. "We have been duped, Sean. But why?" he grimaced as his head bumped against the jolting of the coach. "Does a stinking wee tavern mean so much to yon rich lords that they must steal from the likes of us, when the price of its purchase would never have been missed?" He belched again, sending a spray of vomit down his front. "If ever I lay my hands on those responsible!"

"You might have your wish fulfilled sooner than you think, Davie, for I fear we are drawing to a halt," Sean interrupted, peering out.

No sooner was this said than the coach ground to a halt and the door thrown open to reveal the figure of Neil Stewart, their former host, who stood there, pistol drawn.

"You will both kindly step down if you please," Neil requested in the Gaelic.

"*DIA!* Then the ploy does not lie in *Dunn Eideann!*" McMahon exclaimed, a hint of apprehension in his voice, and recovering sufficiently, to taunt." And you are after having the tongue yourself.

Tut! Tut! my Highland friend, is there no honour amongst us gentlemen?!

"Amongst gentlemen, yes..." Neil pulled the agitator from the coach, a henchman doing likewise to Hamilton.

"We have slept well, Davie. I fear we have travelled far, for I wager I can smell the heather." The Irishman attempted to sound cheerful, as Neil dragged him into a small copse.

"I am not well," Sean heard his friend moan through another bout of vomiting at his back. "That I had a head as thick as yours. Where are we, and why?"

"The why and wherefore will be yours for the knowing and in a short time," Neil answered, pushing the Irishman forward.

Hamilton vomited again and slipped on the wet grass, but somehow succeded in retaining his feet but not his composure as Andrew MacLaren followed by five caterans emerged from out of the trees.

Letting out a cry the Lowlander writhed at his bonds in an apoplexy of fear, in an attempt to retreat as far as he was able from the advancing men.

"Well well McMahon! Hamilton! We meet again!" Andrew MacLaren hissed at the struggling men. "That we should live to see this day!"

"It was ill fortune your lordship!" Sean wailed. "We ourselves were attacked yon side of Stirling. A score or more there were of them. Col Fraser, and poor Dugald, both cut down, the laddie dying in my arms, and I having to leave him there without Christian burial, to save my own worthless soul!" McMahon lamented.

Sean wailed on at the impassive faces of the caterans . "Are you not after seeing what this means?" he pleaded. "With Col and Dugald gone and us fleeing for our lives there was no way we could find our own way back to the *daingneachd*! And as yon wild savages who attacked us took all we had...all you poor folk had entrusted to us, there was nothing left to bargain with, so we bided in *Dun Eideann*, begging for a bite and a sup."

"How came you by the tavern?" This sharply from Johnny MacKellar.

"'Twas a quirk of fate, Johnny, we gambled at the cartes with what little we could barter of our own goods, and won enough to buy yon place. Though it was ever our intentions to sell it and come and try and seek you out when the winter was done."

The blow took everyone by surprise, hurling the wailing man against his captor. "You will not stand there and insult me and mine, Irishman!" Duncan Cameron seethed vehemently. "Do you take us all for fools to be taken in by your tale of lies?"

Startled by the action of this usually placid man, McMahon bowed his head. "It is the truth, I am after telling you. It happened as I said."

"'Tis a pity lying is a sin, MacMahon, for it is sweet to the taste, but it will not help you in this pass." Duncan choked.

"In this you are right, Duncan" Andrew agreed. "Fergus! Bring the garrons if you will!"

"You will not let them murder us your lordship!" Sean shouted out in desperation.

"No, McMahon, I will not let anyone of my own harm either of you. This I promise."

Hamilton at last found his voice. "Then why the garrons MacLaren ? If you mean to dispatch us at all, why not here? Why bother to drag us all the way back to your wild mountains?"

Helped upon a garron Sean cried out to his friend, "Hush Davie, did you not hear the man say he would not let any of his own harm us?"

Ignoring the wailing Sean, Andrew looked up at Hamilton mounted on a second garron.

"There are others beside ourselves you must face. Should your friend's story be true, you shall find us most forgiving. If not..."

Standing beside Andrew, watching the condemned men depart, Neil Stewart, held up a piece of paper. "Now that it is done, what must I do with this?"

Andrew drew in a deep breath. It had been Neil's plan that they use his kinsman's house for the subterfuge, and now that it had succeeded he wanted nothing more. He looked up at the evening sky, then back at the Stewart. "You have gained yourself a tavern my friend. That the name borne on the deed is your own, it follows therefore, that you must be the new owner."

"I cannot accept this man, knowing full well how it was first purchased!" Neil stammered through injured pride.

"Then sell the damned place, Neil, and then you and Isobella can share the proceeds, and should this not sit well with your conscience, then leave a third share for me. Perhaps it will help towards the house Isobella is ever on about that I should purchase each time we meet."

Andrew took a step away. "For I am at a loss to know what other way we can dispose of yon tavern. I well know no cateran will touch this blood money."

Andrew did not know whether it was the mention of the house, or his suggestion to be rid of the tavern, which startled Neil, only that the man stammered. "If this is what pleases you, Andrew, it will be done." Then quietly. "Should you have no other need of my services, I will away, so that I may not strain family connections too fully."

"Aye Neil. Then away. And my thanks...all our thanks go with you, to you and yours, for this days work." Andrew shook the outstretched hand. "Till we meet again Neil Stewart."

The caterans travelled by little known paths, through high corries and passes avoiding all, saying little, until at last they came to the *daingneachd.*

Emerging out of the defile and into the ranks of silently watching people, Hamilton bowed his head in shame, while in contrast McMahon did his best to appear cheerful by greeting those he knew amongst the crowd, both helped to dismount and untied at Andrew's command.

Mairi MacColl pushed through the crowd to where Andrew stood. "You will take a bite and sup, Andrew? As for yon pair they look faint with hunger? Or fear is it?" she said referring to the shivering prisoners.

"A measure of both, I am after thinking, Mairi, for no bite has passed their lips this side of Stirling. So they will be knowing a little of what it was like for some of us in the starving."

"But that must have been days ago, man!" Mairi cried in horror. "The clothes they wear will chill them to the bone, in especial here, where the wind never seems to cease." Then a little quieter, softer, as if justifying Andrew's actions, "It is only fitting that they should reap what they have sown. I mind fine how closely folk would watch when I shared the meal, so I may not give so much as a husk more to one than another. Yet have a care, Andrew MacLaren, that

234

this business does not also consume you. There has already been over and enough death and sorrow as it is."

Here was a woman also changed Andrew thought, from one he had little cared for, to the one he now listened to. One who had seen her friends slowly die, and like others, had done her best to save them.

At a loss to answer, Andrew left the woman to address the assembled throng in an air thick with expectation. Standing there Andrew's eyes swept over faces openly hostile to these whom they had placed their trust...their lives to, and was glad he had placed a guard around them, unsure when someone who had lost a dear one would not reek revenge on these two murderers.

"My friends," he started. "And in especial, those of you who, like myself have known these bitter days, now happily put behind us. You see before you the men we sent south. The same men whose return we waited so long for...in vain. Here they stand, so they may offer an explanation in their own defence for what has passed, so you may judge the truth for yourselves."

Somewhere amongst the crowd a baby cried, and Andew waited while the mother soothed it. "They state, that they themselves were set upon on their journey south, where all was stolen and Col and Dugald slain. Not knowing their way back here, they surrendered all notion of helping us, even though they were aware of our plight, and the trust placed upon them."

"It is true!" McMahon wailed. "Have a pity! What other road was open to us? If only poor Col or Dugald were alive to testify to this, all would be a different colour! Alas, God rest their souls it is not to be!"

"And if it was?" A voice asked from within the crowd.

McMahon strained to spy the speaker, contracting within himself as the questioner pushed his way to the front to confront him.

"Holy mother of God it is an apparition! It is young Dugald himself! Or am I alone blessed with this vision?" Crossing himself, Sean held up his face to the heavens and pretended to weep.

"Enough! Enough I say!" Davie Hamilton stormed in his own tongue. "Enough play acting man. Have the goodness at least to let me die with some dignity. These folk know the truth of it all." He jerked his head at the onlookers. "How else did they find us? And with Dugald there putting the lie to your fanciful tale..." Hamilton trailed off, his final words a whisper. " Leave it be Irishman, it is the end. We both have lost."

"That you have, and it is I who must end it all in the name of Col Fraser, and but for the grace of God my own self," Dugald seethed advancing upon the two men, his dirk drawn.

"There will be no murder done here, Dugald. I have given my word." Andrew gripped the young man by the arm. "This matter is for me alone to conclude."

"You were not left to die as was I. Had it not been for the *troich*, I would not be alive this day!" Dugald retorted angrily, struggling to free himself with a hatred on his young face Andrew had not seen before. "You are not alone in your loss Andrew MacLaren, there are others besides yourself who have known this same grief," he hissed angrily.

Encouraged by the angry growl of congruity from the crowd at his back, Dugald surged on. "By what right alone do you seek to decide their fate?"

"By the right that I am *ceann cinnidh,* here. Or have you so easily forgotten, Dugald Ferguson*?"*

Andrew turned to face his fellow caterans. "Is there a soul amongst you who will speak in defence of these two accused?" he shouted for all to hear, and at their silence. "Is there any who do not seek their death?"

When again there was silence, Andrew swung to Dugald, his words low, deliberate. "It is for me to see an end to this, Dugald. The blood of many is already on my hands. Do not vie for this same notoriety, by yourself staining your own."

Still seething with anger, Dugald did not know what to say, even though he understood what Andrew was trying to save him from; to let the burden of these mens fate lie with him.

Now that it had been put to him, Dugald did not know quite how to save face, especially from those close by who still expected him to strike at these men, as they themselves so dearly wished to do.

However, his indecision gave Andrew time to further order, "Johnny , Sim, ensure all bide here.." He walked past Dugald ignoring the angry shouts of protests, and beckoning the prisoners captors to follow him.

Once out of the defile, the party travelled for a furlong or so until they reached a place marked by mound and rock. Here, some of the graves now quite old were already reclaimed by grass and heather. Others betrayed by the newly turned earth, not so old.

Andrew halted and drew breath, his two prisoners momentarily forgotten while he relived the day all had come here to bury their dead.

Until then, because of ground frozen solid, the bodies as was the custom had lain in the barn at the far end of the stronghold.

He would never forget that day in the barn. The smell of purification, kin struggling to lift dead kin, unwilling to accept that the decomposition lying beneath the winding sheet was that of their own, each attempting to disguise their haste to be away from that place, yet not wishing to give offence, neither wanting to be the last to bury their dead, the continuity which had held them together now broken by native superstition.

At length, no longer able to thole the embarrassing scene, Andrew asserted his authority.

"We shall each help one another in this. You need not fear, my Una will be the last to rest in peace."

Andrew had never forgotten the transformation his announcement had brought. The looks of gratitude and relief, that his Una, as the last to be buried that day would now according to tradition, mean that *she* would watch over all. Each as they trooped silently past reduced to tears mouthing their thanks to him, their *ceann cinnidh*.

Back to the present, Andrew's eyes inevitably wandered to Una's grave, the lump in his throat giving way to an indescribable anger. "Look!" He pointed a shaking finger at the graves. "This is your work! Better that you had both died yon day when trapped by the MacSorley!"

He signalled to Johnny that he lead the party further down the mountainside, where they drew to a halt in a small cul-de-sac of rock.

"You will leave us now," Andrew commanded, drawing both pistols, and waiting in silence until his compatriots had left.

"You promised you would not murder us!" McMahon screamed at Andrew.

"No, Irishman, I promised you I would not let any cateran murder you, I said nothing of myself."

Andrew's shot threw McMahon clutching his side to the ground.

Ashen faced Hamilton awaited his own fate. "Is it sport you seek Heilanman?" he growled at Andrew calmly reloading. For answer Andrew fired, pitching Hamilton on to the ground, a bright red patch spreading over his shirt front.

His legs almost at a comical angle, McMahon struggled in vain to raise himself up, as Andrew stepped forward to shoot him in the back, snapping his spine, the wounded man's screams filling the small amphitheatre.

Slowly and deliberately, Andrew turned on the Lowlander, hitting him in the shoulder as he tried to crawl over the uneven ground. Again, he filled his pistol with powder, and impassively eyed the destruction his weapons had wrought; at McMahon tearing at the earth in pain and desperation, like some wounded animal trying to hide, his paralyzed legs refusing to move.

"For the sake of God have a mercy! What is this!"

Through his brows, Andrew looked up at Duncan standing horrified by the sight of the blood soaked broken men. "Is there no Christian charity left within you man? Do you not think we all sought the same as you, over and over again? In our thoughts, our nightmares? But never in the light of day, Andrew MacLaren, would we have come to do such deeds!"

If the words had reached his *ceann cinnidh*, they had little effect. Standing over McMahon, Andrew fired point blank, and the screaming head dissolved before his eyes. His final shot hitting the struggling Lowlander full in the face.

Sickened, Duncan turned away, believing this was not the same man whose life he had helped save when first they met, and now wishing with all his heart, that the MacIntosh's shot had been better aimed.

Chapter 17

It was almost two years now since the massacre in the glen. Andrew took a long slow protractive look around him at the caterans camped by the woods edge, and at the coming and going to Ness's shore for water for that night's supper.

There was upwards of a hundred men gathered there, with more to come when Johnny MacKellar arrived from his new *daingneachd* in the Cairngorms.

Sitting by himself on a rock, Andrew smiled in amusement at the antics of the *troich* and the big MacAlister, happy that the big man had chosen to bide rather than go with Johnny to the Cairngorms. Though in truth it was Cathal more so than her husband who had refused to move from the bothan she had worked so hard to make a home. So too had Dugald, perhaps he still relished Cathal's bannocks and her looking after him.

Duncan? Well it had taken that man time to mellow towards him after his execution of Hamilton and McMahon. Therefore, Duncan had also remained, not out of any love for him but at the thought of having to uproot himself, even for his old friend the MacKellar.

However, Sim and Mairi MacColl had gone, as had Rob Sutherland, and Hamish MacKenzie, all that was left of his original band of some time ago. Of the rest, now at Johnny's tail, none knew the whereabouts of both *daingeanchds*.

Andrew looked across the turbulent waters of the loch, his thoughts winging to Kintail, to Kirsty, Gregor and young Col. The bairn had grown to be a fine wee lad, with more his mother's looks than his father's, much to the good humoured consternation of Gregor, who took all of Andrew's chiding in good stead.

Always it seemed, Gregor was at pains to make amends for what had passed between them that while back, more so after finding a milch cow or two on his doorstep, the result of some successful raid or other.

It was grand to have such friends, and to be in their homes even for a little while, away from the demanding and Spartan life of the stronghold.

After Kintail, his steps would inevitably lead to Gleidh House, and again to a different world. Now however, he found the road ever harder and had taken to riding a garron, though it meant taking a long protracted way around the corries and braes, a sign, he conceeded of getting old.

Andrew shifted to sit by another rock, away from the wind rising from the loch side.

He could still see Isobella now, when presenting her with some small trinket, a gesture that inevitably would lead cannily to greater things.

"Neil has sold the tavern, Andrew, and at your instructions has kept a third share for himself, the rest he gave to me in trust. It will go some way towards our new home. Mind..." She warned, "I grow no younger."

Taking in this information, and also with it the warning, he lay in bed stretched out on his side, drinking in the beauty of that magnificent body.

She drew a hand through his hair. "What of your caterans, do they not wonder what has become of all that siller stolen by yon two? Do they know a tavern was purchased by the blood money?"

"Yon two!" Andrew scorned. "Never was gear so dearly bought. No, the caterans are well content with what they now have."

The ring he had given Neil Stewart had purchased enough to have seen them through that following winter after the starving, and as long as his folks had their bellies full, they would ask for nothing more.

That he had also stolen from the dwarf's horde back in the wood had done little to prick his conscience. The *troich* as were all other caterans quite willing to live each day as it came, with no thought to the future, unlike himself who was ever planning and scheming for the day he'd at last turn his back on these wild mountains, and not so very long he hoped.

His thoughts turned back to Isobella lying there. "What of your own folks? What would they say to your running off with a landless man, a cateran no less? Leaving the glen to fend for itself, in especial after all you have done. It is your home, lass. Will you not miss it so?"

"Aye, no doubt, Andrew. Yet knowing the *Grant* himself wishes to see Gleidh House in the hands of a man instead of a brainless woman, then perhaps it is for the best."

Isobella drew him to her. "At least there will be no more cold and hungry nights. What say you MacLaren? As for missing my home? My home will be where yon are *mo ghaol.*"

"They are coming Andrew!" Dugald brought him out of the past. "Johnny and the others, see yonder!"

Andrew rose from the rock, blithely waiting whilst the MacKellar lead a score or more caterans down the brae to a mixed reception of good humoured catcalls and greetings. He waved a hand and walked to meet his friend. "It is good to see you well, Johnny." He grasped the outstretched hand warmly.

"And I you, Andrew," the other replied equally warmly.

Johnny looked around him, impressed by the numbers already gathered there. "You have prospered even more since last we met, Andrew."

"Aye, we manage the far side of Crief on occasions. And yourself?"

Johnny shifted the targe at his shoulder, a slight smile playing on his lips. "We 'lift' in the other direction, we cannot both be gnawing at the same bone."

Next morning the camp rose, stirred itself to life, and gathered to arms in the morning mist.

"We have the word aright?" Johnny asked of Andrew, seeking assurance. "The MacSorley is in *Dun Eideann* ?

"Aye, and has been there for two weeks past. This we have from the messengers at the standing stone." Andrew drew a critical eye over the assembled company. "Fergus confirmed that Iain MacKinnon, the same who warned of Quoich's watch on Gleidh House, came especially to verify the fact."

His doubts gone, Johnny nodded. "Then it is set, we reach the glen from its west side, and await the gloaming before venturing through its neck, and so on to MacSorley's own doorstep."

"There must be no mistake in this, MacKinnon, or you forfeit your life this day," MacSorley of Quoich, barked, dismounting.

At his master's icy stare Iain hastened to dispel any doubts the man might have. "It is as I said my lord, MacLaren's caterans believe you to be in *Dun Eideann"* He indicated to the empty glen below.

"They will wait until the gloaming, then pass through yon narrow neck and attack the town and your own tower beyond."

"Then we have this dastard MacLaren and his rabble.! That is unless you play me false?"

"On my word MacSorley Mhor, it is what is planned!" Iain choked. "Fergus MacAlister, told it me by the standing stone as instructed by the MacLaren himself, so that I may save my own gear from their attack when the time comes, this in recognition of my services."

"Strange you have never met your benefactor..your other master," Quoich mused.

"I have only one master, your lordship, as you well know. I sometimes encounter these caterans upon my travels and pass on to you what I have learned....such as to day." Iain MacKinnon, mumbled meekly.

Later, Iain MacKinnon shivered as did all hidden on the ridges either side of the glen, an uneasiness creeping into his mind at the empty glen below. He took another peek over the ridge contemplating that should he have had it wrong, now was the time to be away. Perhaps, he should rise under the pretext of relieving himself and disappear in the fading light.

He took another sharp look below. Yet, should he be right, and the MacLaren taken? Iain's eyes sparkled at the thought of his reward. For, despite all his faults, Quoich would not be ungrateful should the man who had cost him his hand come within his grasp this night. Then in answer to his prayer the first of the caterans appeared from the tail of the glen. "Blessed be to Him, they are here!"

Iain scuttled back from the ridge to where his master sat on a stone, impassively examining his empty sleeve. "They are here my lord!" Iain cried out. "They have just this minute entered the glen!"

Quoich rose as if he had not heard, only his eyes betrayed his excitement, and quickly gathered himself together, reasoning that it would not do to lose restraint in front of his own clansmen, not when he was so close to having his dream realised.

Now his sole fear was that the MacLaren should escape, or worse, be put to death by some other hand than his own, not when he himself had other plans for the accursed man.

242

This was the man who had caused him to be spurned, avoided, worse of all pitied in the higher circles of society in Scotia's capital. No, MacLaren, you will not know what it feels to lose a hand, but you will know what it is to lose both.

Leaning awkwardly on a rock, Quoich's eyes gleamed at the caterans settling down in the narrow glen to await the gloaming, some resting amongst the few trees growing there, others slaking their thirst from the tinkling burn.

"MacSorley Mhor, let us attack! We have them now!" Urged an eager clansman.

"We bide by the plan, see you, man," Quoich hissed. "Let no man show himself until I give the word." He touched Iain on the shoulder. "You have served me well, MacKinnon. You will find me not ungrateful. More so when yon scoundrel is dragged before me.! " Quoich indicated to the glen below. "This is yet the closest you have seen the man? It is he with the pistols."

Iain shaded his eyes against the setting sun, now blood red over the farther ridge. "It is over far to make out his features. The one with the pistols, say you?"

"Aye, MacKinnon, it is a weapon he favours and uses well. The sword is not to his liking, as well I should know, it being the accursed *troich* who did his foul work for him yon fatal day." The man spat vehemently, rubbing his empty sleeve. "Now let us be ready, for the caterans are at last rousing themselves."

The caterans were indeed shaking themselves into some resemblance of order, with the MacLaren at their head advancing to where the glen narrowed to no more than a hundred yards wide.

With bated breath, Iain made out the giant figure of Fergus MacAlister, the unmistakable dwarf at his side, the youthful step of Dugald Ferguson, Duncan Cameron and the MacKellar, the latter he had not seen in an age.

"Seamus!" Quoich barked. "Run. Give the signal now. Careful you bide unseen behind the ridge, see you! "Now we have them.! Now we shall see!" Quoich almost danced with delight as his messenger took off in the direction of the glen's narrow neck.

At first it came as a distant rumble of thunder, interspersed with lightening, the setting sun flashing on breastplate and sabre, the entire breadth of the glen erupting with charging horsemen.

Quoich slapped his thigh in triumph. "We have them MacKinnon! This time no one will escape the net. But what is this! Are they stunned to move?" Bewildered the man put up his hand to shade his eyes.

For in fact instead of scattering before the ranks of charging horse, the caterans ran out a long single line, sword and targe at the ready, awaiting the oncoming onslaught of horse and rider in full cry.

Then it was done. In the blinking of an eye the serried line of military might went down as one, sending rider and mount alike crashing and struggling together as the ground opened up beneath them. Shreiks and screams renting the air as horse and rider were crushed together.

Here and there a broken animal, eyes bulging in terror reared and kicked its way out of the shallow pits, whilst with one terrifying slogan of 'MacVie! MacVie!' the caterans fell upon them.

Beside himself with rage, Quoich rounded on the unfortunate MacKinnon. "You...you MacKinnon!" he stammered with rage, pointing. "This is your work! You have betrayed me.....betrayed us all!" Quoich of MacSorley screamed, all self control now gone.

"No! No! My lord! 'Twas the word given me by the caterans. You must surely mind that others besides myself said likewise," wailed the terror stricken minion.

Quoich would have none of it. "Hamish!" he cried. "Take this..this wretch and find the others who played me false! Take them to my keep of Quoich, this very night and hold them there to await my pleasure."

With a dismissive wave of his hand, and in the same breath Quoich berated his clansmen. "Why do you wait? Be at them before all is lost!" he screamed dragging a reluctant clansman to his feet.

Here and there a clansman braver than others rose at their chief's command and started hesitantly over the ridge top to face the caterans below, in the same instant that a new and terrifying sound reached their ears, as unfamiliar clad clansmen fell upon them from the rear, stabbing and slashing at those who still crouched upon the ridge.

"This way, for your life my lord!" A gillie cried, bringing forth his master's mount. "You must away, for all here is lost!"

Dazed, Quoich allowed himself to be led and mounted. The slap on the animal's rump momentarily jolting him to his senses while he witnessed his clansmen break and run in all directions. And wth one long yell, Quoich held up a handless arm, cursing the man who called himself the Cateran. Then put spur to mount.

"It is done! It is done! MacVie is avenged!" Dugald danced with joy, slapping the dwarf on the back.

Laughing with an inner relief, Andrew searched first one braeside then another.

"Thanks to the assistance of some Grants and Stewarts!"

"What now Andrew?" Fergus asked of his chief, wiping his weapon clean. "Now that all is open to us from here to the great man's house itself."

Andrew waited the arrival of his fellow commander, before venturing, "What say you Johnny, is it the MacSorley's tower you would have us go, and put and end to this once and for all?"

"There will be no end to it, Andrew my friend as I have said before, until one of you lies beneath the heather. Let us first await Neil and Lachlan with news of your adversary before deciding," Johnny suggested moving off to talk to Duncan Cameron.

Momentarily deserted, Andrew stared around him at the carnage, and wondered if any of the horsemen already stripped bare, were those of two years ago. He shivered, uneasy at Quoich's persistence to have him caught.

"Well MacLaren , your plan has worked, all credit to you, for I must confess, I was more than a little skeptical of yon pits," Neil Stewart, cried, striding towards him, Lachlan Grant, by his side.

Andrew grimaced. "No more myself, Neil. It is to Lachlan you must direct your praise, for it was he and his clansmen who dug the pits and watched over them day and night, 'till the time was come."

Lachlan scratched his balding pate, obviously pleased by this praise, if not a little embarrassed.

"Aye, we dug them each night in the gloaming, this week past, and covered them over, all to Andrew's instructions. We feared some body passing through might himself be snared before all was done. But none passed this way."

The big man chuckled to hide his embarrassment. "I tried them out myself, and judged if built aright, they would bear the weight of a man, but not of both man and horse together. Therefore, as I am that bit lighter of both, I dared to try."

"And obviously it worked," Neil grinned. "But now all praise is done, what now Andrew MacLaren?"

"It depends, Neil. All the glen and town beyond lie open to us. Do you Stewarts have a mind for further work? Or is it back to Appin with what you have already acquired from a few poor MacSorleys?" Andrew taunted good humourdly.

"Appin will manage just fine without us for a while, I am after thinking."

"And you, Lachlan? A beast or two would not go amiss in your own glen?"

"In this you are right, Andrew. Lead on before we lose all daylight left to us, for it has ever been my mind to see the inside of MacSorley's grand tower."

"And so you shall, Lachlan. So you shall!"

It was almost dark by the time they emerged from the head of the glen and into the fertile floor of the strath.

"How many was our loss, and how many hurt, Duncan?" Andrew asked, walking beside his old friend.

"Five are dead, and nine hurt by my reckoning at this juncture."

"All our own folk?" Andrew turned an eye to these unknown mountains, almost mystical looking in the growing gloom, resenting it seemed this strange intrusion.

"Two are from Johnny's. A couple are Stewarts and Grants."

"Then it was well done." Andrew sounded pleased. "It is more than I could have hoped, that we should lose so few. It is a great victory over those Lowland mercenaries, and Highland MacSorleys, we are after having this day, Duncan."

"Och aye, Andrew that it is, a grand victory if you do not happen to be one of the unfortunate slain that is. Or that you are not Alasdair MacPherson, he who has a wife and three bairns, and who will never tread the heather again, at least not with *two* feet" Duncan said bitterly, giving his chief a meaningful look. "But it is ever the way of the Highlands, in especial that of the cateran."

Uneasy at the drift of talk, Andrew quickened his step and called out a needless order to no one in particular, but happy for once to be away from the Cameron's company."

"It is no *creach* we are after, Dugald, so I give your MacDonnels fair warning. It is MacSorley's gear that we seek and not the rape of honest folk. You take my meaning?"

"It will be done as you say, Andrew. I will hold the MacDonnels in check. Is it directly to the tower that we go, by passing all?"

"No. There are cattle for the lifting on the way. But only cattle, do you hear? I want no woman harmed."

Frowning at the severity of his chieftain's tone, Dugald nodded curtly, and hurried off to find his band of MacDonnels.

From the head of the glen through the strath to MacSorley's tower, the raiding caterans found to be completely denuded of men and womenfolk alike.

"I'll wager my sword and targe, Quoich himself does not lie within," MacAlister loudly declared, raising an eyebrow at the tower's door.

"You are right, Fergus. It is stoutly held. We cannot afford to bide over long. Quoich at this very minute may be seeking assistance of his patriarch, Locheil himself, so let us see who commands here in his stead."

Cupping his hands, Andrew called out. "There within, I am Andrew MacLaren, and would speak with your master the MacSorley!"

In answer a shot whistled passed giant and chief. A booming voice from the battlements advising them that MacSorley of Quoich did not treat with thieves and robbers, instantly followed by another shot that sent both men scurrying back to the safety of the trees.

"I have a notion the great man himself is not at home. And contrary to our thinking, the tower is not so greatly held, as it is my belief all who followed him this day are yet by his side, either to his other great hall he cries Quoich Keep, or further still to Lochiel's very doorstep." Andrew suggested.

"Then we burn the damned place!" Neil Stewart cried impatiently.

"Only the door Neil, we do not wish to loose all treasures that lie within yon walls."

Fergus rubbed his hands together in obvious joy at the prospect of having further revenge on the hated man. "This is work for your MacDonnels Dugald!"

Dugald peered at his chief standing in the inky darkness amongst the trees. "This we can do fairly well, Andrew." So saying hurried off to the find his company of rogues.

"We cannot afford to bide overlong, man," Johnny agitated.

"Time is not on our side," Duncan added in support.

247

A newly risen moon cast its light between wood and tower. Andrew studied his feet, then up at the gray walls of the tower. "You are right, we must be well on our way before morning for the moving of gear and cattle are a slow business. Dangerous also, when splitting up to go our separate ways."

"So it must be done before this night is out, or not at all," Neil deduced folding his arms, and staring at the ground.

"We might not have so very long to wait." Fergus pointed where bush and tinder heaped against the massive door was already well ablaze, casting quick flickering shadows across the intervening space. A few spartan shots from the battlement confirmed Andrew's suspicions of the tower being sparingly held, but not before two of Dugald's MacDonnels had been brought down whilst fuelling the fire.

"*DIA!* I am hoping not lose more here than we did earlier in the glen," Andrew cursed.

His brain racing, Andrew found Duncan in the dark. "Duncan, a word in your ear! Gather the number you need to take the wounded and yonder beasts away..now.!"

"Better half a bannock than none at all?"

" Aye, if you will," Andrew answered impatiently. "But should this tower fail to fall by morning's light, then it is to leave a trail that a blind man could not but fail to follow. This way we should save some beasts at least, and who better to lead them through this country than a Cameron."

"Och, I can see your reasoning well enough, though even I will not fancy traipsing around these same hills in the dark. Nonetheless, we should see the far side of the glen this night."

Duncan turned to leave. Andrew clutched the man's arm . "Have a care, Duncan, these same braes may hold more than MacSorley women. And I also judge their own menfolk will not be so far away, even allowing for those who may well be with Quoich himself.

With a gesture of appreciation bordering on embarrassment, Duncan left to go about his business.

Finally by midnight, the tower fell in a rush akin to a river in spate of wildly charging caterans through its blazing doorway, Fergus lifting the dwarf over the smouldering debris and into the great hall beyond, and sweeping aside what little resistance was left.

At a more sedate pace Andrew led his fellow commanders into the MacSorley home, amazed to see the ransacking well under way. From every direction it seemed, caterans appeard, carrying armfuls of silver, pewter, lead, before returning for more, whilst others piled tapestries, chairs and other such chattels as could be found, into one great pile.

Here and there angry voices rose above the din as one object or other took more than one man's fancy. The big MacAlister's more so as he pinned a comrade against a wall, his face only inches away from the unfortunate man's face. "The chair is mine. It will suit Cathal fine, I am after thinking!" he shouted angrily.

"Do you not seek it for your own self, Fergus MacAlister, instead of that of your wife? So you might act the fine lord whilst sitting on it in your own bothan," the pinned man choked.

"Aye! And if this is so, what business is it of yours, for should you object, I will take you across my knee and thrash your backside with a stale bannock 'till your nose bleeds!" Fergus shot back with a twinkle in his eye, hoisting the struggling kicking man the higher.

Catching the tail end of the confrontation Andrew called across the hall, "leave him be Fergus, the chair is yours. See you carry it all the way home by yourself."

At mid day they halted by Loch Quoich to gain their breaths and say farewell to the Grants who must strike north by Loyne's shores.

"You have a care, Lachlan. Also give my regards to your mistress, if you please." Andrew addressed the giant fondly.

"And I also," echoed, Neil, cheerfully. "Tell her we both esteem her highly in our own way."

Scarcely acknowledging the requests, Lachlan scratched his balding head as he was wont to do when puzzled. "And you Andrew, are you yourself not heading for Loch Ness? You journey with the Stewarts?"

"Aye man,this is my intention. If you were Quoich now, with the strength of Lochiel's Camerons at your back, would you not split your force, some south to Glen Roy, the rest to trap us when crossing the Great Glen, between yon lochs of Lochy and Ness?"

Lachlan took another scratch at his bald pate. "Mn…this I think I would be doing."

249

Knowing the man was not totally convinced, Andrew calmly explained. "I will continue with my good friend the Stewart here a wee bit further towards Morar for safe measure, so avoiding any Camerons that might already be heading in this direction, then east before swinging north around the great Ben's shoulder and then between Lochs Treig and Ossian and so to the Monadliath."

"It is a goodly plan however long. Though I cannot help but think," the giant stopped to laugh, " that whilst you are on this long dander in the heather, Quoich , for all we know is at this very time making a speedy way to *Dun Eideann,* and not bothering with the likes of you and me!"

"I think you wrong," Neil interrupted. "Quoich has lost overmuch in wealth and pride to let it rest here. No, he will come with what men he can find and try and cut off Andrew and his caterans retreat by way of Glen Mhor."

"Rather you than me," Lachlan voiced wearily. "I wish you well. But how you are from keeping Quoich's spies from off your heels, I do not know, in especial when your steps take you nearer Morar and Cameron country, than it would be to my liking."

"There are ways Lachlan. Nevertheless, leave the worrying to myself. See that you are not yourself less cautious on you own way home."

It was what the Grant had feared. To escape without the MacSorley survivors being aware of which path they took, was no simple task, and numerous were the times Andrew divided his forces to confuse the foe and hasten their escape. So it was that he would gently coax a dozen beasts or so away in the dead of night when MacSorley spies would think them all bedded down.

"We are cutting it fine, Andrew," Neil voiced his concern. "We are closer to Cameron country, as the Grant feared than we are to your own great Monadliath Mountains."

"This I know full well, Neil. However, should we still be watched by other than the MacSorleys, I must make a show of journeying with you to Appin. Then should fortune favour, I will sweep north between yon two lochs when the time is ripe."

"Then see the time is ripe before too much longer, my friend, or Rannoch will see you before I see Appin!"Neil laughed heartily.

It was close on two days later when Andrew felt sufficiently confident to suggest to the Stewart what he thought must be done.

"At least in this wide open space, we have the chance to see who would follow us, Neil. I believe the time has come for us to part. What say you?"

"I think you are right in your decision, Andrew." Neil took a sip of water from his flask, wiping his mouth with the back of his hand, his eyes slowly traversing the wide open moor. "I did not think to bide so long, now it leaves me with nothing short of pointing my feet towards Binnein Mor, and this I would rather be doing whilst this fine weather lasts, and hope for a mist or two to blind the MacIans when nearing Glencoe."

Andrew halted. "It is decided then. We shall part here, and God go with you." He thrust out his hand. "You have ample gear and beasts for your work?"

"Over and enough, my friend," Neil answered gratefully. "The Stewarts and myself are after thanking you for the opportunity." The gleam in his eyes told all. "Have a care yourself man. You are still far and away from home." He shook the outstretched hand. "Till we meet again, Andrew MacLaren!" The voices of his clan behind him also echoing their farewells as they took their leave.

A fine smir blew in their faces, swept by the winds straight from off the shoulder of Leum Uilleim

"I cannot see my hand in front of my face!" the big MacAlister growled.

"And I cannot even see my face!" Hamish MacKenzie jested, wiping his nose. "Yesterday I enjoyed the walk and the view, now I no longer know where I am walking, and there is no view!" He emphasised the point by pulling a brogue out of the sucking quagmire. "At least the Camerons will not find us when we cannot find ourselves."

"Ach, cease your moaning, man," Fergus admonished with a twist of his face.

"It is all well enough for you, MacAlister. All you need do is sit in that grand chair of yours each time we halt," Hamish growled.

"Then you should have done likewise, and it would have served to keep your arse dry when you chose to sit, instead of filling that sack with whatever it may contain." Fergus tapped the sack Hamish carried over his shoulder.

"Enough of your blethering, Hamish," an ill tempered Johnny MacKellar snarled. growing more annoyed by events, and this day he could not just be bothered with the ravings of the MacKenzie.

It had all seemed quite straightforward at the time when told to him by the MacLaren. In and out like a fiddler's elbow. Then away to the Cairngorms with beasts and gear before Quoich's trews were dry from the shock. Now here he was nie on a week later and no closer to his own home. It had ever been the same, the MacLaren was over cautious, the MacSorley and Cameron menace a figment of an over active imagination. Well! Was he Johnny MacKellar not *ceann cinnidh* in his own right? Time he spoke as such to the MacLaren.

"Hamish is right, Andrew, no one will find us in this smir. I am away to the right now, for Loch Garry before I lose my bearings all together."

"You will follow the loch to its end, then head away east, Johnny? Is this your mind?" Andrew condescended, allowing the long column of men carrying their assortments of spoils to clatter past, among protesting beasts, to disappear into the rain. "Aye, you are right, Johnny, we shall separate here, you to Garry and I to Ossian. I thank you for your assistance. I think it was to our mutual advantage, was it not?"

A bolt of lightning lit up the sky, followed by a torrent of rain. Andrew drew his plaid up around his shoulders, rain streaming down his face. "There will be a few friends of ours lying quieter at their rest, now this deed is done to the MacSorley. What think you, Johnny?"

"Aye, Andrew it has taken over long to have the MacSorley pay for yon evil day in Glen Tilt," Johnny agreed, casting an eye after the departing herd. "Come! We must away before we ourselves are lost."

By midday the rain had given way to a warm sun, vapour rising from the heather like steam from a pot.

It was the dwarf who saw them first, and ran to Andrew to signal their coming.

"It is MacBain and Murray!" Fergus shouted dropping his chair and shading his eyes from the sun as the two men bounded through the heather.

Soon proved right, the panting men drew up before their chief.

"What news of Quoich?" Andrew flashed, with little time for greeting.

The MacBain was the first to recover his breath. "We waited behind as Duncan Cameron instructed, Quoich came as Duncan said you knew he would, *ceann cinnidh*, to seal the approach between Lochy and Ness. When you did not appear he sent scouts north and south, and doubtless back to Loy, and still bides by Ness's shore, for he is sure you did not win through."

"The man reasons we are still by Glen Garry, or Moriston, I am after thinking, Andrew!" Dugald applauded.

Donald Murray finished drinking from his flask. "No! No!" he said impatiently. "You are wrong there Dugald, Quoich bides still by Ness side, but the Camerons have pressed on, some north by Glen Spean, meaning to trap us between themselves and Quoich,the rest are headed south in this direction. We feared you would not be so very far in front of the Camerons, and would be caught in their trap,but when we found this was not so, judged you to be behind them, which thanks be to Him you are."

"We had the devil's own work in bypassing their lines to find you here," MacBain interjected.

"It is fortunate we ventured so far south, or instead of being at their backs we would between them and Quoich as you so rightly say." Andrew clicked his teeth. "So now that they lie between us and home, we have no option but to strike east, almost in the very footsteps of the MacKellar," he scowled.

They waited on the edge of the vast moor, Dugald his five remaining MacDonnels, Gilbride and Skene, shooing the half dozed cattle this way and that.

Proud of his responsibilities, Dugald paced up and down, arms akimbo. "Will they never come?" he asked impatiently of Skene.

"When they do, we best be on our way, I am after thinking," was the short response. "Speak of the devil, Dugald they are here!"

Dugald shot a look across the vast moor at the dwarf like shape of men in the distance, having no doubt in his mind that these were the advancing Camerons. "We will move towards Chno Dearg, yet not over fast, not to have them lose us," Dugald commanded, his heart thumping, all urging on the wandering cattle with the flat of their swords.

An hour later from his vantage point amongst the rocks, the young commander watched the tiny specks grow nearer, Cameron scouts well in advance, taking their time to study the ground for tell tale signs of the hunted. All at once, one gave out a cry.

Dugald clambered down from his perch, satisfied, though wary that the ruse had worked.

"They are here. We cannot drive the beasts much further lest we ourselves are caught," he gasped out to his friends.

"How many did you see, Dugald?" Alan Gilbride queried, driving the cattle on.

"Seven scouts are close behind, though they have sent one back over the moor to advise the rest."

"Then the hunters will be six less, shortly."

Undecided, Dugald looked first one way then another, as if seeking a solution in the rocks around him. "I do not know, Alan. Our instructions were to lull the scouts away from Andrew and the column, and have them thinking they were following the tail end of the main drive."

"And so we shall, if we dispatch those immediately following, and force the others to seek us all out again," Alan suggested with conviction.

Less than assured, Dugald demurred. "It will gain us time, as you say."

"That it will," Skene agreed enthusiastically, having had nothing more to do these last days than walk and drive sulky cattle.

Dugald made a moue. "We shall take your advise, Alan. Leave the beasts.! Quickly now! To our places and await our guests."

They were not long kept waiting. Hardly had the last cateran concealed himself when the scouts rounded the rocks, charging past the hidden men at the sight of the unguared herd.

Breathlessly, Dugald waited until all had passed, then with a yell, followed by his tiny band, launched himself upon the scouts so engrossed in retreiving the cattle.

The unequal fight was short and swift, the unsuspecting Camerons going down to a man.

When all was done, the panting leader retraced his steps to his former vantage point. This time however instead of a score or more following in the steps of the scouts, the whole horizon it seemed, teemed with armed men.

Inexplicably, Dugald feared he was about to die. Then why at this time should his thoughts turn to Una, the only lass he'd ever looked at more than once.

When first he saw her in the *daingneachd* she had been the MacIntosh's woman...lass really: cooking and mending and whatever else was his want. Though she was not so much younger than himself he had fallen in love with the bonnie face, flashing eyes, and raven hair. Knowing she belonged to the *ceann cinnidh* , he had been afraid to let his true feelings be known. Then when the opportunity had arisen, brief though it may have been, the MacLaren had come by, and again all was lost to him.

Heaving a sigh which he was certain all of the advancing clansmen would hear, Dugald slid down to warn his comrades.

Strangely he felt no panic or urge to hurry, as if all this had been preordained, and neither speed or stroll would make the difference.

"They come. The scout returns with an advance party of a score or more. The entire Clan Cameron, an hour or so behind I am after thinking." Dugald spoke to his comrades matter of factly.

"We must away then," Skene replied unperturbed by the news, and bent to exchange a Cameron targe for his own. For he had yet to see the day he could not outrun a Cameron, especially if outnumbered.

"If you are all done here, we best away." Dugald nodded in the direction of the partially stripped corpses. "Seeing as our unfriends will want to retrieve what you have stolen from their kin." He rearranged his crossbelt, and loosened his sword in its sheath. "We shall leave the beasts here."

Dugald led his seven caterans even higher amongst the rocks, content that he was leading the hunters away from Andrew and the main column.

Skene grabbed at a boulder to hoist himself over the top of the loose scree. "Should we manage to avoid the Camerons 'till nightfall, Dugald," he gasped, sitting down to rest on a rock. "we can be slipping away in the dark,"

"Only if we bide together, for I am not so sure in myself of where we might be," Ewen MacDonnel suggested, standing over his resting friend. "Though I believe some cousins of mine bide...." Suddenly weak at the knees, Ewen slumped to the ground, the remainder of the company throwing themselves behind what little cover they could find, each at a loss as to where the shot had come, for all had believed the scouts still to be some distance away. As with a blood curling yell, the Camerons fell upon them.

It was with some sense of satisfaction that his premonition had been correct, that Dugald found himself swamped by charging clansmen.

Fighting back to back, his tiny band managed to ease themselves further amongst the rocks, slashing and stabbing at all around. From the corner of his eye, he saw Skene go down, and Gilbride wounded, before he himself was on his back, his sword gone and looking up into the face of a triumphant foe. Then all was black and he knew he was dead and without pain, until realising that for a minuscule of a second the void he had witnessed had been the shadow of Rob leaping over him, in order to give him time to regain his feet.

Grabbing his fallen sword Dugald clambered to his feet, lashing out at all and sundry, laughing and weeping in turn, unable to comprehend what was happening here. He should be dead, perhaps was. Or was it the chill mountain air clearing his brain, that told him it was not so? Whatever it was or not, he was once again in command of what was left of his tiny band.

"Through yon gully, and quickly, see you. Now!" he barked, cutting down a man, and running to slash out again.

It was to no avail, there was no respite. Rasping for breath the caterans strokes grew weaker with fresh clansmen vieing with one another to be at them in this narrow gully.

"Back with us now!"Dugald shrieked. Angry that there was not enough air in this great wilderness to fill his lungs. Slowly the caterans retreated up the gully.

"Is there a way out? Or is it a wall at our backs!" the young leader cried, not daring to chance a look while the Camerons pressed on.

The answer was an eternity in coming, and not to his liking. "Tis a wall!"

"Then we are trapped!" was Dugald's first reaction. It was as if the foe, also realising this, stood back.

It was neither the fact that the caterans were trapped or that they the Camerons needed rest, which made them halt, only the need to let those armed with pistols take the front, which they did, pouring in a deadly fire amongst the men sheltering in the rocks.

Neil MacDonnel fell, as did Alan Gilbride, this time mortally wounded.

"Quick! To the rock wall behind us and over! It is our only hope. Better by far to try than to be shot down like a dog at the Camerons pleasure!" Dugald cried, leading the way, whilst their foe hesitated.

"You can be up and over!" Dugald cried, hoisting the sole survivor up on to his shoulder and, pushing. "Grab, man ! And away!"

"And what of you, Dugald!" came the garbled voice from above his head.

"Never mind me man! Away with you. Tell Andrew MacLaren, we did our best!" Then it was done, the weight lifted from his shoulders and the face with the folds of black hair peering down at him, offering a helping hand.

Turning his back on the nearest Cameron, Dugald leaped for the outstretched hand, gasping as he was jerked upwards and tensing himself against the inevitable shots, unable to comprehend why he was still alive, for they could not fail to miss him at such close quarters. The young man, further bewildered at being alive after the thundering volley reverberated around the narrow gully, and eager hands were helping him up over the cliff wall, and a voice he never thought to hear again saying as he lay there gasping in great lungfulls of air, "You have done well Dugald Ferguson, and have given us time to win through, I am after thinking." And there was Andrew MacLaren ruffling his hair affectionately.

Astounded, unable to digest what had happened, Dugald stared through the billowing gun smoke at a score or more caterans crouched by the cliff edge. "I did not think you would leave the column and come seeking us, Andrew," he rasped shakily.

"Neither did I, Dugald, neither did I!" Andrew helped his young lieutenant to his feet. "Come. Let us be on our way, for there are more than enough Camerons at our backs, and I do not want them on my heels come my own doorstep." So saying, Andrew started off at a trot, still amazed at having taken the risk.

Chapter 18

Andrew knelt by the clear mountain stream, disturbed by the reflection of his leathery face and graying hair, shattering the unwelcome image with a scoop of his hand

His thirst quenched, he rose and drew a hand across his mouth. Should fortune favour him this could be his last 'lifting'. According to Isobella when last they met, they were now not so far short of what they needed for their new home.

Following the meandering stream, Andrew strolled on, sniffing the scent of rock rose, and broom, glad to be alive on so fine a day, under a cloudless sky. Though he would have much preferred to have been free to lie dozing in the heather for a while and let the cares of the day pass him by.

This contentment led him to think of similar happy days in Glen Laidon with Fiona, prior to the MacIntosh's coming; days that would never come again. He sighed. He was growing no younger, and forever climbing mountains or skirting loch and glen, soaked through at times, or near to freezing on others. Hopefully he was close to putting all this behind him.

Andrew reached the high knoll overlooking the river bank, and settled down to wait.

Scarcely had he done so, when from the opposite bank, a half dozen or so cows burst through the thin line of trees, driven on by four of his own caterans.

It was almost time. Andrew drew a pistol from his belt as the caterans and their booty crossed the river a little way downstream and disappeared into the scrub beyond.

From where he lay hidden, the waiting man watched the chase begin; four men at first, one hurrying back to warn his kinsmen which way the caterans had gone.

They grew closer, Andrew perceiving that one of the remaining three was no more than a lad not quite yet in his teens, accompanied perhaps by father and uncle, halt to converse almost directly beneath where he lay hidden.

"*Dia!*" Why did you not send back the lad?" Andrew whispered, steadying a pistol on his forearm and firing at the nearest target.

The shot threw the man splashing into the water, his companion plunging in after him, who, after a time of fighting against the current succeeeded in wrapping an arm around the struggling man and haul him back up the banking.

Now that he saw that his kinsman was not badly hurt, and scarcely giving himself time to regain his breath, the man scanned the opposite banking. Then, having decided what he must do, beckoned the lad to bide by his injured kinsman while he himself attempted to ford the river, and was half way across when Andrew's second shot hit him, the current sweeping him rapidly downstream in a swirl of thrashing arms and legs.

"Father! Father!" the boy cried, running by the river bank, all the while calling out in that high pitched scream of the adolescent.

Impassively, Andrew watched the scene unfold. That he should feel no remorse or compunction for his action came as no surprise. Nor of the sorrow this act would surely bring to at least one household of the great Clan Campbell. Whether or not it made him any different from the MacIntosh when he had come a calling in his own Glen Laidon, he did not care to think.

True, at one time such an action would have left him physically and mentally sick, but that had been another man, and in another time. At present his single thought was the success of his scheme and nothing else. Therefore, should all go according to plan, the MacDiarmids, who held sway in the surrounding country, should now be gathering to arms and chasing after their neighbours the MacDougalls, whom he hoped would be seen as the thieves in this instance, and not themselves, and hopefully the further the MacDiarmids got from their own doorstep and deeper into MacDougall territory, the greater the chances were of both clans becoming embroiled with one another, whilst his caterans slipped in by the back door, and did the 'lifting' on a much grander scale.

Andrew abandoned his knoll and retraced his steps. This time he took no time to drink by the bubbling burn, or smell the sweet scent of the flora. Now all was haste, for his purpose was to be over the river at the next ford, and away in a wide circle to avoid the oncoming MacDiarmids, whom he hoped would be chasing after his own four caterans, and mistaking them for MacDougalls, and the half dozen stolen cattle.

The river scene already forgotten, Andrew reflected on his outlandish plan to raid Argyll.

Over three score caterans were ready to raid the glens, and when this was done, split up and head independently for Appin and the waiting Neil Stewart, who in turn would hold the cattle in their stead until the Autumn trysts.

It was early afternoon when Andrew rejoined his men in the folds of the foothills.

"There will be at least a hundred clansmen down yonder." Dugald lay on top of the braeside nodding down to the small town below, now no longer peaceful but all hurried confusion with men rallying to the call.

Andrew dropped down beside him. "Let us hope none come to the muster at our backs, or yonder hundred will quickly be up here," he chuckled, more bravely than he felt..

At last the mustering over, the clansmen moved off in the direction of the river.

"It succeeds!" Dugald thumped the ground enthusiastically.

"So I believe, young Dugald. We shall give them an hour, no more, then be about our business."

His eyes closed Andrew lay back on the grass, hands clasped behind his head, turning over his plan in his mind for the hundredth time. Now all hinged on the MacDiarmids believing the MacDougalls instead of themselves to be the thieves , and if so, by chasing them in force could induce a confrontation. However if not?. So be it, he sighed.

He must above all avoid a repetition of the MacSorley raid, and the traipsing over hill and around bog. This was now too much physically and mentally for him. And thanks to the Clan Cameron, yon day, could have ended in disaster.

No, if all went according to plan, this 'lifting' could see him end this kind of life for ever. And why not? Was it not so, that others who had joined them, had left with a beast or two to see them on their way? Therefore, would it be so wrong for him to wish for more? After all it had been his planning that had made it all possible.

It was all becoming too much for him. Success could be the downfall of it all. Greater numbers to feed necessitated larger raids. More caterans caused uneasiness amongst local chiefs and lairds, who although willing to tolerate broken men living within their lands, mainly because of the wealth they brought through the 'raiders callop' were unhappy at a rapidly growing strength, which one day might even come to match their own.

It was mainly because of this that he had approached the lairds and tacksmen with a view to allaying their fears by suggesting more of the married men be allowed to settle on their lands, paying rent and allegiance for the privilege, which after some discussion had been done. Therefore, his suggestion having succeeded, he had at one stroke eased the housing situation within the *daingneachd*, with the newly settled caterans helping to supply the stronghold with much needed grain. And as today were 'out' with him on this raid into deep Argyl.

Not that the chiefs were unaware of this, only that they would much prefer to look the other way, providing they in return received their share of the spoils, especially if it was a raid into Argyll against the hated House of Diarmid.

"It is time, I am after thinking, Andrew." Dugald shook his leader's shoulder.

Andrew yawned and turned on his side, taking a sleepy look at his band of caterans some of whom sat in groups quietly chatting amongst themselves, others, like the big MacAlister and the dwarf totally engrossed in cleaning their weapons. He struggled wearily to his feet.

"I am after thanking you, Dugald. Man, I must have dozed off. Gather the men together if you will."

Once gathered, the caterans followed their leader up the grassy braeside, where once on its top they fanned out to descend upon the unsuspecting little town, now bereft of its menfolk.

In no time it was over. And despite barking dogs and screaming women, the raiders went about their business quietly and effectively, driving off the bellowing cattle.

From where he stood a little way up the braeside, Andrew overlooked all. "See none break through our cordon and carry a warning to their menfolk, Dugald!" he commanded urgently, running a pratciced eye over the scene below.

" That I shall, Andrew! " Dugald shouted gleefuly up to his chief. "We have taken the place by surprise, with none to defend it except a few old men! All the clansmen are away crossing swords with the MacDougalls, or so we hope!"

Despite his apparent happy demeanour, Andrew was anxious to be quickly away from the depth of Campbell country. The sudden sound of a commotion having him swing to where Fergus was bravely fighting off the blows of a woman beating him about the chest, whose patience finally exhausted, threw her to the ground where she lay hurling up obscenities at him.

Pushing back his bonnet Fergus grinned up at his leader. "Men I can manage somewhat easier!" he shouted up apologetically.

Acknowledging the apology with a wave, Andrew's eyes strayed to the other end of the town, the sound of the shot jerking him back to where the big man had dropped to his knees, a hand held to his stomach, and a boy no more than twelve years old standing a few feet away a still smoking pistol clutched in his hand, a look of sheer incredulity on his young face at what he had done to this giant of a man.

All at once that inhuman screech filled the air, that Andrew knew and hated, and the dwarf, claymore in hand was rushing at the terrified boy, while he himself leaped down the braeside towards his stricken friend.

Though the leader knew his cries could not be heard by the dwarf, he hoped at least he may be seen. Too late, the tiny man skewered the frightened boy on his claymore, whose tortured cries rent the air, chilling all around.

Instantly from all directions hysterical women rushed upon the scene, the screaming boy, still impaled on that great sword clutching the terrible weapon with blood soaked hands, a look of unbelievable horror on his young face, gulping and choking for breath, legs buckling beneath him.

Impassively the dwarf placed a foot on his young victim's chest and with one bone shattering screech pulled his weapon free, and without a sideways glance at the inert figure ran to kneel by his friend's side, to rock back and forth, tears streaming down his giant face.

"The lad has done for me Andrew." Fergus smiled weakly up at a panting Andrew. "After all the battles and 'liftings', it is no more than a bairn that has seen me dead." He tried to laugh at the irony.

Andrew dropped to his knees and took Fergus's head in his lap.

The giant gave a cough and blood ran down his chin. "Take care of the wee man, he did what he thought was right, but I greatly fear it is an ill omen, this day," he choked.

Andrew wiped the blood speckles from the dying man's lips. "Tell Cathal...." Fergus coughed again, the words faint, hard in coming.

"I am after knowing what to tell her Fergus, my friend," Andrew answered softly.

Tenderly Andrew cradled his friend in his lap until he felt that giant body relax, then gently placed him on the ground.

"It cannot be! It must not be!" Dugald exclaimed, running to the dead man's side, he too, kneeling down and taking Fergus's hand in his, that by so doing it would restore his friend to life.

"Take from him what you can, Dugald, for Cathal's sake," Andrew mumbled, springing up. "We must away from here. We cannot dare wait to give the man Christian burial."

Suddenly Andrew was afraid. Angrily he hauled the grief stricken dwarf to his feet as wailing women passed them carrying the dead body of the boy. Everywhere it seemed his men were running to him shouting out their questions as to what had happened, while in contrast their comrades on the far hillside still quite oblivious to the catastrophe continued to drive on the cattle as commanded.

His head buzzing with what to do next, all Andrew could think of was to be away from here and Clan MacDiarmid country with all possible speed. "Let us away! All is lost to us now!" he barked. "Dugald! Quickly man, before the word reaches their menfolk, for they will not rest easily at this day's work!"

Swiftly the caterans made for the braeside, catching up with those already driving on the stolen herd.

"We will leave the cattle now, if we are to save ourselves, for I fear in this confusion we could not have prevented some of the women or lads from stealing through with word to their menfolk!" Andrew shouted, his anger directed at the innocent drovers, though in truth it was the dwarf he blamed for what had happened.

"And why so, Andrew?" Dugald challenged, seeing this as a final betrayal to his friend Fergus. Nor was he about to return home empty handed and have Cathal thinking her man had died for naught. "The MacDiarmids are as far away as they would have been had the boy not died," he protested, standing squarely, defiantly before his chief.

Seething with anger Andrew answered his haughty young lieutenant. "True. Yet the MacDiarmids will come after us more speedily for the murder of the lad than for their cattle. 'Tis a matter of pride and honour, not to mention revenge. Do you not agree, Dugald?"

Dugald was in no mood to acquiesce. He would not return to Cathal's doorstep empty handed.

"Doubtless you are right in this, for you are well known for your planning and caution. Yet I am after thinking all is not lost. Though we do not have the number of cattle we had hoped for, it is to our advantage that we have fewer then to drive. I say we can salvage some profit from this day still."

Andrew glared around him at the murmur of agreement that met this suggestion. "Very well Dugald," he said testily. "You may take those who will follow you. I will not hinder you in this. Though have a care, for now I am sure the MacDiarmids will no longer see the MacDougalls as the villains in this piece, and will come after you...and I... with every able man they can muster, and I for one do not wish to be hindered by beasts loath to leave their own pastures."

Now not so sure as to have challenged the man who had trusted him so many times in the past, and who had raised him to this position of respect above older, if not wiser men, Dugald dropped his eyes to his feet, reluctant to retract his words. Twin spots of colour appeared on his cheeks as he said with something akin to a murmur, " You are ever over cautious, *ceann cinnidh.*. I say it can be done." With this Dugald swung on his heel, calling out to those who had a mind to follow him.

A few hesitated at Dugald's back, one asking of Andrew. "Will the gain be shared by us only, who take the risk to see the cattle back with the Stewart?"

Disappointed by the number choosing to follow the younger man, Andrew merely nodded.

In order to confuse the watchers in the sacked town below and give Dugald and his band time Andrew led his men off in a different diection.

Later in the day, a cateran pointed to where Dugald's band had left a score or more beasts grazing in a gully some time before. "At least they have had the good sense not to have taken all their spoils with them, the man declared."

For a moment Andrew's anger and disappointment prevented him from thinking, or even caring. It would serve the young popinjay right, if he and his band were to be overtaken. No! It would not do, he was still *ceann cinnidh* , and was responsible for all under his command, even those so ill advised as to have followed the young upstart. Besides, did he not owe it to all those waiting anxiously back in the *daingheachd* for the safe return of a husband, father, or loved one.

Certain that Dugald and his band, despite having left an amount of cattle and gear behind, would be overtaken once the MacDiarmids returned and had a whiff of the scent, Andrew made up his mind.

It would mean of course that he would have to alter his intentions of veering away east, and well away from those who would chase Dugald, if he was to save the daft laddie and those with him.

"MacMaster! MacAdam! Follow those fools. Keep me well advised how far the MacDiarmids are at their backs. We shall meet by yon braes we rested in this morning. You two!" Andrew singled out two others to his side. "Take five men each, divide yon beasts the others have left behind between you, and head in the direction allotted to you as before. Hopefully this may help confuse our pursuers for a time. And time is what Dugald...the devil take him...needs. When you reach the braes scatter them there. Meet me in the same place as MacMaster and MacAdam. Quickly now before all is lost!"

At last all being ready, Andrew gave the signal and the columns moved off in their various directions.

"We shall give them another half hour,"Andrew decided, looking across the moor in search of his two scouts.

It was almost an hour since the two columns, minus their herds had gathered in the hollow. Now they awaited word from the men he had sent to spy on Dugald and the pursuing MacDiarmids.

"They come!" A man tugged at Andrew's sleeve.

A little distance away the dwarf sat hunched forlornly against a tree, knees drawn up to his chin. Andrew did not know whether to feel sorrow or anger at the tiny man. Although the rest of the company had no such qualms, all seeing him as the reason for their ill fortune. Thanks to him their long trudge into Argyll had been for nothing.

Only Andrew thought he knew what had gone on in the *troich's* head. In killing the boy, he had acted instinctively to his big friend's death. It was that simple.

"They are here!" The same man touched Andrew's arm again.

On reaching them, MacMaster was the first to speak. "The MacDiarmids are less than an hour behind, Dougald!" he exclaimed, still out of breath.

"Less by now, I should say," the second man added hurriedly.

Andrew grimaced. "Devil take the man, and all who were gullible enough to follow him." He absently toyed with his pistol. "However, they are still our folk, and although it goes against my better judgment, we shall do what we can. Come! Let us be on our way."

"We are scarcely here in time,"Alan Fraser, whispered in Andrew's ear.

"Now we start our plan, Alan. Let Him be with us." Andrew backed away from where they hid along the short ridge.

Beneath them the MacDiarmids, now not so far behind Dugald and his party had entered the gleannan. Ravens took to the air at their rapid approach, squawking their protests at these strange intruders to their domain, and on the far ridge, the sun, a red ball of fire dipped behind the opposite ridge, and with it the heat of the day.

A little distance beneath where Andrew hid, his eight caterans rose from the gorse covered braeside to fire into the midst of the pursuers, then turn and sprint back up the brae. Who with a howl of rage and alarm gave chase, only when nearing the top to run into a second line of fire from another row of hidden caterans.

Again it was the turn of the first line to fire, though now, the MacDiarmids had sought cover amongst what boulders they could find on the slope

"They are wise to us now, Andrew," Fraser gulped at his chief.

"Aye. They seek to outflank us. They will be more cautious now, besides suspicious, I am after thinking, for they must surely know we cannot have the herd up here, and are not the party that they seek, or only partly thereof."

In answer to Andrew's deductions, the MacDiarmids were cautiously retreating back down the brae, intent on resuming their chase after Dugald and the original band,where upon reaching the glen floor were attacked again by another band of Andrew's men from the opposite slope.

Confused and taken aback by this unforseen situation, the MacDiarmids retreated some way back down the tiny glen to gather out of range and to take stock.

Crouched behind a rock, Alan Fraser said cheerfully,"They will not try and force a way through the glen, so Dugald and the lads are safe meantime. What think you, Andrew?"

"There is honour and vengeance to be satisfied, Alan. What think you, if in their place?"

Not awaiting an answer Andrew led his caterans, hidden by the rim, along the ridge until they were almost directly above the foe, where some slaked their thirst by a burn, and others bound the wounds of their fellow clansmen,until a command had them trotting off in the direction they had first entered the glen.

"They are beaten! They have had enough!" a cateran cried.

Andrew held up his hand for silence. "No. They mean to outflank us. Come at us along the ridge from further down the glen. Come! We shall halt them as they climb, though we are vastly outnumbered."

Running and slipping, the caterans worked their way along the jagged ridge, until at last they looked down upon the ascending clansmen once more.

Andrew threw a quick look at his men drawn up behind the ridge, reloading or leaning on their swords to regain their breath, and to the *troich* standing some distance away from the others.

There was no time to waste, they must attack now. Andrew gestured hastily to the dwarf what he had in mind and hoped he would understand, but at this juncture and after what had happened earlier that day, he was in no mind to deliberate. He turned to the rest. "Await my signal. Those with pistols will fire upon my command, then it is at them with the sword, then away. We seek only to draw them away from our lads, not fight a clan battle."

Cautiously, Andrew peeked over the rim where the MacDiarmids, intent on their climbing were unaware of their presence. Suddenly Andrew and his men were on their feet, yelling and crying out their own individual clan slogan and running down to meet the foe, Andrew firing his pistols, the *troich* somewhere in the midst of a sea of tartan reeking havoc with his terrible weapon, anxious to be at them, seeking revenge for his big friend's death.

Andrew, his pistols empty was in no hurry to reload, or seek a fallen sword. He had been already more than brave this day, a trait he did not mean to duplicate.

Shouting a command he turned and ran back up to the ridge top, followed by his obedient band, a panting dwarf amongst them. Over the top they ran, through a line of rising caterans whose turn it now was to attack the chasing foe.

It was enough. Once again an unexpected attack had caught the MacDiarmids unawares, reducing their numbers, their wounded lying bleeding on the ridge top.

"They quit, I am after thinking!" Fraser gasped, running down to where Andrew stood at the foot of the brae on the further side from the glen.

"For the time being,"Andrew gulped in air, and cast a look back up to the ridge top. "We must keep going. Even in this direction we can lead them away from Dugald. Though be wary, these clansmen know this country better than we do ourselves."

They ran until certain there was no pursuit, when Andrew drew them to a halt to count their losses and tend the wounded, and praying for those they had left behind to the mercy of the MacDiarmids.

They had done what they could for their fellow caterans, it was now up to that young man to lead his band to Appin, then safely back home, to the *daingneachd.*

A line of women, some with bairns in their arms or at their skirts cast worried eyes at Andrew and the returning men, each woman searching for a loved one amongst the few. Cries of dismay when not sighting a husband or son.

"Have no fear!" Andrew cried a reassurance. "there are many more to come, Dugald has taken a party to Appin as arranged, and will be back in a day or so."

"And I suppose that great mountain of a man of mine has gone with him?" Cathal MacAlister cried in mock dismay, amidst shrieks of laughter, which was mingled with relief from the other women nearby.

Her eyes still twinkling with amusement, Andrew stared at the woman, unable to take his eyes away, not knowing what to do or say.

Cathal saw the look. "He is not with them, is he Andrew?" The woman's gaiety replaced by a note of finality, an acceptance, waiting Andrew's look to soften and tell her she was wrong, although she already knew it was not so.

A slight shake of Andrew's head confirmed her worse fears. Beside him the dwarf stood head bowed clasping and unclasping his hands, childlike, a queer wailing sound emanating from within that giant head.

Cathal nodded her understanding, and from all around, women converged to offer their condolences, for all had witnessed this so many times before, and would no doubt do so again, and together they led the greiving woman back to her bothan. While at their back Andrew let out a slow breath of relief at not having to tell the woman of how her man had died. The wailing of the *corranaich* already at his back as he strode for his own empty bothan.

Cock-a - hoop, Dugald quickened his step to meet the caterans that were grazing the beasts by the burnside a little distance from the stronghold, and changed direction to seek out Andrew.

"It is done, Andrew, and all are safe! We won through to Appin as planned!" Dugald's eyes gleamed with pride, his recent confrontation with his chief all but forgotten.

"You have done well then Dugald. What was the Stewart's mind in all of this?" Andrew returned stonily, for he had not forgotten.

Dugald answered as if nothing was amiss. "Yon man was after thanking me for my effort, and was somewhat amazed that you should run before such as the MacDiarmids!"

Instead of giving his cocky young lieutenant a suitable retort, Andrew cast an experienced eye over those at Dugald's back. "I feared not all would return with you Dugald, though I see the opposite to be the case, that you have in fact gained in numbers, if I am not mistaken, see you?"

Dugald shrugged, a wide grin on his face, and pointed to a group drinking their fill by the burn.

"Yon four are they who supplied you with much needed information at the standing stone these years past." Dugald chuckled. "The MacSorley believes they have betrayed him, especially after our wee raid on his....house. He had them held in his keep by Loyne side. They had just newly escaped when we came across them in the Monadhliath and were making for the standing stone. It was their hope that some of us would eventually find them there. The one nearest slaking his thirst is, Iain MacKinnon, he who warned you of Gleidh House being watched, if you mind Andrew?"

Iain MacKinnon was near enough to have heard the tail end of the conversation. So this was their *ceann cinnidh*. After all those years in the service of the caterans, he would at last meet the man face to face, and as he rose from the burnside to meet the chieftain, saw not the figure who now strode towards him, but a much younger man, a man who had stood on a river bank firing at a man scrambling up the river bank. With he, Iain MacKinnon, standing amid stream, screaming vengeance on the devil who had done this foul deed to Gregor MacKinnon, his younger brother.

Grateful that the MacLaren, having sensed nothing to be amiss, or recognised him, had moved on to greet the other escapees, Iain, his senses in turmoil reflecting on the events that had led him to leave his own folk for that of the MacSorleys. Yet, if this was the man who had ended his brother's life by the river the day of the battle against the MacKerlichs, who then was the man he himself had slain yon night in the rain, at the croft of *an iasgair ?* The one everyone in the district knew as the fisherman?

He remembered his own MacKinnon chief's suspicions that one of his own clan had been responsible for the death of the MacLaren,' the fisherman' and that his patriarch, not wishing further reprisals after their defeat by the MacKerlichs in the battle of the glen had hunted high and low for the assassin. It was then he had decided it best to be away, and had come at length to settle in MacSorley land.

Therefore, whether he liked it or not, this was the man responsible for his present predicament and his brother's death. This, however could be easily remedied, once he knew the whereabouts of the caterans *daingneachd.*

Looking around him at the high mountain fastness, Iain smiled for the first time in years it seemed. There was still a wrong to be righted, and in this MacSorley of Quoich himself would play a part. He would have his revenge...and a little besides. So thinking Iain MacKinnon followed the caterans up the mountainside.

270

Chapter 19

It was one of those rare September evenings when a man found it hard not to be at peace with the world. So deciding, Andrew strolled down the heather to his favourite spot by the tinkling burn. Inhaling deeply, he drank in the beauty of the scene; of heather in full bloom, the black serrated ridges of the mountains beyond Ness.

He kicked out at a stone, sad that Una could not be here to share these moments with him, and rounding an outcrop of rock almost stumbled over the lounging figure of Duncan Cameron.

"*DIA* Duncan, I did not see you sitting there!" Andrew apologised, recovering from his surprise.

"No matter, Andrew, I myself was thinking it was awhile since last we spoke," the elder man answered, leaning back on the rock.

"You have something on your mind that needs saying?"

"Only...." The man shrugged. "I am wearied Andrew, and growing over old for this life of mine." Duncan continued before Andrew could voice that this was not so. "It is true...and you yourself have seen this. Do you think me so niave not to be aware of your concern? Or your consideration not to include me in the longer forays? Of which I thank you. No, Andrew, I am weary and advise you, that unless you yourself look to the future, then it will be to see yourself in me."

Andrew sat down beside his old friend unable to find the right words. Duncan went on. "You are not yet too old to start anew, before it is too late. Be the crofter you once were...before all of this. Before, God help us, we came to change you to what you are today."

Wagging a finger in warning, Duncan stared at his young chief. "It is true Andrew, if you can but mind as I do. You *were* a gentle man when first we met, incapable of such deeds...."

"Such as killing the Irishman and his friend?" Andrew cut in angrily.

"No Andrew, not for killing them, for the good Lord knows they deserved to die, and each man who watched a loved one perish during the starving would gladly have done the deed himself. No. It was the manner in which it was done. *This* made me afraid, made me despair for you. The crofter lad could not have brought himself to have done such a thing my friend, but the cateran could and did."

Duncan plucked a blade of grass and put it between his teeth to give the younger man time to digest his words. "Do you mind when we lifted yon *spreidh* of cattle from Moray? It is a long time ago now." Duncan's voice softened. "You left me to watch the town we were passing by." He paused to catch his breath. "I mind hearing the sound of the kirk bells yon Sabbath norning, and peering down at the honest folk trudging to their worship, and wishing with all my heart to be one of them. Do you take my meaning, Andrew? It is over late for me, but not for you. Do you wish to end your days here, dependent on the charity of others? Such as old Finlay or his like? Or God forgive me, myself?

Shaken by the man's words, Andrew rose to stare across the wild purple vista, hearing his old friend say. "Man is to those same mountains Andrew, as the May Fly is to man, both are over quick in their passing.

"I did not choose this path entirely Duncan, if you mind. Though I confess my steps grew easier on it for a time," Andrew reminded his friend. "I admit I made mistakes. What humble man not born to this life would not?

I left my native glen because I was afraid, thinking to leave my fear buried beside my sweet dear Fiona, and start anew. I came away leaving all that was dear to me in yon far glen, only to find the fear was buried deep within myself, and there it bides. Perhaps it is this which makes me act thus. What say you, Duncan?"

Andrew turned to look down at his friend dozing there, his eyes closed, the blade of grass drooping from his open mouth.

"I see my soul searching has the same effect on you as it has on the *troich*" Andrew chortled, bending down to stir the man, who at his touch slumped forward.

"Duncan!" Andrew exclaimed, kneeling down beside his friend, and unable to believe that anything could be wrong with the man who had just finished talking to him.

Andrew cradled the old man's head in his lap, his last words still in his ears. Had the man come here to pass his last hour? Or had death found him just as suddenly?

The mountains were still there. The loch and burn still flowed. Nature would not know of his passing. Only he and a few others would mourn this good man, who had been right. It was time to be away, and leave this life behind.

Dugald and his party emerged out of the morning mist, the driven beasts huddled together seeking comfort from one another in the eariness of the surrounding mountains.

Dugald broke away, climbing the steep barren slope, winding a way through isolated clumps of whin to meet his chief, who stood reflecting on how much the young man had mellowed and matured in such a short space of time: mellowed; since Fergus and Duncan's passing: matured; after learning of the part he, Andrew had played in diverting the MacDiarmids in the Argyll raid.

"I thought to find myself here before you Andrew, since we found no trouble at all in the 'lifting', evidently you had less." The man's words echoed hollowly in the morning air.

Andrew refrained from stating the obvious. Alarm registered on his weathered countenance. "Where is the MacKinnon? I charged you to keep him close," he asked forcefully, for he had never fully trusted the man since first meeting him by the burn. The *troich's* behaviour had confirmed his growing uneasiness, despite the trouble the MacKinnon had found himself in by being in the caterans' employ.

"Have no fear Andrew!" Iain is in good company with the Rattrays, he brings up the remainder of the herd some ways back. Besides, we cannot always be watching him like a sow with her litter." There was a hint of annoyance in Dugald's voice.

True, Andrew thought, the man had done nothing to give rise to suspicion. Indeed, the opposite had been the case, working well at any chores given him, and plainly grateful to be free once more, besides content with his lot. Still? There was something...and the *troich* was seldom wrong.

"You are right there, Dugald," Andrew agreed. He lifted his face to the weak struggling sun. "The mist will not be long in lifting, I am after thinking, and with any luck after the 'raiders callop' has been paid to Neil MacPherson, we shall see home by nightfall." The last of his words drowned out by a volley of shots echoing earily around the mountainside.

"Dia! What was that?" Andrew screwed up his eyes to peer up at the mist hidden crags.

"It is hard to know Andrew, for the great mountains themselves are playing with the sound." Dugald squinted in the opposite direction from which they had just come. "That it is a fight of some sort there is no doubt," he declared categorically.

"Neill! Peter!" Andrew beckoned both Fedriths to him with a flick of his hand. "Away with you now, and find out what is taking place up yonder, for I believe the sound comes from there." He indicated the direction he wished them to take. "You will find us in the corrie that we passed not long since," he threw after them. "Gang warily, see you!"

The Federiths were no sooner away than it seemed they were back, rushing to their chieftain's side, stammering that it was none other than Neil MacPherson himself who was engaged with a passing band of strange clansmen, who would not submit to paying for the herd passing through his land and would be grateful for any assistance that he or his kind might decide to offer.

"What think you, Andrew?" Dugald chuckled, amused by the situation. "It might serve our purpose to help the man, since we ourselves are dependent upon his goodwill."

"Aye, but cautious mind, for we must see how the land lies."

"In this mist?" Dugald shot back good humourdly.

Smiling broadly, Andrew flashed back. "Away with you man!" Then in afterthought added, "But since your wit is as sharp as your sword this morning, Dugald Ferguson, perhaps you should bide behind and guard the herd." Then at Dugald's crestfallen expression slapped him on the back. "Come on then man," he chuckled, unable to keep a straight face. "Lets see what this business is all about."

Cautiously, the Federiths led them back up through the swirling mist to the heights above, the only sound now heard in that eerie silence, that of their own laboured breathing.

"We are too late, it is over" Dugald cursed at the prospect of perhaps adding to their good fortune and the MacPherson's discomfiture, for he would dearly loved to have seen that man's face when asking for their assistance.

"No. There stands MacPherson." Peter Federith gestured to the crags above.

Reaching the top, Neil made his way to them. "I am over glad to see you MacLaren!" That man greeted Andrew warmly. "We are sorely pressed to hold them. It is this mist solely that hides our lack of numbers...or they would have broken through by now. I have sent for more of our own, but I fear they will be some time in their coming."

"They come again!" a voice shouted anxiously out of the mist.

Clearly alarmed, Neil drew Andrew aside. "You will help?"

Nonchalantly Andrew brushed an invisible speck of dirt from his sleeve. "We have a herd of our own to attend to, Neil." He gave his sleeve his full attention. "Though...if it was to pass through your lands without reduction....?"

"It is a bargain MacLaren! No raiders callop will I ask this day!" Neil pivoted on his heel, drawing to an abrupt halt when Andrew made no sign of moving. "You will help? *Before* it is too late that is?

Andrew folded his arms and appeared to deliberate. "Aye, and a third these rascals clansmen possess."

"A third!" the MacPherson choked, his patience on the brink of explosion. "A quarter, or the next time you see your *daingneach* it will be in Hell, MacLaren! And that is a long way from the Monadhliath!"

"Aye and a lot warmer forby, Neil."

Andrew, knew Neil had the means to stop his caterans from passing through his lands in future should he choose, and was pleased with his bargain, though he would have settled for less. Pretending to be disappointed he shook his head. "A quarter it is then." Then signalled his men to follow him at the trot.

They sent the strange clansmen reeling back with the impetus of their unexpected attack, where one could scarcely make out friend from foe in the swirling mist.

His own safety ever paramount, Andrew took his time in reloading his pistols, now quite useless under the circumstances, for he could just as easily hit friend as well as foe. When suddenly out of the mist came a fair-haired youth, who seeing Andrew pick up a sword but without the customary protective targe, charged at him, forcing him back.

Within seconds Andrew knew this young man was much too quick and agile for him, his only hope lying in coming to grips with him, where his greater strength would come to his advantage.

Again the lad came at him, missing his chest by inches. Disadvantaged without a targe, Andrew backed away, slashing defensively with his hated weapon. Once more the youth missed him by a hairsbreadth, before nimbly dancing away as Andrew thrust at him. He came again. This time their swords caught by the hilt, and Andrew seized his chance by grabbing for his pistol as his opponent caught him a glancing blow with the edge of his targe.

Blood blinding his vision, fear filling his belly, Andrew tore the pistol from his belt and fired it into the young lad's stomach in a swift upward movement. The boy reeled back, held upright only by the still locked blades, his fear filled face turned heavenwards.

Andrew freed the swords, and let the boy sink to the ground.

"Uncle!" the boy choked clutching his belly. "Uncle!" he cried again and lay still.

For a moment, Andrew felt a twinge of remorse at having given the lad a lesson he was never likely to profit from, quickly followed by the thought that it could just as easily have been himself lying there.

"They flee! They flee!"

Andrew looked up at the cry of triumph, his victim already forgotten.

"We sent them back, MacLaren, and there is no other way past us here, for it is a sheer drop at their backs. Though, granted desperate men could find a way down, but without their precious herd!" Neil cried out to Andrew, now by his side.

A figure appeared out of the mist. "Neil, we have prisoners here for your inspection."

Neil's smiled faded. "Then let us have a look at these strange folk who would rather die in these cold mountains than pay the MacPherson his dues."

Andrew followed the chief further up the trackless mountainside until they came upon a group of despondent men huddled together in the lee of a rock overhang.

"Who amongst you will act as spokesman here?" Neil barked, his eyes darting from one to another.

"I will." A man, rose from where he had been attending a wounded comrade.

Neil! Neil!" A clansman rushed to his leader's side. "Tis your cousin, Rory! Man he is sorely hurt!"

Neil swung to Andrew. "See if you can make sense of this MacLaren, whilst I am away to my cousin." He swung back to the prisoners, glaring, "And the Devil help you all should my cousin be the worst for this day."

"MacLaren?" the prisoner who had arisen, asked, a look of curiosity on his face. "You cannot be Andrew MacLaren of our own Glen Laidon?"

Andrew stepped closer, it coming to him as to the opening of a door that the man who stood here was his own good-brother. "Rob MacLaurin!" he cried in disbelief. "You, Rob, my own wife's brother..it cannot be you?"

"One and the same," Rob answered, drawing closer to his kinsman. "It has been many a year now since you quit the glen. And to where? Still, if I were to believe we'd meet again, I'd never in a hundred years wager it would be to see you thus."

Andrew saw the hurt through his kinsman's disbelief. "It was never always so Rob, less you judge me over harshly, see you." He wiped the blood away from his eyes. "But why here Rob? What brings you to such a God forsaken place..and with beasts?"

"It was not by choice I can assure you. We came to buy cattle for ourselves, the remainder to sell in the Lowlands, for there is siller to be made there." At first all went well, until one chief after another demanded toll for passing through their lands, forcing us to leave the drove roads for higher ground. Then your friend came upon us, demanding more than the all the others put together. What is left of the tale you can easily surmise. We were driven ever higher until at length we found ourselves here with nothing but cliffs at our backs."

Though Andrew listened, his mind reeled with thoughts of Glen Laidon, and in particular his son. But dare he ask? After all, he had done nothing less than desert him.

He desperately wanted to know if the lad was well, prospered back home. Something that he could take away with him, a memory..or if he could help him in some way. He had a little siller put by, and should it come to it, the house he would share with Isabella Grant could wait a little longer.

Andrew cleared his throat, it taking as much courage to ask the question as it had done to face the fresh faced lad a wee while back. "Calum ? He fares well?"

"Well enough the last time I saw him, unless you and yours have treated him otherwise." Rob glanced around him. "Since he is not here, he must be amongst those free to fight on."

Andrew could not stop himself from shaking. "He is *here*?"he shouted incredulously, those nearby staring in his direction. "You have brought a child with you, on this....?" he stammered.

Rob's intended angry retort melted away in the knowledge of how well Calum had turned out to be, and the man he had made of him in the absence of his cowardly father...a father who now stood before him. Now let Calum see for himself what manner of man his father was... A common robber. "Scarcely a child, MacLaren, he is all of seventeen years old, and tall as yourself, with the same fair hair of his mother. Aye, and if the tales I have heard about you back in the glen are right, much better at the sword play than you ever were yourself, which is a mercy in itself," Rob added with a sarcastic chuckle.

Andrew felt weak. A pain deep within his gut rose red hot to his chest to throb in time to the pounding of his heart. He shifted his glazed eyes to the other prisoners, recognising some, though it meant nothing, and fighting all the while to erase those last fateful words of his kninsmen from his mind.

It could not be, Satan himself could not be so cruel as to let him destroy his own flesh and blood, and with his own father's pistol.

Andrew drew a hand across his eyes. Perhaps it had been another he had slain, and spurned his own naiveté.

"What is amiss, man?" Rob challenged. "Do not have me thinking you have a concern for your son?" he asked at the pained expression on the cateran's face. "Or is it you do not wish the lad to see his father in this pass..to see him for what he really is?" Now all he wanted to do was hurt the man, humiliate him; make him suffer for all those awkward questions Calum had asked him about his father.

"He is dead, Rob. I saw the lad you described lying there as I came here with the MacPherson," Andrew lied, unable to tell his kinsman the truth, and cursing at ever being destined to bring grief to this entire family all of his life. He cleared his throat. "Unless there is another fits your description?"

Rob shook his head. "The poor laddie," he whispered. "And I after telling his grandmother I would take a care for him." He turned to stare unseeing to where his fellow prisoners still sat huddled around the rocks. "Last year my own father gone, and now Calum. It will surely break her heart." Head bowed the distraught man wiped away a tear.

278

A few of Andrew's former clansmen rose and moved slowly towards him, one of whom he recognised as the man who had berated him the day they had come to carry his dear Fiona away.

"So it is you yourself, Andrew MacLaren, it surprises me naught to see you in such brave company . Brave company that is to take a laddie's life. What manner of man..or men is it that needs kill the laddie, when he could just as easily have been taken prisoner?

"Then it is true, it is my own son who lies there? There can be no doubt?" Andrew stared at each in turn.

Their silence confirmed what he already knew, what he had feared in his heart. Andrew's mood changed. At least there was something he could do to make amends, however small. "I cannot save my son, but at least you men I can."

"You MacLaren?" his former tormentor laughed sarcastically.

Andrew's reply was as sharp as a pistol shot. "You must take yourselves back up the cliff top. I will send you a man to guide you down the other side to the glennnan below."

"We shall not leave without the beasts," another broke in, "we have already paid a high price,"adding with a scowl at his would be rescuer. "This you should know."

Andrew threw a glance at Rob MacLaurin and in turn encompassed the others. "You will leave the beasts here," he commanded, his hand on his pistol butt, "for I am *ceann cinnidh*, to all caterans here at my back!"

The sting in Andrew's voice halted the protesting unarmed clansmen, and silencing those who had gasped at the notion that this man...this coward could be leader of these wild men.

"Soon the MacPherson's men will be here in strength," he went on. "Then you will lose more than your beasts, I fear."

Stepping to his kinsman he seized him roughly by the arm. "I have cattle of my own not so very far distant. Allow the man who I send lead you to it. They are yours for the taking."

"And those, Andrew? What of those?" Rob jerked his head in the direction of the guards, more than a hint of suspicion in his voice. "Will they not have a word or so to say in all of this?"

"Perhaps. We shall see. Will you do as I suggest?"

Rob complied with a mere shrug of his shoulders. "But why put your own self at risk for us man, we who are nothing short of strangers to you?"

"Maybe it is for you all. You, my Fiona, and for all the trouble I have caused you and yours. In the end, for a son I never knew. Who can say? Whether you scorn me or not, a part of me lies out there this day."

For a fleeting second, Rob MacLaurin felt some sympathy for the man. It could all have been so different. His fellow clansmen drew away. "You should not have left the glen, Andrew, not in the manner in which you did. Nonetheless, the fault does not lie with you alone. Should I win back home, I will tell them there who we had to thank for all of this."

Andrew drew the pistols from his belt, and held them so that the other man could see the inscription on both weapons, and as Rob peered closer, Andrew informed him, "It is too long a tale to relate how I came by this one. He weighed the one he had taken from the MacIntosh; ironically also the same weapon responsible for his own son's death, in his hand. "But tell them back in Glen Laidon, that I found the man who took the pistol from my own *tigh tughadh* yon black day." Then roughly. "Come! You must be away before the MacPherson returns!"

Andrew crossed to where the MacPherson sentinels stood guard, bidding his former clansmen to follow discretely behind. "The MacLaurin here, will take his men back up the mountainside and persuade the remainder of his clansmen to lay down their arms,whereby the MacPherson can win the entire herd without further bloodshed." He motioned to Rob and the others not to halt as he spoke.

"It is not for you to decide," one sentinel flung at him angrily, his hand dropping to his sword hilt. "You will leave them be until the MacPherson himself, returns."

Andrew drew up inches away from the dissident, arms akimbo, eyes bulging. "Listen you puss on a sow's arse, did you yourself not hear Neil MacPherson ask me to see what I could make of this?" And as the man stammered to reply, thrust his face into that of the other. "Well! Will you brave the wrath of your chieftain when I inform him that it was you who prevented me from doing what I thought best, and in doing so perhaps save many a MacPherson life into the bargain?"

Realising by the man's expression that he had gained the advantage, Andrew drove home, "*Dia!* Stand aside man, let them all pass! You may tell the MacPherson if you will, what I have done, should you meet him before I myself do."

"Let them go," another advised, not wishing to be on the wrong side of his chieftain's wrath. "It is the MacLaren's head that will fall, not ours, if he is wrong in this."

Gratefully, Andrew watched the men of Glen Laidon disappear into the mist, and wishing with all his heart to be going home with them, the possibility not far from his mind, until remembering the single reason for doing so lay in the heather not so far away.

Sadly, Andrew made his way back down the mountain coming upon a group of MacPherson's in the very act of stripping his son, the sight of which brought all of his pent up anger to the boil.

"Let him be! You are worse than carrion crows! He is but a lad, see you!" he shouted furiously at the would- be robbers.

Quickly recovering from Andrew's verbal onslaught, one cried out, "You will have his *feileadh mor*, and his weapons for yourself? Is that the way of it?" He took a hasty step back as Andrew surged to his dead son's side.

"Seeing as I slew the lad it is my right, and none shall gainsay me!" Andrew flashed, whipping out both pistols. While somewhere in his brain he hoped one would be foolish enough to challenge him; help ease the pain in his chest.

"Leave it be," another suggested, "there are more pickings to be had than this slip of a boy."

Andrew watched them go, more than a little annoyed that he could not vent his spleen on the grumbling scavengers, before dropping to his knees beside his son, to let his eyes roam over the still form, searching for a likeness of himself, and in its stead found a face so like his own Fiona.

Gently he touched the cheek, tracing a finger to the lips already cold, contemplating on what might have been, and cursing the day the MacIntosh had so brutally entered their lives.

With a tremour, the father closed the eyes of his dead son.

"Andrew, man, what do you do there?"

The voice reached the mourning man through a void. He looked up at Dugald Ferguson and Calum Gunn, standing there and rose shakily to his feet. "Dugald, see the lad is buried decent, if you will. Let no one lay a hand upon him."

"You will take nothing?" An astonished Gunn asked.

281

"No, Calum. The lad is my own son, and yon clansmen, my kinsmen from Glen Laidon."

"Andrew, I did not know...!" Dugald burst out, clearly moved.

"'Tis all right, Dugald, but do as I ask."

Andrew turned to the other man his voice now stronger, more resolute. "Go you up yonder, my kin await you. Lead them to our herd, let them take what they will, and guide them out of the Monadhliath."

It was an indication of the respect for the MacLaren that neither man challenged the implications of such a command, for the herd did not belong to Andrew alone. Yet without the merest hint of hesitation Calum left to do as he was bid.

Andrew turned to Dugald, his hands spread in apology. "I must seek out the MacPherson, for I fear he will be greatly displeased at what I have done." Then remembering he was still *ceann cinnidh* , and should not be justifying his actions, even to his young lieutenant, continued more coarsely. "After all they are my kinsmen, and I will not stand by and see them slain."

His chieftain disappearing in to the mist, Dugald let out a long low whistle and turned to look down at the silent figure of the young MacLaren. "So you are the son of the Cateran himself. *Dia!* The man is deep. Deeper than Ness itself, I am after thinking. Yet he leaves me here to see you laid to rest, whilst he himself hastens to make his peace with the MacPherson."

Disconcerted, Dugald started off in search of assistance.

Andrew found Neil MacPherson in none too pleasant a mood. "My cousin Rory is maimed; he will never tread the heather again. Now these invaders will feel my wrath when my men come up!"

It was almost the last straw, Andrew thought. How was he now to appease the man?

"'Tis sad I am to hear this Neil, but you shall have your revenge. I have the strangers foxed, see you. I have sent some of my caterans around the base of the mountain, where they will await the strangers descent from the cliffs up yonder." Andrew indicated with a quick flick of his hand. "I advised those strange folk it would be more prudent to leave without the herd and save themselves before the rest of your clansmen arrived. So, should everything work to plan, you shall have your herd as well as your revenge, Neil."

"So that was your plan when you spoke to my man as you did." Neil guffawed, his maimed cousin temporarily forgotten. "Hamish swore you were after conniving with yon clansmen!"

"And to what purpose, think you, Neil, with a quarter of the herd at stake? It was difficult enough to convince them to leave the beasts behind, and save themselves. And to show my good faith I have dispatched Calum Gunn, to guide them down the cliff, see you."

Admiringly, Neil answered, "It is a masterly plan of deception, MacLaren, the likes of which you are well renowned. Though for what has happened to Rory my kinsman, it should be the MacPhersons that await yon brood and not your own caterans."

Thinking quickly at this unforeseen suggestion, Andrew ventured, "Aye, you could have your revenge if the strangers were not half way down the cliff by now. Besides, my own men will already be in position," he lied.

Neil gestured his resignation. "Och ! We will leave it be then Andrew. My men will bide here should any of those heathens decide to climb back up, either way we have them."

When Andrew left the MacPherson, it was to gather the dwarf and what men that had not already left, and lead them around the base of the cliff.

Once there he anxiously scanned the heights above for any of the Macpherons, hoping that the unprotected heard gathered there would occupy their attention for a time.

"Do not fire upon the strangers!"Andrew called out to his men. "They are not our unfriends in this! Pass the word, so that all may know."

"It is a hard thing to read your mind, Andrew, I am after thinking." Alan Fraser, expressed dully. "Not so long ago you would have us fight these same folk, which you now wish unharmed. This I cannot fathom."

"I will explain later Alan, much later. For now, suffice to say I crave your indulgence. I would have the strangers spared."

Fraser turned a puzzled eye on the clansmen who now having reached the valley floor through a mist quickly dissipating before a conquering sun, were led by Calum Gunn and Rob MacLaurin who ran to where he and Andrew stood.

283

"Quickly now!" Andrew cried out, urging his kinsmen to keep moving. Then to Rob, "Have your men follow Calum, and be away before the MacPherson realises what is afoot!"

Rob halted, tossing his head in the direction of the cliff. "And what will be your fate when the MacPherson finds out he has been duped?"

"There is enough time for that later. We shall survive. Now go, or all is for naught!" Andrew urged.

Rob took a few steps away, halted, then having made up his mind said quietly. "You can aye return with us to the glen, now the account is settled , and my sister rests in peace." He pointed to the pistols in Andrew's belt.

"There is nothing for me in yon glen now Rob, I fear. What is done cannot be undone, mores the pity." Andrew moved away, terminating the conversation. Then with a final gesture, implored of his kinsman. "Go for pity's sake man, while there is still time!"

As his kinsmen, led by Calum Gunn ran down the mountainside, Andrew searched the empty ridge above. "We shall give those clansmen of mine a minute or so to be away before we start our battle."

"Andrew! Those are your kinsmen?" Alan exclaimed. "How come they here?"

"That they are, Alan, and how came they here is another tale."

"I hope this entire deception is worthwhile. Mind you, we must bide here at the MacPherson's sufferance when all this is done," an anxious Alan Fraser admonished

"Let me be the best judge of that my friend. Now let us make the MacPhersons believe we have apprehended those kinsmen of mine." So saying Andrew fired both pistols in the air, shortly followed by that of his caterans, who seeing the business as a strange masquerade, wholeheartedly joined in, fencing with one another, with some even going to the extent of falling down dead upon the heather.

In no mood for levity, Andrew peered into the thinning mist, awaiting Dugald's return, to be joined by the Fraser.

"Our play acting is almost done, Andrew, shall we start anew?"

Suddenly Alan found himself on the ground and half on top of his chief, the dwarf on top of them both, rolling to one side, the sound of shots hitting a boulder close to their heads.

Recovering from the shock, Andrew struggled to his feet, now comprehending the *troich's* action, for not more than a hundred yards away a score or more of dismounted horse men rushed towards them.

Andrew shouted a warning to his caterans, many like himself with empty pistols. "'Tis the MacSorley, and yonder the treacherous MacKinnon!"

"See Andrew!" Alan spun his chief around, pointing through the remaining coils of mist. "See Andrew, the brae fairly swarms with them as far as the eye can see in this smir!"

"You are right, Alan, the MacSorley has his entire clan at his back, and some Camerons thrown in for good measure, I am after thinking. If only this mist was not for lifting so rapidly, we could win free. As it is...."Andrew trailed off despairingly.

Breathlessly Dugald found his chief huddled behind a rock in the act of struggling to think and reload his empty pistols. "Andrew!" he shrieked. "I have seen the MacSorley, and yon devil McKinnon in his company!"

"This I aready know," Andrew replied haughtily. The fear of what Quoich had in store for him gave way to anger and desperation. "You assured me, man, Iain MacKinnon was in safe company. How then has he had time to be away warning the MacSorley and back?" While asking the question Andrew's eyes were rivetted on his task.

"It was yesterday I last saw him, but was sure the Rattrays knowing my instructions would not let him out of their sight," Dugald pleaded, focusing on the approaching enemy.

Andrew thrust his powder horn back into his belt. "Plainly, Quich has been following us, all the while awaiting the right time to strike...and this is the right time," he rapped out.

"Will, Neill help?"

"Only if he has not found out that I meant to dupe him, for if he has, who do you think he will support, if any?"

A MacSorley clansman charged towards them, Andrew cooly shot him dead and ducked behind his shelter again. "Perhaps our friend Neil will let us fight it out, and pick up what is left of the spoils?"

Outnumbered, the caterans were being pushed back to the base of the cliff where only a short time ago Andrew's kinsmen had descended, leaving Dugald and himself isolated behind a rock, Alan and the dwarf having run to help their hard pressed friends.

His reloading complete, Andrew stepped out from behind his shelter,firing into those MacSorleys who had turned in their direction, shouting at the disconsolate Dugald by his side, "We must both be away to warn the *daingneachd* , Dugald!"

"You will not bide to lead the men?" the young lieutenant shouted incredulously of his chief, who had already broken into a trot, away from the scene of battle. "If you are not, I will command them in your stead, for I will not leave them here leaderless!"

"No Dugald you must come with me, you and I are the only ones here who know of the second way out of the *daingneacd*. All is lost here. We are outnumbered and must surely break, and when this happens all will take to their heels for home, Quoich at their backs. Quick now, before we are cut off.! And thank the good Lord no one has as yet recognised me, or all will be quick to be at our heels!"

Andrew slid down a heather banking, Dugald close behind. Momentarily out of sight of the fight, Andrew gasped at his lieutenant. "Your legs are younger than mine, do not wait for me. All now depends upon you, Dugald." He slipped and the younger man threw out a hand to help him.

"Quoich will do the women and bairns no harm, it is the fighting men he seeks to break, and you above all to have within his grasp," Dugald gasped back, scarcely daring to believe he too was running away.

"Doubtless you are right, but with no fighting men spared, who is to tend for them? In especial through the winters." Andrew plunged on at the doubt on the others face. "The only chance we have of saving the others back in the stronghold is for you...us, to help them reach, Johnny MacKellar in the Cairngorms! Do you not agree?" Andrew grasped at the heather pulling himself up and over a rise; the sound of the battle still ringing in his ears. "We are almost clear now. Make you for the higher ground where the mist will help hide you until you are sure that none follow. I myself will go this way, for I know it well. Should I be seen I will lead them away from you and the *daingneachd*. Now go! And may good fortune go with you."

For a moment Dugald hesitated, his conscience rebelling at the thought of deserting his friends, although his head told him otherwise, that his chief was right. It was up to him to save those back in the stronghold.

Chapter 20

Andrew looked up at the young man standing a few feet away from him at the top of the slope, who with a shrug of resignation turned and trotted off into the mist.

Running, and climbing, Andrew paced himself for the long road home, his conscience only partly bothering him at not having stood and fought alongside his fellow caterans. He knew full well what the upshot would be should Quoich take him alive, therefore, his concern for those back in the stronghold was only partly true. In truth he was again running away, fear of what that grand man would do to him, propelling him on.

The ground he panted and stumbled over in fear and exertion fell away, to rise again at some distance. Andrew gasped for breath and steadied himself to leap a burn, landing in the soft marsh on the other side, his brogues squelching as he ran clear.

Now having ran some distance from where he had left his men, his legs ached. He grasped at the heather and levered himself over a steep slope, and as he sat down for a moment to rest, saw the ant like figure of the dwarf far below.

An hour later, Carn Odhar lay to his west. He hated this part of the mountains, with its never ending steep slopes and dark gullies. Usually when returning with a *spreidh*, he would swing closer to Ness, but today all was haste, he must reach home by the shortest possible route.

Andrew levered himself over the top of some craggs, the sun rolling back the mist like surf to the shore, and caught another glimpse of the dwarf. A tinkling burn drew his attention and he knelt to slake his thirst. It was to be his last halt until he reached the *daingneachd*.

Today there were no women or bairns tending cattle on the lower slopes, confirmation of Dugald having reached the *daingneachd* before him. Andrew passed through the empty defile.

Now a different scene met the cateran leader's eyes. In contrast to the tranquility of the deserted mountainside, here confusion and panic reigned. A cateran ran passed and he caught the hurrying man by the arm demanding of him Dugald's whereabouts. A shaking finger pointed to the end of a row of bothans where an exasperated young lieutenant was endeavouring to create some sort of order in a long line of women and children, most laden with every vestage of conceivable household belongings they could manage to carry, and all pushing towards the narrow passageway.

"Dugald!" Andrew blared out. "How in the name of all that is holy are you allowing this! You know full well man, none can pass through yon hole in the wall with all they carry. And even so, how far will they travel with such burdens all the way to the Cairngorms? Do you want Quoich to follow such a trail all the long road to Johnny's door?"

Dugald gestured helplessy. "None will listen, Andrew. No doubt they will, now that you are here."

Andrew threw a look at the open bothan door. "How many are within the pasageway helping folk through?"

"Five, Andrew."

"How many are left to defend the defile?"

"Eight, maybe nine."

"*Dia!*. Where are all the rest? I did not leave so few behind."

"Gone! Except for a few married men helping their wives and bairns through the passageway."

Andrew placed a calming hand on the desperate man's shoulder. "First" he began, his voice composed as if confiding a confidence, "find two or three men, and have them coax these gathered here into some sort of line. Instruct all they may take with them are extra food and clothing, all else must be left behind. Clear? When this is done, you must get yourself through the passage and lead them to Johnny. Take as many as you can. I will send the *troich* with more after the wee man arrives. Then should all go well, I myself will follow with the remainder."

For a moment as on the slope earlier that day Andrew thought his lieutenant was about to protest, and rushed on to explain for he had no time to debate the odds. "Know one here knows where Johnny bides besides ourselves, Dugald."

Now understanding, Dugald replied with a rush. "This I will do Andrew. How long think you before Quoich arrives with yon traitor MacKinnon? And how long can the defile be held if not all our own are through the passage?"

"It depends. It will be hard to hold the defile if our own men are mingled with theirs. And although I need our mens help, I hope those who have managed to escape scatter all over the Monadliath, rather than find their way back here, though this is too much to expect of men who have women and bairns here." Andrew gave the young man's shoulder a gentle push. "But, first let us get these folk to safety."

A full half hour later the dwarf arrived, and despite the tiny man's obvious exhaustion, Andrew allowed him no rest. Miming and signing in the strange cipher they'd invented over the years, Andrew gave out his instructions, only having just done so when word of Quoich's approach filtered through from the sentinels on the rocks above.

"How many of ours can you see man?" Andrew shouted up to the nearest sentinel.

"A dozen *ceann cinnidh* ! With ten times that number at their heels!"came the anxious reply.

Ordering all who were not helping the women and bairns through the pasageway to follow him Andrew led them to the entrance of the defile, where he climbed on to the saucer shaped rock which helped to block and hide the same, and had hardly done so when the first of his men came staggering through.

"You down there! Stand with the rest!" Andrew shouted out.

Alan Fraser jerked his head up at the voice, unable to believe he was being ordered to stand and fight, and he nearer to exhaution than ever he had been in his life. "How come *you* are here MacLaren? Did you take fright at the first sign of the MacSorley? Leave us to fall where we stood!" he screetched up at his chief.

Wounded by the accusation which came so close to the truth, Andrew hurled back. "Stand with the others Alan Fraser, you will soon learn where my loyalties lie!"

A cateran who had followed Andrew up onto the rock touched his shoulder, drawing his attention back to the defile where the last of the caterans to return were fighting a rearguard action against the first of the foe.

"We cannot yet fire for fear of hitting our own men, so sorely mixed are they," Andrew snapped at the man.

Quickly kneeling by the rim of the rock Andrew shouted down to his men waiting at the end of the arena. "Quoich and his like are here. Have a care you do not fire upon your own when they come rushing through!"

Hardly had Andrew's warning been given before the first of the caterans squeezed past the rock into the arena.

Andrew rose and fired his pistols into the pursuing foe. "Now!" he shouted to his waiting men, who, with a wild cry launched themselves past the rock into a defile scarce wide enough for two men to weild their weapons, and so into the advancing foe.

In one fearful attack the defenders drove MacSorley's men to the furthermost reaches of the narrow defile, before rushing back to the narrow neck of the bastion of rock where Andrew and his fellow cateran lay.

"Andrew! All are now through the passageway!" Alan Fraser called up breathlessly to him. "Now I see why you hurried back here. I did not know there was another way out." Then as a means of an apology, added. "Tis thanks to you the womenfolk are saved."

Fear and desperation put steeliness into Andrew's voice. "They are not yet safe, Alan Fraser, it all depends on how long we hold here. We must give them time to hide within the mountains, or Quoich will find it a simple matter to prevent their escape." Then a little less sternly to the desperate man. "I have Dugald and the *troich* guiding them to meet Johnny MacKellar, though it is a long hard road for the very young and old."

The cry that the attackers came again terminated all further conversation. "It is now all up to us, Alan!" Andrew shouted down. "Quoich will pay dearly to win through."

However, it was not the wild halloo of the clansmens cry which reached their ears, but the high terrified neighing of stampeding garrons, driven on by the invaders at their backs.

Hidden by the rock at the entrance to the defile where Andrew and his companion perched, the waiting caterans were unaware what was afoot until Andrew shouted down as to the intentions of their attackers.

Waving his understanding, Alan Fraser shouted Andrew's warning to his companions, that as they could not hope to halt the charging garrons they must he mindfull of the MacSorley and his like at their heels.

As Alan shouted his warning, Andrew fired at the leading garron, bringing it down to its knees, those, close behind, crashing into the stricken beast in a tangle of legs and bodies, the stricken animals that struggled to rise, again brought down by further pistol shots, until the defile was nothing more than a tangled mass of writhing horseflesh.

Gradually, ever gradually, a silence settled over the defile, broken here and there by the nervous whinnying of the remaining garrons making their way back the way they had come. Now only the dead filled the passageway.

Andrew rose cautiously, wanting to know what was happening from the lookouts above, to be informed that the foe were now gathered around a mounted man who, they surmised to be Quoich himself.

So the MacSorley himself had arrived. Now what would that great man do? Ride the long way round the mountain in the hope of finding another way in? Or sit outside and bide his time? Either way time was on their side. It would give the womenfolk more time to be away.

However, whilst in the midst of turning these thoughts over in his mind, a shout from above informed him Quoich was in no mood to wait, and his men were attempting the passageway through the defile in strength.

"So! The MacSorely would rather risk his men than wait," Andrew thought out loud, firing into the midst of the first of the foe charging round the rock into the waiting caterans, who in turn slashing and hacking with their swords drove the attackers back, for all knew full well that to fail and let the foe win into the open space of the arena would spell disaster.

Furiously, Andrew worked to reload, unaware of an adversay climbing up on the rock, who with a snarl launched himself at the cateran chief, the sound dying in the attackers throat when finding himself impaled by MacNeil's blade, that man wrenching his weapon free to fend off another climber, whilst Andrew's pistol dealt with a third.

"We cannot hope to hold out much longer Alistair, their numbers are too great. Hold here as best you can, I must away and improve matters."

Andrew dropped to the ground. He found two wounded men and hauled them to their feet, cajouling them to follow him, with an order to help him drive the penned cattle at the far end of the arena back to the entrance of the defile.

"Hold them here lads, and await my signal. We must not bring them too close to the fighting lest they stampede in the wrong direction, for all depends on timing" he emphasised firmly.

Andrew cupped his hands and shouted to the heights above. His message clear that the boulders were to be launched into the defile at the commencement of the next attack, and that they were to join him immediately this was done.

Hardly had he spoken than shouts arose that the attackers came again. Giving the signal Andrew returned to join Alastair upon the rock.

At first it came as a low rumble, increasing, as rocks pounded into the soft flesh of the dead garrons lying on the defile floor. The screams of maimed and dying clansmen buried beneath a massive fall of rock. A few who had been fortunate enough to have survived the carnage retreating to the far end of the dust filled defile.

"The passageway is now completely blocked, Andrew!" Alistair exclaimed in unbridled delight, sword held high. "They will not win through now!"

"I think you are wrong there, Alistair! Andrew pointed a pistol. "They come again," his warning drowned in a high explosive yell from the MacSorley clansmen coming on again, angered by their losses and the savage way in which their kinsmen had died. On they came, stumbling over piles of rubble, broken men and beasts.

At the stern determine faces of his foe, Andrew again knew fear. The caterans had made Quoich pay dearly, and in a way that man had least expected. Still they came on unbeaten.

Andrew ran to the rim of the rock which faced into the arena. "Now!" he shouted to his two wounded caterans guarding the herd.

Helped on by other wounded, the caterans whooping and yelling drove the terrified cattle into the defile, as their attackers won free of the fallen rocks, the sheer weight of the herd turning the invaders back the way they had come.

"It is done!" Andrew shouted down from his perch, "get you all back to the end bothan! We must be away before the MacSorley and his kind recover!"

Catching up with the running caterans, Andrew led them to the escape route in the bothan, returning to stand guard by the door to await the tailenders who had done so much damage with the rocks from the heights above.

No sooner had the last cateran lined up to pass through into the caveran beyond, when the first of their adversaries exploded into the arena.

"Quickly lads, they are following the trail left by our womenfolk across the arena?" Andrew cried, failing to keep the alarm out of his voice.

Peat smoke rose from the further end of the *daingneachd* where Ewen Finlay and his cronies had elected to bide and await the coming of the invaders. There was nothing he could do. He had brought this on all of them.

Sadly, Andrew scanned the length of the stronghold, seeing again the giant figure of the big MacAlistair stride from his bothan; his friend Duncan Cameron, and although he could not see his own dwelling from here, his mind overflowed with thoughts of Una and their happy life together. A lump in his throat, he closed the door.

"Andrew! All are through!" The anxious voice of Alan Fraser jerked him back.

Andrew crossed the floor and wriggled through the small aperture, straightening up on the other side. "Quickly now!" he ordered the small band gathered there. "Some of you help the wounded on their way, and have a care of the caverans on either side. Follow the tapers light. Once clear, make for the high mountains on the far side of the corrie!"

Those caterans swiftly followed their chief's instructions, the remainder arranging themselves on either side of the passage wall to await the foe.

Andrew filled his powder horn, pocketing what lead shot he could carry. "Take yon powder barrel some ways down the passage, then you too be away. There are sufficient here to hold until all are safe within the mountains," he requested of a man.

"Andrew," Alan Fraser whispered, drawing his chief's attention to the hole they had just crawled through, where an inquiring sword blade waved about and was then slowly withdrawn.

Andrew put a finger to his lips in a gesture of silence, all there waiting in the tapers flickering light like a cat awaiting a mouse.

All at once 'the mouse' emerged, first the head and shoulders of a man on all fours, then half turning to look around, Alan struck, almost severing the head from the body,the chin bouncing and scraping on the stone floor while his fellows struggled to pull him back through.

It seemed an eternity to the defenders in their mountain catacomb before a volley of shots eventually poured through the hole, the lead whining and ricocheting from wall to wall. No one however ventured to follow. It was when one of the caterans had been hit on the knee, that they decided to move further back.

Andrew looked around him. "Calum, Alan and myself will bide here to defend the passage. It is now time for the rest of you to leave."

"We shall not leave you now Andrew," Neill replied indefatigably, stabbing his sword point into the floor. "You may need the assistance of more than two should the MacSorley mount a serious attack. The man does not care how many he may lose. Only that in the end he has you in his clutches."

"I thank you for your loyalty and concern, Neill. But again yon crew out there may believe all here are trapped within this mountain, women and bairns forby, and therefore be content to sit and wait, and hope we starve. Or yet again at this very minute may be making their way around the mountainside in search of another way in. Should this be so, we may indeed be trapped. So, it is best you may be gone. You yourself have a wife and bairns, Neill, and will serve them best by helping them over the mountain to Johnny MacKellar, in the Cairngorms. Our folks will not yet be so far distant that you cannot find them."

Andrew pointed sternly. Now go! And God willing we may meet again in not so long a time."

Reluctantly the caterans shuffled away, Neill with a despairing gesture, the last to leave.

"You yourself should have gone, Andrew," Calum said in his soft sing song voice, his eyes on his departing friends, less by looking at his chief that man would conclude he thought him to blame for all that had come to pass. "It is you above all, Quoich seeks. It will go badly for you, I am after thinking should that man take you alive."

Andrew tried to make light of his friend's anziety, though in truth he felt that same jab of pain at his heart when thinking of what the MacSorley had in mind for him. "And you, Calum? After the havoc you have wrought with those boulders from above, Quoich will not be so inclined to clutch you to his bosom, lest he grasps a dirk in his one good hand!"

The caterans laughter echoed eerily down the passageway at the unexpected humour of their chief.

Calum shook his head in mirth. "Perhaps in that pass we best both be leaving." He winked at Andrew. "Or we could leave Alan here to sing our foes to death."

Well known for his lack of tone, Alan pulled a wry face. " I could give them a few notes, if you like, Calum, maybe bring down a few rocks into the bargain!" and jumped back when a tartan bundle rolled through the hole, pushed further, by a sword blade, quickly followed by dry whin and bush.

"Quickly! Kick them aside!" Andrew barked, rushing forward to kick further lighted combustibles away, the billowing smoke driving them back coughing and holding tear filled eyes.

"They mean to burn, or smoke us out !" Calum cried, beating at the flames.

"Have a care they will not be far behind! They will use the fire as a shield!"

Coughing and sputtering, Andrew beat at the flames with a plaid he'd first kicked aside, all the while forced, as were his comrades to retreat from the aperture.

"They will be on us presently," Andrew coughed. "Trail the gunpowder from the keg someways to the exit. I will set it alight after I hold them for awhile."

"You will not hold them alone." This decisively from Calum.

"I shall...with these two pistols! Now go quickly whilst there is still time."

Kneeling behind a column of rock amidst the swirling smoke wafted by draughts from deep within the cavern, Andrew kept his eyes on the aperture while his friends departed, awaiting the first of the foe to appear. Then, believing through smoke filled eyes he had seen the first to emerge, fired.

Whether he had hit someone, Andrew did not know, nor was it the time to find out. Backing down the passageway, he snapped off a shot and ran passed the keg with its trail of black powder, where once at the exit he snatched a taper from the wall and set it to the powder, waiting only to watch while it hissed and sparkled on its way to the keg. Then he was out into the open, bounding down the scree to the corrie floor, as a far off explosion at his back proclaimed his success. A cloud of smoke, blown out of the exit, spiralled upwards, dissapating in the warm midday breeze.

Crossing the corrie floor, Andrew lifted his pace, satisfied that he had done his work well, and was not quite aware of the horsemen until they were almost upon him, a dandified figure at their head.

Even as the cateran broke into a wild desperate run he knew he could not reach the safety of the opposite slopes before the horsemen were upon him. He lifted his pace again and for a brief moment believed upon reaching the first of the rocks littering that side of the corrie that he may yet survive, when suddenly a flying body crushed him to the ground, and as he landed in an unceremonious heap, heard the high angry cry of his attacker, and the contorted face of Iain MacKinnon glaring down at him.

"At last MacLaren! This is for my brother!" Iain screetched, stabbing at him.

Only just succeeding in deflecting the blow with a rock he had picked up with his free hand Andrew's attacker again lashed out at him. His vision clouding, Andrew fought off the sea of blackness which threatened to engulf him, knowing that to lose conciousness was to lose his life. He groped for a pistol, his other hand grasping the MacKinnon's dirk, believing the fight to be useless, for even should he succeed in defeating his antagonist, there were others close by equally willing to see him dead, none more so than Quoich himself, and in a final desperate act dragged an empty pistol from his belt to lash out at the man.

However, it was not Andrew's blow that hurled Iain MacKinnon to the side, but the blow of Alan Fraser, who had miraculously appeared out of the rocks and in so doing was in turn. transfixed by the blade of Kenneth MacSorley. The whole episode an eternity to the cateran leader who lay helplessy looking up into the gloating face of a mounted enemy savouring every precious second of his fear.

Emitting a high shreiking laugh of triumph, Quoich gently coaxed his mount forward, the movement deliberately protracted to extract every ounce of fear from the helpless man on the ground.

"No, MacLaren, for you it is not yet done. Now you will know what it is to be without *both* hands!"

296

At a signal, willing clansmen ran to obey their chief, pinning Andrew's outstretched arms to the ground.

Andrew MacLaren closed both eyes and prayed that it would soon be over, and therefore did not see the downward thrust of the giant claymore as it split the MacSorley from shoulder to hip, or the caterans falling upon the remaining horsemen, until he felt his arms free and was staring up into the face of a grinning tiny man with a gaint head.

Not until a cool breeze from the mountain top returned him to full senses did he understand what had just taken place. His men had come back for him! Kenneth MacSorley of Quoich was no more.

It was indeed all over at last.

Chapter 21

A miscellany of elderly, women and children helped by caterans wound a long slow way up the steep slope of the desolate mountain.

"You will not bide then, Andrew?" Dugald asked, his eyes on the straggling column.

"No, Dugald, Johnny will not thank me for imposing on what he now regards as his own domain. Besides, he will be needing a good right hand like yourself to help with yon," Andrew nodded to the slow procession of refugees.

"You think he will see me as that, Andrew?" Surprise etched on the youngster's face.

"Aye, that I do. I have watched how you have and matured over these past years. You are a good man Dugald, a better man than I could ever hope to be."

Embarrassed by such flattery, Dugald looked away. "What will you do now? And where will you go?"

"Och, back to what I was at first and never should have left."

"Back to yon Glen Laidon of yours? Or Kintail? Why must it be so?" Dugald entreated, not wishing this man...his friend to leave. "Now the MacSorley is dead, we could return to the *daingneachd*. No one else will seek to harm us...except...perhaps, Neil MacPherson, and surely we can come to some arrangement."

Angry with himself for mentioning the latter, Dugald hurried on determindly. "Besides, what of old Finlay and his like, back there? Surely you will not turn your back on them, for you are still *ceann cinnidh!*"

Andrew eyed the column of humanity now some distance away, choosing his words carefully, more than a little annoyed by Dugald's perception. "I will not return to the *daingneachd*. Though after a time you may wish to return there as chieftain yourself, with whoever else may chose to follow you. This I believe would sit with Johnny well enough."

"I could not command as you have commanded, Andrew. Nor do I have the gift for planning the' lifting'. Many broken men are alive today because you kept them fed. I could never hope to do likewise."

"Do not underestimate yourself my young friend. My planning did not always come to fruition as it should have done. There is many a man not alive because of it." Andrew shuffled a foot "No, I made many a mistake, Dugald, not least of that with the MacSorley. You can do no worse than I."

Reluctantly, Dugald grasped Andrew's outstretched hand. "We may never meet again, *ceann cinndh,*" the emotion welling up in the younger man.

Andrew made a pretence of making light of the situation. "Never is a long time, Dugald my friend. Though, should I return to Kintail....if they will have me, I might someday take a stroll to the high Monadhliath to visit Dugald Ferguson , cateran chief who reigns there."

Squeezing the young man's hand, Andrew gently pushed him away. "It is time we were both on our way. Go Dugald they are in need of you."

Andrew waited until Dugald had rejoined the column and had stopped to wave a farewell salute, then pretending to be unaware of the dwarf hiding some distance away took his first steps towards Loch Ness.

Andrew sat watching the insect on the wall which he had done for close on an hour, his thoughts intermittently interrupted by the snoring of the dwarf stretched out at his feet on the eathern floor of his tiny bothan.

Sadly, the bothan had fallen into disrepair since the little man's leaving. The alcove now bare from where he had produced his miracles of meat and wine. Andrew sighed. It must be done, and if so must be done now.

Through the gaping roof he judged the dawn to be less than an hour away. His eyes strayed to his sleeping friend, unable to comprehend his feelings at this exact time. Though equally certain that where he intended going, there was no place for the tiny man, for Isabella, he knew would not welcome him in their new home. Nor could anyone blame her.

Here amongst wild men such as himself, the dwarf had come to be accepted. Eventually one had come to overlook his grotesque appearance, seeking to look behind the features to the man beyond. This same man, who on occasions too numerous to mention had undoubtedly saved his life, and who he had repaid by continually robbing him of his horde in order to fund this self same house south of the Highland Line. This then was he, who he now intended leaving from where he had first found him, and without as much as a fare you well.

Damn the man! He, Andrew must think of himself. After all, did he not deserve some sort of reward for all of his planning, as Duncan had so rightly pointed out?

Angry now, Andrew let his self loathing simmer. Had his traipsing in the heather, braving the elements, freezing or starving in the *daingneachd* not been for the one purpose? In the end to live as his own master with, Isabella Grant, and as far away as possible from this kind of existence. Therefore, was it not so, that the *troich*, however regrettable it may be, must be left behind.

His decision made, Andrew rose noiselessly, and holding his breath swung the door back on its creaking hinges, listening intently for a change of breathing that would tell him the dwarf was awake. Hearing nothing he stepped quietly outside, the sharpness of the morning air dispelling the mustiness of the bothan and any doubts he may have had concerning the leaving his tiny friend, and without a backward glance made his way through the woods.

At last Gleidh House lay before him, and he smiled at the thought of the welcome within.

True, the last two 'liftings' before Quoich had struck had been less than successful. Nevertheless there should be sufficient saved for the house and land by Stirling which, Neil Stewart had been assigned to purchase when the time was right; and now the time was right. As for Isabella, she would have to accept him as he was, for he had nothing more to give.

Reaching the door, Andrew rapped keenly on it with his dirk handle and stood back to await its unhurried opening by Helen the maid, who would as on other occassions proceed to present him to an equally unflustered lady of the house.

"It is yourself, Mister MacLaren." The small voice seemed to squeeze through the mearest crack in the partially open door. Helen smiled shyly up at him. "If it is the mistress you are after seeking, she is not at home?"

The voice got no further, when the door itself was thrown wide open and the figure of a total stranger to Andrew stood there, arms akimbo.

"And who would this Mister MacLaren be, Helen, may I ask?" The small middle aged dumpy man demanded sourly, eyeing the caller up and down, through beady eyes.

"Tis a friend....an acquaintance of the mistress," Helen ventured timidly.

"Thank you Helen, I can speak very well for myself," Andrew retorted, angry as well as mystfied at being greeted and kept on the doorstep by someone he did not know, and an impolite one at that. "I might ask the same of you sir!" he growled back.

The frown slackened on the older man's face, and his hands dropped to his side. "In this you are right, Mister Maclaren, my courtesy.....or lack of it is unpardonable." He stood aside with a flourish. "But come away in man! Come away in!"

Andrew was shown to the same massive table at which he had sat on many a happy occassion. Where, his host pouring him a glass of wine ushered him to be seated, while he, Andrew looked expectantly to the far door where Isobella's appearance would put an end to this mystery.

"You will forgive my ill manners, MacLaren," the man apologised, "but it has come as a shock...a great shock." He dabbed at his brow, his lip twitching nervously. "I am Hector Grant, Isobella's cousin germain. It was not until last week that I heard of this cataclysm, and was told..." He mopped his brow again in one sharp movement of his hand. "No..instructed by the *Grand* himself to make haste here to Gleidh."

In order to give himself time to recover, Hector sipped at his wine. "Tis a sad business this...and the affrontry of it all!" He sat down heavily, the incongruity suddenly too much for him.

From the time he stood in the doorway, Andrew knew something was far wrong, not least of all concerning Isobella. Taking up his glass he asked calmly, "Isabella? She is not at home?"

"No, that lady has departed in company with yon rascal Neil Stewart, these two weeks past."

"Departed with her cousin to where?" Andrew asked dumfounded.

"Cousin?" Hector Grant furrowed his brows, a lack of comprehension on his face. "Neil Stewart is no more cousin to

301

Isobella than I am to the King of France!" he mocked, sweat oozing out the collar of the irate man's shirt. "As to where she has gone, France sir! That is where the lady has departed!"

Hector finished off his wine in a gulp. "To France, MacLaren. Though lord knows how came she by the siller, considering the goodly debt she has left behind, with no thought to her own folk here in the glen; not that she cares *that* for them!" He snapped his fingers.

His mind only partially on what his host was saying, Andrew felt suddenly tired. He had been duped. Now he had nothing left but the siller in his sporran and the tartan on his back. He had stolen, maimed and killed for this beautiful woman, and she had led him to her bed, while her suitor Neil Stewart had never raised a hand against it; all to what end?

At least all his doubts and misgivings at wondering whether or not he could fit into Isobella's circle of society was no longer an issue, Andrew thought, heaving a small imperceptible sigh. The issue now was, whether or not to return to the *daingneachd* and attempt to start all over again, or ask Johnny MacKellar for sanctuary...at least until he came into his own again, and his step led him once more to Kintail, where, cap in hand he would ask Coll MacKerlich for a wee bit land to start his life anew.

"You are unwell, sir? You must bide the night." The anziety in Hector Grant's voice brought Andrew back to the present.

"Och it is nothing a bite and a good night's rest will not cure. Besides, I believe I owe you an explanation for my unexpected arrival.

Andrew sat with his back to the boulder gazing dreamily over the black empty mountains, half heartedly fighting not to doze in the mid-day sun. It was grand and peaceful here, and for the first time in a while fine to be at one with the world, neither having to fret at what was in front or behind him. At last the sun found him and he succumbed to closing his eyes.

Andrew decided he would return to the stronghold, start anew and bide there until he had enough to carry him to Kintail. This was of course if old Ewen Finlay and who else was still there, pardoned him for his errors. Should they not? He sighed.

Feeling a sudden coolness and believing a cloud had obscured the sun, Andrew opened an eye, starting up in fear and apprehension at the sight of the *troich* standing over him, his gigantic face expressionless.

What had the tiny man in store for him he wondered, with him stealing away in the night? Had the man found his cache in the rocks empty? And if so, it would take little deduction as to who was the thief.

Fearful of the speed by which the dwarf could draw his awesome weapon, Andrew made no move towards his own pistols, instead, he lay for what seemed to be an eternity staring up at his silent observer, who, with a shake of his enormous head pointed back down the bare slope.

Puzzled Andrew drew himself to his feet, and glimpsed the receding figure of Lachlan Grant disappearing amongst the trees . "So this is how you have come to find me. At least the servant has had the decency not to have followed the mistress. But were you aware of her intentions all along?" he asked of the diminishing figure.

Now standing with his back to the dwarf, Andrew slowly reached for a pistol, and in so doing felt a gentle touch on his shoulder. Swallowing hard, he turned to face a grinning *troich* , who it appeared was only too happy to be reunited with his chief again.

Whether the dwarf knew of his perfidy or not, all at least appeared to be forgiven.

Ginning in relief, Andrew pointed down the mountain in the direction he meant to take, for he intended to see Kirsty, Gregor and the bairn before his feet led him back once more to the *daingneachd*, and the life of a cateran.

It was almost dark of that second day when Andrew and the dwarf first saw the long black spirals of smoke on the horizon. With a quickening of their step they crested the brae.

Beneath them a trail of desperately fleeing women, bairns clutched to their breasts, or trotting at their sides, small fists knotted in the folds of their mothers skirts, hurried by, while some distance behind, a ragged line of a score or so of their menfolk, some wounded had halted to rest briefly to await the pursuing foe.

Andrew felt a tug at his sleeve, the dwarf drawing his attention to a group of women, away to their right.

"Dia!" Andrew exclaimed, and was running down the brae before the word had left his lips. "Kirsty! Kirsty!" He leapt over the boulder strewn slope, the dwarf not far behind.

Too intent on escape no woman gave these two strangers a second glance, but continued to claw at the heather in their desperation to gain the top of the slope. Now and again one would halt to look back in terror, the bairn at her knee crying hysterically at something it did not understand.

"Kirsty!" Andrew cried again, cutting through the exhausted women to her side.

KIrsty looked up, a far away look in her eyes, "Andrew! You are here?" she whispered in incomprehension.

"Where is Gregor? He is safe? What is happening here?" Andrew's fear for this woman and her son made him bark out the words.

Kirsty clutched Coll to her skirsts, the small boy looking up at this man he knew. Dazed, she pointed down the slope. "Gregor is with the menfolk...or what remains of them."

Mustering all her strength she drew herself together. "Fergus MacRae, the same who bides in your croft, came to warn us, that his *tigh tughadh* and some others had already been put to the torch by the MacKinnons!" Kirsty took a tired step up the slope anxious to be away.

Her eyes flashed with fear. "It is no 'lifting' Andrew, this is a *creach* ! The MacKinnons mean to have their revenge for the battle in the glen yon day. Gregor, the bairn and myself would now be dead had it not been for Fergus's timely warning!"

The MacKinnons! Andrew cursed quietly. Had he not had enough of that name?

Out of the turmoil he heard his own name called aloud, and Gregor leading a small band of clansmen through the straggling women came hurriedly to meet him.

"The fiddler gripped his hand. "You have chosen an ill time to call, I am after thinking, Andrew MacLaren." He forced a smile, though obviously glad to see his friend, and the dwarf.

"Would that I had a score of my caterans at my back my friend, it would be to teach yon mongrel MacKinnons a lesson they would not readily forget."

"That as may be, MacLaren," a clansmen interjected with a nod down the slope,"but lest we move, yon same mongrels will up here at our throats...and soon."

Andrew darted a quick look at the backs of the fleeing women. "The women folk will not travel far before the MacKinnons are upon them, lest we hold them for a time." He swung back to Gregor. "Think you, Coll Mackerlich knows of this?"

Gregor stepped round some whin. "No Andrew, we had scarce the time to save ourselves far less send for help. We had little warning. Even less had poor Fergus MacRae, now himself lying dead back yonder, not come to warn us."

"Aye Kirsty was telling me the same," Andrew panted. He drew to a halt on the brae top. "We must hold them here awhile...give the women time to be away."

A young lad ran passed intent on catching up with his mother who lay exhausted after her climb. Andrew grabbed him by the arm. "What are you called, my young friend?" he asked.

"Donald MacKenzie!" the strartled boy answered, trying to break free, surprised that any should want to know his name, under such circumstances.

Andrew crouched down in front of the lad, his voice calm, gentle almost, amidst the wailing and crying all around. "Now then young Donald MacKenzie, can you run like the deer on the hill?" The lad nodded. "Can you run as far as Monar House, as if your life depended upon it...and those forbye?" Andrew swung the boy round to face the huddled women.

Donald swung back to look up into the face of a man standing close by.

"Answer the man, Donald," the wounded man prompted with a nod.

The boy drew himself up to his full height. "That I can," he annouced proudly.

Andrew held the boys arms by his side, and looked him straight in the eye, the look one of trust. "Run, Donald. Run as fast as your feet will take you to Coll MacKerlich Himself. Tell him to come as quickly as he can, and with what men he has, and not to wait to gather more. Tell him what is happening here. Do you have it my young warrior?" Andrew asked, standing up.

"That I have. I am not a bairn!" This stubbornly, for had he not been entrusted with such a mission?"

Despite himself, Andrew smiled down at the boy. "Then begone with you Donald MacKenzie." He gave the boy a gentle push.

The young messenger took two steps then halted, his eyes on his father.

"Go my son. And may He go with you," the wounded man commanded.

With a last look at his father the boy was gone.

"He will not fail you MacLaren," the man said adamantly.

"I never doubted that he would, my friend. It is us who must not fail him and all the others."

Swiftly and without challenge, the cateran took command.

"Lie here hidden behind the crest. Those with pistols wait until they draw close then be at them."

Andrew caught Gregor by the arm. "Go with the wounded old friend, and help the women. Take the *troich* with you. When...if the MacKinnons break through our lines, hide the women as best you can. The *troich* will help."

"No!" Gregor exploded. "You are thinking a one armed fiddler is of no use to you! Then ask the MacKinnons!" Gregor shouted, shaking his sword.

Andrew blushed, for what the man had said was true. He wanted Gregor safe, if not for his own sake, for that of Kirsty and the bairn, yet he could not shame the man by telling him this. Neither would Gregor leave his friends to stand alone.

Angry at this obstnacy, Andrew tried another tact. "Yon wee lad Donald cannot fully explain what I have told him. You can do this, Gregor!"

"And more so the lad's own father!" Gregor shouted back. "Send him for he is wounded and stands with us here! Send him if you feel the MacKerlich must know what is happening here this night!"

Still angry but knowing he was beaten it was on the tip of Andrew's tongue to ask the man if the loss of one arm was not enough,but said instead, "You were ever the stubburn one Gregor MacVinish, but I have no time to argue with you, for, see you , our unfriends are already on the move."

Leaving Gregor to his post, Andrew ran along the short line of prone clansmen.

"No one will fire until you hear my first shot."

Signalling the dwarf to follow him, Andrew ran down behind the rim of the slope to its far end, then in a crouch, to a massive lump of rock some ten feet high, a quarter way down the brae, where hoisting himself up on to the outcrop, signalled the dwarf to hide in the nearby whin.

Now hidden on the enemy's flank Andrew waited until the first rank had passed, then firing, brought down those nearest him, his clansmen simultaeniously pouring fire into them from the crest of the slope.

Andrew succeeded in reloading and firing again before his hiding place was discovered. With a yell the foe turned in his direction, coming at him from across the intervening space.

Practiced though he was at speedily reloading, Andrew's hand still shook. A shot pinged and hummed off the rock, followed by another, then they were swarming round the base of his rock like bees round a honeypot. One pistol loaded he fired down into those trying to scale his bastion, before being forced to stand and draw his hated weapon, and relying on the advantage of height to keep the foe at bay.

Suddenly the dwarf was amongst them, taking the assailants by surprise, his great claymore swinging, forcing them back before the impetus of his attack; some unsure whether this grotesque figure was human or otherwise.

While the dwarf was busily engaged below, Andrew reloaded, firing into the converging Mackinnons, bringing two down,then with the smoking pistols still in his hands leaped down from the rock over his opponents, at the same time as the dwarf launched a new attack.

Too much for the three remaining attackers, they turned and fled back to meet the second wave of their clansmen climbing the brae.

Taking advantage of the temporary respite, Andrew and the dwarf swiftly returned to the crest of the brae, intent on helping those awaiting the second wave of the MacKinnons, when almost there Andrew slipped, covering his hands in gore, and as he tried to haul himself to his feet, stared through the fan of his bloodsoaked fingers into the glazed eyes of a dead man with one arm.

The scream of anguish still in his throat, Andrew wiped Gregor's blood on the heather, sick at the thought of what had befallen his friend and what this would mean to Kirsty. The sight of young

Donald's father dragging himself on his hands and knees from the fight, blood spurting like a fountain from a gaping hole in his chest, adding to his anguish.

With a cry born out of anger and despair, the dwarf and all else forgotten, Andrew hurled himself to his feet, and with all caution gone, strode straightbacked down the brae to meet the next line of MacKinnons.

For the first time in days, Andrew felt at peace with himself, the prospect of not having to face the future now no longer relevant. No more struggling, either cateran or crofter. No more guilt at what he had done. Soon it would be all over, and ironically by the hands of the clan which had involunarily made him a hero.

Amongst these emotions, the man wondered how far young Donald had ran.

Miraculously they had halted the first two lines of MacKinnons , but could not hope to halt a third. Poor Kirsty! Poor Coll! And young Donald and his like.

Andrew drew his sword and struck it into the ground, oblivious to the shots thudding around the course heather at his feet. He had no time to reload. His favourite weapons were of no use. Perhaps after all, he was destined to die weilding the hated sword, and as he pulled it free, they were upon him, and he jabbing and thrusting in a way that would have made his old grandfather proud. Then he was down, and hours later, or was it only moments, a giant head peered anxiously into his face, and somewhere through a red mist, a mounted man was grinning ruefully down at him.

"It is a strange way to be retuning home, fisherman, I am after thinking. But do not be lying there overlong, for should you choose to bide, you have a new *tigh tughadh* to build." Then the face and voice were gone.

Epilogue

On the walls of the *tigh tughadh* , the scorth marks, as had the memories of that fateful day had never completely faded. Once again the house stood proudly over rows of neatly stooked corn.

From the braeside, the plaintive cry of the whaup broke the stillness of the September evening as the man and woman walked hand in hand by the sea loch. Then, as if in a prearranged signal the man walked alone to the waters edge, where, for a moment he stood staring across the loch. Slowly his hand slid to his belt and he took out the solitary pistol, to run a finger over the engraved butt. Finally, with a sigh, he hurled the weapon into the air, following it with his eye as it described a near perfect arc to land with a splash in the still waters of the loch, equating the disappearing weapon to that of his past, and the ever widening circles of the centrifugal force to that of the major events which had affected his life. Then, and only then, was the man aware of the woman's hand in his.

Out of that cathedral stillness came the shrill laughter of a child, both man and woman in turn laughing at the antics of the small boy being chased, caught and thrown up on to the shoulders of a tiny man with a gigantic head.

Squeezing her hand, Andrew MacLaren, led Kirsty to the *troich* and Coll. Together the family strolled for home.

The End

Printed in Great Britain
by Amazon